"I KNOW I SHOULDN'T BE GOING HOME WITH YOU."

Meg's voice dropped as she looked down at her hands. "But I don't know what else to do."

The man beside her took his eyes off the road for a moment. He spoke softly. "I'm your husband. Why shouldn't you be going home with me?"

"Because I don't know you, Victor. I have no right to be living in your house."

"Lisa, I—"

"Please don't call me Lisa. My name is Meg. Meg Howell."

Victor sighed and concentrated on driving.

Meg leaned against the back of the seat and closed her eyes. She thought longingly of her cool white bed in the hospital, safely removed from this man and his house and all the terrifying situations that lay ahead.

But she'd had to make a decision. She couldn't hide in the hospital forever. Until she was strong enough to get back to Las Vegas and uncover the truth, she'd simply have to accept what people were telling her.

It was time to start living her life—or whoever's life she was in.

MARGOT DALTON

Tangled Lives

MIRA BOOKS

ISBN 1-55166-047-4

TANGLED LIVES

Printed in U.S.A.

Tangled Lives

Prologue

From the desert plains of Nevada, silent and endless under a starlit sky, the freeway lifted to the canyonlands of southern Utah. Darkness began to fade and a heavy gray mist rolled through the valleys, pierced by the headlights of oncoming traffic. Gradually, a faint shimmer of light appeared in the sky to the east, glowing above the jagged horizon. The wind died, and the stars vanished one by one.

On the freeway, a five-ton truck hauling a load of glass pulled over to the shoulder and stopped. The driver got out, stretched his arms, then zipped his jacket and hunched his shoulders against the chilly dampness of early morning.

It was only August—hot summer on the desert—but the coolness up here carried a hint of autumn.

The other side of the freeway was about twenty yards away on the high side of the cliff, so the lights of southbound vehicles seemed to be floating overhead through the swirling mist. Except for the occasional throb of passing trucks, the silence was profound, almost palpable.

The man strolled around to examine the straps and fastenings on his load. Satisfied, he paused and glanced into the steep ravine that fell away from the road.

There was no ditch, just a sharp-angled drop. He couldn't see down the slope without moving closer.

He turned and walked around his truck, heading for the driver's side. Suddenly, something caught his attention in the brush-filled gorge. He stopped abruptly and peered into the shadows. Then he saw it again, a pale shape in the darkness, a faint glimmer of metal.

Cautiously, he edged his way into the brush. As he neared the object, he could make out its form—a car, caught and teetering partway down the slope. It was a white 1957 Thunderbird, its distinctive rear fins and taillights unmistakable even in the dim light.

From above, the car looked almost intact. But as he crept alongside it, slipping and skidding on the damp grass, he saw that the front was badly damaged. The car had obviously gone over the edge of the freeway and plowed down the cliff, smashing into a sturdy metal post that was the only remnant of a fence once strung along the side of the ravine.

He shivered. There was something eerie about the stillness, the dense mist creeping along the valley floor below him and the car perched precariously on the slope, like a white ghost among the sage and juniper.

After a moment, he moved closer to the shattered window and looked inside. The bloodied form of a woman sprawled across the gearshift console.

Horrified, he stood looking at the delicate nape of her neck, the matted dark hair and slim, twisted line of her back. Finally, he turned and scrambled wildly back up the incline, heading for his truck and the CB radio inside the cab.

1

The room was large and comfortably furnished, almost elegant. A few paintings hung on the walls, framed in dark oak that matched the furniture. Only the flashing, beeping equipment near the bed, and the masses of flowers showed that it was a hospital room.

Dr. Clara Wassermann sat near the window with a clipboard in her lap, looking at the woman in the bed. It was difficult to recognize Lisa Cantalini in this bruised and battered face. Lisa was a beautiful young woman, and more conscious of her looks than anyone Clara had ever encountered. Her eyes were very dark blue, a startling contrast to her black hair and creamy skin. They were almond-shaped, giving her an exotic look that she liked to accent with cosmetics and a dramatic wardrobe. But now, stripped of makeup, she looked young and vulnerable. It was almost as if that powerful and self-absorbed personality had vanished. Heavily bandaged and sedated with painkilling drugs, she seemed strangely unformed.

Suddenly, Lisa's left eye fluttered open and she rolled her head on the pillow. Her right one—purple and livid—was swollen shut.

Lisa glanced around the room with a panicky expression. She grimaced and raised a bandaged arm, trying to touch her eye, then winced and dropped her hand. Clara drew her chair closer to the bed.

"My head hurts," Lisa whispered, her voice slurred. "Where am I? What happened?"

"You had an accident with your car, Lisa. You drove off the freeway and crashed into a post."

The woman in the bed looked up at her blankly.

"You've got some nasty cuts and bruises, and a mild concussion. That's why Victor called me to come over and talk with you," Clara went on carefully. "He says you've been conscious once or twice since yesterday, but you seemed quite confused. He thought I might be able to help."

"Who are you?"

Lisa's voice was clearer now, her undamaged eye beginning to focus on Clara's face.

"I'm Dr. Wassermann." Clara pulled her chair around so Lisa didn't have to look into the glare of the window. "Remember, Lisa? You came to see me several times this past spring."

"But I don't...I don't know you," Lisa said, looking panicky again.

"Of course you do." Clara was familiar with the symptoms of posttraumatic shock, and not at all surprised by Lisa's reaction. "Try to remember, Lisa. We talked quite a lot about your childhood, and some of the problems you and Victor were having."

Lisa gazed at the therapist uncertainly. "I don't know what you're talking about," she said at last, trying to heave herself upright in the bed, then falling back with a groan. "I don't know who you are. What's going on? What's happening to me?"

Clara reached over and gave the younger woman a soothing pat on the shoulder. "You mustn't be alarmed," she said. "Your condition is quite normal after an accident. You must relax, Lisa, and try not to worry about anything."

"But I'm not... My name isn't Lisa."

Clara grasped the clipboard tightly. "You're not Lisa? What's your name, then?" she asked.

"Meg," the woman whispered, closing her eyes with sudden weariness. "My name is Meg."

"Meg?" Clara asked, struggling to maintain a calm, conversational tone. "That's your name?"

But Lisa was asleep again, her dark fan of eyelashes casting a dense shadow on the pale unbruised part of her cheek. Clara watched her in silence for a moment, then got up quietly and left the hospital room.

Clara Wassermann was in her early fifties, a tall, willowy woman with a streak of pure white in her dark hair. She wore well-tailored clothes with an air of artful elegance. Her gracious manner concealed a degree of professional ambition that probably would have surprised even those closest to her.

She entered her office building, a restored brick three-story in downtown Salt Lake City, rode up impatiently in the elevator and hurried through the halls to her professional suite. Clara had several rooms on the upper floor, comprising a small reception area for her secretary, a consulting room decorated in soothing earth tones and a sparse private office lined with shelves of books and audiocassettes.

Inside her office, she moved without hesitation to one of the lower shelves and knelt to examine the tapes of her sessions with Lisa Cantalini. She frowned briefly, then selected one of the cassettes, consulted the label and flipped it into the tape player on her desk. She settled in the chair to listen, drawing a notebook toward her.

"Thursday, May 12," she heard her own voice saying. "Therapy session with Lisa Cantalini. How are you today, Lisa?"

"I'm fine. Look, do you really need to have that thing on while we're talking?"

"I can turn the tape recorder off if it makes you uncomfortable. It's helpful for me to have a record of our discussion, that's all."

"Some discussion," Lisa's voice said scornfully. "I talk, you listen. You call that a discussion, Dr. Wassermann?"

"It's not really our purpose to listen to my conversation. Have you talked with Victor about any of the things we discussed last week?"

"Victor's never home. How can I talk with him?"

There was a silence on the tape. Clara waited and jotted notes.

Eventually, Lisa's voice began once more, sounding reluctant and annoyed. "He says he's working late every night. How the hell do I know if it's true? To tell you the truth, I don't much care. Are you married, Dr. Wassermann?"

"I have been," Clara said neutrally. "I live alone at present."

"I live alone at present." Lisa mocked the doctor's precise tone.

"Would you prefer to lie on the couch, Lisa? You might feel more comfortable."

"Nobody lies on couches anymore. You're from the Dark Ages, Dr. Wassermann."

"Really?"

"Besides, I can't see your face when I'm on the couch."

"Sometimes that's helpful. Perhaps you could just try it. You can adjust the back so you're sitting more upright if you prefer."

"Oh, *shit,*" Lisa muttered.

Clara looked down at the tape recorder and smiled at the resentful note in the young woman's voice. There was another break in the conversation while a series of shuffling noises gave evidence that despite her objections, Lisa was moving onto the leather couch.

"Is that all right?" the doctor asked quietly.

"It's okay. What were we talking about?"

"You were discussing Victor's work."

"He tells me he's got money problems," Lisa said. "The man's so rich he hardly knows what to do with all his money, but he fusses like an old woman and keeps saying I have to be more careful about the clothes I buy."

"You always dress so beautifully, Lisa. You have a wonderful clothes sense."

"A person learns that," Lisa said offhandedly. "After fifteen years in the business."

"What business do you mean?"

"The beauty-pageant business. I know I've told you all this before. My mother entered me in my first pageant before I was three years old. 'Baby Spring Blossoms,' it was called. I won it. By the time I was eight years old, I'd already been in forty-three pageants."

"And your last pageant was when you were... eighteen?"

"Right. Five years ago. By then I'd won just about every title in the state, and I was all set to go on to Miss Utah, then Miss America. I would have won, too. Everybody thought so. I'd have a terrific career and tons of my own money, and I wouldn't need Victor."

There was another brief silence on the tape, then Lisa's voice again, light and challenging.

"Does that shock you, Dr. Wassermann?"

"Very few things shock me. Why didn't you go on to enter the Miss Utah pageant?"

"My mother died when I was eighteen, just after we started preparing for the pageant. She had liver cancer. And afterward it turned out that she'd made a real mess of our finances. There was no life insurance, not even enough money saved for me to live on. I had to drop out of college and go to work."

"If you'd already qualified, why couldn't you enter the pageant anyway?"

"You really don't know much about it, do you? It costs thousands of dollars just for the evening gowns. The girls have them custom-made by designers in New York and California. And you have to take voice and dance lessons to prepare for the talent competition . . . It costs a lot to be in a major pageant."

"Couldn't you have found a sponsor, considering your previous success?"

"Not really. Not somebody who'd be willing to support me and pay my college tuition, besides everything else. You see, a girl can't be working for minimum wage somewhere and expect to impress the judges. She doesn't have a chance unless she's in college, working toward a definite career, and all those things are the family's responsibility. The pageant business is pretty cutthroat."

"So your mother didn't leave you with enough money to pursue your career?"

"That's what I just said."

"How about your father? Couldn't he have helped?"

"I never had a father."

"But I thought..."

"Oh, sure, there was Greg," Lisa said impatiently. "But he was only around for a few years. He left when I was four or five. I hardly ever saw him again, and I was glad."

"Why?"

"He and Terry used to fight all the time. Mostly they fought over me."

"Terry... That's your mother?"

"Of course. Greg hated the whole idea of pageants. He was such a jerk. I still remember the fights, and how nice it was after he was gone and there was just Terry and me."

"How did he treat you when he lived at home?"

"You mean, was he abusive, right? That's what therapists always want to know, if your father was abusive."

"Was he?"

"Of course not," Lisa said coldly. "My mother would have killed him."

There was another silence while the tape whirred and Clara made notes on her pad.

"I know what you're thinking," Lisa said at last.

"What's that?"

"How it's strange that she'd love me so much and become so involved in my life. After all, I was adopted, not her real child. Aren't you thinking that?"

"Is that how you feel?"

"I don't know. Tell me, do you think I'd be a different person if I'd grown up with my real mother instead of with Terry?"

"I don't know. There are differing opinions over the importance of genetics and environment on a person's development. Do you know anything about your birth parents, Lisa?"

"Not a thing. I always had this fantasy when I was a kid, you know...?" Lisa's voice softened and took on a wistful note. "I thought my real mother was a rich, glamorous movie star, and someday she'd come and get me in a big white limousine, and take me away to live with her. I waited and waited, but she never came."

Clara sat up intently and looked at the tape player, waiting.

"After Terry died," Lisa's voice went on, sounding dreamy and faraway, "and life was so hard for me, I actually tried to find my birth parents, you know. I contacted the lawyer's office where they'd arranged the adoption, but nobody was looking for me. That's what the letter said. 'None of your birth family is conducting a search at this time. If a search should be instituted, you will be notified immediately.' Nice, hey?"

"How do you feel about that?"

"About being adopted? I don't know. Sometimes..." Lisa's voice slowed and took on a strange, hesitant tone, markedly different from her usual air of brash confidence. "Sometimes I don't really know...who I am. Like I'm...different people, you know?"

"Different people?"

"Well...more like there's different people living inside me. It's...really confusing."

Clara's stomach tightened again as she thought of her recent encounter with Lisa in the hospital. She poised her hand over the notebook, listening to her own voice on the tape.

"I'm not entirely sure what you mean, Lisa."

"Well, like when I was a little girl, I felt as if this other little girl lived inside me. She looked like me, but she was . . . nicer, somehow. She was better than me."

"Where did she come from?"

"Out of the mirror. I told you, she looked just like me."

"Was she a comfort to you? An imaginary friend, so to speak?"

"God, no! She wasn't my friend. I hated her. Her name was Griselda. I don't remember making up that name but I guess I must have done it because subconsciously it was the ugliest name I could think of."

"Why did you hate her?"

"She was prettier than me," Lisa said simply.

"I thought she looked exactly like you."

"She did. But she was still prettier, somehow. I couldn't stand her. Whenever I looked in the mirror and she came into my mind, I almost went crazy. It took years for me to get rid of her."

"Is she gone now?"

"Of course she is. I got rid of her a long time ago."

"How?"

"By winning pageants. Every time I stood by myself on the stage and they gave me the crown and the sash, I knew I was really, truly the prettiest girl of all. It felt so good."

Clara watched the tape recorder with a frown of concentration.

"When I was eleven," Lisa went on, "Terry took me to see *Snow White*. It was just like Griselda all over again. The poor queen kept saying, 'Mirror, mirror, who's the fairest of all?' and the mirror told her it was somebody else. God, I hated that movie! I wanted to stay and watch the queen try to kill Snow White, but I just couldn't stand it. I made Terry get up and leave right in the middle, and she was so upset. But after that day, Griselda never came back."

"Never?"

"Not that I can remember. She was...she was gone. But now there's..." Her voice trailed off.

"Lisa?" Clara's voice prompted gently. "Are you falling asleep?"

"No," Lisa said, sounding distant and childlike. "I'm just...thinking."

"Yes?"

"Sometimes I feel like...somebody else lives inside me, too. Somebody totally different from me, just like... Griselda was."

"Does she have a name, as well?"

"I think so," Lisa said almost shyly. "I think she's called...she's called Maggie...something like that... Isn't this weird? Am I going out of my mind?"

"In my opinion," the doctor's voice said neutrally, "you are entirely sane. Now, could you tell me more about Maggie?"

But Lisa's voice was growing sleepier, muffled and heavy. After a few more disjointed sentences, the tape whirred into silence, then clicked off.

Clara felt a cold shiver of excitement.

She was already fairly certain that the voice on the tape, and the broken woman in the hospital bed, represented a prize beyond imagining. Lisa Cantalini's case was going to be the professional coup that finally brought Clara Wassermann the recognition she craved.

But Clara had to be meticulous so that no criticism of her methods and procedures would discredit her published work.

She had to be very, very careful.

2

The following afternoon, Victor Cantalini strode down the hall toward his wife's room, thinking how much he hated hospitals. He liked to be on his feet, in charge of things, moving easily from place to place. The thought of all those people lying sick and helpless behind closed doors gave him a suffocating feeling.

Victor hadn't been confined to a hospital since a humiliating, painful bout with mumps when he was a teenager. The memory still haunted him at times like this.

He stopped by Lisa's door and hesitated for a moment, a tall handsome man with a thick head of curly gray hair and an air of calm power. Though he was almost thirty years older than his wife, Victor Cantalini was still muscular and vigorous. Today he was wearing lightweight pleated slacks and a chocolate brown shirt open at the neck.

He patted his hair with an automatic gesture, then edged the door open and stepped quietly into the room. The first thing he saw was a woman's shapely body straining against the white fabric of her uniform as she leaned over the bed.

Victor smiled as the nurse straightened and turned to look at him. She was young and attractive, with red hair tucked under her cap and an ample bosom stretching the buttons of her jacket. Her expression was gently sympathetic, so appealing that Victor responded with interest until he realized that her attention was all on her patient, not him.

"Hello, Mr. Cantalini," she murmured. "Your wife fell asleep a few minutes ago. She sort of drifts in and out. If you sit here for a while, she might wake up and talk with you."

Victor moved over beside the nurse and stood looking down at Lisa, assailed by conflicting emotions.

He found it strange to see her lying so still and vulnerable, her face bruised and without makeup. It was almost four days since her accident and the heavy swelling around her right eye was beginning to recede, though it was still badly discolored.

But despite the livid marks on her face, Lisa was more beautiful than he'd ever seen her. The clean line of her cheek and jaw, the high cheekbones and fine molding of her face, the dark wings of eyebrows and the delicacy of her mouth were incredible.

"God," he murmured aloud. "She's really gorgeous, isn't she?"

"Yes." The nurse reached out to adjust the intravenous drip attached to Lisa's arm. "Yes, she's a lovely woman."

"She won a lot of beauty contests when she was a teenager, you know." Victor was still gazing at Lisa's quiet face. "She was working in television when I met her. Doing commercials, things like that."

They were both silent, watching as Lisa stirred restlessly and murmured something.

"Is she all right?" Victor asked. "I thought the doctor said the concussion wasn't serious. Should she be sleeping like this in the middle of the day?"

"She's still under light sedation," the nurse said, gesturing at the IV stand. "And there's—" She stopped abruptly.

"What?"

"Well, she seems to have picked up a mild infection sometime in the last couple of days. Her temperature spikes up and down, but it's well under control. She's also getting some antibiotics in the IV drip."

"An infection? What does that mean? What kind of infection?"

"You'll have to talk to Dr. Bartlett." The nurse gathered up her clipboard and equipment tray. "I have to go now. If you need anything, Mr. Cantalini, just press this buzzer, all right?"

"I sure will, Joanne," he said, reading the name tag on her left breast pocket. He flashed her a warm smile, which she returned in a detached, professional manner.

Victor watched her leave the room, enjoying the way her hips moved invitingly under the crisp cotton of her uniform. After the nurse was gone, he settled in an armchair near the bed and looked at his wife with a familiar mixture of hunger and concern.

Her frail, battered look notwithstanding, Victor felt a troubling and wholly unexpected surge of sexual desire as he watched her sleeping. No woman had ever satisfied him the way Lisa did. The memory of her naked body in his arms, her beauty and the thrill of possessing her, aroused him so powerfully that he shifted in the chair, feeling hot and awkward.

As if any man could ever possess Lisa, he thought bitterly.

Suddenly, her eyes opened and she looked up at him in silence, blinking in the muted light that filtered through the drapes.

Victor was puzzled—and a little frightened—by the blank look on her face. "Hi, honey. It's Victor. Remember me?" he said, trying to make her smile.

"Victor," she murmured.

"Your husband. I know it's hard for you to remember sometimes that you have a husband, but here I am."

All at once, he felt too big for the chair, too rough and masculine for this sterile quietness. Lisa watched him in silence.

"You know, this is the first time I've really talked to you since you...since the accident." She continued to regard him with that bewildered, helpless look. "Those must be some terrific drugs they're feeding you, sweetheart," he joked.

"Victor," she said again as if testing the name, trying to make sense of it.

His uneasiness mounted. "Lisa," he said cautiously, "are you all right? Is there anything you need? Because I can..."

Color rose suddenly in her cheeks, probably from the fever, he thought, and her forehead began to dampen. She brushed at her face and rolled her head on the pillow, then turned to him again.

"I don't understand," she whispered, "why everybody keeps calling me Lisa."

"Well, of course they do." Victor bit his lips and glanced nervously toward the door. "That's your name, isn't it? What else would we call you?"

"My name is Meg. I live in Las Vegas and I need to get back to work. I'm late for work."

Victor stared at her, appalled.

"Lisa," he muttered in a hoarse whisper. "Honey, don't say things like that. You live with me out in the canyon, remember? As soon as the doctor says it's okay,

I'll take you home and then you'll feel a whole lot better. Just wait and see."

"I don't know you. My name is... My name is Meg. I don't know anybody called Lisa." Her eyes closed, and she appeared to be falling asleep again though her cheeks remained flushed.

"Oh, Christ," Victor muttered. He watched her for a moment. It was eerie, as if another person had taken up residence inside Lisa's body. Finally, he got up and rushed from the room, forgetting all about being quiet in the hallway.

Dr. Wassermann was at the nurses' station when Victor approached, and so was Saul Bartlett, the balding, elderly doctor who'd treated Lisa a few times since their marriage, for menstrual cramps and other minor complaints.

Victor stalked over to them, his fear giving way to a bracing flood of anger.

"What the hell's going on?" he demanded, pausing near the desk where the two doctors were conferring in low tones. "What's wrong with her?"

Clara Wassermann gave him a soothing pat on the arm that only served to make him angrier. "Victor," she said gently, "you mustn't be alarmed."

"Not alarmed!" he shouted, conscious of the other doctor's sudden tension and the disapproving looks from the nurses behind the desk. "My wife's going out of her mind and I'm not supposed to be *alarmed?*"

"Please, Mr. Cantalini," Dr. Bartlett began.

"Lisa hasn't gone out of her mind," Clara said calmly. "Victor, come into the staff lounge with us for a few minutes so we can talk about this, all right?"

Victor glared and shifted on his feet, finally allowing himself to be led down the hall to a room filled with shabby leather furniture, used disposable cups and dog-eared magazines.

"Coffee, anyone?" Clara asked, pausing by a small urn on a table in the corner.

"A little cream, no sugar," Saul Bartlett said. "Thanks, Clara."

"That's fine. Victor?"

"No," Victor said, "I don't want *coffee.* I want answers, dammit!"

"Saul, have you and Victor met?"

"Not formally. I saw you here the morning your wife was admitted."

The doctor got up and extended his hand. Victor shook it.

"Victor owns several automotive dealerships in northern Utah," Clara told the other doctor. She sat in one of the leather chairs and looked at the two men. "I can understand how upset you are, Victor," she said at last. "It's a rather unsettling phenomenon. I wish I'd had the chance to warn you before you spoke to Lisa."

Saul sipped his coffee and looked from Clara to Victor in silence.

"I believe Lisa is displaying the initial symptoms of a very rare dissociative condition known as MPD," Clara went on.

"What does that mean?" Victor asked. "MPD, what's that?"

"It stands for multiple personality disorder."

Victor gaped at her, thunderstruck. He struggled to find his voice. "Like...like those television movies where somebody thinks they're two different people, and one of them does things the other doesn't know about?"

"Those dramatizations tend to be highly inaccurate," Clara said. "For one thing, they suggest that MPD is a much more common phenomenon than it really is. In fact, there are not that many completely authentic, fully documented cases."

"I thought there were hundreds of them nowadays," the other doctor said.

"Oh, there are lots diagnosed," Clara said dryly, "but very few are actually authenticated and verified."

"And you think my wife's one of them? For God's sake, Clara, this is so..."

Saul gave Clara a skeptical frown. "MPD arises from particular kinds of stress, right? I've seen Lisa a few times in the past, and she's always seemed to be a very confident and self-assured young woman."

"Appearances can be deceiving," the therapist said. "Lisa has a number of unresolved conflicts from her childhood. Negative feelings about her mother, an absent father, deep insecurities about having been adopted.... There are a host of contributing factors. And," she added with a glance at Victor, "she's also been under considerable strain in recent months."

"That's true. Things haven't been perfect between us lately," Victor said. "What marriage *is* perfect all the time? But she always has lots of money to spend, and she knows how to have fun. I don't see why she should go off the deep end like this, all of a sudden."

"It's not 'all of a sudden,'" Clara said. "Lisa's alter personality has probably been present since her childhood."

"Come on, Clara," Saul said. "Let's look at a couple of alternative diagnoses for a minute, shall we? The girl's had a bad knock on the head. I treated her initially for shock and a mild concussion, and now she's got a fever spiking up at two-hour intervals. Don't you think a little disorientation is natural under the circumstances?"

"Perhaps, but this isn't the first time I've heard about Lisa's alter personality. She mentioned Meg in several of her last therapy sessions, over three months ago. Soon afterward, she quit coming to see me, and gave no explanation."

"What do you mean, she mentioned Meg?" Victor shifted angrily in the chair. "I can't believe I'm hearing this."

"Lisa wasn't sure of Meg's name at the time," Clara told him. "But she knew of her existence."

Saul moved a little closer and placed a sympathetic hand on Victor's shoulder.

"What happened that last day, Victor?" Clara said. "Just before Lisa's accident, I mean. How did she seem?"

Victor shrugged. "The same as always, I guess. When I left in the morning, she was still in bed. She planned to get up and spend the day lazing by the pool. I think she had somebody coming over, a cousin of hers or something. I was working late, and she was gone when I got home around eleven that night. No message, nothing. Just gone."

"Was that unusual?"

"For Lisa?" He laughed without humor. "Nothing was unusual for Lisa."

"So the next thing you heard was that she'd been found unconscious in her car."

"No. She called me just after midnight from her car phone."

Clara looked at him with interest. "Really? Where was she?"

"Somewhere on the freeway, south of Cedar City. She sounded really funny. Strange, I mean."

"In what way?"

"Just strange. Maybe a little quieter than usual, kind of sleepy. She said she'd had an impulse to go down to the condo in Vegas for a few days, then changed her mind. She told me she wanted to come home and talk with me, see if we could work things out and try once more to make a go of our marriage. She...said she loved me," Victor added with some reluctance.

Clara nodded thoughtfully. "And did you find *that* unusual?"

"Yes. That was pretty unusual."

"And soon after that, she must have fallen asleep and driven off the freeway. Her car was heading north when she left the road, wasn't it? She'd already turned around and started back to Salt Lake?"

"That's right. Lisa always drives like a maniac. When she hadn't made it home by five-thirty, I was starting to get really worried. Then I heard from the police."

Clara nodded, looking satisfied. "I think when she called from her car phone and said she loved you, it's possible that you were already talking to Meg, not Lisa," she told Victor. "I think at that time Meg must have known about Lisa's life and situation, though she doesn't seem to have any awareness of it now. It's likely that the trauma of the accident was enough to temporarily..."

The other doctor looked at Clara thoughtfully. "I've only tended her physical condition," he said at last. "I wasn't aware she'd suffered this kind of trauma in her life, and I've never seen a documented case of MPD."

"Few people have," Clara said. "As I said, it's very, very rare, but it does happen, Saul."

"I know. Still, I can't help finding it odd, the way you talk about these women as if they're two separate people."

"In a way, they are," Clara told him. "In a true case of multiple personality, the alter personality can have its own artistic talents, even an IQ markedly different from the host personality's. It registers different blood pressure and brain-scan readings. It can be right-handed while the host is left-handed, speak languages and be knowledgeable in subjects unknown to the host, and emerge as a completely separate personality on handwriting analyses and psychological-profile tests."

"My God," Victor breathed, gazing at her in stunned amazement.

"I've been reading all the literature I can find on the disorder, and I've talked with Lisa...or Meg," she added with a brief smile, "several times in the past couple of days. Her case is classic in many ways but there's one very significant difference."

"What's that?" Saul asked with a glance at Victor.

"Well," Clara said, frowning, "in all the cases I've researched, the host personality is initially quite unaware of the thoughts and activities of the alter. Or alters," she added. "There are usually more than one. The alters, on the other hand, are well aware of the host personality. In Lisa's case, this seems to be reversed."

Victor listened in silence, feeling rising panic when he began to comprehend the full import of what the therapist was saying.

"Lisa knew about Meg a long time ago, or at least suspected her existence," Clara went on, "but Meg now seems to have no knowledge of Lisa. She insists that she comes from Las Vegas and that she's a waitress and kitchen worker in a casino. She even recalls her address and phone number in Las Vegas, but nothing at all about Lisa's life. It's really quite bizarre. Although, of course, the accident could have affected her memory."

"So what do you think?" Victor asked. "Will she get better? I mean, will she come back to reality?"

"I don't know. First, I have to find out why..." Clara fell silent for a moment, then waved her hand. "Never mind. I'll let you know more about the process of integration when I've finished my research. In the meantime," she said, "the best thing for you to do, Victor, is accept her as she is and help her to recover her physical strength."

"As she is. What does that mean?"

"Exactly what I said. The alter personality—Meg, in this case—is usually created in early childhood to cope with some kind of trauma that the child finds unbearable. The alter is a very important part of the patient's psychological makeup, and it's vital that the therapist and others close to the patient accept its existence. Otherwise, integration cannot take place and the personality will remain fragmented."

"So what are you advising, Clara?" the other doctor asked. "We should all start calling her Meg, and treat her like a different person?"

"That's her name. Lisa is completely absent at the moment. I'm not even able to call her up under hypnosis. The only woman in that hospital bed, for the moment at least, is a person named Meg."

"I can't do it," Victor said flatly. "I can't take her home and call her Meg. It's just so crazy. You have to help her, Clara. I'm not sure I can handle something like this."

"Okay, call her Lisa, if you insist," Clara told him, her tone hesitant. "She'll likely answer to it, and it might jog some memories for her."

"How long is this going to last?" the doctor asked. "What's your prognosis?"

Clara shook her head. "I'm afraid nobody can predict what will happen in a case like this. We just have to give her as much comfort and understanding as we can, and hope for the best."

3

Meg wandered under a scorching sun. She was burning up with thirst, and so weary that her feet refused to carry her any longer. At last, exhausted, she collapsed onto the parched sand and began to whimper.

A carrion bird circled overhead and watched her with cold yellow eyes. In the shadows, snakes and other loathsome creatures crept nearer to her on the sand, waiting.

Somewhere beyond the leaden blue of the sky, a gentle voice asked why she was crying, but she couldn't answer. The voice was small and faraway, nothing at all to do with her, and the glaring sky hurt her eyes when she looked up.

With part of her conscious mind, Meg understood that she was trapped in a nightmare. Despite its horrors, she was reluctant to wake up. Somewhere out there, beyond this parched desert, was a real world that had suddenly become treacherous, a waking nightmare, more frightening than anything that came to her while she slept...

Meg sobbed and rolled her head on the pillow. Her hair was drenched with sweat, and the sheets felt stifling.

She sensed the murmur of women's voices around her, and hands working over her with soothing competence. "The poor thing, she's burning up with fever," one of the women said. "She keeps muttering something. It's all right, Mrs. Cantalini." The voice was louder now, addressing her directly. "Can you hear me? It's your nurse, Joanne."

Meg nodded and opened her eyes, focusing on the pretty, freckled face above her.

"Joanne," she muttered hoarsely, licking her lips. "Thirsty," she added.

"I know you are." The nurse held out a glass of crushed ice chips swimming in water, tilting the straw so Meg could drink. Meg lifted herself and gulped quickly, refreshed by the burst of coolness. She settled back onto the pillows, and watched while the nurse bustled around the bed, replacing the hot twisted sheets with drifts of white cotton that felt as cool and sweet as fresh snow.

Meg sighed, nestling in the coolness, then stiffened when she saw another woman sitting quietly by the window. It was the tall woman with the clipboard, wearing a long gray tweed skirt and a silk blouse the color of dried rose petals.

The woman was writing, her elegant silver-streaked head bent over the clipboard.

Dr. Wassermann, Meg recalled. That was the woman's name.

Meg looked at the doctor though half-closed eyes, battling a fear that she didn't fully understand. She only knew that this woman had the power to look into her soul and change her life in some monstrous way.

"Isn't her temperature going down yet?" Clara asked the nurse. "It's been four days since she started getting these spells of fever."

"Dr. Bartlett has an antibiotic in her IV drip, and she seems to be responding quite well. She peaks only a few times a day now."

"Nevertheless, the temperature fluctuations make her therapy more difficult. A good deal of the time, she's too disoriented to respond."

The nurse busied herself with the contents of a small metal tray. "A lot of patients have picked up this same staph infection," she said over her shoulder. "It's gone through the hospital like wildfire. Mrs. Cantalini is lucky, actually. She's getting over it faster than some of the others."

The nurse smoothed the damp hair on Meg's forehead and made a small adjustment to the heavy bandage over her eye. Then she turned to leave, taking her tray and the bundle of twisted bed sheets. Meg was alone with the woman in the silk blouse, who leaned closer and studied her face, smiling gently.

"Well, hello there," the older woman said. "How are you feeling this morning?"

Meg tried to answer, but her lips were swollen and cracked from fever.

"Hard to talk?" Clara asked with calm sympathy, looking deep into her eyes.

Meg nodded.

"All right. You don't need to say too much if it's difficult. Just nod yes or no when I ask questions. Do you understand?"

Meg nodded, keeping her eyes fixed on the woman's face. Clara Wassermann had remarkable dark eyes, almost mesmerizing in their intensity.

"Now, first we need to establish who I'm talking to. Are you still Meg, or is Lisa back today?"

Meg tensed and gripped the edge of the sheet.

"Perhaps I should rephrase that." Clara said. "Are you Lisa today?"

Meg shook her head and looked away.

"All right," Clara said, making a note on her pad. "Meg is still with us, I gather. Have you developed any consciousness of Lisa since we spoke yesterday?"

Meg closed her eyes. "I don't know what you're talking about," she muttered.

Clara looked at her intently. "You sound angry. Why are you upset, Meg?"

"You keep talking about Lisa," Meg said. "And the nurses call me Mrs. Cantalini. I don't know what's happening. I want to go home."

"Soon you'll be well enough to go home." Clara touched Meg's forehead with a cool, soothing hand. "In a few more days. Right now, I want you to answer some questions for me. Is that all right, Meg? Just a few questions?"

Meg nodded wearily.

"How do you feel at this moment, Meg?" the doctor asked. "If you could describe your emotions in a single word, what would be uppermost?"

Meg searched her mind. "I guess," she said reluctantly, "that I'm mostly scared. Scared and confused."

"Why are you scared? You're safe here. You're in a warm bed in a hospital, surrounded by people who want to take care of you. I'm here with you, and your nurse is outside, and Victor's waiting to see you. What are you frightened of?"

Meg didn't answer immediately. "I don't know what's going on," she whispered at last. "I don't know how I got here, or who these people are. I don't know who Lisa is."

There was a silence while the therapist calmly watched her.

"You keep telling me," Meg went on with difficulty, "that Lisa...lives inside me somewhere. It doesn't make sense. I keep trying to understand, but I can't. I've never heard of Lisa, and I don't want to talk about her. My name is Meg Howell. I want to get out of here."

Clara leaned back in the chair. "Why should you be afraid of Lisa? After all, you and Lisa have shared this body for a long time, haven't you? You have memories going back to when you were three years old."

"But that's not true!" Meg said desperately. "I didn't share a body with anybody. I grew up with Hank and Glory, and...and lived in Las Vegas and played baseball, and helped Hank with the horses. I know I did. You're all trying to make me believe I'm crazy, but I'm not."

"Hank and Glory were good parents, weren't they?" Clara said. "Very kind and loving?"

Meg nodded. "They were so...so good to me. They loved me. Glory was small and fat, and when she laughed..." Meg paused wistfully, then went on, "And Hank was tall and big, slow-moving and really gentle. He shod horses for a living. After Glory died, we—"

"Glory died?" Clara interrupted, suddenly alert. "Your mother? When?"

"Can't...hard to remember," she whispered, rubbing her bandaged forehead. "Getting hot again."

Clara held the glass of ice water to Meg's lips and supported her while she drank.

"When did your mother die?" she repeated. "Was it an accident?"

"I was about fourteen," Meg said softly. "She was...run over by a car at a stock-car race. We always went to the car races. Hank loved them. Then Hank and I were all alone."

"Was that a problem?"

"With Hank? No, I loved him, too. But he started to drink after Glory died, because he missed her so much. I had to look after him a lot of the time. We had a job at a dude ranch, and I was usually the one who..." Her voice trailed off.

"So your mother died when you were fourteen. What happened to your father?"

"I can't remember. We were at the ranch and then... It's all a blur. It's like a movie screen going blank. I can't remember."

"Was he always kind to you?"

"Always," Meg said. "Even when he..."

"What?"

"Nothing," Meg said. "Hank was good to me. I loved him."

"Lisa never had a father, and she was hostile toward her mother," Clara said gently. "But you were completely different. You had a father who loved and needed you, and you also had a tender, understanding mother whom you adored. Exactly what Lisa wanted and never had."

"What do you mean?" Meg asked the therapist warily.

"We'll talk about it another time, okay?" Clara scribbled on the pad for a moment, then smiled at Meg. "Now, tell me more about this Little League baseball team we talked about yesterday. You were quite a tomboy, weren't you, Meg? Not at all the type to... well, to enter beauty contests, for instance?"

"Beauty contests?" Meg looked at the other woman blankly. *"Me?"*

"You're a very lovely girl, you know, Meg. You could probably win a beauty contest if you were to enter one."

Meg laughed hoarsely, then began to cough, and Clara helped her take another sip of water.

"That's just... silly," Meg said, sinking back into the nest of pillows. "I'd never enter a beauty contest."

"You know, I think you're right. And *that,*" the doctor added, making another note on her pad, "is a very interesting point. In fact, it's quite fascinating."

Why? Meg wanted to ask. What was so fascinating about a beauty contest?

But she was already drifting back into the hot, confusing, light-sparkled world of her dreams, and she couldn't find a way to frame the question.

Maybe it was all part of her nightmare, this whole dreadful experience. Maybe when she really woke up, she'd be in her bed in Las Vegas, getting ready to put on her uniform and head out for work. And none of this would have happened.

Clara Wassermann sat in her office, gazing through narrowed eyes at the city skyline. The night was black and rich with stars, and a full moon beamed across the eastern mountains while the vast salt flats to the west of the city lay in darkness.

She sighed and stretched, then caught her reflection in the mirror near the coat tree. Clara studied it without emotion. Her face in solitude was sharply etched, cold and remote. She'd paid a high price to reach her present status, she thought.

A woman didn't rise to this level in a tough occupation without making sacrifices. Clara blamed the demands of the job for her failed relationships and the loneliness of her existence. However, the choice had always been hers and she'd never hesitated to put her work first.

She smiled bitterly, musing over the irony. For a woman who made a career of mending damaged psyches and broken relationships, her personal life was as sterile and clinical as a laboratory.

But the case of Lisa Cantalini and her dissociative-personality disorder was going to make it all worthwhile. When Clara finished documenting the therapy and had it published, she'd be famous. That kind of recognition was worth more to her than anything. It was what she'd wanted all her life, and now, miraculously, it lay within her grasp.

She chose an audiocassette and popped it into her machine, then took her pen in hand and prepared to listen.

"Thursday, May 26," her own voice said. "Therapy session with Lisa Cantalini. Hello, Lisa."

"Hi, Doc." Lisa's voice was bright and breezy, almost impudent.

Clara felt an icy chill, thinking about the bruised, frightened woman lying across town in a hospital bed. It was the same voice on the tape, the same woman a scant three months earlier, and yet the differences were overwhelming. After thirty years of medical training and professional practice, Clara Wassermann still found herself astonished by the complexity of the human personality.

"You're looking well, Lisa," her voice went on courteously. "Are you comfortable there on the couch?"

"Yeah. Actually, I'm getting used to it. It feels...kind of sexy."

Lisa's voice grew languid, almost teasing. Clara remembered how the young woman had stretched and displayed herself on the leather couch during that final session. She'd worn denim shorts and a yellow jersey halter top, her breasts pressing against the soft fabric, nipples clearly visible....

"I'm glad to hear it," Clara said, her own voice sounding dry and crisp.

"Hey, what's up, Doc?" Lisa asked. "Am I upsetting you?"

Pages riffled briskly on the tape. "Not at all, Lisa. I'm glad you're comfortable. Now, would you like to talk about the girl in the mirror again? I think you called her Maggie."

"No!" Lisa said emphatically. "I don't want to talk about Meg."

"Meg?"

"That's her name. Not Maggie. It's short for Megan. I just...found that out."

"Why don't you want to talk about her?"

"Because she's boring. She's so uptight. Besides, she's not even real."

"If she's not real, why does she have a name?"

There was a silence on the tape, then the sound of Lisa's body moving impatiently on the couch. "That was all kid stuff, that Meg thing. Let's talk about Victor, okay? Isn't that why I'm supposed to be here, to find out what's wrong between me and Victor?"

"All right," Clara's voice said neutrally. "Let's talk about Victor."

There was a long silence on the tape.

"I hate this, you know," Lisa said sullenly.

Clara was silent.

"I hate it when you say we're going to talk about something and then you just shut up."

Another silence.

"Victor's exactly the same. He keeps insisting we've got to talk, and then he won't say a thing. He just sits there looking at me like I'm some kind of bug."

"I'm sure that's not true. You're an exceedingly beautiful young woman, Lisa."

"Victor used to think so, too. When he first met me, he fell like a ton of bricks. Poor man, I almost felt sorry for him. I was working at the television station then, and he kept calling every day, sending me flowers and presents, begging me to go out with him..."

"But you wouldn't?"

"Not a chance."

"Why not? Were you bothered by the age difference?"

"No, I wasn't," Lisa said scornfully. "The fact that he was fifty-one and I was twenty didn't particularly matter to me," she added, mocking the doctor's precise tones as she often did. "Victor's a good-looking man. Handsome and sexy, just the way I like them."

"So why didn't you respond to his advances?"

"Because he was married."

"I see. You had moral objections, then?"

Lisa laughed, a peal of genuine mirth that made Clara smile involuntarily at the tape machine. "Yeah, right," Lisa chuckled. "Moral objections. That's really funny."

"All right, what were your objections?"

"I just knew it was impractical," Lisa said, her voice suddenly cold.

"Impractical? In what way?"

"I know what happens to young girls who get tied up with married men. They get a lot of money and presents, a few nice holidays and a polite kiss-off after they've wasted ten good years of their lives. No way, baby. Not for Lisa Bauer."

"So what happened?"

"He chased me all winter. In the spring, we sent a film crew out to Victor's place to do a series of commercials showing luxury cars against a country background." There was a pause, then, "Do you know where Victor lives?"

"Why don't you tell me about it?"

"Well, he's got this big, really beautiful house. It's sort of a castle, actually, built of pink granite, out in the canyon at the foot of the mountains. It's got acres of land around it, and a little creek running through the property, and everybody who lives out there is so rich it just makes you sick. God, when I saw that house I wanted it so much. I wanted Victor and his house."

"So what did you do?"

Lisa giggled. "I went inside and had a little chat with his wife, Pauline."

There was a brief silence on the tape, then Lisa's voice again, sounding faintly defiant.

"Don't you want to know what I said to the nice lady?"

"I'm interested in your entire story, Lisa."

A series of gentle sounds indicated that Lisa was settling herself more comfortably on the couch.

"Well, Pauline was kind of pitiful, actually," the young woman began. "She had to be at least as old as Victor, with frizzy yellow hair in a perm, you know, to hide the gray, and that fat belly most women get when they're old. No style at all. I honestly didn't know how he could stand her. I went inside to ask for a glass of water while the crew was filming, and Pauline did the gracious-hostess bit and offered to show me around the house. You know what I said?"

There was another silence on the tape.

Lisa giggled again. "I smiled sweetly, all girlish and wide-eyed, and said, 'Oh, thank you, Mrs. Cantalini, but I've already seen the house. I was here with Victor one day when you weren't home. You've done such a beautiful job of decorating the bedrooms.' "

"Was that true?"

"Of course not. But it shook *her* up, I can tell you."

"So what happened? Did she confront Victor?"

"Right away. He came to the station the next day, so mad he was practically shaking, and asked me why I'd told his wife a lie like that."

Clara waited.

"I told him I couldn't help myself," Lisa went on. "I told him I wanted him so much that I just kept having those wild fantasies about being alone in his house with him."

"And?" Clara prompted gently.

"And we went to Las Vegas together that weekend. I let him make love to me, then cried and said it could never, ever happen again because of his wife. Seven months later we were married."

"That was a speedy divorce," Clara observed neutrally.

"Well, it sure didn't start out that way," Lisa said. "At first, Pauline made all kinds of threats. She said she was going to clean Victor out, drag both of us through the mud and take every cent he had. But then she died, so there was no messy court scene, after all."

"That was convenient."

Clara glanced quickly at the tape, troubled by the dry tone in her own voice. She made a stern mental note to try harder to avoid expressing value judgments of any kind during therapy sessions.

But Lisa sounded undisturbed, just dreamy and pleased. "It was, wasn't it? After Pauline died, there was no problem at all. We just got married and I moved into that beautiful house."

"How did she die?"

"Pauline was a lush," Lisa said coldly. "She drank a lot. One day she tripped on her housecoat, fell down the stairs and broke her neck. The housemaid witnessed the whole thing."

"I see. So then you and Victor were married..."

"And it was great for a while. We really had a good time. But now it's—"

The young woman stopped abruptly.

"Lisa?" the therapist said.

"Hmm?"

"You were telling me about your marriage."

"Not much to tell. Maybe I need a lover." Lisa's voice grew coy and seductive. "Do you think I need a lover, Doc? Should I find some big, sweaty, young hunk who can do me the way I like? And then I'll come back here and tell you all the juicy details. You'd really like that, wouldn't you?"

Clara frowned, recognizing this blatant manipulation of the therapist. A quick change of subject was always the best defense, as her next question demonstrated.

"Tell me, Lisa, when did you first learn you were adopted?"

There was a brief, shocked silence, then Lisa's voice, confused and defensive.

"I didn't... What did you say?"

"Tell me about the moment when you learned you were adopted. Did your mother tell you?"

"No, she didn't." Lisa's voice was low and uncertain, not at all the brash, seductive tone she'd been using just moments earlier. "She . . . I guess she couldn't bring herself to. She kept putting it off. Finally, when I was seven or eight years old, I . . . I heard it from the kids."

"What kids?"

"The other kids on the playground. All the girls hated me because I was so much prettier than they were, and my mother always bought me these beautiful clothes. One day, they told me I was adopted, like it was some awful sickness or something. I had to go home and ask Terry what it meant."

"How did you feel when she told you?"

"I *hated* her," Lisa whispered. "Oh, Jesus, I hated her so much. . . ."

Her voice trailed off. Soon afterward, the tape clicked to an end.

Clara sat in silence looking at the machine for a long time while the night deepened beyond her office windows and the empty building creaked and sighed in the summer wind.

She thought about the brazen woman on that tape, and the baffling alter ego that Lisa Cantalini had long ago created to shield herself from her pain. This other personality—Meg—was more real and vivid than the doctor had anticipated, and strangely vulnerable. Clara realized that the persona of Meg had probably been bearing Lisa's pain for years, and now it was almost destroying the core personality.

But Clara felt no particular sympathy for either of Lisa Cantalini's personalities, only a clinical interest and an intellectual challenge that was becoming all-consuming.

Suddenly, acting on impulse, she picked up the telephone, consulted a number among her notes and dialed.

"Willows, Las Vegas," a receptionist said courteously. "What station, please?"

"Could you connect me with the lower kitchen?" Clara asked.

She waited tensely until someone answered, amid a clatter of pans and crockery and the hollow shouts of many voices.

"Kitchen here," a cheerful voice said, sounding richly Italian. "What I can do for you?"

Clara took a deep breath and crossed her fingers. "I'd like to speak to Megan Howell, please. Is she there?"

"Sure. Just a minute. Meggie, *telephone,*" the voice bawled into the uproar.

4

The lower kitchen in the big casino was fully into its late-evening rush, preparing the red-eye specials for gamblers who spent all night at the gaming tables. Through the small hours of the morning, dinners and breakfasts would be served simultaneously, while the staff scrambled to clean the kitchen and make salads for the next day.

In one corner, a thin woman in a stained pink uniform bent over the fry grill, scrubbing at the blackened surface with a wide spatula. The grease came away in crusted, oily mounds, and she scraped them into a plastic barrel under the grill.

"Meg!" A blond girl passed by, carrying an armful of plates. "Carlo says you're wanted on the phone."

The woman glanced up and pushed a lock of hair back under her white hair net, leaving a smear of grease on her forehead. "Me?" she asked.

She looked across the kitchen at Carlo, the busboy, who waved the phone and gestured frantically.

"Meggie! Hurry up!"

Puzzled, she put down her spatula, wiped her hands on her apron and went over to take the phone.

"Hello?" she said into the receiver.

"Is this Megan Howell?"

"Yes, it is."

A woman's voice said something that Meg couldn't hear over the clatter in the kitchen.

"Excuse me," she shouted. "Could you speak a little louder? It's really noisy in here."

"I said, you don't know me. My name is Dr. Clara Wassermann, and I'm calling from Salt Lake City."

Meg frowned and shifted the phone to her other hand. She rubbed at the small of her back, which always ached when she scrubbed the fry grill. "I think you must have the wrong number or something."

"Do you know a woman called Lisa Cantalini?"

Dana, the kitchen supervisor, passed by and glared at Meg. "Make it snappy," she hissed. "That grill won't clean itself, you know."

Meg tensed and looked at the telephone, then held it back to her ear. "I don't... What was the name?" she shouted.

"Lisa Cantalini."

"What does she look like?"

"She's in her early twenties, tall and slim, dark hair and blue eyes. Very attractive, well-dressed, drives a white Thunderbird..."

"Oh, *her,*" Meg said. "Yes, I know her. I mean, I've talked to her a couple of times, but I never knew her last name."

"Could I call you at home tomorrow and talk to you about this?"

"I don't have a phone at my place." Meg licked her lips nervously and glanced at Dana, who was studying the fry grill with a hostile expression. "Look, there's nothing to tell," she said hastily. "I just met her one day last spring when I was getting off work. She dropped her purse in the parking lot and I helped her pick the stuff up. We started talking and she bought me a drink in the lounge."

"Was that the only time you saw her?"

"A couple of times after that, she came by when I was getting off shift and took me out to dinner. She really liked to talk."

"What did she talk about?"

"Me, mostly," Meg said hesitantly. "It was kind of weird. She was really interested in my background and my family, all that kind of stuff."

"And your parents?"

"Especially my parents. She wanted to know all about them."

"Could you tell me their names?"

Meg stiffened. "Look, what is this, anyhow? What kind of doctor did you say you are?"

"I'm a psychiatrist, Meg. I'm sorry I can't explain the details of this, but I can assure you that it would be very helpful to Lisa if you could just answer a few more questions."

Meg shifted on her feet, then nodded reluctantly. "Okay. My parents' names were Hank and Gloria Howell. They raised me on a little farm outside Las Vegas where my daddy tended horses for a living."

"You told Lisa that?"

"Yes, I did."

"And you told her a lot of details about how you grew up in Las Vegas, and played Little League baseball, and helped your father with his horseshoeing business?"

"I probably told her all that stuff. Why?"

"Meg, please, I'd like you to think very carefully. Is there any reason that Lisa Cantalini would identify with you?"

"Meggie! Cut it short! We need this grill in ten minutes!"

Meg gestured helplessly at the telephone, then turned away and hunched her shoulders to block some of the noise. "Identify? What does that mean?"

"Well, for instance, do you look at all like Lisa?"

Meg glanced down at her stained uniform and dirty sneakers, and gave a harsh burst of laughter. "Like *her?*"

"Do you have similar coloring or anything? Are you close to the same age?"

"Oh, I see what you mean. Well, I have dark hair like she does, but that's about all. I'm not...I sure don't have her looks. And I'm quite a few years older than she is."

"So the two of you wouldn't have anything at all in common?"

"Not much. Except that she was..."

Meg fell silent.

"Meg? I'm sorry, I didn't catch what you said."

"She was really interested to hear that I was adopted," Meg said at last, raising her voice. "She kept wanting to talk about it all the time, how it felt and how my parents dealt with it, all that kind of stuff. She said it gave us a common bond."

"I see."

Even through the uproar in the big kitchen, Meg could hear a note of satisfaction in the other woman's voice.

"What's all this about?" she asked.

"It's quite a complex situation," the doctor said. "To put it briefly, Mrs. Cantalini seems to have assumed your identity."

Meg's eyes widened. "What do you mean? She's pretending to be *me?*"

"Not really, Meg," Dr. Wassermann said quietly. "I think it would be more accurate to say that she believes she *is* you."

Meg shifted uncomfortably. "Look, this is really weird," she muttered. "Is there anything I should do? I mean, is she crazy? Is she going to...come here and try to hurt me, or something?"

"Not at all. Lisa is certainly no threat to you. She's in the hospital at the moment, and won't be well enough to go home for some time. It might be helpful for her to speak with you at some point in the future, but I'll let you know if I feel that's indicated."

Meg shifted awkwardly and cast an anxious glance at Dana. "I'm sorry, but I really have to go," she said at last. "I can't talk anymore right now."

"Meg, is there somewhere I can call you if I need to talk to you again?"

"I told you, I don't have a phone at my apartment. I guess you'd have to call here, but I'd really rather you didn't." Meg looked at the supervisor, then pressed her mouth closer to the receiver. "I'll get into trouble if you call me here. I could lose my job."

"All right, I'm sorry. I'll try not to bother you again. Thank you, Meg."

Meg murmured something and hung up, then stood looking at the phone for a moment. Finally, she trudged back to the fry grill and picked up her spatula.

Dana paused and watched, hands on hips. "So," the supervisor said with heavy joviality, "who's calling you at work, Meggie? Got a boyfriend?"

Meg ignored her and went on scrubbing.

"Meg? Who was on the phone?"

"None of your business," Meg said curtly, keeping her back turned.

Dana raised her eyebrows. "I don't know what's gotten into you lately," she said coldly. "You're acting like you don't want to keep this job."

Meg straightened, her cheeks flushed with annoyance. She shook the spatula into the grease-filled pail, deliberately splattering the hem of Dana's white uniform. "Don't be silly," she said sarcastically. "Who wouldn't want to keep this job?"

The supervisor gave her a long, level glance, then shook her head. "I truly don't know what's gotten into you," she repeated.

Meg stood sullenly by the grill with the spatula gripped in her hands. Dana glared at her a moment longer, then turned and headed toward the back to check on the rows of teenage dishwashers who labored over stainless-steel sinks.

Meg watched the woman go, her face expressionless. Then she bent over the grill once more and began scraping methodically at the mounds of congealed grease.

It was just after 2:00 a.m. when Meg's shift ended and she left the casino. The air in the small hours of the morning was cool and crisp, a welcome respite from the blistering August heat. A few die-hard gamblers were still hurrying along the wide streets, carrying their plastic tubs of coins from one casino to another while the wash of neon lights created a kind of garish, artificial daylight.

Meg moved among the tourists to the bus stop and stood leaning wearily against the shelter, her head drooping. After a few minutes, she gathered herself together, rummaged in her handbag for some coins and went into an all-night drugstore to use the phone.

"Hi," she said briefly when her call went through. "It's me."

She waited a moment, then grimaced at the phone.

"Yeah, that's right. It's *Meg*, damn you. Look, I got a call tonight at work, from this Dr. Wassermann in Salt Lake City."

Again she listened, then nodded.

"She was asking all kinds of questions about a woman named Lisa Cantalini. Apparently, this woman thinks she's me. She's assumed my identity."

She held the phone to her ear and glanced at the boy behind the drugstore counter, then lowered her voice and spoke again.

"The doctor didn't say. Just that Lisa is in the hospital and won't be able to go home for quite a while. What do you think?"

Meg listened, apparently not pleased by the response. "Look," she began with some heat, "you said I wouldn't have to work there for more than another week or so. I can't stand that bloody job. If you knew how hard it is... I almost got fired tonight. I came really close to telling that supervisor what to do with her greasy spatula."

The other party spoke for a long time and Meg nodded, looking somewhat mollified.

"I know, I know. But, Jesus, it's awful. I'm not even waiting on tables anymore. I've been demoted to full-time kitchen work. And that dumpy little apartment I'm living in... Okay, a little longer. Just a few more days. When should I call you?"

She listened, then grinned briefly.

"Oh, did I wake you up? I'm sorry, sweetheart, but this is when I get off work. If you had a job, you'd understand better."

The response clearly amused her. She threw her head back and laughed, all her anger vanishing for the moment.

"Is that right?" she murmured. "Well, I miss you, too. When I see you again, I'll show you how much. G'bye, baby."

Clara walked into the flower-filled hospital room, holding her clipboard and a couple of files. She found Lisa propped against a mound of pillows, wearing a jade silk housecoat instead of the cotton hospital gown. Her short black hair was freshly washed, curling softly around her face. The dark bruises on her face had faded to a dull grayish yellow, and most of the swelling was gone from her right eye.

Victor was lounging in a chair nearby. He glanced up when the doctor entered and rose courteously to hold out a chair for her.

"Thanks, Victor." Clara seated herself and turned her attention to Lisa.

After a week of therapy, the doctor no longer had to inquire which personality was dominant. She could tell immediately just by facial expression and body language.

Even weakened and battered, the persona of Meg had a different expression, an air of gentleness that Lisa had always lacked. Strangely, she seemed to have a sense of humor, as well, something that Clara had never detected in the beautiful young woman who'd first come to her for treatment.

But today, something was different. The woman in the bed had the familiar, vulnerable look of Meg, but also something of the hostile expression that Lisa had so often worn during those final therapy sessions in the spring.

"Hello, Meg," Clara ventured. "You're looking a little stronger today."

Victor shifted abruptly at Clara's casual use of the name. His handsome face twisted with embarrassment but he said nothing, merely turned aside and looked out the window.

Lisa gave the doctor a cold glance. After a long moment, she closed her eyes deliberately and turned her face away.

Clara glanced at Victor, who nodded. "Saul said she'll be ready to go home in a few days, but she'll need to stay in bed for another week or two. Filomena will look after her."

He made an abrupt warning gesture, then leaned toward Clara with a look of appeal that was surprising in such a strong and forceful man.

"You'll have to talk to her, Clara," he whispered urgently. "She keeps saying—"

"I won't go home with him," Lisa said, her eyes still closed. "I don't even know him."

"He's your husband," Clara said calmly. "Look, I need to explain a few things to both of you. Last night, I called—"

"He's not my husband! I've never seen him before. Why won't anybody listen to me?" the young woman asked in despair, opening her eyes. "I keep telling you, my name is Megan Howell. I live in Las Vegas and work in the kitchen at the Willows. I'm *not Lisa!*"

She sat up to give emphasis to her words, clenching her hands into fists. Her exotic dark blue eyes were almost violet with emotion. Then abruptly, her face twisted and she crumpled against the pillows, putting both hands to her forehead.

Clara placed a hand on the young woman's arm. "Meg," she said gently, "there's something I need to tell you. It's very important, and you're probably going to find it upsetting."

Victor looked at his wife in concern. He got to his feet and murmured something about leaving them alone to talk, but Clara motioned him back into his chair. "You'd better hear this, too, Victor. We all need to understand." She looked down at Lisa's huddled form. "Last night," she said, "I called the Willows in Las Vegas. I asked to talk with a kitchen worker called Megan Howell."

Victor hitched his chair closer, gazing at Clara. "And?" he said. "What did they tell you?"

"Megan Howell was on duty at the time, so they sent her to the phone. I spoke with her at some length. She lives in the city and works night shift at the Willows kitchen. She told me her parents were named Hank and Gloria Howell."

The woman in the bed stared up at her, wide-eyed with shock and horror. The color drained from her face, leaving the bruises looking dark and angry on her pale skin.

"That's impossible. What are you saying?" she whispered. "I'm Megan Howell."

Clara reached out again to touch Lisa's arm, but the young woman pulled it away.

"You're wrong. Why are you doing this?" she shouted.

"Calm yourself, my dear. Please be calm and listen." Clara flipped through the notes on her clipboard, taking a few moments to collect her thoughts.

"It's early for me to make a firm diagnosis," she said at last. "Especially in a case as unusual as this. Most of my conclusions are speculative at this point, but I can tell you what I think is going on, and after some further therapy sessions, I hope we'll be able to confirm it."

The others watched her in silence; the tension in the room was almost palpable.

"I believe this is what happened," Clara went on. "Lisa, you had a traumatic and emotionally unrewarding childhood, complicated by the lack of a father image, conflicts with your mother, fears about being adopted, which your mother did nothing to ease, and deep concerns over your body image, which your mother actually intensified by concentrating so heavily on beauty pageants. At some point, possibly very early in your childhood, you created the personality of Meg as a source of comfort and escape."

Clara looked from one face to the other, both of which were blank with astonishment.

"You're talking about me, right?" Lisa said at last. "But how could I have created her? If she's living and working in Las Vegas, she could hardly be a figment of my imagination. This is all so crazy," she added bitterly. "It's just crazy."

"It's a most unusual case," Clara agreed. "I believe you created another child and communed with her as an imaginary friend, so to speak, but didn't give her a name. Or, more accurately, you gave her a variety of names depending on how you felt and what purpose she served in your life at the time. She was unnamed and unrecognized, but her personality was very distinct. She grew up along with you."

Victor shook his curly gray head, looking baffled and uncomfortable. Clara turned to him.

"Victor, you've lived with Lisa for several years. Have there been times when she seemed different? Sweeter and more loving? Even humorous?"

Victor looked at the doctor, then at his wife. "Sometimes," he said at last. "Usually she's...pretty touchy.

But there were times when . . . yes, she seemed different. She was a lot more gentle and loving."

"Almost like a different woman?"

"Definitely."

Clara nodded. "I believe those were the times when Meg was in ascendancy, even though she hadn't been given a name or any validation by Lisa, the core personality. Perhaps that's why Meg has no memory of those times now. As I told you before, in cases of multiple personality, the alter personalities are aware of the host, but the reverse is usually not the case until the separate personalities become acquainted with one another through therapy. This is the first case I know of where the opposite is true. Although she usually denied it, Lisa has always had some awareness of Meg, but Meg now has no knowledge of Lisa's personality or situation although I still think she may have known of Lisa in the past. But the fact is that at present she claims an entirely different background."

Victor shook his head, still looking confused. "But . . . where does this woman in Las Vegas come in?" he asked. "What's she got to do with anything?"

"That's the fascinating thing. Apparently, Lisa met this woman by chance last spring, and they talked at some length. When Lisa found out the woman was also adopted, she identified strongly with her and went back several times to see her."

Victor smiled without humor. "God knows, she spent a lot of time in Vegas during the spring," he said, glancing at his wife, who still looked dazed and uncertain. "She was almost never home."

"She was talking with Megan Howell, learning all about her life. Somehow the woman must have closely matched the alter personality that Lisa had created. In time, the two merged and became one in her mind. Her alter personality now had a name and a history, and it began to assert itself. After the shock of the car accident, the new personality was the one that emerged, fully in control, when Lisa regained consciousness."

She turned to Lisa, who stared at her, wide-eyed.

"Are you telling me... You're saying I don't *exist?*" Lisa whispered. She looked down at her hands with a helpless expression, touching her arms uncertainly as if she expected her body to vaporize and float away in the sunlight. "I'm only a copy of somebody else?"

"Lisa," Victor said, putting an arm around her. "Honey, don't..."

She pulled away from him and turned to the doctor. "What's going on?" she whispered. "Why are you saying all this? I *know* I'm Megan Howell. I don't understand why you're making this up!"

"Personality is a very complex matter," Clara murmured soothingly. "Don't we all invent ourselves in some fashion, Meg? In fact, what part of us is actually *real,* in any tangible, visible way, other than our bodies?"

"But... my memories," the young woman said, her burst of anger fading into uncertainty. "I remember Hank, and Glory, and working with the horses, and bread baking in the trailer... How can you possibly expect me to believe that wasn't real?"

"All of it was real," Clara said. "All of those things really happened, but they're from someone else's life. Think of it this way. They're memories that you've borrowed for a time because your own are too painful."

"So I'm..." She fell silent, frowning. "You think I'm really Lisa, pretending to be somebody else? You're saying that I'm out of my mind?"

"This has nothing to do with sanity," Clara stated. "Nor is it pretense. In cases of multiple personality disorder, the subject is not pretending in any way. Each personality exists and is a distinct being. Meg certainly exists. At the moment, you *are* Meg."

"So where's Lisa?"

"In abeyance," Clara said. "Just as you were during all those years after Lisa created you but wouldn't give you expression."

Lisa studied the doctor's face, her own looking weary but skeptical. "If you're right, then who gets to exist?" she asked finally. "Who wins, if there's only one body?"

"That's what the therapy needs to explore." Clara glanced at Victor. "We need a lot of sessions to determine which personality is going to be dominant. Sometimes the final, integrated personality will turn out to be a blend of the others, a different entity altogether."

"With a different name?" Victor asked.

Clara nodded. "That's possible."

He shook his head in despair and looked out the window again, while Clara turned back to her patient.

"I *know* I'm Meg," Lisa said. Her face was still pale, and perspiration beaded her forehead and upper lip. "I have no memory of being anybody else."

"Than we'll call you Meg," Clara said, "and we'll go from there."

She put her notebook away and got to her feet.

"In a few days, Victor will take you home and see that you're looked after," Clara said. "And I'm going to get in touch with Ms. Howell again in Las Vegas, and see what else I can learn from her." Clara turned to Lisa's husband. "Victor, I'd like to see Meg at least twice a week, in my office, if possible, or at your home if she's too weak to come to the city. All right?"

"Of course," Victor said.

Clara walked to the doorway then paused to look back at the couple.

Victor was wringing out a cloth in a metal basin on the nightstand. He placed it on his wife's forehead while she closed her eyes and moved her hands restlessly over the blanket.

5

August sunlight washed over the sprawling city of Salt Lake, filtering through the lush Wasatch Mountains and sweeping across the white desert country to the west. In the hills east of the city, costly homes glowed like jewels, half-hidden among the spreading juniper and cedar.

Meg looked up at the houses through the tinted windshield of the Lincoln, then glanced over at Victor, whose face was concealed behind a pair of dark glasses as he drove aggressively through the morning traffic.

She examined his hands, gripping the wheel. They were strong and square, the fingers dusted with springing dark hairs. Victor was supposed to be her husband, but she couldn't imagine those hands touching her body, holding her in an intimate embrace...

He looked over at her with raised eyebrows, and her facc flamed. She turned away quickly.

"Do you remember any of this?" he asked.

She shook her head. "Not a thing."

"You must have driven this road a thousand times. It's hard to believe you've forgotten it altogether."

Meg stared quietly out the window at the houses and passing cars.

He shifted uncomfortably on the leather seat, and Meg felt a touch of sympathy. Victor was such a blunt, straightforward man. There was no doubt that this bizarre situation upset and embarrassed him.

"I'm . . . really sorry," she murmured, gazing down at her hands.

"About what? Being sick? I guess you can't help that, can you?"

"About everything," Meg said. "I know I shouldn't be going home with you, but I don't know what else to do."

"Why shouldn't you be going home with me?"

"Because I don't know you," Meg said simply. "I have no right to be living in your house."

"For Christ's sake, Lisa—"

"Please," she said. "Could you call me Meg? I'm not . . . I don't like being called Lisa."

He sighed and concentrated on his driving.

Meg leaned against the seat and closed her eyes, feeling weak and shaky. She thought longingly of her cool white bed in the hospital, safely removed from this man and his house and all the terrifying, awkward situations that lay ahead.

But she'd had to make a decision. She couldn't hide in the hospital forever. It was time to start living her life again, no matter how confusing and disjointed it seemed. And until she was a little stronger, this seemed to be the only option.

"What's it like?" Victor asked. "I mean, is it like amnesia? Do you remember what foods you like, your favorite television programs, stuff like that?"

Meg frowned, her eyes still closed. "I remember a lot from my childhood," she said at last. "But I don't remember much about the last couple of years."

"That's what I find so hard to understand," Victor said. "I mean, last week you talked to me at breakfast, then left the house, got in your car and headed to Vegas for a holiday. Today you're supposed to be a completely different person, with a different name and everything. I don't see how something like that could happen."

"I don't, either."

Meg looked out the window again. The houses were getting bigger and farther apart, spread along the canyon floor and surrounded by wide green lawns and shrubbery. She turned to Victor.

"Dr. Wassermann brought me some books and articles," she said. "Information about multiple personality disorder. I've been reading them for the past couple of days, ever since she told us about it. And she and I have been talking a lot about my memories and feelings, and . . . and Lisa," she added, suddenly awkward.

"Yeah?" He glanced at her, his eyes unreadable behind the sunglasses.

"I'm beginning to understand a little more about it. I mean, how two personalities can coexist in the same body, and both of them can be real."

"Well, I sure as hell don't understand it. At first I thought you were just making it up, pulling another of your stunts, but I can see you're not. Not even you could be such a good actress."

Meg looked up quickly, startled by his bluntness, but didn't respond.

"Clara seems to understand what's going on," he said, "and she's one of the best therapists around, so I guess we have to accept her diagnosis."

She surveyed his profile for a moment, then gazed out the window once more, thinking about the books she'd read on multiple personality disorder. Meg was beginning to develop her own theory about the baffling things that were happening in her life. And she wasn't convinced Dr. Wassermann's interpretation was correct.

But it was still so confusing, and she was too weak to sort everything out. As soon as she was strong enough, she intended to go back to Las Vegas and see what she could learn. Meanwhile...

"Right, honey?" he asked, interrupting her thoughts. "We have to follow the doctor's orders."

"I suppose so. But I think I probably need to get away by myself for a while. I need to spend some time finding out who I really am, and why all this has happened to me."

He turned onto a side road and drove toward the creek, passing houses that were bigger and costlier than any they'd seen so far, with lavish grounds and landscaping.

"So what do you want?" he asked. "You want to get an apartment in town for a while, or what?"

"I don't know. I can't remember anything about this city. I honestly feel like I've never been here in my life."

"Clara thinks you should live at home until you're stronger. Then we'll decide what to do. Maybe you'll get over it," he added hopefully. "Maybe you'll just wake up one morning and be Lisa again."

Meg thought about his words, and the fragility of existence. The doctor had shown her a number of case studies where that kind of abrupt and lasting shift of consciousness had occurred, just as it apparently had with her after her accident. It was incredible to realize that a whole human life could somehow be wiped out in the blink of an eye, replaced by another personality with different feelings, memories, attitudes and abilities.

Meg stared blindly at a field where a couple of horses grazed in front of a big white clapboard house with green shutters.

For some reason, the sight of the horses soothed her, made her feel stronger. "Look," she said to Victor. "They're beautiful, aren't they?"

"That's the neighbor's place. Don't you remember Jim Leggatt?"

Meg shook her head.

Victor thumped the wheel in exasperation, then sighed and said patiently, "Jim's sort of a part-time cowboy. He runs a big construction business and goes to rodeos on the weekend."

Meg studied the horses. "What events?"

"Beg pardon?"

"What events does he enter? At the rodeo, I mean? Is he a calf roper, or what?"

Victor laughed. "Damned if I know. Some kind of roping, I guess. You were sure never interested in rodeo before, Lisa. You always said Jim Leggatt was a real barbarian, and you didn't like him at all."

Meg looked wistfully at the horses again, then glanced up in alarm as Victor pulled the Lincoln to a stop in front of a triple garage fronted with pink stone. Beyond the garage, she could see a massive two-story house built of the same rosy pink granite, set behind wide lawns and surrounded by trimmed flower beds and masses of shrubs. The creek ran through the back of the property, heavily shaded by trees, making the whole setting look private and serene.

"It's so beautiful," she whispered.

"Well, at least *something* hasn't changed," Victor said, getting out of the car and reaching into the back for her suitcase.

"What do you mean?" Meg climbed out and stood in the wash of sunlight, looking around uncertainly. Her head began to throb. She swayed and clutched the fender of the car, feeling weak and dizzy.

Victor gave her a humorless smile. For a moment, his face looked cold behind the dark glasses, almost brutal.

"You've always liked my house, haven't you, Lisa?" he said quietly, then strode across the flagstones to the pink mansion.

Despite the seclusion of Victor's house, at least one of his neighbors witnessed the arrival of the Cantalinis.

Jim Leggatt was sitting with his brother on the screened side veranda of his big house, drinking coffee and reading the morning papers. Both men glanced up with interest when Victor parked the Lincoln in the adjoining driveway, then got out to reach for his wife's suitcase.

Dean Leggatt raised his eyebrows, whistling with warm admiration when Lisa Cantalini climbed from the passenger seat and stood on the gray flagstones. She was wearing white cotton slacks and a cherry-red sweater, and her tousled black hair shone with glossy highlights in the morning light.

"Very nice," Dean said appreciatively, lowering his coffee mug to give the neighbors his concentrated attention. "Very, *very* nice."

Jim gazed thoughtfully at his older brother. The Leggatt men were both in their early thirties, tall and muscular, with a rugged, blue-eyed handsomeness that concealed widely different personalities. Dean was dark and ambitious, quick-moving and impatient, while Jim, the fair-haired one, was quiet and steady.

When women were nearby, Dean tended to be the one who flirted, while Jim watched in silence. But these appearances, too, were largely deceiving.

Dean Leggatt was a loving family man, faithful to his wife of twelve years, passionately devoted to his three young daughters. Jim, on the other hand, had managed thus far to sidestep marriage and commitment by the narrowest of margins.

"Hey, Dean," he said, lowering his paper. "Are you ogling my neighbor's wife? A happily married guy like you?"

Dean grinned. "There's a difference between ogling and admiring. And *that,* my boy, is truly an admirable woman."

"I guess," Jim said offhandedly, glancing out through the screened porch.

He watched Lisa Cantalini hug her arms in the morning breeze and follow her husband up the walk. She looked tense and not too steady on her feet.

"Victor's bringing her home from the hospital," Jim told his brother. "She's been there almost two weeks."

"Having a baby?" Dean peered through the lattice and across the expanse of green lawn as if waiting for a bassinet to materialize.

Jim gave a short burst of laughter. "Lisa Cantalini's hardly the mommy type. She had an accident with her car," he explained, leaning forward to pour himself more coffee from the carafe. "Drove off the freeway down by Cedar City and crashed into a fence post halfway down the cliff. She hung there most of the night, apparently, until some trucker came along and found her just before dawn."

"Was she badly hurt?"

Jim shook his head. "Doesn't look that way, does it? Actually," he added, reaching for the sugar bowl, "it's amazing she survived at all. The woman usually drives like a bat out of hell. She's got this snazzy little 1957 white Thunderbird that Victor had fully restored for her."

"Just like the one in *American Graffiti?*"

"Yeah. Just like that." Abstractedly, Jim stirred sugar into his coffee.

He was wearing dusty riding boots, jeans, a yellow T-shirt with the logo Caesar's Palace on the front, and an old baseball cap pulled casually over his blond hair. Dean, who was dressed in vacation attire of corduroy slacks and a blue polo shirt, gave his brother a speculative glance.

"So, what's the story?" he asked finally.

"What story?"

"Come on, Jim. I can always tell that look in your eye. You and the neighbor lady have a bit of mutual history, right?"

Jim shook his head and leaned back in his chair, draping one arm over the back. He smiled, his eyes sparkling with amusement. "Why do you always take such an interest in my love life?"

"Because I don't have one of my own," Dean said cheerfully. "The only way I get to have any variety in my sex life is vicariously, through you."

"Annie would kill you if she heard you say that."

"I know." Dean folded the sports section and reached for the comics. "But Annie knows I love her. She'd certainly rather have me adventuring vicariously than firsthand."

"Well, I'm afraid there's not much enjoyment, vicarious or otherwise, to be had in my stories about Lisa Cantalini. I don't like the woman, Dean. Never have."

"You're kidding. A gorgeous woman like that, and you don't *like* her? Does she vote Republican, or mistreat your horses, or what?"

Jim looked over at the neighbors' well-manicured grounds. "To start with," he said quietly, "I really liked Pauline. I liked her a lot."

"And that's..."

"Victor's first wife. She was a sweet woman, Pauline Cantalini. She was like a mother to me from the first day I moved in here, and we were friends for more than ten years. It really tore me up when she died. Then, seemed like just a few weeks later, Victor announced that he was marrying this girl called Lisa Bauer, a 'former beauty queen,' as he described her. And before anybody could blink, she was living in Pauline's house, tearing everything up and redecorating, acting like the queen of the whole canyon."

"She's...quite a lot younger than he is," Dean ventured, looking at the broad oak door behind which Victor Cantalini had vanished with his wife. "Isn't she?"

Jim looked at his brother and raised an eyebrow. "About thirty years," he said dryly. "But then, we're hardly in a position to criticize, are we?"

Dean nodded, brooding over his coffee mug. "You know, Jimmy, sometimes I wonder," he said at last, "if either of us will ever really escape from the old man's shadow."

Jim's thoughts turned to his father. Dean and James Leggatt were the only offspring of Ezra Leggatt, an early land developer, notorious throughout the Utah-Nevada frontier for his arrogance and voracious greed, both in business and in sexual matters. Not one of his first three wives had survived life with Ezra long enough to give him a child, although there were a number of miscarriages and stillbirths.

The fourth wife, Amelia, was nineteen when she married Ezra Leggatt, then sixty-seven.

Even so, he outlived her by almost twenty years. Poor, gentle Amelia died when Jim was four and Dean was a toddler. Ezra was still alive when Jim left home to follow the rodeo circuit, and Dean went to Harvard to train for a legal profession. When Ezra Leggatt died, both his sons became enormously wealthy, and the brothers responded to this good fortune in different, but characteristic, ways.

Jim Leggatt came home from the rodeo circuit after Ezra's death and settled down to start a construction business, stubbornly determined to build a fortune with his own hands to match the one his father had left. He was now well on his way to accomplishing that goal, but the glossy quarter horses in the pasture and the rodeos he attended on weekends were still the love of his life.

Dean had gone on to finish law school and sail through his bar examination. He moved to California where he now had a town house in Los Angeles, a beach house near Topanga and a winter chalet in the San Gabriels. Dean was busy and prosperous, happy with his marriage and successful in his practice. But he never forgot his Utah roots. He stopped off in Salt Lake City whenever his business travel allowed, enjoying the chance to spend a day or two with his brother and catch a wistful glimpse of a life so different from his own.

"So is that the only reason you don't like her?" Jim heard his brother say. "You just figured she was a sorry replacement for Victor's first wife?"

Jim shook off his memories to answer his brother. "Not really." He looked down at his coffee mug. "Things never seemed quite right over there after Lisa came. And they couldn't have been married more than six months or so, when Lisa started to get restless."

"Restless?"

Jim shrugged. "She took to dropping by, just to visit, she said. She hung around the barn and pretended she was crazy about my horses, but that was a pretty weak excuse. She doesn't know a thing about horses. In fact, she's terrified of them. You can tell by watching her walk past the fence."

"So she was only interested in stud services?" Dean asked with a significant grin, which his brother didn't return.

"I guess so," Jim said. "But I didn't feel like playing, and I let her know. She wasn't very happy about it."

"Why weren't you interested? That's a gorgeous woman, Jimmy."

"She's my neighbor's wife, for God's sake! Victor Cantalini may not exactly be a prince, but I don't hate him. I'm not about to jump on his wife whenever his back's turned."

Dean sighed. "So, did she find diversion somewhere else?"

"Maybe," Jim said in a noncommittal tone. "She seems to have a few male visitors when Victor's away, but I wouldn't know who they are."

"I'll bet Trudy knows."

"No doubt, but if I started gossiping with Trudy about the neighbors, I'd never get any work done."

"Did I hear my name taken in vain?"

Jim's housekeeper appeared in the doorway, a small, plump woman in jeans, sweater and a bib apron made of heavy denim. Her gray hair was piled loosely into a bun on the top of her head, and a lot of bright makeup made her face look like a decorated cookie.

"Hi, Trudy," Jim said, waving the carafe. "We're out of coffee."

"Already? I just filled it."

Her employer gave her a winsome smile. "I know, but it's so good, Trudy. We purely can't resist your coffee."

Trudy whacked him on the arm with the folded magazine she was carrying, making him wince, then beamed at the other man.

"Could I get you anything, Mr. Dean? Some fresh-baked scones, or a bit more toast? Maybe a little fruit and cheese on a platter?"

"You always treat him so nice," Jim complained. "If that was me, you'd haul me off to the kitchen and make me fix my own."

"Your brother is our guest," Trudy told him sternly. "Besides," she added, smiling at Dean, "he looks so thin. Out there in California, they don't even know how to eat. Raw fish and sprouts, that's likely all he ever gets."

Jim snorted, then gave his housekeeper a glance of beguiling innocence. "How was the dance, Trudy? Did you have fun?"

"What dance?" Dean asked, leaning back in his chair.

"Trudy went to a singles' dance in the hall at Sandy last night. Didn't you, Trudy? She's joined the One-and-Only Club."

"It was all right," Trudy said, lowering herself into one of the padded wicker chairs and addressing herself to Dean. "But no matter how they fancy up those singles' dances," she added, "they still feel like a meat market. Everybody's shopping, and that's the plain truth of it."

"If you were a piece of meat," Dean told the housekeeper gallantly, "you'd be a prime cut of filet mignon, Trudy. You'd be top of the menu."

"Oh, you," Trudy protested, her plump cheeks turning even pinker under the rouge. "Isn't he a caution?" she asked Jim.

"Yeah," Jim agreed dryly. "He's a caution, all right, Trudy. By the way, what happened to the business section of this paper?"

"It's in the kitchen. I noticed some good recipes on the other side."

"You didn't cut it up, did you?"

Trudy winked at Dean. "He always gets so upset when I cut recipes out of the paper," she confided. "As if there isn't going to be another whole paper in the mailbox tomorrow."

Jim stood up, his lean body looking powerful and muscular within the screened confines of the porch. He towered over the housekeeper with a look of menace that made her giggle.

"If it wasn't so hard to get household help," Jim complained darkly to his brother, "she'd be gone in a minute. Along with her mangy goats and her seven hundred jugs of moonshine."

Trudy and Dean both ignored him. Jim hesitated in the doorway a moment longer, still trying to look stern, then strolled into the house in search of the rest of the news.

"Hey, Trudy, got any exciting new vintages coming up this fall?" Dean asked, hitching his chair out into the sunshine and leaning back to enjoy the warmth on his face.

"The rhubarb is coming along nicely," she said. "And I made some dandelion wine this year, too, that I have high hopes for. Manny was upset about *that,* I can tell you."

She looked through the window at the gardener, languidly trimming a hedge down near the stables.

"Why was Manny upset?" Dean asked, always intrigued by the lively give-and-take of his brother's household.

"Because when I told Jim I wanted dandelions to make wine this year, he wouldn't let Manny do any spraying all summer. We picked them by hand, thousands of them. Jim even helped when he was home in the evening."

Dean tried to picture his cowboy brother squatting on the wide green lawn at sunset, picking dandelions with his housekeeper and the Mexican gardener. He shook his head.

"You amaze me, Trudy," he said solemnly. "You constantly amaze me."

Trudy nodded placidly, then looked up as Jim returned to the porch carrying the missing business pages and another jug of coffee.

"Why?" he asked. "What's so amazing about her?"

"Everything," Dean said, helping himself to more coffee. "Trudy, can I watch when you milk the goats tonight?"

"You can milk 'em yourself," Trudy said, "if you're so excited about the idea. Crystal hardly butts at all anymore."

Jim grinned, then sobered when she turned to him with a thoughtful air.

"Jim," she began.

"Hmm?" He flipped through the business section, looking for the commodities prices.

"Did you see Victor and Lisa coming home just now?"

Jim nodded. "We were watching through the lattice. Lisa looks okay, but she seemed pretty shaky."

"She's shaky, all right. But that's not all," Trudy said mysteriously.

Both men looked at her. "What do you mean?" Jim asked.

"I was talking to Filomena this morning before they got home," Trudy said. "She came over to borrow a cup of brown sugar."

"I think you're the only person in the world who actually talks to Filomena. That's Victor's housekeeper," Jim told his brother. "Very grim, dark and silent. Kind of a scary woman, Filomena is."

"Oh, pooh," Trudy scoffed. "Filomena's a perfectly nice girl, and she's a wonderful mother to that little boy of hers. She just keeps to herself, that's all."

Jim raised his eyebrows and returned to the paper.

"And I would, too," Trudy muttered, "if I lived in *that* house." She peered through the latticework at the pink granite mansion across the lawn.

Dean was clearly fascinated. "What did Filomena tell you?" he asked. "About Lisa, I mean. Is she badly hurt, after all?"

Trudy leaned forward and tapped her forehead, giving both men a significant look.

"She's mentally disturbed?" Dean guessed. "Some kind of head injury?"

Jim lowered the paper and listened, while Trudy leaned back expansively under the concentrated attention of both men.

"Lisa doesn't know who she is."

Dean was the first to speak. "You mean she's got amnesia?"

"That's what I asked. But Filomena says it's something more complicated. Apparently, Victor tried to explain it to her, but he's not exactly the best person at explaining things. Besides, he and Filomena hardly ever talk about anything if they can help it."

"I wonder what that would be like," Jim addressed the ceiling with a wistful sigh. "Having a housekeeper who just goes quietly about her work. I can hardly imagine it."

"What do you mean, more complicated than amnesia?" Dean asked. "Is she having hallucinations, or something?"

"Something like that," Trudy said. "She thinks she's somebody else."

"Marie Antoinette, no doubt," Jim commented cynically. "Or Cleopatra. Maybe even Scarlett O'Hara."

"You're not very sympathetic, are you?" Trudy observed.

Jim put the paper in his lap and looked at the other two. "A couple of months ago," he said, "on a hot day in spring, I was riding down along the creek on that trail out of the hills. I was right behind their property, and Lisa was out on the deck of the swimming pool, suntanning. She didn't see me through the trees."

"What was she wearing?" Dean asked with warm interest.

"Not much," Jim said. "A white bikini panty."

"No top?" Dean breathed.

Jim shook his head. "She sat up to put on some tanning oil, and she was a pretty sight, let me tell you. I don't like the woman much, but she sure got my attention. I felt like a real jerk, spying on her through the trees like a schoolboy. I was about to spur my horse and get out of there, when that little kid of Filomena's came wandering onto the pool deck."

"He's so cute," Trudy told Dean. "His name's Domingo, but Filomena calls him Dommie."

"How old?" Dean asked.

"Let's see." Trudy frowned. "He was born in the spring just before Pauline died." She turned to Jim.

"Remember how excited Pauline was about the baby, and all the things she bought for him?"

Jim nodded, smiling wistfully. "She was so happy, you'd think it was her own baby. Of course," he added, "Pauline and Victor never had any kids of their own."

"And she just had about two months to enjoy him before she died, poor thing," Trudy said with a faraway look. "Anyway," she added, giving herself a little shake, "that was two years ago this spring. So Dommie's about two and a half, the darling."

"Go on with your story," Dean said to his brother.

"I don't know why I sat and watched," Jim said. "It made me nervous for some reason, seeing Lisa and the little kid all alone there on the deck. He had something in his hand, and he was trying to show it to her. He kept touching her arm and talking to her."

Jim fell silent, his face cold with memory.

"And then?" Trudy prompted.

"She hit him," Jim said. "She just hauled off and smacked him so hard that he sat down, plop, right at the edge of the pool. Lisa gathered up her towel and stuff and left him there, crying. She walked through the trees to the house and didn't even look back."

Dean stared at his brother in horror. "She left a two-year-old alone by the pool?"

Jim nodded grimly. "She sure did. I was all set to tie up my horse and wade across the creek to get him, when Filomena came running out. She picked him up and hugged him, then took him away."

"Do you think Filomena saw Lisa hit him?"

"I doubt it. I don't think Lisa would have hit the kid if she thought she had a witness. That's the kind of woman she is."

Jim turned back to the paper with a dismissive air, while the other two watched him.

"You'll have to forgive me," he said coldly, "if I can't spare a lot of sympathy for Lisa Cantalini, whatever her problems might be."

6

She paused just inside the front doorway, conscious of Victor looking back at her and waiting for her to react. To her relief, he stripped off the dark glasses and folded them into his shirt pocket. The strange air of menace seemed to vanish along with the glasses, leaving him warm and hearty, not threatening at all.

"Well, Lisa," he said. "Does it feel good to be home?"

She looked around uncertainly. Large rooms opened into one another beyond the foyer, quiet and beautiful, with masses of plants and gleaming wood surfaces. The color scheme was pleasantly muted, a combination of cream shades highlighted by soft touches of gold, pale rust and turquoise.

Her head was pounding, and the nightmarish sense of confusion was growing more intense. She had no memory of this place, yet everything was eerily familiar. It dawned on her that if she'd been entrusted with the task of decorating a big house and given an unlimited budget, this was exactly how she'd choose to make it look. Everywhere she turned, in all the drapes and furnishings, the thick carpets and oak-framed paintings, she saw her taste reflected.

Victor watched her in silence. "You recognize it, don't you?" he said at last. "You remember the house. I can tell."

"I... Not really," she whispered. "But it's... very beautiful."

"It should be," he said. "You spent enough money on it, Lisa."

She wanted to correct him, to ask him again if he would call her Meg, but suddenly she was too weary to make the effort.

"Hey, Dommie," Victor said with pleasure, addressing someone just beyond the arched entrance to the living room.

Meg looked down the hall and saw a small child wearing striped denim overalls and a blue T-shirt. He was about two years old, with glossy black hair and huge dark eyes. He stood solemnly on the gleaming tiles, holding a red plastic truck in his hands, clutched tight against his chest.

"Got a truck?" Victor asked gently, moving toward the child who looked up at him with quiet trust. "Dommie got a truck?"

The child nodded and held up his toy for Victor's inspection.

Victor put down the suitcase, took the truck and examined it carefully. "That's a great truck," he said to the little boy. "Four-wheel drive, right?"

He grinned and ruffled the child's hair, then turned to his wife. "Look at Dommie's truck, honey."

She gazed down at the little boy, enchanted by his beauty. His face was smooth and flowerlike, delicately molded, and his eyes were enormous, golden-brown beneath dark lashes. He looked neat and well cared for, from the top of his shining head to his small blue running shoes.

"Hello, dear," she whispered, kneeling in front of the boy and reaching out to touch him. "How are you?"

The child's brown eyes widened in panic. He shrank against Victor's leg, seeming on the verge of tears. Victor bent to hand the child his red truck.

"I guess Dommie doesn't remember you, Lisa" he said, clearing his throat. "You've been away for quite a while, you know."

She looked into the child's face and was stunned by the terror that she saw reflected there. She glanced up in confusion as a woman came running along the hall and snatched the little boy up in her arms.

The woman was thin and small, probably in her late twenties, wearing a charcoal-gray uniform and white apron. Her hair and eyes were as dark as the child's.

"I'm sorry," the woman muttered to Victor. "Dommie, you shouldn't be out here," she whispered fiercely. "Mama told you to stay in the kitchen."

"It's all right, Filomena," Victor said. "He isn't hurting anything. Say hello to Mrs. Cantalini."

The woman looked over her son's dark head, then glanced away quickly. "Hello, ma'am," she muttered.

"Hello, Filomena," Meg said. "How are you?"

"Fine," the woman said, still holding the little boy in her arms.

"Mrs. Cantalini's doctor wants her to spend the next few days in bed," Victor told the housekeeper. "She won't be coming down for meals."

"I'll take her a tray for lunch," Filomena said curtly, addressing Victor. "I'm sorry if he bothered you," she added, turning away and starting down the hall. "It won't happen again."

"Filomena," Meg said.

The housekeeper stopped and turned, keeping her eyes lowered. "Yes, ma'am?"

"I'm...not very hungry," Meg said. "Please don't go to any trouble for my lunch. Just a bowl of soup or something."

"I'm making an omelet."

"That sounds nice," Meg said awkwardly.

She hesitated, embarrassed by the idea of this woman waiting on her, making meals for her and carrying them to her room. She searched for something to say that would ease the tension in the room and make the housekeeper relax.

"He's such a beautiful little boy," she said at last, smiling at the big-eyed child nestled in his mother's arms. "You must be very proud of him, Filomena."

The housekeeper glanced up in surprise and looked at Meg for a moment. Meg stared back, appalled at what she saw in the woman's face, suddenly needing to lean against the wall as Filomena hurried off down the hall with her child.

Meg rubbed her forehead and shivered, then followed Victor as he began to climb the stairs with her suitcase, but she was still shaken.

What had prompted that brief flash of recognition from the housekeeper, and the cold, implacable hatred in the woman's eyes?

Her confusion increased when Victor led her into a big square room and set the suitcase on the carpet by a row of mirrored doors.

She sank into a padded armchair near the door, looking around in awe. This room was as richly furnished as the rest of the house, but beautifully feminine. She could see the head of a bed in an alcove, and a tiled bathroom beyond a partly open door. And everywhere, on walls and dresser tops, in antique frames and on small easels, she saw pictures of herself.

She was surrounded by images of her own smile, her eyes and hair and body, like shattered reflections in a room full of mirrors. On the wall above the bed hung an oil painting about four feet square, showing her seated on the grass beneath trailing willow branches. She was wearing a soft white dress, pulled down off one shoulder, and her long dark hair surrounded her face like a cloud.

Victor followed her gaze. "I always liked your hair that way," he commented. "You should let it grow long again, Lisa."

She stared at the painting, then reached up automatically to touch her hair. It was short, almost boyish, trimmed neatly above her ears and at the nape of her neck. She couldn't remember wearing it long.

"When..." She paused and bit her lip nervously. "When did I get it cut?"

Victor made a gesture of annoyance. "Not long ago," he said. "Sometime in July, I guess. You said you were tired of looking after it, and it bothered you in the heat. Remember?"

She shook her head, barely hearing him, still gazing at her smiling face in the big oil painting.

"Can you manage by yourself?" Victor asked. "Do you need help getting into bed or anything? I can ask Filomena to come up if you want."

Meg thought about the housekeeper's parting glance and shuddered. "No thank you," she murmured. "I can... I'll be fine. Thank you, Victor."

She was anxious for him to leave so she could be alone. But after he strode from the room and closed the door behind him, it took all her strength to drag herself from the chair, get her clothes off and change into one of the silk nightgowns she found in the vast mirrored closet.

She climbed into bed, pulled the soft covers up around her face and sank gratefully into a cool world of peace and stillness.

For several days after she came home, Meg drifted in and out of sleep, struggling to maintain some sense of reality. But she felt herself slipping away, growing more disoriented all the time. Her fever returned and Dr. Bartlett came to see her, bringing medicine and instructions. The world seemed foggy and dense, and conversations were hard to follow. Her consciousness began to ebb and flow again, as it had in the hospital.

Filomena moved silently about the room, changing bedding, folding clothes, carrying in neat trays of food and taking them away again, never looking directly at her.

Meg changed her nightgown each morning, struggled from her bed to the bathroom and occasionally rested for a few minutes on the padded window seat when she felt strong enough. Sometimes she saw the neighbor's horses grazing in the pasture below. Looking at them brought her a fleeting sense of peace.

She was sitting there one afternoon, watching the horses as her mind circled wearily around the same track, examining the disjointed events of her life.

Meg understood what Clara Wassermann had told her about multiple personality. But in a private corner of her mind that she never allowed the doctor to explore, Meg believed that Clara had it all backward.

Lisa wasn't the dominant personality. It simply wasn't possible, because Meg's childhood memories were too vivid to be secondhand.

Instead, Meg believed that she really had experienced the childhood she remembered. She'd grown up with Hank and Glory on their rented farm, played baseball and loved horses and been a tomboy. And then, sometime in the jumbled years that she couldn't remember, she'd changed into Lisa.

Immediately afterward, she must have come to Salt Lake with a story about a childhood spent winning beauty pageants and being admired for her beauty, an existence completely different from the one she recalled. She'd married Victor, moved into this house and established herself in a comfortable, luxurious life-style.

But she'd obviously continued to have flashbacks, times when the Meg personality became dominant again for brief periods. Those were the times when she went back to Las Vegas, even worked as casual labor in the casino...

It was all so confusing, and so utterly terrifying.

At first, the fears were vague and formless, like a continuation of her nightmares. But as time passed and her mind cleared a little, Meg began to realize what frightened her the most.

Always uppermost, of course, was the shattering knowledge that Lisa's personality could reappear at any time and drive her out of existence again. The other fear was less urgent, but equally troubling. There was a woman in Las Vegas, claiming to be Megan Howell. Obviously, this woman had known Meg at some time in the past and had assumed her identity when she vanished. Meg had no recollection of the woman. Who was she, and why was she saying she was Meg?

There were all kinds of reasons, Meg supposed, that somebody might want to take on another person's identity. Debts, trouble with the police, perhaps a relationship that she wanted to escape from.... Any of these were a possibility.

What terrified Meg was the knowledge that this impostor had obviously met her again when she was calling herself Lisa Cantalini, and calmly taken advantage of Meg's personality dissociation. According to Dr. Wassermann, the woman—the one who called herself Megan Howell—had talked with Lisa as if they were strangers meeting for the first time. They'd gone out for meals and drinks and she'd talked casually about Meg's childhood as if it were her own.

The brazenness of it was infinitely chilling.

Meg put her hands to her temples, wondering if she should confide in Dr. Wassermann. But Meg was aware of the doctor's power over her life. She didn't want Clara to know about her suspicions, at least not until she had a better idea of what had happened to her.

If only she could get her strength back, and go to Las Vegas...

A knock sounded at the door. Meg turned around, wondering who it could be. Victor was never home during the day, and Filomena didn't come to her room unless it was time to bring a meal.

"Come in," she whispered, then licked her lips and tried again. "Please come in."

The door opened and a man entered.

"Hi, kid," he said, smiling as he crossed the room. "I just got back from Vegas and heard about your accident. How are you feeling?"

Meg stared at him, her awkwardness increasing as he grasped one of the upholstered chairs, hitched it close to the window seat and straddled it, resting his arms on the back and studying her intently.

He was the best-looking man she'd ever seen, so handsome that he took her breath away. He was tall and slender, with a catlike grace and a look of tensile strength, like shining tempered steel. His hair was dark and crisp, trimmed close to his beautifully shaped head. His eyes were a very light gray, wide and clear under dark lashes and eyebrows, and his gaze was as innocently direct as little Dommie's.

"Well," he asked, still smiling, "aren't you going to say something? It's the first time I've seen you since you were practically at death's door, honey. I thought you'd have lots to tell me."

Meg shifted on the window seat and pulled her quilted housecoat tighter around her, fiddling with the belt at her waist. She took a deep breath and glanced up.

"I don't... know who you are," she whispered. "I'm sorry. I've been sick, and I..."

He gave a disbelieving laugh, his handsome face startled and hurt. "Don't *know* me? Your own cousin? Lisa, kid, what the hell are you talking about?"

"My name is Meg," she said, staring down at her belt again. "I have... no memories of being Lisa."

He gaped at her, then turned away quickly and looked out the window at the horses grazing in the field below.

"Jesus," he whispered at last. "I came back from Vegas on Tuesday, planning to come and see you as soon as I had a chance. When I went to the bar last night, Smitty told me you'd been in a car accident and nobody had seen you for a long time. He heard you'd been released from the hospital, so I took a risk and came over. What's going on, kid?"

"I remember the accident," she murmured, searching for something to say. "Not how it happened, or anything like that. I remember waking up in the car and wondering where I was, and then the ambulance and the paramedics coming. A few things like that."

"But you don't remember me, Lisa? You don't remember a thing about me?"

"I don't even remember Lisa," she said wearily.

"You've got amnesia, then? Something like that?"

Meg shook her head. "That's what Victor keeps saying. But it's not amnesia. It's called MPD. Multiple personality disorder. I know it sounds crazy."

"Not really," the man said calmly, leaning back in the chair and extending his legs. He was wearing a pair of well-cut pleated slacks and a yellow polo shirt that rested easily on his broad shoulders, complementing his tanned skin and dark coloring. "Actually, you know, I always thought you had a few other people living in there, Lisa. You're far too complicated to be just one person."

"You thought..."

"God knows, I'm no expert on psychological disorders. But I used to wonder sometimes when you were talking...when *she* was talking," he corrected himself, giving Meg a disarming smile. "Damn, it's really confusing, isn't it?"

She looked down at her hands.

"So," the man went on agreeably, "you're one of the people who's been living inside Lisa. Well, then, let's introduce ourselves, okay? I'm Lisa's cousin, Clay Malone. Lisa and I grew up together in Provo. Our mothers were sisters."

Meg watched him in shocked silence.

"Who are you?" he asked gently. "What's your name?"

"I'm . . . Meg," she whispered.

"Hi, Meg." He reached out and took her hand, squeezing it tenderly, then lifted it to his mouth and kissed her fingers and her palm. "Glad to meet you. What are you like?"

"Me?"

"I mean, are you quiet or noisy? Shy and cautious, or really bold? Refined or crude? What kind of personality do you have?"

"I'm . . ." Meg hesitated, struggling for words to describe herself. It was difficult because her personality seemed to be vanishing, receding deeper and deeper every day into mists of sickness and confusion. And the vestiges of herself that remained were obscured by the dazzling smiles in the photographs all around her, images of a woman who was herself, and yet so different.

"Come on, kid," Clay said, leaning forward to stroke her hair with a soothing hand. "Tell me what you're like."

"I guess I'm kind of quiet," Meg said at last. "I like to work hard, and . . . and be alone. I like children and animals. I like to read. I'm kind of athletic, not much for clothes and makeup."

He nodded, looking fascinated, and swung himself out of the chair to pace around the room.

"I think maybe I've met you before," he commented, picking up an antique paperweight and hefting it idly, then replacing it. "A few times when I've been with you in the past . . . with Lisa," he corrected himself, "she'd change completely, and it was like a different woman was looking out through her eyes, speaking through her mouth. I guess maybe that was you. But you don't remember?"

"I have no memories of sharing a body with Lisa. My memories are completely different. I remember growing up in Las Vegas, playing Little League baseball, helping my daddy with the horses. I even remember little things, like having a pet hamster named Abigail," she said, trying to smile.

"Do you have a last name, too, or are you just Meg?"

"I'm Megan Howell."

He stared at her, his eyes widening with recognition. "Megan *Howell?* That skinny woman who works in the casino kitchen? Lisa, you've been talking about that woman for months. Now you think you *are* her?"

Meg flushed painfully and gripped her hands tight in her lap. Her head ached, and she glanced longingly at the cool softness of her bed.

"Sorry, kid," Clay said instantly. "I didn't mean to upset you. Are you tired? Ready to go back to bed?"

She nodded. He stooped and lifted her effortlessly, carried her over to the bed and put her down. Then he removed her housecoat, tucked her under the covers and pulled them up around her shoulders.

"Want some pillows to prop you up?"

She nodded again, gazing at him quietly.

He plumped a couple of lace-trimmed pillows and arranged them behind her, then drew the chair closer and looked down at her again, his handsome face worried. "I suppose you've talked about all this with your shrink . . . what's her name?"

"Dr. Wassermann."

Clay laughed. "Yeah, that's right. Remember how you used to make fun of her last spring, when you were supposed to go to her for marriage counseling, or whatever it was?"

She shook her head, and he smiled. "No," he muttered. "I guess you don't remember, do you?"

"She comes to the house to talk to me," Meg said. "A couple of times a week. She asks me about the kind of things I remember, and tells me more about...about Lisa."

"But doesn't she know that Megan Howell's a real person? Somebody you met last spring and developed a kind of obsession with?"

Meg nodded. "Dr. Wassermann called and talked to her. She heard about how Lisa...how Lisa met Megan Howell and spent time with her. The doctor thinks Lisa first connected with the woman because they were both adopted. Later, as she learned that the woman's family had dealt with the adoption so much better, and Meg had had the kind of childhood Lisa would have liked, she simply became Meg."

"So Lisa just sort of chucked her own life and borrowed someone else's for a while. And that's where you came from."

"That's what the doctor thinks."

Suddenly, he laughed, a peal of genuine humor that startled her. "That sounds like Lisa," he said with a fond smile. "If Lisa likes something, she takes it no matter who it belongs to. Right, kid?"

Meg stared at him quietly and he sobered, looking contrite. "So, what's the doctor's prognosis? Who will you turn out to be when all this therapy ends?"

"I'm not sure. Maybe a sort of...blend of the two personalities. Apparently, that's what often happens."

"Part Lisa, part Meg?"

She bit her lip and turned away.

"Does that scare you?"

Meg nodded.

"Don't be scared, kid. Whatever happens, I'm with you all the way. Remember that, okay? You might not be able to remember anything else right now, but you and I, we've been friends since we were babies. You can always count on me." He got to his feet and touched her forehead and cheek with a gentle, lingering hand. "I'd better go," he murmured. "You're getting tired. Listen, kid..."

"Yes?" she asked.

"I know you don't remember a lot of things, so there's something I have to remind you about."

"Yes?" she said.

He leaned close to her, his strange, light gray eyes suddenly luminous with intensity. "Don't tell Victor that I was here to see you."

"Why not?"

"Your husband's never met me," Clay said with a brief smile, "and I don't think he wants to. He's jealous of us, kid, and the way we've always been so close. Victor could make big trouble for me if he ever found out I was coming to see you. So it'll just be our little secret, okay?"

"I hardly ever talk to Victor," Meg said tonelessly. "He doesn't even come up to see me anymore."

"Poor baby." He bent and kissed her cheek, holding his face close to hers for a moment. She had a confused impression of clean-shaven skin, of strength and smoothness and expensive cologne. Then he headed for the door, pausing to smile at her before he disappeared into the hallway with a springing tread.

When he was gone, Meg felt a growing sense of unease. His words and manner had been comforting, but the impression he'd left was somehow disturbing. It was as if the room had been visited by something beautiful but feral, a wolf or lynx who padded through the underbrush and lurked in the shadows with glittering eyes.

She gripped the bedspread and stared at the ornate plaster cornices on the ceiling, trying to calm herself and think rationally.

The most terrifying thing, of course, was Clay Malone's casual reference to his shared childhood with Lisa.

If he was telling the truth, then Dr. Wassermann was right. Lisa had really been the dominant personality all those years, and Meg was no more than a figment of another woman's imagination.

7

Jim Leggatt sat at the table in his sun-room, relaxing over a second cup of coffee and reading the morning paper. He looked up with a smile when his housekeeper came in to clear the table.

"I love Sundays," he told her.

"You work too hard." She gathered a couple of plates in her hand and swept briskly at the toast crumbs on the tablecloth. "I don't know why you have to be there all the time when you're the boss."

"Things just seem to run smoother," Jim said wryly, "if the boss tries to show up at the job site occasionally."

"I see there's a letter from Dean and Annie." Trudy gestured at the pile of mail by his elbow. "Seems like he just left."

"That was two weeks ago, Trudy." Jim picked up the opened letter and handed it to her. "Annie's already thinking about Christmas. She says they're all going up to the chalet this year, and I should come out for the holiday."

"That sounds nice. Are you going?"

Jim surveyed the peaceful scene beyond the window. It was September, one of his favorite months. The morning sun was clear and cool, and the faded grass shone like beaten gold. His horses grazed in the pasture near the creek, while a couple of Trudy's little brown goats skipped and butted horns nearby in ferocious mock battle.

"I don't know," he said at last. "Maybe I should."

"Well, you know how much you love those kids."

Jim nodded, thinking wistfully about his nieces. Dean's three girls were a laughing, merry group, all of them turning out to be as pretty and warmhearted as their mother. They adored their handsome cowboy uncle, and fussed over him lavishly whenever he went to Dean's house for the holidays.

"Yeah," he said at last. "I love those kids, all right. Annie says they're all getting rid of their skis and learning to snowboard. She says Kate's likely going to be state champion in a few years."

"Kate's always been a daredevil," Trudy said fondly. "So, are you going out there for Christmas?"

"I guess so. Do you want to come along? Dean wrote a special note at the bottom of Annie's letter to say you're invited."

"Well, that's real nice of him," Trudy said. "But," she added, "I don't think I'll go this year."

"Why not? It'll be pretty lonely around here," Jim said. "I'll pay for your ticket," he added. "Call it a Christmas bonus."

"That's real nice," Trudy repeated. "But I may have other plans."

She hesitated in the doorway with her hands full of plates, looking almost shy.

"Other plans?"

"I met this fellow at the One-and-Only dance a couple of weeks ago," Trudy said awkwardly. "He's a nice man. He used to own a barbershop in Salt Lake, but he's been retired for a few years and he likes to travel."

Jim's eyes widened in surprise.

"He's planning to go away for the holidays, on a cruise to the Caribbean." Trudy took a few steps back into the room, and looked out the window at her goats. "He asked if I...might want to come along," she said, her cheeks turning pink.

"Trudy!" Jim exclaimed in delight. "You're having a romance!"

Her color deepened. "What's so strange about that?" she asked, gripping the plates tensely. "Just because I'm old and fat, you think there's no possibility of romance in my life? Is that what you think?"

Jim realized that she was upset, and felt ashamed of his carelessness. "No, Trudy," he said gently. "I don't think that at all. I think you're a real fine woman, and any man would be lucky to go on a tropical cruise with you."

She nodded, her displeasure fading to embarrassment. "I've never done anything like this," she murmured. "Never in my life. I guess I'm a little nervous."

"There's no need to be nervous. You'll have a wonderful time." He got up to refill his mug from the silver carafe on the sideboard. "Sit down and have a cup of coffee with me, okay? Tell me what's happening next door."

Trudy put down the plates, accepted the cup he gave her and settled into the chair opposite him, adopting a confidential tone.

"Lisa's been home for almost two weeks now, and Filomena says she's hardly getting any better at all. I guess Victor tried to warn her, but Filomena still wasn't prepared for it. She says Lisa's really strange."

"Strange?"

"Crazy." Trudy gave him a meaningful glance. "I told you before, the woman's crazy. She's gone out of her mind."

Jim sipped his coffee thoughtfully.

"She caught this fever in the hospital, some kind of staph infection, and it keeps coming back. But that's not the worst part. Filomena says she's like a totally different person."

"In what way?"

"She talks different, acts different . . ." Trudy lowered her voice dramatically. "She even calls herself by a different name."

Jim put down his cup in astonishment. "You're kidding."

"She calls herself Meg."

"That's strange, all right."

"I guess Victor's so upset, he hardly talks to her anymore. And Filomena hates her, you know. The woman just sits all alone up there in her room, looking out the window."

"I know," Jim said. "I've seen her." He hesitated. "It can't be much fun," he said at last, "being shut up in that big old house with a husband who won't talk to you and a housekeeper who hates you."

"Oh, she's not alone all the time." Trudy gave him another significant glance. "She has company."

"Who?"

"That guy who's *supposed* to be her cousin," Trudy said with heavy emphasis.

As a rule, Jim avoided this kind of gossip about the neighbors. He'd only raised the topic this morning to make up for his thoughtlessness about Trudy's cruise, but now he was interested in spite of himself.

"Supposed to be?" he asked.

"I saw the man one day this summer when I was looking after Dommie while Filomena went to the doctor. Lisa told me he was her cousin."

"But you don't believe it?"

"Not for a minute," Trudy said darkly. "For one thing, he's never there when Victor's around. And for *another* thing, they were acting far too chummy to be cousins, if you ask me."

Jim grinned. "Maybe they're kissing cousins, Trudy."

She snorted and took a gulp of coffee.

"What does Filomena say about this guy? The cousin, I mean."

"She won't talk about him. Not a word. If I mention him, she just clams up and changes the subject. Not that Filomena's ever been all that chatty at the best of times," Trudy added ruefully.

Jim thought about the couple who lived next door, remembering Lisa's seductive behavior toward him, and that summer day when he'd glimpsed her half-naked by the pool. Again he saw the casual, brutal way that she'd hit the little boy.

"Well, I guess it's none of our business," he said abruptly, getting up and pushing in his chair. "I won't be home until late," he added, heading for the door. "Don't worry about supper."

"Where are you off to?"

Jim paused in the doorway. "I'm going to load up Cochise and run down to Provo for a jackpot team roping this afternoon."

Trudy gave him a fond smile. "When will you ever grow up and stop playing cowboy?"

"Not for a long time, I hope," Jim said, returning her smile.

He took his jacket and cap from the closet near the back door, then strolled outside and headed for the barn, where he tipped some oats into a pail, took a halter from the wall and carried them out to the pasture, whistling softly.

Both horses threw their heads up and listened, then came trotting toward him with joyful nickers of welcome.

Jim held the pail to each of them in turn, stroking their glossy necks. He fitted the halter onto his sorrel gelding and led him toward the barn while the other horse, a dainty mare called Amber, trotted behind them looking downcast.

"Next week," Jim told her, pausing to tug at her forelock and rub her velvety ears. "You'll go next week, girl."

He paused suddenly and glanced up at the pink granite house across the yard.

Once again, the woman was sitting in one of the upstairs windows, looking down at him. Jim could see her pale face through the leaded-glass casement, her blue silk housecoat and dark hair.

There was something inexpressibly sad about her wistful pose, the droop of her shoulders and the way she sat so quietly, watching him with his horses. He shivered and turned away, heading toward the barn without looking back.

"Is Lisa there?" Clara asked, looking into Meg's eyes with a dark, mesmerizing gaze. "Could I speak with Lisa today?"

Meg tensed in the chair. "No," she said. "No!"

Clara continued to watch her steadily. "Are you sure you feel strong enough to be out of bed?"

"I'm fine." Meg gripped the arms of the chair tightly. "I get so tired of being in bed," she said. "Sometimes I sit by the window for hours and watch the neighbor's horses."

"Do you like horses, Meg?" Clara asked.

"Yes, I do. He has beautiful horses," she said. "They're both sorrels. A gelding and a little mare. He takes good care of them, too."

"Have you met the neighbor?"

"I've only seen him down there with the horses. He's tall and blond, quite young. He's a good rider," she added. "Victor says he goes to rodeos."

Meg shifted nervously. She was growing more tense with every visit from the doctor, worried that Clara could somehow reach inside her mind and draw Lisa out against her will.

"Meg," Clara asked softly, "why won't you let me talk with Lisa?"

"I'm afraid," Meg said at last.

"What are you afraid of?"

"I'm afraid that if you bring Lisa out, she'll stay and I won't exist anymore."

"What if I promise that won't happen? Would you let me talk with Lisa if I give my word that you can come back afterward?"

Meg shook her head. "I don't want to. I don't want to think about Lisa."

"All right," Clara said. "I'd like to do some hypnosis therapy today," she said casually. "I think we should review some of your memories."

Meg looked at the doctor in alarm. "Hypnosis?"

"Trust me, Meg." Clara fixed her with that steady, intense gaze. "I'll only talk to Meg. We'll only talk about

Meg's memories. We'll talk about when Meg was a little girl. When Meg was a very small girl..."

The monotone voice and the repetition of her name were lulling and seductive. Meg found herself drifting against her will, floating into a distant, childlike world.

"You're going back," the voice told her. Meg followed, knowing that it was her lifeline. The voice carried her deeper into the mists of time, past scattered images and random bits of emotion.

"Back, back... still further... you're three years old, Meg. Where are you?"

"I'm in the kitchen," Meg said. "I'm sitting with Mama."

"Are you happy there?"

"Yes," Meg whispered. "I love my mama."

"What's she doing, Meg? What's your mama doing?"

"She's telling me a story...."

Meg understood that the story was not being told for the first time, that it was a favorite story, repeated over and over again for her pleasure.

She could feel her mother's plump arms enclosing her, and the pillowy softness of Glory's breasts and thighs while Meg cuddled within her embrace, as small and light as a feather. There were comforting smells, too, of cookies and baking bread and a roast in the oven, and the pleasant oily scent of the rawhide strips that Hank braided into headstalls and reins.

"Tell," Meg commanded, sinking blissfully into Glory's softness with her thumb in her mouth.

"Tell what, punkin?"

Meg removed her thumb. "Tell 'wheniwuzzadoptid,' she said, running all the words together into one pleasing sound.

"You've heard that story a million times, honey. How about *Cinderella?*"

"No," Meg said firmly, and Glory chuckled.

"All right, then. It was in October but it was still real hot. Hank and I were living in this very same trailer house, but it wasn't here on the farm. It was in a trailer park south of the city. Hank was doing horseshoeing at the racetrack, and I'd been working for three years at a pretty good job, dealing blackjack at the Flamingo. We were saving every penny because we knew that someday *you...*"

Glory paused to hug the little girl, and Meg wriggled in delight.

"We knew someday you'd be coming along," Glory continued, "but we didn't know when. And then one Sunday morning the phone rang, and a man said, 'Is this Gloria Howell? Mrs. Henry Howell?' "

Glory dropped her voice to a low, thrilling pitch, imitating the man.

"I said, 'Yes, sir, it is. How can I help you?' And he said, 'Well, I might have a little package waiting for you up here in Reno, if you and your husband can get here by tomorrow.' And I almost died of excitement."

"Because you knew right away that it was me," Meg said.

Glory hugged her again. "Not right away. Not till I saw you. But I can tell you, chickie, it's more than four hundred miles from Las Vegas to Reno, and Hank and I must have flown, because I don't remember that old truck touching the ground even once."

Meg especially loved the image of Hank and Glory flying through the sky in their rusty old truck, coming to get her. When her mother fell silent, staring out the window with a dreamy expression, Meg reached up and tugged impatiently at Glory's collar.

Glory shook herself and smiled, bending to kiss the little girl's cheek. "It was a lawyer's office we went to," she said. "All fancy oil paintings and dark wood. Hank and I went in and told them who we were, and in a minute a lady came out from another room carrying something in a pink blanket. She walked over and handed it to me, and it was..."

Glory's voice faltered and got husky with emotion, as it always did at this point.

"It was *me,*" Meg said, bouncing happily. "And you loved me."

"Oh, honey, I loved you," Glory whispered, burying her face in Meg's shining dark hair. "I loved you so much, Hank had to hold on to me real tight or I would've keeled over, right then and there, with you in my arms."

"So you took me home."

"We sure did. From that minute, I didn't want anybody else to touch you or change your diaper or do a single thing for you. You were just this big..."

Glory held out her hands to indicate a shape like a shoe box.

"I was only six days old," Meg said.

"That's right. And Hank and I signed all those papers in a flash and spent a hundred dollars buying the things we needed to look after you, and then we brought you home. We named you Megan, for Hank's mother, and I thought it was the most beautiful name, but Hank was calling you Meg before a week was over, and pretty soon everybody else did, too...."

Meg wanted to stay in the warm kitchen, safe in Glory's arms. But the voice kept intruding from some distant place, drawing her forward again. She followed obediently.

"You're older now, Meg. You're eleven years old. How do you feel about your parents now? Is your home still a happy one?"

"Yes, but Daddy has to go away a lot, and that makes Mama sad."

"What are you doing?"

"I'm playing baseball this summer." Meg's spirits plummeted.

"What's the matter?"

"There's a boy..."

"Tell me about the boy. Is he playing baseball, too?"

"No. Not yet."

"Is it daytime? Is the sun shining?"

"No. It's after supper. Daddy and Mama can't come to my game because Daddy's away. He's at Laughlin, shoeing horses."

"Where are you, Meg?"

"I'm going to the game. I'm on my bike."

"All right. Let's go forward a little. Are you playing now?"

"Yes. It's windy and dusty. We're winning. But afterward..."

"Tell me, Meg..."

She was packing her ball glove and cleats into an old duffel bag. The opposing pitcher came up and stood watching her. He was a tall, muscular boy of thirteen, with bold dark eyes and a manly swagger.

"You got a couple nice hits," he said, grinning. "You're not bad, for a *girl.*"

Meg heard things like this all the time. She ignored him, tugged her cap low over her eyes and started toward her bike, which was chained to a backstop. The boy followed and watched while she fastened her duffel bag onto the rack behind the seat.

"And you know what else?" he said, his voice suddenly cracking though he was obviously trying to sound grown-up and cool. "You're real pretty. You're just about the prettiest girl I ever saw."

Meg turned and gave him a quick look of surprise and displeasure, then bent to unfasten the lock on her bike. But the boy moved forward with disconcerting swiftness, grabbed her shoulders and kissed her full on the mouth.

Meg gasped in outrage and kicked his shin with such force that he doubled over in pain, causing a burst of laughter from the scattered onlookers. She wrenched her bike into position, jumped onto it and pedaled away furiously, bending low over the bars, her legs pumping like pistons.

The wind tugged at her clothes and the desert spun past as she flew up the road toward their farm with the boy's words ringing in her ears.

Pretty... just about the prettiest girl...

"I *hate* him," Meg shouted.

The wind caught her voice and whipped it away from her. She began to cry, but the tears dried on her cheeks as soon as they fell.

Glory was in the kitchen, knitting, with the neighbor's baby sleeping nearby in its portable bed. Meg burst into the room so noisily that Glory looked up and shook her head in warning. She put a finger to her lips and pointed at the baby.

Meg subsided and tossed the duffel bag into a corner of the porch, then came in more quietly and got a glass of milk. Glory dropped the knitting into her lap and watched her daughter with concern.

"What's the matter, punkin? Did you lose?"

"No, we won." Meg sat by the table, hooked her feet around the legs of the chair and wiped milk from her lip. "There was a dumb boy there, Mama. The pitcher on the other team. He... After the game, he..."

"What?"

"He...kissed me," Meg said, her face turning scarlet. "Real quick, before I even knew what he was doing. And he said I was...pretty."

Glory relaxed and picked up her knitting again. "Well, that's certainly the truth," she said calmly. "Why are you so upset?"

"I don't *want* to be pretty!" Meg said with such passion that Glory cast another concerned look at the sleeping baby. "I hate all that dumb stuff, Mama. I just *hate* it!"

Glory looked at her in surprise and began to protest, but Meg got up and raced down the hall to her room, flinging herself onto the bed. She lay and stared at the ceiling, stormy with anger.

After a while, she heaved herself to her feet and stood in front of the mirror on her dressing table, tugging off her baseball cap and studying her reflection.

Glory trimmed Meg's hair about once a month, while Meg perched on a kitchen stool and tried to keep still. Her hair was very short, parted boyishly on one side, but it was thick and shiny and looked even darker against her white skin. Meg never seemed to tan even though she spent most of her life outside.

Meg hated her looks. As the years passed and she grew more conscious of the image in her mirror, she began to feel increasingly isolated by the difference between herself and her parents. Hank was stocky, muscular, slow-moving and quiet. He had pale gray eyes and shaggy blond hair. Glory was short and fat, hazel-eyed, with wild ginger hair and freckled skin.

Meg would have given anything to look like them. It would have made her feel so *safe,* somehow, if she had a chunky body and light hair and an ordinary-looking face. Sometimes Meg would catch sight of herself unexpectedly in a mirror or a store window and feel a cold shiver of dread, but she had no idea what she was afraid of...

"Meg? Let's go forward."

There was that voice again, coming from far away.

"You're fourteen now. It's September, and you're at the car races. Tell me what's happening."

Meg recoiled in terror. "No," she whispered. "No, I don't want to."

"You're safe, Meg," the voice said, gentle and soothing. "You're just visiting. You can leave whenever you begin to feel uncomfortable. Now, tell me who's with you."

"Mama and Daddy," Meg said reluctantly. "It's a holiday."

"What are you doing?"

"Daddy and I are looking at the cars. Mama's up in the grandstand."

"Tell me about the cars. Do you like cars?"

"Not as much as horses. But Daddy really likes them, even though he works with horses all the time. Isn't that funny?"

"Yes, it is. Tell me about the cars."

"There's such a lot of them, all over the place. It's warm and sunny, and the crowd is really excited...."

Meg followed her father around the pit area, feeling comfortably nondescript in her jeans, sneakers and ball cap, peering at engines and listening to drivers and mechanics while they discussed handling and suspension, horsepower and track conditions.

Glory was waiting for them up in the grandstand. Meg's mother wasn't the least bit interested in cars or engines but she always enjoyed the fun of being in a holiday crowd. When the races started, Hank and Meg went up to sit with her. Both of them were tickled by Glory's enthusiasm, and the unlikely cars she chose to bet on because she liked the color of the driver's helmet, or the name sounded lucky.

After a few races, Glory grew restless and decided to go to the refreshment stand for ice cream, taking their orders for snacks but refusing to accept Meg's offer of help.

"You stay here with Daddy," she said. "You're more interested in this stuff than I am. Here, chickie, bet a dollar for me on that car with the pink stripes. I'm real partial to that shade of pink."

Meg watched fondly as her mother made her way down through the grandstand. Glory was a bright splash of color in the crowd, wearing a loose sundress of brilliant blue cotton and the swinging turquoise earrings that Hank had bought for her years ago in Virginia City.

The next race started before Glory got back. The cars roared around the track with dizzying speed, glittering in the desert sunlight, while Meg and her father shouted themselves hoarse up in the stands. Suddenly, one of the cars spun out of control, crashed through the barrier in a cloud of dust and plowed into the crowd along the sidelines, scattering people in all directions.

They gasped in horror and peered down at the wrecked car while screams and the wail of sirens filled the air. The crowd fell away to admit the medical personnel and Meg saw the bodies on the ground, bent every which way like rag dolls.

And nearby, crumpled in the dust, a bloody mass of bright blue cotton....

Meg began to scream. Hank patted her shoulder, dazed and silent, then got to his feet and stumbled down the stairs toward the track.

Meg sat alone while people nearby looked at her in horrified sympathy. She was unaware of them, or of anything at all except the dazzling sunlight, the clouds of dust that settled in the desert, the warm wind on her face....

Tears ran down her cheeks. She wiped at them with the sleeve of her housecoat while Clara sat opposite and watched her in silence.

"Why are you crying, Meg? Are you sad about your mother?"

"Partly," Meg whispered, looking out the window at the horses.

"What else?"

"It all seems so *real* when you take me back like that," Meg said at last. "It's a lot more real than the present. I feel like I'm being swallowed up. Like I only exist in the past and none of this..." She waved her hand at the luxurious bedroom. "None if it is really happening."

"Now that you're awake, do you still remember the baseball game, and the boy who kissed you?"

Meg nodded.

"That's very interesting." Clara frowned thoughtfully at the notes on her clipboard.

"Why?"

"Because in that memory, we see Meg expressing a definite consciousness of her own sexual attractiveness, as well as strong concerns over adoption. Both of those are new."

Meg glanced up at her, suddenly cautious.

"You haven't expressed those emotions before," Clara said quietly. "And by her own admission when she spoke to me on the phone, Megan Howell has never considered herself particularly attractive, either. I'm sure that was one of the things that drew Lisa to her when they met, the lack of a physical beauty that Lisa would find threatening. I wish I could speak with Megan again," Clara added, looking annoyed.

"Why can't you?"

"Because Megan Howell seems to have vanished. Apparently, she quit her job rather abruptly just a few days after I spoke with her, and she has no telephone at home. Nobody seems able to contact the woman. Her supervisor was quite angry about it."

Meg shrugged this away, reluctant to think about the "real" Megan Howell.

"Why is that memory so significant?" she asked. "About the baseball, I mean."

"Until now, except for Glory's death, all of Meg's memories have been happy and positive."

"But now..."

"Now, in addition to her terror over her physical attractiveness, which she is quite strongly aware of, Meg also seems to have developed some powerful feelings about adoption. This is the first time we've recovered a memory like that."

"So what does that mean?"

"It seems that Lisa's attitudes are now beginning to color Meg's memories, as well, even though you constantly refuse to allow me to bring Lisa out, even under hypnosis. It's evident to me that Lisa still has influence over the basic identity, even when she's not present."

Meg gave her doctor a quick glance.

"Does that trouble you, Meg? You should be encouraged by this. It may well be the first step to full personality integration."

"But that means Lisa will still be the dominant one, doesn't it?"

"You mustn't be so afraid of Lisa," Clara said with unusual gentleness. "Lisa is merely another part of you. You're two sides of the same coin. Two aspects of the same person. If you can bring yourself to accept that, your life will cease to be so fragmented and confusing. You can begin the process of replacing these borrowed memories with something closer to reality, and fully merge your two separate identities."

"Look, did you ever consider..." Meg looked down at her hands, gripped tightly in her lap.

"What, Meg? What were you going to tell me?"

"Nothing," Meg said. "I wasn't going to say anything."

She turned away and looked out the window again, hiding her face so Clara couldn't read her thoughts.

8

September deepened and mellowed, and the morning sun took a long time to climb above the Wasatch Mountains and flood the plains with light. When Jim finished breakfast and headed down to his truck, the yard was still in shadow, bathed in the pearl-tinted radiance of early dawn. The spectacular autumn foliage remained shrouded by dense mists rising off the creek.

He paused by the truck, his mind already on problems that he needed to deal with before noon. His firm was building a warehouse complex on the northern outskirts of the city, and there were all kinds of delays. One of the larger electrical workers' unions was out on strike again, and a truckload of plumbing supplies that he'd ordered weeks ago was still inexplicably delayed somewhere in Kansas...

He tossed his thermos into the truck, then turned up his jacket collar and headed for the little pen behind the barn where his horses spent the night. They were both there, standing along the fence near the water trough. Jim let himself through the little gate and started toward them.

Suddenly, he paused in shock and stared at the horses. A slim form, almost invisible in the shadows, moved between the two animals.

Jim stepped closer and recognized his neighbor, Lisa Cantalini, wearing a gray down-filled jacket, blue jeans and running shoes. She emerged from behind Cochise and stood looking at him, clearly as startled as he was.

She seemed different than Jim remembered, thin and fragile, and her skin was very pale. Jim remembered Trudy's account of the woman's sickness and fever. He recalled the shadowy face he'd seen at the upstairs window so often.

Still, despite her physical weakness, she was even more beautiful than he remembered. Maybe it was because she was wearing no makeup, and her face seemed young and vulnerable. Her exotic eyes were a very deep blue in the morning shadows, and her hair, glossy and dark, lifted casually with the breeze.

But the main difference was her manner, and the strange expression on her face. She looked shy and timid, not at all the confidently seductive young woman that he remembered.

Finding her in his corral, alone with his horses in the early morning, was so bizarre that he could scarcely believe it. Jim looked into her wide, startled eyes and felt a chilly touch of the irrational fear that people sometimes experience when confronted by mental illness.

"Hello, Lisa," he said, trying to sound casual. "I'm surprised to see you out here."

"I... thought you'd be gone," she murmured, looking down at the dusty ground beneath her feet. "You've usually left by this time."

"I'm on my way. Just stopped in to check my horses. Can I help you with something?"

"I noticed..."

Her voice was so low that he stepped forward, straining to hear. She gave him a wary glance, like some timid woodland animal, and edged back closer to the horses.

"I noticed from my window yesterday that the gelding was lame," she said. She bent and lifted one of the big sorrel's rear hooves, running her free hand along the cannon bone. "There's quite a lot of swelling down here above the fetlock."

Jim gaped at her, speechless with shock and some other, less definable emotion. Lisa Cantalini, of all people, in his corral alone with his horses, was startling enough. But the sight of her standing there with the gelding's hoof in her grasp triggered a distant memory, faint and elusive.

In the nature of memories, he couldn't pin down the image, but sometime in the past he'd seen a dark-haired woman standing just like this, next to a horse, holding one of the rear hooves and saying...

"Sorry," he muttered, abashed. "I had no idea that you knew so much about horses."

She turned away quickly and lowered the sorrel's leg to the ground, patting his hindquarters and looking in concern at the injured fetlock.

Jim cleared his throat awkwardly. "Lisa...does Victor know that you're over here this morning?"

She shook her head, still patting the horse. "Victor's in Las Vegas at an auto dealers convention. I think he's going to be away all week."

"I see."

He moved closer to Lisa and knelt to run his fingers over the gelding's lower leg. Cochise shifted and moved away a little, then submitted to the touch. "I used him at a team-roping event in Provo on the weekend," Jim said in a conversational manner, glancing over his shoulder at the woman who stood silently next to him. "I'm not sure when he hurt the fetlock, whether it was in the arena or the trailer, but it's pretty tender."

"What are you doing for it? Just liniment?"

Again he felt that chill of alarm. He and Lisa Cantalini had never had much to say to each other. There'd been a few exchanges—heavily flirtatious on her part—that Jim remembered with distaste. To his recollection, she hadn't ever touched any of his horses.

It was so utterly implausible to find her hanging around his barn in the early morning, inquiring about his veterinary procedures . . .

He glanced over at the pink granite mansion, silent in the misty light. "I've been trying to put liniment and hot wrappings on it twice a day, but I usually don't have enough time in the mornings." He looked at his watch as he rose to his feet. "In fact, I should be gone by now. I'm late already."

"I can do it in the mornings," she said, her face lighting up.

Jim stared at her. Though undeniably his neighbor's wife was a fine-looking woman and the memory of her lovely naked breasts sometimes haunted his dreams, her type had never really appealed to him. He had no taste for overstyled hair, careful makeup, and designer clothes. But this morning, he couldn't take his eyes off her.

The silence lengthened. Lisa's cheeks flushed with embarrassment and she looked down at the ground again, moving the toe of her sneaker in the soft dirt.

"If you want me to," she murmured awkwardly. "I mean, I've got nothing to do all day, and it would be easy for me to put hot dressings on his leg while you're gone. I'd really like to do it."

"Lisa...I can't believe you know how to doctor a sick horse. I've lived next door to you for more than two years and you've never shown much interest in horses. In fact, you've always seemed to be a little afraid of them."

"I've had lots of experience with horses. It was...I guess it was before I came to Salt Lake." Lisa kept her head turned away while she stroked the horse's withers.

Looking at her glossy dark hair, Jim remembered Trudy's chatter about mental illness and different personalities. Again he felt that icy shiver of fear.

"You actually know how to put on a hot dressing?"

"I've done it hundreds of times."

"Okay," he said. "If you really know something about horses and you want to do this, I guess I can use the help. I'll show you where I keep the supplies."

"I can manage by myself. There's hot water in the barn, isn't there?"

"If you want to be my veterinarian," he said curtly, "you'll have to know where everything is. Come on."

Quietly, she walked with him toward the barn.

Sharply conscious of her presence next to him, Jim was more than a little concerned about the wisdom of his own actions.

Did he really want to leave this young woman alone with his horses, playing amateur veterinarian?

Despite her confident words, he didn't believe Lisa Cantalini had much experience with horses. On the other hand, if she really wanted to do this, the application of hot dressings was a relatively simple procedure. There wasn't much chance that she could hurt the gelding, and she seemed so anxious to help...

Again that scrap of memory flitted across his mind, then vanished before he could grasp it.

They reached the barn and went inside. She looked around with pleasure at the neat stalls, the saddles and tack hanging on the walls, the sacks of feed and baled hay, the shelves of veterinary supplies.

"It smells so good," she said. "I'd almost forgotten how wonderful a barn smells."

He watched as she moved over to examine a braided headstall on one of the hooks. "When were you last inside a barn, Lisa?"

She looked up him, her smile fading. "I don't know," she said abruptly. "Where do you keep the liniment?"

"Here on the shelf. I've been trying out this new brand."

She took the bottle and glanced at the label, then nodded and set it back on the shelf. "Okay. And the dressings?"

"There's some clean burlap in the stall over there. I always hang it out to dry afterward on the edge of the stall."

She went into the stall to collect an armful of the coarse wrappings, carried them back and set them down by the sink with a businesslike air.

Jim watched her, fascinated, then caught himself and straightened when she turned to look at him.

"I'll be all right," she said. "You can go now, if you need to get to work."

"Okay." He lingered by the stalls. "Are you sure you can manage, Lisa?"

She reached up to get a halter from one of the hooks by the door. "I'll be fine," she repeated, heading for the corral.

He pulled himself away reluctantly and went out the opposite door toward his truck while she fitted the halter on Cochise and led the gelding back inside the barn.

Jim got into his pickup and sat behind the wheel, watching as they vanished into the shaded depths.

At last, he put his truck in gear and drove off toward the city, shaking his head, wondering just what had happened to Lisa Cantalini.

Meg worked carefully over the big gelding, applying the hot dressings to his leg, then rubbing the warmed area with liniment. The horse shifted uneasily, lifting the hoof and setting it down with a clatter on the heavy plank floor. Meg murmured and patted him soothingly until he calmed under her touch, reaching back to nuzzle her shoulder as she knelt beside him.

When the treatment was finished she took a brush and currycomb from the shelf and groomed him thoroughly. She went out, brought the little mare inside and brushed her, as well, reluctant to leave the comforting warmth of the barn for her luxurious house and empty bedroom.

But after a couple of hours, she felt herself growing weak and shaky from the unaccustomed exercise. Her forehead was clammy and the strength seemed to have left her hands. She turned both horses out into the pasture, tidied the barn and dragged herself home, almost too weary to climb the stairs.

In her room, she shed her clothes, pulled a nightgown over her head and climbed into bed. She stared moodily at the ceiling, wondering if she would ever be strong enough to go to Las Vegas to search out the truth about her past. She could barely manage being out of bed for a couple of hours; how could she possibly drive four hundred miles by herself?

She rolled over and settled into the blankets, her mind full of troubled thoughts. It was a long time before she fell asleep.

She woke to a dazzle of sunlight and stared at the window in confusion, trying to remember where she was. A dark shadow fell across the bed, startling her until she recognized Filomena standing silently next to the bed with a pile of folded sheets in her arms.

The housekeeper gestured at a tray on the table near the window. Meg heaved herself up on one elbow and saw plastic-wrapped sandwiches, a steaming bowl of soup, a glass of milk and some fruit.

"Is that my lunch?" she asked, still uncertain of the time.

Filomena nodded without looking at her and set the sheets on a nearby dresser.

"I'll get up," Meg said. "I need to go the bathroom, anyhow. I'll get up so you can change the bed."

Filomena watched impassively as Meg struggled to sit up, then dragged herself from the bed and fumbled for her housecoat.

As soon as Meg was on her feet, the housekeeper began to strip the bed, working with brisk motions as she pulled sheets from the mattress and tossed them onto the floor. Meg paused for a moment to get her balance and began to move toward the bathroom.

She almost stumbled over Dommie who was sitting just outside the bathroom door, playing with two bright cloth dolls. Meg recognized them as Bert and Ernie, the Sesame Street duo. She knelt on the floor by the little boy, her head clearing gradually.

Dommie looked up at her and shrank back against the bedroom wall, putting two fingers into his mouth.

Meg gave him a reassuring smile. "Hello, Dommie," she murmured, settling more comfortably on the floor. "May I see your dollies?"

Dommie hesitated, then held one of the toys up for her to look at. Meg took Bert in her hands, examining his shock of black hair and his impudent grin.

"Look," she said. "They're hand puppets." She drew Bert onto her hand and held him close to Dommie's face, making the doll talk.

"Hello, Dommie," the puppet squeaked, waving his little hands. "How are you? I'm Bert."

Dommie looked at the toy in astonishment, then up at Meg.

"Hi, Dommie," Bert repeated. "I'm Bert. Can you say hi?"

"Hi," the little boy said huskily, surprising Meg who'd never heard the child speak.

"Hey, kid, can I talk to Ernie?" she squeaked.

She helped Dommie fit the other puppet on his hand, then grinned at the deep voice the child affected when he made the puppet talk.

"Hi, Bert," he growled.

"Ernie!" Bert squealed. He bounced forward, propelled by Meg, and drew the other puppet into a rapturous hug.

Dommie laughed aloud at the embrace, a delighted, childlike peal of merriment.

Meg smiled and was about to make Bert initiate further conversation, when she became aware of Filomena watching them.

The housekeeper was glaring at Meg fiercely, gripping a pillowcase tight in her hands. Her thin dark face was so angry that Meg scrambled to her feet, handed the puppet to the disappointed-looking child and went into the bathroom, upset at Filomena's reaction.

When Meg came out, the bed was neatly made and Filomena was dusting. The housekeeper moved briskly around the room, clearing objects from table and dresser tops to clean beneath them, then putting them back.

Meg passed Dommie, who fitted one of the puppets onto his hand and held it up solemnly.

"Hi," he muttered, his voice deep.

"Hi, Ernie," Meg whispered.

She paused wistfully, then cast a nervous glance at Filomena and went to sit in the chair by the window. After a brief hesitation, she drew the lunch tray closer and began eating.

"This soup is so delicious," she said, putting down her spoon to take a sip of milk. "How do you make it, Filomena? What's that flavoring?"

The housekeeper ignored her questions as she always did. Filomena never spoke to Meg unless it was to discuss something related to her work or the running of the household. All Meg's timid attempts at conversation were brushed aside as if they hadn't been offered.

"I've never learned to cook very well," Meg said, her loneliness prompting her to try again. "I'd love to learn. I'd especially like to bake cookies."

She gazed out the window at the rich palette of fall colors in the trees along the creek.

"My mother used to bake cookies," she said, remembering her last therapy session and the vivid memories that Dr. Wassermann had recovered.

Nowadays, it seemed that Meg could only recall her mother under hypnosis. Her image of Glory was getting dimmer all the time, fading into the mists, where all her memories were piled in a disorderly jumble of confused images and half-remembered faces.

Filomena continued stolidly with her task, finally disappearing into the bathroom with the discarded sheets.

Meg heard the clatter of the hamper lid, followed by the sound of cabinet doors and running water.

Meg took a banana from her tray and peeled it, then cast a cautious glance at Dommie, who was still sitting near the bathroom door playing with his dolls.

"Want some?" she whispered, holding the banana up for him to see.

The little boy looked at her with interest and scrambled to his feet, edging closer to the window.

Meg broke off some banana and held it out to him. He stuffed it solemnly into his mouth and stood watching her, his eyes huge and dark. Meg felt a sudden hunger for warmth and contact. It was all she could do not to reach out and pull the child into her arms.

"Dommie," she told the little boy softly, "do you know that I can't remember the last time somebody hugged me? I honestly can't remember."

He moved a little closer to her, gazing up at her curiously. Meg glanced at the half-open bathroom door, then reached out a cautious hand and touched his head. His dark hair felt like silk, soft and warm under her fingers.

"Dommie," she murmured, smiling down at his little jeans and shirt. "You're so sweet..."

"What's all this?" a voice asked from the door, making both of them jump.

Meg looked up and saw Clay Malone leaning in the doorway, smiling and handsome in a black leather jacket and jeans. He was carrying a brightly ribboned package in his hand, along with a bunch of yellow roses wrapped in cellophane.

9

Clay strolled into the room and looked down at the little boy and the woman in the chair.

"Hey, Lisa, I know you've always liked men," he said, "but don't you think this guy's a little young for you?" He dropped one hand onto Dommie's head and smiled at the child.

Meg was searching for a reply when Filomena came in from the bathroom and saw Clay. The housekeeper went rigid and her face turned white. She rushed forward, took the boy into her arms and ran from the room, leaving the cloth puppets on the floor.

"And hello to you, too, Filomena," Clay said with a grin, watching the housekeeper's hurried departure. "That's sure a friendly woman, isn't it? Her chatter must drive you crazy, kid."

"I can hardly get her to say a single word to me. She always ignores me. I think the houseplants get more attention."

"Well, she's never liked you much. Come to think of it, I don't think she's ever liked anybody. Except the sainted Pauline, of course."

"Who's Pauline?" Meg asked.

Clay went into the bathroom to get a vase for the yellow roses. He put them on the dresser, then settled himself in the opposite chair.

"Thank you," Meg said. "They're lovely. Who's Pauline?" she asked again.

Clay looked at her in concern. "You really do have amnesia, don't you, kid?" he murmured. "You can't remember anything."

"Oh, I remember lots of things," Meg said with a touch of bitterness. "The only problem is, nobody believes my memories are real."

"What does your shrink say? When does she think you'll get back to reality?"

"She thinks it's starting already. She says my 'borrowed memories,' as she calls them, are starting to be changed and shaded by Lisa's personality, and eventually everything will merge into somc kind of reality."

"That's really fascinating, you know." Clay stretched his long legs and threw an arm over the back of the chair, glancing at the sandwiches on the tray. "Hey, egg salad! Your all-time favorite," he said. "Eat up, kid. You need to get your strength back."

"How did you know that egg salad's my favorite?"

Clay sighed. "I've known you since you were a little kid, Lisa. I guess I'm pretty familiar with your tastes. Come on, eat your lunch."

He took off the plastic wrappings and handed her the sandwich. Meg took it and began eating, looking at him cautiously.

Clay Malone arrived every few days on his motorcycle, always in the afternoon, and stayed for an hour or so. He was the only person in her life who actually talked to her, except for Dr. Wassermann, who hardly counted. The psychiatrist, after all, was paid to talk to her.

"Have you had lunch?" she asked, feeling guilty for eating in front of him. "I could . . ."

"Ask Filomena to whip something up for me?" he suggested when she paused awkwardly. "Who'll check it for arsenic?"

"Well, I can't make anything for you," Meg said. "I don't even remember where the kitchen is."

"That's okay," he told her. "You never *did* know where the kitchen was, kid."

"Dr. Wassermann says I should talk with you about the past, and see if you can help me recover some of Lisa's memories."

For a moment he looked alarmed. "You told the shrink about me?"

"Why shouldn't I? She's interested in every contact I have, especially someone like you who's familiar with Lisa's childhood."

"I guess she would be." Clay shifted in the chair. "I just wouldn't want her to tell Victor about these little visits, that's all," he said. "Victor doesn't know I've ever been in Utah, and it would probably be just as well if he didn't find out. If you know what I mean."

Meg felt a familiar twinge of confusion. She finished her sandwich and reached for the napkin.

"Come on," Clay urged. "There's still another one. Eat it all."

"I don't think I can. I haven't had much appetite lately."

"But you're getting better, right? You look a lot stronger today. Not so pale and shaky."

"I was up early this morning and outside for quite a while. It was so good to be out," Meg said, looking down at her hands. "I feel like I've been locked up in this house for my whole life."

"Speaking of your whole life," Clay said casually, "are you starting to remember anything? I mean real memories, not all that Las Vegas crap. Things about our life when we were kids, and the stuff we did?"

"Sort of," she said at last. "But it seems really faint and faraway. It's just a lot of grainy shadows, like one of those old silent movies, you know?"

"Does the doctor think that's normal?"

"She says it's hard to establish what normal is, since there are so few cases of dissociative personality and mine's apparently different from all the ones that have been written up."

"But?" Clay prompted.

"But," Meg went on, trying to recall the doctor's words, "she says it's normal that Lisa's memories wouldn't be all that clear in my mind since to all intents and purposes I'm a distinct personality. She says that when I begin to recover Lisa's memories, I'll still see them as an outsider would. I'll be watching Lisa doing and saying things that don't really have anything to do with me."

"I see," Clay said. "Like half of you is sort of standing back, totally detached, and watching the other half?"

"That's what the doctor says. But she points out that it's not really so unusual. She says that everybody behaves that way to some extent. We're all fragmented in many ways, she says, and multiple personality disorder would probably be a lot more common if people could recognize and acknowledge the symptoms."

"But what causes a case like yours, where the two personalities split right in half and one of them actually disappears?"

Meg shrugged. "The doctor gave me a lot of books to read, but none of them say anything about a situation like this. I guess," she added, "it's sort of like amnesia, caused by some kind of stress that my mind needs to escape from. Since I can't seem to recover any of Lisa's memories, I don't know what stress she was under. The doctor says I need to accept her pain and feel a genuine desire to help her before I can begin to integrate the two personalities."

"And do you?"

Meg thought about Lisa, that frightening, opposite personality that had somehow sprung from her own mind.

Or the other way around, if Clay and the doctor were right...

"I don't know. Sometimes I do, but other times I actually hate Lisa. I feel like she's just waiting to...come back."

Meg shivered, and Clay reached over to pat her shoulder. "Hey, kid, no need to be so melodramatic. Lisa isn't so bad, you know. She's always been one of my favorite people. In fact," he added, "it's real hard for me to call you Meg. I wish you could just be Lisa again, and everything would be like it was. I'm getting a little tired of all this."

Meg felt a shudder of alarm. "Well, if you want things to get back to normal," she said at last, "then you have to help me, Clay. Why don't we do what the doctor says, and get you to tell me things about the past that might fill in the blanks?"

"Okay," he said. "What do you want to know? Ask me some questions."

Meg thought for a moment. "We grew up in Provo?" she said.

Clay nodded. "Our mothers were sisters from North Carolina. Terry and Gerry, the terrible twosome, short for Teresa and Geraldine. Cute, hey? Your mother was married for a while, but her husband left when you were about four years old and never came back. My old man,” he added bitterly, “didn’t even stay around that long. In fact, he never bothered to marry my mother. She always wore a ring and pretended her husband was killed in Vietnam. You know, it must be a hell of a relief for her,” he added thoughtfully, “now that she can leave all that behind.”

“Your mother’s still alive? My aunt?”

“Of course she is,” Clay said in surprise. “She married an insurance salesman about ten years ago and we moved to Florida with him. I suppose that’s where Victor thinks I am right now,” he added. “Still in Florida, working for the Miami police department.”

“You’re a policeman?”

“I used to be. I joined the Miami force about six years ago, then quit two years later to become a private investigator. But we’ve never told your husband that I quit, kid. He likes to think I’m safely out of the way, thousands of miles from you. I guess you don’t remember, but he told you once that if I ever came to Utah, I’d be really sorry.”

“Why?”

“I told you,” Clay said patiently. “He’s insanely jealous of me. Once he actually threatened to hire some muscle to deal with me if I ever showed up here. Victor’s a pretty tough dude, you know, even if he hides it well.”

“Then why aren’t you afraid of coming to the house like this? What if he finds out?”

“Who’s going to tell him?” Clay asked mildly. “Filomena? She never talks to anybody.”

“What if he comes home in the afternoon and finds you here?”

"What would he come home for?" Clay asked, laughing. "To grab a quickie? I don't think you and Victor are all that friendly these days, kid."

Meg flushed and turned away.

"So, what else do you want to know?" Clay asked.

She looked down at the food on the table, wondering what to make of this man. If Meg's own theory about her past was correct, then Clay Malone was the most blatant and outrageous of liars.

But he seemed so convincing....

And if he was telling the truth, then Meg was truly lost in a nightmare she couldn't even begin to understand.

"Were you around when I entered all those beauty pageants? I can't imagine doing something like that. The doctor says I entered seventy-nine beauty pageants starting before I was three years old, and won most of them. I don't remember a single thing about it."

"Oh, God, you were beautiful, Lisa," he said with a faraway smile. "But my mother always thought Terry went overboard with the beauty-contest stuff. That's why Greg left, you know."

"Greg?"

"Your father. Terry's husband. Greg couldn't stand it, all the attention she gave you. You were Terry's whole life. Pretty dresses and dancing shoes, crowns and flowers... That was what she lived for from the moment they got you."

He gave her a cautious glance.

"You remember that part, don't you?" he asked gently. "About being adopted?"

She nodded. "It's just about the only thing I *do* remember. The doctor thinks it's one of the keys to my condition."

"Okay," he said in relief. "I thought maybe you'd blocked that, too. It was always kind of a sore point with you. You were really upset when you found out, especially when Terry wasn't the one who told you. It hurt pretty bad, I guess."

Meg thought about the memories that remained so clear in her mind, of Glory with her frizzy ginger hair and plump floury arms, sitting in the shabby kitchen of a trailer house and telling her how much she was loved and cherished....

"Who's Pauline?" she asked abruptly.

Clay cast her a quick glance. "Now, what made you think of that?"

"A while ago, you said Pauline was the only person Filomena ever liked. I just wondered who she is."

Clay turned to finger one of the glossy leaves on the yellow roses. "She was Victor's first wife," he said.

"What happened to her?"

"She died."

Meg sat erect in her chair and put the other sandwich back on the tray. "How did she die? Was it a long time ago?"

Clay sighed and settled back in his chair. Again Meg was conscious of his good looks and the controlled power of his body.

"Not long," he said at last. "Two or three years ago, I guess. It was in the spring before you and Victor got married."

"How did she die?"

"She fell down the stairs."

"*Those* stairs?" Meg asked in horror, gesturing toward the hallway. "The big curved staircase in the foyer?"

Clay nodded. "She tripped on the hem of her housecoat and took a swan dive. Apparently, she was drunk at the time. Filomena testified at the inquest that she saw Pauline trip and lose her balance, and the coroner found a lot of alcohol in her blood."

"She was drunk? I thought you said she was a saint."

He grinned. "Even saints can have a drinking problem, kid. I guess Pauline was one of those closet drunks. An alcoholic housewife who drowned her sorrows in a gin bottle when she was all alone. Come to think of it," he added thoughtfully, "Victor can't have been all that much fun to live with. Especially when—" He fell silent abruptly.

"What?" Meg asked. "What were you going to say?"

"Nothing. Come on, eat your sandwich, kid."

"I'm not hungry anymore." Meg looked out the window at the horses. "What was she like? Pauline, I mean. She must have been a nice person if Filomena liked her so much."

Clay made a gesture of irritation. "How would I know? I never met her. I was in Miami when all this was going on."

"So how do you know all the details?"

He grinned. "You told me, Lisa," he murmured softly. "You told me everything."

Meg felt a sudden, inexplicable fear. She struggled to get herself under control. "Was Pauline a lot younger than Victor, too?" she asked. "Like . . . like me?"

Clay laughed. "Hell, no. She and Victor were high school sweethearts. I guess the poor lady didn't age all that well." He glanced out the window, still smiling, then turned back to her. "You used to tell such a funny story about how you first met Pauline and made her so jealous by hinting that you and Victor were having an affair when it wasn't even true."

"That's not funny," Meg said coldly. "It's not funny at all."

Clay shrugged and sprawled in the chair, avoiding her eyes by toying with the flowers.

"But was she..."

"Leave it alone," he said quietly. "Why don't you leave it alone?"

"Why should I?"

"Because," he said, turning to look at her directly, "if you keep asking questions, you might find out some of the things you've been trying so hard to forget."

He got up and prowled around the room, looking at her makeup bottles, picking ornaments up and setting them down, studying the big oil painting over her bed.

"God, you were so beautiful." He sighed, gazing at the painting. "Are you going to let your hair grow again, Lisa?"

"I don't know. Was Pauline... Why did Filomena like her so much?"

He turned to her, his jaw tight and angry. "Look, why can't you just drop it?"

"I only want to know if—"

"Yes, she was a nice person," Clay said, obviously controlling his patience with an effort. "She took in stray cats and gave money to orphans. She was fat and plain and boring, but people liked her. When Filomena got pregnant, Pauline was good to her. Apparently, she helped Filomena learn some English and get her citizenship papers, and made sure she saw a doctor regularly. She helped with the baby when he was born, too. Filomena appreciated her generosity. Does that answer your questions?"

Meg was silent a moment, frightened by his intensity. Finally, she nerved herself to ask a question she'd been wondering about for several days.

"Clay...who was Dommie's father?"

"Dommie's father?" he asked blankly. "Filomena's kid? Now, why would you be asking that?"

"Was it...was it Victor?" Meg asked.

Clay threw back his head and laughed, genuinely amused. "No," he said. "No, kid, I don't think it was Victor."

Meg thought about the vigorous gray-haired man who occasionally shared her meals and whose attitude toward her veered between detachment and a tentative, clumsy sort of kindness. The only time her husband seemed genuinely happy and relaxed was when he was playing with Dommie.

"He really loves that little boy," she ventured. "I keep wondering if—"

"Well, forget it," Clay said curtly. "When you start getting your memory back, you'll realize how silly that idea is."

"Why?"

Clay sighed. "Because," he said, "from what I understand, Victor couldn't have had anything to do with Filomena's baby. In these days just before Pauline died, there was only one woman Victor was interested in climbing into bed with, and it sure wasn't the housekeeper."

"Who was it?"

"You," Clay told her softly.

Meg twisted her hands in her lap, feeling tired and miserable.

"Hey, kid." Clay patted her shoulder. "Don't be like that. Look," he added, moving away to take the wrapped package from behind the flowers. "I brought you a present."

Meg looked at the gold foil and satin ribbons. "What for?"

"Think about it," he said. "See if you can remember why I'd be bringing you a present today."

She gazed up at him, her eyes widening in astonishment. "It's my birthday." she said. "Today's my birthday, isn't it?"

"It sure is. September fifteenth. See, you *can* still remember a few things." Clay smiled. "Do you remember anything about the parties we used to have on your birthday? Terry always acted like it was some kind of royal occasion. She spent so much money on special designer cakes and decorations, and expensive presents for you..."

Meg's face clouded. She fingered the gold foil, then unwrapped it slowly to reveal a satin box with a perfume bottle nestled inside.

"It's your favorite," Clay said. "Halston. Cost me a small fortune."

"Thank you," she said, wondering how she could remember that she liked egg salad sandwiches but have no memory of her favorite perfume.

Clay bent to hug her, gathering her into his arms and holding her tenderly. Meg had a confused awareness of male strength and warmth, of hard muscles under soft leather and stubble that scraped against her face.

"Hey," he said, drawing back and looking at her in surprise, "speaking of perfume, what's this I smell?"

"I don't know," she said. "I'm not...not wearing anything."

"I'll say." He wrinkled his nose, still looking astonished. "You smell like *horse,* kid."

She moved awkwardly in the chair. "I was... over at the neighbor's place today," she murmured. "One of his horses has a swollen fetlock and I told him I'd put some heat dressings on it while he was at work."

"Told who?"

"The neighbor. His name is Jim Leggatt."

"I know his name. Since when are you so fond of horses, Lisa? Or," he added coldly, "is it the *neighbor* you're fond of?"

"I don't know what you mean," Meg said. "I just noticed from my window that the horse was limping, and went down to have a closer look at him. And the neighbor... Jim... he was there, so I told him I'd put the dressings on in the morning when he didn't have time. That's all."

"God, I don't believe this," Clay said in a flat tone. "I don't think you've ever touched a horse in your life. You're scared of horses."

"*Lisa's* scared of horses," she said. "But I'm not. My name is Meg, and I love animals."

He shrugged and looked away. "Okay," he said at last. "If you want to keep on being this way, go ahead. Just be real careful of the neighbor."

"Jim Leggatt?" Meg thought about the man who lived next door, his sunny blond good looks and engaging smile. "Why should I be careful?"

"That guy's bad news," Clay said over his shoulder, gathering up the scattered gift wrappings and taking them into the bathroom. "He almost killed a woman last year in a hotel room in Salt Lake."

Meg looked at the empty doorway in disbelief. Again she thought about Jim Leggatt's easy smile, his friendly cowboy manner.

"Why?" she called.

"I don't know. I guess they had a disagreement." Clay came back into the room and stood looking down at her. "That guy's got a real ugly temper, kid. In my business, you hear about these things. You can hang around his horses if you want to, but try not to be alone with him or talk to him very much. Okay?"

Meg shook her head, appalled.

"Lisa?" he said. "Promise me you won't take any chances."

"All right," she said, turning away to look at the two horses grazing quietly in the pasture.

10

Meg woke early the next morning, feeling a surge of anticipation when she remembered the sorrel gelding down in the neighbor's pasture. Despite Clay's warning, she could hardly wait to get back to the barn.

She slipped from her bed, feeling stronger than she had since the accident. She dressed rapidly in faded jeans and a sweatshirt, brushed her hair and went downstairs. In the foyer, she paused for a moment to glance upward, shuddering as she thought about Victor's first wife plunging to her death at the bottom of those oak stairs.

Could Pauline Cantalini have known what was happening to her? On the way down, did she have time to realize that she was about to die?

Probably not, Meg told herself, trying to shut out the terrible image. After all, her own car had plunged over a cliff and plowed down the hillside into a metal pole, and she had no memory of the incident. She couldn't even recall getting into the car.

With a reluctant, gruesome kind of fascination, she looked down at the carpet by her feet, searching for faded bloodstains or other evidence of trauma. But everything was clean, silent and luxurious.

Of course there wouldn't be any trace of Pauline's tragedy. Both Clay and Victor had remarked several times about the way Lisa had redecorated the entire house after her marriage.

There was no doubt that the house reflected Meg's taste, although she had no recollection of choosing these colors and furnishings...

Suddenly, Meg became aware of another sensation that had been absent from her life in the weeks since the accident. She was hungry. She needed to eat something before going over next door to work on the sorrel's heat dressings.

After a brief hesitation, she began to move tentatively down the hall toward the back of the house, following the fragrant scent of bacon and fresh coffee.

Meg paused outside a closed door, then knocked briefly, opened the door and stepped inside a big, gleaming kitchen decorated in white ceramic tile and pale oak. She paused when she found three pairs of dark eyes looking at her in astonishment.

Victor was sitting at the table, eating a hearty breakfast of bacon and scrambled eggs. Dommie was beside him in a high chair, a yellow bib tied around his neck, glowering at a bowl filled with hot cereal. Filomena stood at the counter stacking dishes in one of the sinks. All of them stared at Meg in shocked silence.

Victor was the first to speak. "Well, well," he said with forced heartiness. "Look who's up early this morning. Dommie, say hello to Mrs. Cantalini."

Dommie's face brightened. He reached into the recesses of the chair and pulled out one of his hand puppets, holding it up to show her.

Meg smiled at the little boy, then at the puppet. "Hi, Bert," she said. "Hi, Dommie."

She sat down at the table while Filomena set a place mat and a cup of coffee in front of her.

"Thank you, Filomena," Meg said. "I'll just make myself a couple of slices of toast," she added, getting to her feet. "If you could show me where the bread is..."

"I'll scramble some eggs," Filomena said, breaking eggs into a pan without looking at her. "And there's more bacon."

"All right." Meg sank into her chair again. "That would be really nice of you, if it's not too much trouble."

"It's her job." Victor leaned back casually in his chair and stroked Dommie's shining black hair. "But Filomena's not used to giving you breakfast, Lisa. You've never exactly been an early riser."

In the weeks since her accident, she hadn't exchanged more than a few scraps of conversation with Victor. He lived in his own quarters in the big house and apparently didn't like visiting his wife in her room as if she were still a patient in the hospital. For long periods of time, Meg actually forgot that she was married, and always felt a little shock when she encountered the man unexpectedly like this.

Meg looked at the stranger who was her husband. Victor Cantalini was well-dressed and handsome in a cool, hard-edged kind of way. Despite the obvious difference in their ages, and the fact that she had no real memory of him, Meg could understand what had first attracted her to him, back in that misty past that she couldn't recall.

Her husband had an air of competence and masculine strength that was both reassuring and a little intimidating, yet he showed real tenderness to the small boy in the high chair. Maybe he'd once shown his wife that kind of tenderness, as well, in the days before he became so baffled and annoyed by her strange mental condition...

Meg gave him an awkward smile. "I thought . . ." She paused and cleared her throat. "I thought you were going to be staying in Las Vegas all week."

Victor held a spoonful of cereal in his blunt fingers, coaxing Dommie to eat. He turned to her in surprise. "Why? Did you miss me, Lisa?"

"I just wondered why you came home early." Meg looked up gratefully as Filomena set a plate of food in front of her. "Thanks, Filomena. That really looks delicious."

But the housekeeper was already moving back to the sink, her thin back rigid under the neat gray uniform.

Victor got up to pour himself another cup of coffee, then settled in his chair and smiled at his wife. "I get a little tired of all the hoopla at those conventions," he said. "I'm too old to be throwing water bombs out of hotel windows."

Meg nodded and attacked her food hungrily. "I'd think," she said after a moment, "that *anybody* would be too old for that."

Victor made no comment, just raised an eyebrow and sipped his coffee. "I see you've been making friends with Dommie," he observed when once more the little boy held the puppet up to show her, his dark eyes sparkling.

"Dommie and I are both puppet fans," Meg said, uncomfortably aware of Filomena's cold glance. "I'm Bert, and he's Ernie."

"Are you Ernie, kiddo?" Victor asked, leaning toward the little boy. "Which one is Bert?"

Dommie produced the dark-haired puppet, and Victor grinned. "I see. Eat your cereal, Dommie. Hey, Filomena," he asked over his shoulder, "is the poor kid supposed to eat all of this? It's a pretty big bowl you've given him."

"He'll eat it," Filomena said with an edge, "if everybody just leaves him alone."

Victor and Meg exchanged furtive, guilty smiles that suddenly made her feel much closer to the man.

"Put the puppet away and eat your breakfast, Dommie," Meg murmured. "Maybe we'll play some more when you're finished, all right?"

Dommie's face clouded with disappointment, but he attacked his cereal obediently.

"These scrambled eggs are so good." Meg sighed. "I wish I could get Filomena to tell me what seasonings she uses."

Victor looked at his wife in astonishment. "You've never been interested in cooking, Lisa."

"I know, but I'm different now," she said quietly. "I'm a different person."

Victor shifted uncomfortably at this reminder, and an awkward silence fell.

"So," he said at last, "what are you doing today, honey? Are you feeling strong enough to stay up this morning?"

"I'm not sure. I thought I was strong enough yesterday, but I wasn't. I had to go back to bed even before lunch."

"Did you have any calls or visitors while I was away?"

Meg exchanged an involuntary glance with Filomena. The housekeeper was the first to turn away, her face impassive.

"Not really," Meg said, looking down at her plate. "It's been pretty quiet. But," she added impulsively, "I met one of the neighbors. From the white house over there."

"Trudy?" Victor asked.

Meg looked at him in confusion.

"Jim's housekeeper," Victor explained. "Don't you remember Trudy? She's a nice little fat woman with gray hair, keeps a couple of milking goats in their pasture."

Meg shook her head. "I didn't see anybody like that. It was the neighbor that I met," she said. "Jim Leggatt. I was looking at his horses through my window and I noticed that one of them was lame. I went over there yesterday morning to have a better look, and Jim was there."

Victor nodded and drained his coffee mug, then looked at it thoughtfully.

"You don't remember anything, do you?" he said at last. "People or places or anything. Everything's just gone."

"Not everything," Meg said. "There are a lot of things I remember."

"But they're all made up, right? They're from this woman in Las Vegas."

"They're from my childhood."

"So, did you get along any better with Jim? You used to hate the man, as I recall."

"He seemed all right," Meg said. "I didn't talk to him very long. He just showed me where the dressings and liniment were, and then he had to leave."

"Dressings?" Victor asked. *"Liniment?"*

Meg's cheeks colored with embarrassment. "I told him I'd put heat dressings on the horse in the mornings because he doesn't have time. I'm going over there again today, as soon as I finish breakfast."

"My God." Victor was gazing at her in openmouthed shock. "You've never touched a horse in your life, Lisa."

She took a deep breath and forced herself to meet his eyes. "But I'm not Lisa," she said. "I'm Meg."

Victor got up abruptly and pushed his chair in. "Well, I'd better get going," he said with false heartiness. "Dommie, you be a good boy, okay? I'll be home late," he told Filomena. "I'm having dinner in town."

The housekeeper nodded without looking around. Meg watched in silence as Victor collected his briefcase and headed for the door. She put down her fork, got up and followed him to the foyer.

He turned, clearly surprised to find her watching as he took a black nylon gym bag from the closet.

"Racquetball at noon," he told her, holding up the bag. "I'm playing with a couple of the salesmen from the downtown dealership."

"Are you good?" Meg asked.

He gave her a wolfish grin. "Not too bad, for an old guy."

Meg looked at his thick shoulders, his flat belly and powerful athletic torso.

"But do you have the killer instinct?" she asked.

His eyes narrowed and he gave her a startled, wary glance. "Say again?"

"The killer instinct," Meg repeated. "It's essential for racquetball, isn't it? I've heard it's a pretty fierce game."

Victor relaxed visibly, smiling. "Well, of course I have the killer instinct, baby. Hey, I'm a car salesman, right?"

She smiled back at him, then hesitated. "Victor... about the neighbor, Jim Leggatt..."

Victor riffled through his pockets and swore mildly, then raised his head to shout down the hall.

"*Filomena!* Have you seen my car keys?"

Within seconds, the housekeeper appeared. She opened the top drawer of a large console and silently handed Victor his keys. Then she turned and went back to the kitchen.

Victor muttered again as he put the keys in his jacket pocket. "Jim Leggatt?" he asked his wife. "What about him?"

Meg shifted nervously on the soft carpet. "Just...I don't know. I thought I heard somebody say something bad about him. That he has a tendency to violence, or something. I wondered if—"

"Now, who'd be telling you something like that?" Victor looked at her intently. "Filomena? Clara? You don't talk to anybody else, do you?"

"Not really. I...I guess not," Meg faltered, her nervousness increasing. "I just...thought I overheard a bit of conversation about him. That he was a dangerous man, something like that."

Victor moved forward and suddenly took her in his arms, startling her. Except for an occasional hand to steady her on the stairs or a courteous peck on the cheek, it was the first time he'd ever touched her.

"All men are dangerous, baby," he whispered into her neck. "You should know that."

Meg shivered in his arms, conscious of the thick strength and firmness of his body and the expensive cologne he was wearing.

She drew away and looked up. "But is he..."

Victor bent and kissed her mouth, then drew her into a fierce embrace again.

"God, you're beautiful, Lisa," he whispered. "You're even more beautiful than you were before the accident. I think you actually look better without makeup. Not many women can say that."

She trembled, trying not to pull away and scream. After all, the man wasn't an invading stranger. He was her husband, and had every right to hold her.

If only she could *remember*...

"All men are dangerous," Victor repeated, drawing away to look at her. "If your instincts are warning you about the neighbor, honey, you'd better pay attention to them. I know you never liked him much. Maybe you've got a good reason. Okay?"

"But did he..."

A small flurry near the kitchen door made them both turn. Dommie was trotting down the hall toward them, pursued by Filomena, who looked grim and purposeful.

Victor swept the little boy up in his arms, kissed him soundly and tossed him into the air while Dommie screamed with delight. Filomena watched in silence, her hands gripped tensely in her apron.

"Well, I'm off. So long, everybody," Victor said. "You know, this is kind of nice," he added, giving Meg a meaningful smile. "I like having my wife and a little kid at the door to kiss me goodbye in the morning."

Then he was gone, striding across the rosy flagstone terrace toward the rear of the house.

She closed the door and turned to look at Filomena by the carved oak newel post at the bottom of the stairs.

Pauline had plunged down those stairs to her death, while Filomena watched....

Meg caressed Dommie's soft hair as the little boy paused beside her, holding up one of his hand puppets with a hopeful look.

"Very nice," she murmured, then looked over at Filomena. "Would Dommie like to see the horses?" she asked.

"No," Filomena said, moving back down the hall toward the kitchen.

"But the little mare is really gentle," Meg said, following. "After I've finished the heat dressings and the grooming, I could come over here and get both of you, and we could give Dommie a chance to sit on the horse. You could even hold him while I lead the mare around the small corral."

"Ride horsey!" Dommie shouted, dancing with excitement. "Ride horsey, Mama!"

Meg was pleased and astonished by his exuberance. She'd never heard Dommie, who was normally so grave and silent, express noisy enthusiasm about anything.

His mother, too, watched him for a moment, then cast Meg a bitter glance. "What do you think you're doing?" she asked in a low voice.

"I just..." Meg quailed in the face of the woman's obvious hatred. "I just thought he might enjoy sitting on the horse for a little while. But if you—"

"Mama!" Dommie yelled, his face red with urgency.

Filomena threw her hands up and stamped into the kitchen.

"Filomena?" Meg asked, pausing in the doorway.

"All right," the housekeeper said grimly. "But I come, too. You don't take him over there alone."

"Of course," Meg agreed. "You'll be there every minute."

Dommie ran over to hug Meg's leg, bouncing and shouting. Meg peeled him away gently, gave him a kiss and left the kitchen. She collected her jacket from the hall closet and ventured out into the crisp autumn morning, heading for the barn.

Jim Leggatt had clearly anticipated her visit, because everything was laid out for her, neat and ready. The two horses greeted her with almost as much enthusiasm as Dommie had displayed.

As Meg worked over the horses in the warm, dusty fragrance of the barn, she marveled at the strange workings of the human mind. If her therapist and the people around her were to be believed, she'd never done this kind of thing before in her life. Yet it had a rich, satisfying familiarity.

Her hands remembered the feel and weight of a horse's body. Her back drew upon long-stored reserves of strength when she lifted and moved the animal's leg. Even her nose greeted the scent of hay and horse with joyful recognition. It wasn't possible that she'd never been around a horse before.

Perhaps she'd worked with horses during one of those blackouts Dr. Wassermann had alluded to. In one of the therapy sessions, Clara Wassermann had questioned her closely about blackouts. But since Meg couldn't remember any of Lisa's life, she couldn't recall if Lisa had suffered any "telltale blackouts," as Clara had described them.

"Why telltale?" Meg had asked.

"Because those would be previous times when Lisa was in abeyance and you had charge of the body. It's possible that you had some fairly long periods of existence before the accident, but Lisa was never aware of them, simply because she refused to acknowledge your being. In fact, that's a much more normal clinical profile for MPD."

"So when Lisa was blacked out somewhere, I'd be the one who was out doing things? I'd be Meg, working with horses and all the other things I enjoy?"

"It's possible. But you do recognize the obvious flaw in our theory, don't you?"

"Somebody would have noticed," Meg had said after some thought. "If Lisa started behaving so drastically out of character, somebody in her life would have been aware of it."

"Except . . . ?" Clara had asked, waiting for the answer like a schoolteacher with a bright pupil.

Meg wrung out the damp burlap and drew more hot water. She watched as it steamed gently in the pail, still recalling her conversation with the therapist.

"Those trips to Las Vegas," she'd suggested while Clara waited. "It could have happened then, right? Lisa went to Las Vegas all the time, especially in the past six months. She sometimes stayed for long periods of time. Nobody knew what she did down there. Not even Victor."

"Not even Victor," the doctor had agreed, looking satisfied.

Meg shook her head and lifted the pail, troubled by the memory of that therapy session.

She hated the disjointed confusion of her past. It was bad enough not to be able to remember recent events. Far more distressing was the knowledge that two separate personalities had quite possibly occupied her body over a period of many years, pulling her in utterly different directions.

Meg carried the steaming bucket into the stall and knelt by the gelding. She reached for the liniment bottle and began briskly rubbing medicated cream into the hot damp hide above the horse's swollen fetlock, murmuring soothing words as the animal shifted restlessly on the heavy plank floor.

Maybe she should ask Victor if they could terminate the therapy. Everybody had different theories about what had happened to her, and the sessions with Dr. Wassermann weren't doing anything to shed much light on her recent past.

Especially since Meg couldn't bring herself to confide her own beliefs. She was afraid all the time these days, fearful about what she might learn next.

Or when Lisa might choose to reappear...

Suddenly, a shadow fell over the floor, touching her back and shoulder. Meg gasped and turned around, her heart pounding noisily in alarm.

11

Filomena stood in the doorway wearing an old green coat over her uniform. She carried Dommie in her arms, bundled in a red jacket and knitted hat. The little boy was gazing at the horse in wide-eyed astonishment.

"Horsey!" he shouted, wriggling impatiently. "Put me down, Mama."

Meg got to her feet, brushed dust from the knees of her blue jeans and went over to lift the child in her arms.

"The horse is called Cochise," she told Dommie. "Can you say that?"

He struggled with the unfamiliar syllables, making them sound rather like a sneeze. Meg laughed and kissed his cheek while Filomena looked on grimly, her arms folded tight against her chest.

"That's close enough," Meg said, still smiling at his pronunciation. "Cochise has a sore leg. See, Dommie, where his leg is all swollen down here? I'm putting bandages on it."

Gently, she set the child beside the big sorrel gelding, holding Dommie's hand while he bent forward to examine the slick damp hide above the fetlock, his dark eyes grave and worried.

"Horsey hurt a foot?"

Meg nodded. "He's got a pretty nasty bump, but it's getting better. Here, I'll lift you so you can pat him."

She held Dommie close to the gelding's head, showing him how to caress the broad forehead, how to scratch behind the velvety twitching ears. When Cochise nickered softly and butted at the boy's hand, Dommie bounced in Meg's arms, laughing with delight.

"He likes me!" he called to his mother over Meg's shoulder. "Horsey likes me!"

Filomena said nothing, merely gave an abrupt nod and kept watching.

Meg put Dommie down beside his mother and reached for one of the leather halters from a row of pegs on the wall.

"I'll catch Amber," she said. "That's the little mare out there. She's really gentle. Do you still want to ride the other horse, Dommie?"

He was too excited to answer, but he dragged at his mother's hand until reluctantly, Filomena crossed the floor and watched Meg approach the mare out in the small corral. Meg slipped the halter onto the horse, spoke a few words to her and caressed her withers, then led her back to the barn.

"Ready?" she asked Dommie, who was dancing from one foot to the other, clearly breathless with anticipation.

Filomena held him back, gazing fearfully up at the horse. "This is safe?" she asked Meg.

"Yes, it is," Meg said. "See, Filomena, I'll put Dommie up on Amber and you can walk along beside him while I hold the halter shank."

Filomena moved closer while Meg lifted the little boy and settled him on the mare's glossy back. Dommie clutched a handful of the coarse mane and took a deep breath.

"You mustn't kick, sweetheart," Meg warned him. "She's been trained to think that if you kick, you want to go faster."

Filomena gripped the small red sneaker nearest to her and kept her other hand on the child's waist, while Meg took the halter shank and led the mare slowly out into the corral, down past the gate and back toward the barn. Dommie laughed, his cheeks red with excitement.

Suddenly, Meg had a confusing flash of memory, so vivid that she stopped for a moment and stood gazing at the bright autumn sky.

I've done this before, she thought. And it wasn't very long ago. I've led a horse like this, with a little boy sitting up there and his mother walking alongside. It was even a fall day, just like this, but it was somewhere else...

"Okay," she said after a moment, circling back toward the barn. "Was that a big enough ride?"

Dommie was about to protest, when an unfamiliar voice caused them all to turn and look at the doorway.

"Domingo Xavier Morales, as I live and breathe," a woman called cheerfully. "How did you get way up there on that big horse?"

"Dommie's a cowboy!" the little boy shouted, starting to bounce again. "Like Jim!"

"You certainly are. And a very fine-looking cowboy, too."

A small fat woman came out of the barn and stood grinning at them, her arms akimbo. Meg felt an instant affinity for her. She had the same plump little body, the same round face and sparkling eyes that Glory had had. But this woman's hair was gray, not frizzy ginger, and it was piled in an untidy knot on top of her head.

The woman was leading a goat, black with white patches. The goat butted furiously at her leg and strained against its small red halter.

"Look, Crystal," Dommie said, addressing the goat as if it were another child. "Ride a horsey!"

"Stop that, Crystal," the woman told the goat. She jerked at the halter. "Behave yourself. Can't you see we've got company?"

Meg lifted Dommie from the horse and set him carefully on the ground near the black goat, who stopped struggling and regarded the little boy with lively curiosity.

"Hi, Lisa," the woman said. "I hear you've developed a real fondness for Jim's horses."

"Are you... are you Trudy?" Meg asked.

The woman gave her a shrewd glance. "That's me. Trudy Westerby. How are you feeling, Lisa?"

"Fine, thank you. I'm getting a little stronger every day."

"Well, that's real good news. Especially since Jim's got you doing veterinary work for him. Where did you learn so much about horses?"

"I don't know," Meg said.

The other two women exchanged a glance, and Trudy smiled with forced heartiness. "Tell me, are you any good with goats? This animal's been so restless lately, she's driving me to distraction."

Meg knelt and ran her hand over the goat's silky hide, assailed by more of those vivid memories.

Glory had kept a milking goat for a little while, until Hank started complaining bitterly about its messy, destructive habits. Meg tried to remember the goat's name, but the memory seemed to vanish as quickly as it had come.

Crystal responded to Meg's touch, bleating with pleasure and wriggling under her arm for more patting.

Meg looked up at Trudy. "Is she in heat, do you think? I don't know all that much about goats."

Trudy frowned. "She shouldn't be. Let me see, it was about..." Her plump face puckered with concentration.

Meg got to her feet and took the halter from the mare's head, turning her loose in the corral.

"Crystal ate Jim's favorite blue jeans right off the clothesline yesterday," Trudy told the others. "The man was some upset, let me tell you."

"Crystal, you're a bad girl," Meg said to the little goat, who cast her a roguish glance and skipped daintily to one side.

"Do you all have time to come in for coffee?" Trudy asked.

Filomena shook her head. "Not today," she murmured, looking quickly at Meg and then turning away.

Meg realized again just how much the housekeeper disliked her. It was even more distressing when she saw Filomena with Trudy, who was obviously a friend to the young mother and her little boy. Somehow, Meg had never pictured Filomena relaxing with anybody, sipping coffee and chatting like other women.

Apparently, it was only the people in her own household that the woman hated.

"Oh, come on," Trudy urged. "I baked a whole batch of cinnamon rolls. Dommie, tell Mama you want a cinnamon roll. You come along, Lisa, if you're not too tired. Filomena tells me you're still a little shaky these days."

"Yesterday was my first time out of bed for any length of time," Meg said. "I guess I overdid it a little. By the time I got home, I was so tired, I went straight back to bed and Filomena had to bring my lunch on a tray."

"No wonder," Trudy said, yanking at her goat's halter. "It's real hard to get up and around when you've been in bed for a long time. Do you feel better today?"

"Much better."

"Good. Then you can come in for coffee and a snack. Filomena, bring that child and come along. There's no earthly point in your having lunch over in that big lonely house when I've got fresh cinnamon buns on the table."

Filomena moved reluctantly toward the door with Dommie tugging at her hand.

"I just have to finish with Cochise and turn him out," Meg said. "I'll be in right away."

"Well, don't dawdle," Trudy said in the same firm tone she used with her goat. "Those buns are getting colder every minute."

"I'll be right there," Meg promised, once again warmed by the woman's resemblance to Glory. For the first time in weeks, she felt a stirring of optimism, almost happiness.

She rubbed some more liniment into the horse's leg, wiped away the dampness and turned both horses into the pasture. Then she walked up to the large white house, hesitating a moment before she climbed the pillared veranda. She heard sounds of merriment through a screen door around the side, so she went up and knocked.

Dommie opened the door and admitted her into a kitchen that smelled like all of Meg's childhood memories. She stood in the doorway, sniffing appreciatively, then paused in shock when she saw Jim Leggatt sitting at the table next to Filomena. He was listening to some story of Trudy's, laughing with enjoyment.

For the first time, Meg really noticed what a handsome man Jim Leggatt was. He was bareheaded, and his smooth blond hair glistened like corn silk under the overhead light. His eyes were almost as dark blue as her own, and when he laughed there were deep creases in his tanned cheeks. He cast an aura of warmth and good humor all around him, so that even Filomena seemed more relaxed in his presence.

"Hi, Lisa," he said.

"Hello," Meg whispered, suddenly overcome with shyness.

He raised his coffee mug in greeting. "I heard there might be fresh cinnamon buns today, so I thought I'd come home for lunch. How's my horse?"

"He's better than yesterday. The swelling's gone down quite a bit."

"Thanks to you," Jim said casually. "I appreciate it, Lisa."

She nodded, her cheeks turning hot with embarrassment.

"Guess what Crystal did," Dommie said in his husky voice. "She ate a pie and now she gots a tummy ache."

"I never thought anything could make that goat sick," Trudy gestured Meg to a seat at the table. "But that's her problem, all right. She made such an awful pig of herself, she'll probably have cramps for two days and hardly give a lick of milk."

Meg sat down opposite Jim, conscious of his blue eyes resting on her with thoughtful speculation. She tensed, remembering Clay's warning about this man's violent tendencies. It was hard to believe, seeing him relaxed and laughing in his sunny kitchen, surrounded by women and smiling at the little boy.

But lots of people had dark, hidden sides to their natures, Meg reminded herself. She, of all people, should be the first to realize that.

Late that evening, Jim sat behind his desk working over masses of quotes and invoices from the new building project he'd recently contracted. A moment later, he pushed the papers aside and sipped from a heavy tumbler filled with ice and whiskey, gazing out the window at the silvered pasture where his horses drowsed by the fence, dark shapes in the moonlight.

Finally, he took a medical text from a pile of books on the computer stand, studied the index and flipped rapidly through the pages, then began to read. After a while, still deep in thought, he got up and wandered through the house to the kitchen with the book under his arm.

Trudy was making butter from two gallons of curdled goat's milk. She sat at the table with her little silver churn, cranking rhythmically while she watched a game show on television.

"The Andes Mountains," she shouted.

"You're supposed to word your answer in the form of a question," Jim said, sitting opposite her and looking up at the screen.

"Oh, pooh," Trudy said. "Salvador Dali," she added.

"Hey, that's right. You're not just another pretty face, Trudy. I hope your new boyfriend appreciates you."

"Of course he does," Trudy said placidly. She opened the lid of the churn to examine its contents. "Starting to clot," she reported. "It won't be long now."

She glanced at the book Jim was carrying and raised an eyebrow.

"I stopped by the library this afternoon," Jim said. "I checked out some books on psychiatric disorders."

Trudy cranked energetically. "Are you planning to change jobs?"

He grinned. "Do you think I'd make a good shrink? I could start smoking a pipe, get a bunch of those baggy tweed jackets with leather patches on the elbows. . . ."

Trudy smiled back at him. "Somehow, I really can't see it."

She got up and took a plastic bowl from the cupboard, then began lifting out masses of milky yellow butter from the churn and packing them into the bowl.

"You're thinking about Lisa, right?" she asked.

Jim watched as she kneaded and shaped the butter into a glistening mound. "Doesn't the whole thing seem really strange to you?" he asked.

"Of course it's strange. She's like a whole new person. She's even given herself a different name."

"Then why does everybody seem to take it so much for granted?"

"What do you mean?" Trudy asked.

"Well, nobody seems all that amazed or puzzled, do they? We just accept that a month ago she was a shallow, selfish woman, hitting little kids and running around in her fancy car, and now she's over here in blue jeans, playing with the same little boy she used to hit and rubbing liniment on my horse. If I were her husband . . ."

Trudy looked up from her mound of butter. "What would you do? If you were Victor, what would you do?"

"I don't know. It's just . . ."

"Come on, tell me. Would you lock her in her room, or put her away in an institution, or what?"

Jim shifted uncomfortably. "I don't mean that. I'd just . . . be a lot more interested in her condition. I'd be looking for some answers, I guess."

"Everybody knows the answer. She's got a multiple personality. It's not like she isn't getting lots of medical attention, you know. The psychiatrist told Victor all about it."

"But don't you think that's really amazing? It's a pretty rare condition, you know."

Trudy shrugged and worked a couple of spoonfuls of salt into the fresh butter, then began shaping it into blocks. Jim watched the brisk movements of her hands, fascinated as always by his housekeeper's varied skills.

"I guess we aren't so amazed anymore," she said at last, "because we see it all the time. Folks with multiple personalities are on every afternoon talk show these days. It's even used as a defense in murder trials."

"It is?"

"Sure. I saw a woman on a show just last week who claimed one of her other personalities committed the murder while she was blacked out. The jury acquitted her."

Jim watched as she lined up the pale yellow blocks on a sheet of waxed paper, then began to wrap them.

"Well, TV always plays up the sensational," he said. "But this whole situation with Lisa... it still seems really bizarre to me. Somehow, I can't bring myself to believe it."

"What?" Trudy asked. "What can't you believe?"

"I don't know." He got up and moved restlessly across the kitchen to gaze out the window again.

"Do you think she's pretending? Making the whole thing up?" Trudy asked.

"I wouldn't put it past her. Lisa Cantalini's a pretty devious woman, you know."

Trudy carried the blocks of fresh butter over to the fridge. "Well, I don't know what to think. Actually,

Lisa's just the kind of person who'd develop some kind of exotic medical condition. But I happen to know that Filomena believes she's faking. Filomena doesn't trust her at all."

Jim looked at his housekeeper with interest. "What would be the point of all of a sudden pretending to be a wholesome girl who likes kids and horses?"

"Filomena hints that maybe Lisa's doing it to worm her way back into Victor's good graces. I guess that marriage was in real big trouble before the accident, but now he's being nice to her again because she's acting so different."

Jim thought this over, still looking out at the silvered pasture.

"Want some fresh buttermilk?" Trudy asked.

He shook his head. "No thanks. I've still got a glass of whiskey in the office.... How bad was it?" he asked. "The situation between her and Victor, I mean."

"I don't know. Filomena doesn't like to talk much about things in that household. She really hates the woman, you know."

"I'm always surprised that Filomena talks to you at all. I've hardly ever heard her speak."

"Oh, she talks, all right. But there's always something..." Trudy trailed off.

"What?" Jim prompted.

"I don't know. It's like she's afraid of something. I don't know what it is. Maybe she's afraid of Lisa," Trudy added thoughtfully. "That girl couldn't be much fun to work for, let me tell you."

Jim picked up the medical book and flipped through it.

"'Multiple personality is always caused by severe childhood trauma,'" he read aloud. "'The personality fragments so that the alternate persona can help to endure a situation that the host personality finds intolerable. Multiples tend to be artistically talented people with higher than normal IQs,' " he went on. " 'The host personality seems to be initially unaware of the alter or alters, though the latter usually have strong opinions about the activities of the host. However, the personalities can at first seem unrelated and exhibit widely divergent tastes, backgrounds and memories.' "

"No kidding. Different *memories?*"

"There's a case history in one of these books. A girl who was a ballet dancer in New York. She'd grown up in Pennsylvania, spent all her life obsessed with dancing and never went beyond high school. She had six alternate personalities. One was an Englishwoman who spoke with an upper-class British accent, had vivid memories of her childhood in London and claimed to have been educated at Oxford."

"Oh, come on. That hardly sounds possible."

"I know. But it was authenticated by a whole panel of psychiatrists."

Trudy frowned skeptically. "So how did she get the education? Did one personality go to England all the time without the other knowing about it?"

"Apparently, she was educating herself from library books for years while the host personality, the dancer, was experiencing long blackouts. The blackouts were what made her go for help in the first place."

Jim tossed down the book and went to the fridge to get himself a glass of ice water.

"But there's another thing that's so..." He fell silent, gazing into the depths of his glass.

"What?" Trudy said.

Jim looked up, frowning. "You know what it's like when you have one of those memories you can't quite grab hold of?"

"Drives you crazy," she agreed, pouring buttermilk into a glass jug.

"Well, when I first saw Lisa with my horses, I had this flash of memory, but I can't pin it down. I could swear I've seen her before."

"Of course you've seen her before," Trudy said. "She's been living over there for two years."

"Not there. Somewhere else. I felt as if I'd seen her somewhere else, a long time ago. Something to do with horses."

"Lisa Cantalini?" Trudy stared at him. "You mean, before she married Victor and came to live here?"

Jim nodded. "God, I wish I could remember."

"It's probably one of those déjà vu things," Trudy said. "They talked about it the other day on 'Oprah.' You have the really strong feeling you've done this same thing before, but it's just some kind of mental illusion."

Jim drank his water, rinsed his glass and set it in the sink, then collected his medical book. "You've got to stop watching all that daytime television, Trudy."

"Go away," she said, settling back in her padded rocking chair and picking up the remote control. "My favorite show's coming on."

Jim smiled and wandered out, pausing in the foyer to open the front door and breathe deeply of the autumn night, pleasantly scented with wood smoke and damp earth. He gazed at the lighted windows of the house across the way, thinking about Lisa Cantalini's beautiful face, her tilted eyes and creamy skin.

Again he saw her standing in his corral with the horse's hoof clutched in her hands, giving him that shy, friendly smile that contrasted so sharply with her former hard-edged sophistication.

Suddenly, with blinding certainty, he remembered where he'd seen the woman before.

12

Victor glanced at his watch and cleared his throat, then leaned across the shining expanse of the dining table.

"Almost eight o'clock," he said. "I think I'll slip down the hall and say good-night to Dommie before we have our dessert, all right?"

Meg nodded, watching as he got up and strode from the room. He was still wearing the well-cut jacket and dress slacks that she'd seen him in earlier in the day, and his shoulders looked broad and masculine in the doorway.

Filomena was at the sideboard, serving portions of strawberry shortcake onto dessert plates and covering them with whipped cream. She turned and glanced at Meg, then looked away quickly.

"Victor really loves that little boy, doesn't he?" Meg ventured.

Filomena nodded curtly and looked down at the sideboard. "Would you like some more whipped cream, ma'am?"

"No, I think that's enough. Thank you, Filomena."

She sipped her coffee in silence, relieved when Victor came back and seated himself at the head of the table. Light from the chandelier glistened on his hair, softening his blunt features. Meg wondered what kind of things

Victor had done in his youth, and whether his nose had been broken at some time....

"Thanks, Filomena," he said, watching the housekeeper as she served the rich dessert.

Filomena nodded without speaking, put the crystal bowl of whipped cream on the table and quietly left the room.

Alone with her husband, Meg picked at the strawberries and cake, feeling uncomfortable. Tonight, she had on a soft dress of pale blue jersey with a cowl neck and long draped skirt. It was the first time she'd eaten her evening meal downstairs with Victor, and she'd decided, after some hesitation, that blue jeans didn't seem appropriate for the luxurious dining room.

But she'd found it hard to choose from the array of clothes in her vast mirrored closet. Many of them were too expensive and dressy to be comfortable. Still, they were beautiful. The dress she was wearing was exactly her taste, and fit her perfectly. She simply had no memory of buying or wearing it before.

"Delicious, isn't it?" he asked. "Filomena makes a great strawberry shortcake."

"Yes," Meg murmured. "It's very good."

"You look like you're feeling a lot better today, honey."

"I guess I am. I still get a little weak and dizzy if I'm up for a long time, but it's not as bad as it used to be."

Victor raised his wineglass in a brief salute. "I've always liked that dress. You look like a million dollars in it, Lisa. What a figure."

She flushed at his frank, admiring glance, and looked down at her plate.

"Dommie told me he went for a horseback ride today," Victor said. "It was all pretty garbled, but I got the impression a whole crowd of you were over there. Is the kid imagining things, or what?"

Meg shook her head. "You should have seen him, Victor. He was so excited."

"So, how did you all come to be over in Jim Leggatt's barn?"

Meg gripped her wineglass. "I told you this morning, didn't I? I offered to put heat dressings on his gelding's swollen fetlock. I have nothing else to do," she went on, "and Jim said it would be a help to him if I..."

Victor was gazing at her in astonishment. "You're really serious about this, aren't you? I thought it was some kind of joke."

"You don't mind, do you?" Meg said, recalling her cousin's dark warnings about Jim Leggatt.

"Why should I mind? I'm just a little surprised, that's all. Like I told you, Lisa, you never used to be very fond of Jim Leggatt. And you sure didn't show much interest in his horses."

Meg sipped her wine.

"I guess this is the multiple-personality thing, isn't it?" Victor said heavily. "You're not Lisa anymore. You're a completely different woman who likes horses. I keep forgetting."

"I don't know how different I am," Meg said. "I have no memory of the way I used to be."

"None? Like, you still don't remember meeting me, getting married, anything like that?"

Meg shook her head. "Not really. It's all hazy. Kind of a blur, like...like it happened to somebody else and I just heard about it."

"Do you still remember all that stuff from Las Vegas?"

"Yes. But some of those memories are starting to fade, too," Meg said. "The Las Vegas memories. They don't seem as real as they used to."

"Does that mean your own life is going to come back now?"

"I don't know. The doctor thinks it might be like that."

"So what do you remember about this summer?" Victor asked. "I mean, just before the accident. If you don't remember being at home, do you remember being this waitress in Las Vegas?"

"Sort of."

"I always wondered what you did down there all the time," he said with a faint grin, "but I sure as hell never figured you'd be working in a casino kitchen. What was it like?"

"Actually, other than the fact that I had a job, I have no clear memory of the job itself," she said, looking at the wilting remains of her dessert, the mingled streams of red and white.

Like blood on skin...

She shivered and looked away. "I remember lots of things from my childhood... or Megan Howell's childhood," she corrected herself. "But the last year or two are really garbled. I don't remember much of anything from either life."

"Maybe there's another personality in there," Victor suggested. "Maybe she was doing something this summer that neither of the other two knows about, and that's why you can't remember."

Meg looked up at him, startled and appalled. He shifted awkwardly in his chair.

"I was talking to Clara this morning," he said, taking another gulp of wine and reaching for the bottle. "She suggested that might be a possibility."

Meg gripped her fork. "The doctor thinks there could be a *third* personality? She's never said anything like that to me." She stared at him as the full implication of his words dawned on her. After a moment, she dropped her head into her hands and moaned.

"Oh, God," she whispered. "I can't stand any more of this."

"Hey, baby." Victor got up and came around the table to drop a hand on her shoulder. "Hey, don't feel bad. Come on, Lisa," he urged. "Come with me. I want to show you something."

She got up and walked beside him through the carpeted hallways to a door that opened onto the big triple garage at the rear of the house.

"Look," he said, holding the door and flipping a light switch.

Meg looked blankly at the vehicles. She recognized the black four-by-four that Victor sometimes used on weekends, but there was no sign of his dark blue Lincoln. The only other car in the garage was an antique white Thunderbird with the convertible top lowered to show off its red leather interior. The freshly painted body of the car gleamed under banks of harsh fluorescent lighting.

She looked up at Victor, who was watching her with boyish anticipation. His face darkened and he made a gesture of annoyance, then turned aside and locked the garage door.

"You don't remember your car, either? The boys in the body shop have been working on it for weeks. They just finished the paint job yesterday."

"I'm sorry, Victor. Did you . . . It must have cost a lot to get it fixed." Meg glanced at his rugged profile as they started back toward the dining room.

"It doesn't matter," he said curtly. "I own a whole string of body shops, you know."

"But it's a real antique, isn't it? That's a 1957 model, and it's in such beautiful condition. There are hardly any of them around."

Victor stopped in the entry to the dining room and looked down at her. "You remember the year and the make of your car?"

"It's . . ." Meg trailed off, then smiled up at him. "I guess I do. Thanks, Victor."

He grinned, looking happier, and dug in his pocket. "Anytime you're feeling better, baby," he said, handing her the keys. "Maybe you shouldn't drive until the doctor says it's all right, though."

She weighed the bunch of keys in her hand and looked down at them, wondering what doors they fit.

"I wish somebody could give me a set of keys like this," she told her husband ruefully, "to unlock all the doors in my mind."

He smiled again and dropped his arm around her shoulder to give her a hug, then drew her into his arms with more purpose. Meg pulled away and hurried into the dining room.

"We should finish eating our dessert," she said without looking at him. "If we don't, Filomena's going to think we didn't like it."

They sat at opposite ends of the table, eating their plates of shortcake without speaking. The only sounds came from the trees rustling softly beyond the window, and the screech of an owl somewhere in the tall cedars down by the creek.

* * *

Hours later she stood in the bathroom, brushing her hair and gazing at her reflection. She was still upset by Victor's suggestion that a third personality might have been dominant during the summer, someone unknown to either Meg or Lisa.

Nobody could ever know, she thought desperately, how terrifying it was to lose yourself like this and have no idea what was happening to your mind, or where your body had been. She envied other people, the confident ones like Trudy and Clay, Dr. Wassermann and Jim Leggatt and Victor.

Even Filomena, as dark and troubled as she seemed, knew who she was and what her life had been.

Only Meg was lost and wandering in some alien landscape, at constant risk of betrayal by forces within her mind that she couldn't recognize or control.

She pulled on a housecoat, then left the bathroom and stood looking around the luxurious bedroom, which was gradually beginning to feel less unfamiliar. The colors were soothing and the furnishings were lovely.

For the first time, Meg felt a powerful stirring of curiosity about the part of her existence that had been controlled by Lisa's personality. Until now, she'd shunned all thoughts of Lisa, frightened to learn too much about the past for fear Lisa would take over.

But if Victor's and Dr. Wassermann's suggestion about the possible existence of yet another personality was true, then Meg and Lisa could *both* be in danger....

It was time to look for Lisa, she decided.

The desk and armoire had been locked ever since her arrival. Meg found the keys on the ring Victor had given her and opened both pieces of furniture, her heart pounding as she sorted through masses of paper.

Lisa's personality obviously hadn't been as neat and well-organized as Meg's. She'd tossed things at random—sales receipts, newspaper clippings, photographs and pages torn from magazines displaying fashions in hair and makeup that she found interesting.

Meg sifted through the jumble in growing confusion. She didn't even know what she was looking for. Maybe some trace of their shared childhood, something that might jog her memory and help her to remember.

After all, one of them had been present in some fashion during all the years the other was growing up. Dr. Wassermann still felt it likely that Meg had been observing Lisa during their childhood, even though she was never allowed to emerge. The psychiatrist spent a long time with Meg under hypnosis, probing for those buried memories, and was beginning to report some progress.

Meg had to acknowledge the possibility that the doctor was right, and that Clay was telling the truth about Lisa's childhood. If so, she wanted to see a picture of Terry and Greg or the house they lived in, or perhaps even a childhood photograph of herself with Clay, something to trigger the memory process.

But there was simply no trace of Lisa's childhood, or of the one Meg remembered, either. The more Meg sorted through the messy drawers, the more conscious she became of a total absence of girlhood souvenirs. She widened her search to include dresser drawers, boxes piled at the back of the closet and stacks of leather-bound albums.

All of them contained pictures and chronicles of Lisa's life, but only for the past few years. There were photographs of her and Victor vacationing at some Caribbean resort, playing on the beach, waving drinks at the camera. There were also some pictures of Lisa suntanning topless, and others, much more explicit, apparently taken by Victor in their hotel room.

Meg's face and neck burned with embarrassment when she looked at the nude photos, showing her own slender body twisted into lewd poses, and her face sultry with sexual desire.

She hid the pictures at the bottom of a box and opened the scrapbooks, most of which contained a messy chronicle of the changes made to the big house. Lisa had saved scraps of decorator fabric, wallpaper samples, even price quotes for everything from plumbing to window shades. Meg was shocked when she tried to calculate how much had actually been spent on the renovation.

At the bottom of one box, hidden behind the shoe rack, she found a bunch of clippings that made no mention of Lisa or of home decoration.

Wealthy Businessman's Wife Suddenly Dead At Age 53, one headline said, and the article went on to describe the accidental death of Pauline Cantalini. The housekeeper, Filomena Morales, had called 911 to report her mistress's body at the foot of the stairs in the family home. Foul play was not suspected, but an inquest had been ordered.

Meg riffled through the papers, feeling uneasy, almost sick.

Cantalini Devastated By Wife's Death, another headline said. The news story was accompanied by a photograph of Pauline Cantalini, a woman with a round, sweet face and gentle smile. The article described the prominent couple's loving thirty-year marriage, and how disappointed they had both been in their childlessness.

But Pauline Cantalini had apparently found other outlets for her maternal instincts. "Local children's charities mourn the loss of Pauline Cantalini, whose generosity and hard work will be sorely missed," one article began.

The last clipping was a brief mention of the inquest, at which the death had been deemed to be accidental. No further action was expected, the story reported.

What troubled Meg as she rocked on her heels and brooded over the old newspaper clippings, was that Lisa had saved them. She tried to imagine what would motivate a woman to collect the newspaper reports of her predecessor's death.

Lisa must already have been involved with Victor during the inquest, because they were married just a couple of months later.

"What kind of person are you?" she whispered to the inner recesses of her mind, the dark place where Lisa hid in wait. *"Who are you?"*

But there was no answer.

Dr. Wassermann still couldn't bring Lisa out, even under hypnosis. She blamed the failure on Meg's fear and refusal to cooperate. But Meg might be willing to try now if some of her questions could be answered. Having Lisa so near, but unknown and silent, was like being locked in the darkness with a dangerous animal.

She replaced the clippings about Pauline's death and looked around, searching for something, anything to cast some light on that lost childhood.

Wouldn't Lisa have kept crowns and sashes from all those beauty pageants? Wouldn't she have hung onto her trophies for singing and public speaking, newspaper articles about her triumphs? But Lisa's history didn't seem to extend further back than two or three years.

Finally, Meg bundled up the scraps and clippings, closed the albums and put them all away. She hesitated by the dresser, picking up a framed photo of herself and

Victor on their wedding day. In the picture Meg was wearing a white suit, some kind of costly designer outfit with a sheath skirt, a frogged jacket with padded shoulders and a pillbox hat and veil. Victor was in black tie and tux, looking happier than Meg had ever seen him.

Meg studied her own face in the picture and tried to read her expression. Had she been happy to be married to Victor? Had she truly loved him, or did he merely represent security and warmth?

The beautiful face in the picture gave her no answers. Meg looked calm, satisfied and unreadable. She stood like a model being photographed in a trendy wedding outfit, her shoulders back, chin high, her smile gently amused and a little contemptuous when contrasted with Victor's eager happiness.

Meg set the picture down, slipped from her housecoat and climbed into bed. She turned off the beside lamp and stretched out on the cool silk sheets, suddenly almost unbearably tired.

But sleep came slowly, drifting into her mind, bringing confused images of horses, Dommie's laughter, Trudy with her naughty goat and Jim Leggatt's sparkling grin...and those nude photographs, so dark and erotic...

Suddenly she jerked awake, then gasped in terror. There was a man getting into her bed, reaching for her, his breathing loud and ragged in the scented darkness.

Meg struggled to sit up, flailing at the intruder.

"Hey, baby," Victor whispered, grabbing her wrists. "Relax, Lisa. It's just me. I didn't mean to scare you."

Meg looked at him, appalled. Her eyes adjusted gradually to the darkness and she could make out his silver curls, the rugged line of his jaw and nose, the curve of his mouth. He was apparently naked, his heavy bare shoulders glistening faintly in the moonlight.

"Victor," she whispered. "Please, I..."

"If you're not up to it, that's okay. I'll just hold you for a while. C'mere, sweetheart."

What should she do? she wondered frantically. The man in her bed was a virtual stranger to her, and yet he was her husband. And in his own fashion, he was trying to be gentle. Resisting his approach, even though he was clumsy about it, seemed graceless and cruel.

Reluctantly, shivering with distaste, Meg let him draw her down into the bed and hold her. He was so strong, and despite the difference in their ages his body was hard and muscular, heavily sprinkled with hair from his chest down to his legs.

He held her close, sighing with pleasure, and began to run his hands over her body, pulling her nightgown up to caress her thighs and buttocks.

"So sweet, baby," he murmured in her ear. "God, I remember this body. Nobody's got a shape like yours."

His hand moved around, crept up to her breasts, cupped and fondled. He pulled her nightgown aside and lunged forward to fasten his mouth greedily on one of her nipples.

Meg shuddered with revulsion and pulled away. A dreadful memory was beginning to thrust at the back of her mind, making her head ache.

"Please, Victor," she begged. "Please, I don't think I'm... ready."

"Like hell," he muttered, his breath hot on her skin. "You're always ready. You're so hot to trot, I can't keep you at home. Maybe it's time your husband got a bit of it. What do you think, baby? Can't you share the wealth a little bit, now that you're acting so sweet and lovey-dovey to everybody else?''

Abruptly, he clutched at her nightgown and plunged his hand between her thighs. Meg shouted and began to pound him with her fists.

He laughed. ''Wanna play rough, Lisa? We used to have a great time doing this, remember? God, those wrestling matches were fun.''

He was so aroused that Meg could smell his excitement, and it sickened her. He knelt above her, pinning her shoulders to the mattress.

''Get out!'' she whispered, sobbing and straining in his grasp. ''Go away, or I'll kill you. I swear I'll kill you, Trapper!''

Victor stiffened and pulled away. ''Who's Trapper?'' he asked, gazing down at her in the moonlight.

''I don't know,'' Meg whispered.

He climbed out of bed, naked and hairy, still visibly aroused, his face twisted in disgust. ''You haven't changed, have you?'' he muttered. ''You're being as sweet as pie these days, but you're still just the same cheating little bitch you always were.''

She looked up at him from the pillow, her terror subsiding. ''Don't swear at me,'' she said coldly. ''What's that going to accomplish? I don't remember you. Until I do, I don't want you in my bed.''

He made an impatient gesture, then grabbed his bathrobe from a nearby chair and stalked out of the room.

13

It was almost a week since Jim had last seen the neighbor's wife, and most of that time he spent wondering what to do about the disturbing memory he'd recovered. He had a powerful urge to stay out of the situation, keep himself from getting involved.

But whenever he thought about the woman's shy smile, her gentleness and the competent way she'd looked after his horse, his resolve gave way to confusion and uneasiness.

After breakfast, he took his cap and jacket and went outside, heading for the barn. The autumn morning was clear and sunny, fragrant with the scent of warm cedar. Jim glanced at the hills to the east, wondering if he had time to saddle Cochise and go for a ride. The gelding was a lot better now, getting fat and lazy from two weeks without exercise. A long ride would probably be good for both of them.

When he went into the barn, he saw a slim figure vanishing through the big door at the back.

"Hey?" he called. "Who's there?"

Lisa Cantalini came hesitantly back into the barn. "I just... came over to look at the horses," she murmured. "I'm leaving now."

Jim examined her with growing concern. She seemed pale and listless, and her eyes were smudged with weariness. She had a lost, troubled expression that tore at his heart.

"So, how's my horse?" he asked, moving over next to her in the doorway. The two horses had followed her into the small corral, where they stood looking hopefully at the barn.

"He's fine," Lisa said. "The swelling's all gone."

"I think he needs a ride. In fact, I was planning to take the morning off and go up into the hills for a couple of hours. Would you like to come along?" he asked as casually as if they were in the habit of riding together every morning.

Her eyes widened in surprise. "Where? Riding, you mean?"

Jim looked at her intently. "Why not? You know how to ride, don't you?"

"Yes, of course. I used to..."

She fell silent and looked at the horses with a wistful expression. Jim turned away, got a couple of bridles from the tack room and tossed one to her. She hesitated a moment with the bridle in her hand, then went outside to catch the little mare.

"What saddle can I use?" she asked.

He gestured at the barn. "There's a small roping saddle at the far end. You can adjust the stirrups if you need to."

He busied himself with the big sorrel, watching covertly while she found a pad and blanket, then lifted the saddle onto the mare's back with easy familiarity. She threw the stirrup over the padded leather seat and fastened both cinches, checking them for tautness, murmuring to the horse as she worked.

He almost said something then, but decided to wait until he saw her in the saddle.

Anybody with a decent instruction manual could learn how to bandage a horse's leg, or how to put a saddle on and tighten cinches. Horsemanship, though, was something that only came with practice.

Jim swung himself onto the sorrel and sat watching while she shortened her stirrups a couple of notches, then gathered the reins and mounted.

She sat erect in the saddle, her eyes shining, her dark hair lifting and tossing gently in the breeze, and gave him a luminous smile that made his heart beat faster. "Oh, this feels so good," she said. "I haven't..."

The mare lowered her head and danced sideways, skittish in the crisp morning air. Lisa murmured to the horse, sitting with her hands relaxed on the reins.

Jim watched in admiration as she trotted the mare across the corral and back, her slim body swaying gracefully. He followed, heading for the edge of the pasture that bordered the hills.

She reined in next to him and looked down at the gelding with a critical frown. "He looks fine," she reported. "He's not favoring that leg at all."

Jim nodded and swung out of the saddle to open the wire gate, then closed it behind them after she passed through.

They rode in silence for a while, and he kept stealing glances at her, captivated by her beauty and her childlike enjoyment of the ride.

"What's your name?" he asked quietly.

She flushed and looked away. "Meg," she said in a low voice. "My name is Meg."

"But you used to be Lisa?"

She nodded, and he sensed her painful embarrassment. "It's... I have multiple personality disorder," she said. "I don't understand it very well."

"I guess most people don't. I've been reading about it."

"You have?"

He nodded, squinting beneath the peak of his cap at the sandy trail that wound through sagebrush, juniper and tumbled rocks, up into the dry hills above the creek. "It's a pretty rare condition," he said.

"I know. I've lived this whole life that I have no memory of. I'm supposed to be Lisa, but she feels like a stranger."

"How about Victor?" Jim asked. "Do you remember him at all?"

He saw the way her hands tensed on the reins, and felt another rush of sympathy. "No," she said. "I don't remember anybody. Not from here."

"But somewhere else?" he asked, suddenly alert. "You remember some other kind of life?"

"It's all so confusing," she said. "The doctor thinks that Lisa met a woman who works at a casino in Las Vegas, and learned all about her life, and then...borrowed it."

"Whose life?" he asked.

"Meg. The woman in Las Vegas. Her name is Megan Howell. The doctor says that my personality was present in Lisa's mind for years, ever since she was a little girl. But when Lisa met this woman, I started to gain dominance because I assumed Meg Howell's name and history and got too strong for Lisa to control."

"What kind of history?"

"Just...a completely different childhood from Lisa's. I remember growing up on a little farm in Nevada, working with horses, playing baseball...things like that."

"No beauty pageants? No fancy clothes or jobs in television?"

She gave him a wry, bitter smile. "Nothing like that."

"So when did you appear?"

"Right after the car accident. Lisa was sick and badly hurt and I came out," she concluded. "That's what the doctor thinks."

"But you don't?"

Meg shook her head. "I don't know."

Jim gave her a keen glance, wondering if it was right to tell her what he knew. Maybe he should talk to Victor or her doctor, and let them deal with it.

He listened to the creak of saddle leather, the soft clomp of hooves, the harsh call of a red-tailed hawk that was hunting mice in the brush nearby.

"Meg," he said gently. "Where did Lisa learn to ride?"

She glanced up at him, suddenly cautious.

"Look at you," he said, gesturing toward her. "You've got a better seat on a horse than anyone I've ever seen. You understand equipment, feeding, medication, everything about horses. Did Lisa know any of that?"

"I don't think so. We're completely different personalities."

"So when did she learn to ride like this?" he persisted.

"The doctor thinks maybe there were times when Lisa had blackouts and I was...there," Meg said. "But I don't remember them."

"It takes years to learn this kind of horsemanship. Hundreds of hours."

"What are you saying?"

"I've seen you before, Meg," Jim told her gently, trying not to alarm her. "Years ago. I never recognized you when you were...when you were Lisa," he went on. "But the first time I saw you with my horse, it triggered a memory. Took me almost a week to track it down and recall where it was."

She waited, tense and silent.

"It was about six or seven years ago," he said, gazing at the sparse trees beside the path. "I was at a rodeo in Arizona. A little place called Parker, right on the Colorado River south of Las Vegas."

"I know where it is."

"There was a guy at the rodeo doing some custom horseshoeing. Kind of a nice-looking fellow, tall and slow-moving, a great hand with horses."

Her face paled. She turned to stare at him, but said nothing.

"He had a girl with him," Jim said, smiling at her. "The damnedest thing I ever saw. This girl couldn't have been more than sixteen, a slim, pretty little thing, but she could shoe horses like a pro. I remember that I stood around and watched her working for most of an afternoon."

"And?" she whispered.

"And it was you. Now that I remember, I'd know you anywhere. I didn't recognize you when you turned up next door as Victor's wife, but seeing you like this..." He waved his hand at her blue jeans, the horses and sandy brush and saddle leather. "It all comes back."

"But..." She reined in abruptly, trembling with shock. Jim dismounted quickly and reached up for her, lifting her down from the saddle.

For a moment, she stood near him in the sunlight, and his whole body ached to hold her. She was so beautiful, so sweet and troubled and vulnerable....

She was also his neighbor's wife.

Jim took a deep breath and turned away, gesturing toward a large flat rock by the trail. He led the horses over and held the reins loosely while Meg sat down next to him.

"It was *me?*" she whispered. "You're sure?"

"I'd bet my life on it. Not many women look like you," he added. "You're kind of unique."

She stared at a line of cedar trees etched against the sky. "Then I was right," she said slowly. "I was right all the time."

"About what?"

"I believe Meg was always the dominant personality. I think I really had the childhood I remember, and Lisa was the one who appeared suddenly a few years ago."

"What does the doctor say about that?"

"I've never talked to her about it. I'm not even sure she'd listen to me," Meg said. "She seems so intent on proving her own theory."

"What's her theory?"

"I told you. This whole idea that Lisa was always dominant and I lived inside her, and suddenly came out when Lisa met this other woman who gave a name and identity to her alter personality."

"It seems a little farfetched," Jim said. "I can't see why she'd be so convinced. Are there any pictures of Lisa as a little girl, for instance? Any real evidence of all those beauty pageants she was supposed to have entered?"

Meg shook her head again. "I looked the other day. There's nothing from her childhood. No pictures of her mother, no news clippings about the beauty pageants, nothing at all."

"I remember Trudy saying the same thing about a year ago. She asked if she could see some of your trophies and scrapbooks, and you said you never saved anything like that. Trudy thought it was pretty strange. So," he added, "did you ask the doctor about it?"

"I mentioned yesterday that there doesn't seem to be any trace of Lisa's past. She said that Lisa had so much hostility toward her mother, she must have destroyed everything in a subconscious desire to wipe out her childhood. She thinks it was Lisa's resentment of her childhood that finally allowed me to appear."

"Well," Jim said, extending his booted feet as he leaned back on the rock, "I think *you're* probably right, and your doctor's got it backward. I just can't see why she's not willing to consider any other possibilities."

"Maybe the case is more interesting to her this way," Meg said quietly. "Sometimes I get the feeling that she really wants to have an unusual case."

He raised an eyebrow. "More than she wants to help you?"

"I don't know. Of course," she added with some reluctance, "there's the fact of that other woman, too. The doctor's actually talked to her."

"What other woman?"

"The woman who's calling herself Megan Howell. After my accident, I told the doctor I wasn't Lisa Cantalini, and gave her my name and a number at a Las Vegas casino. Dr. Wassermann called the number and Meg Howell was working in the kitchen. That's what really convinced the doctor that her theory was right. The woman was actually there."

Jim looked at her, bewildered. "So, who is this woman? Do you know her?"

"Not that I recall. I've been searching my memory, but the past few years are so confused. She must be somebody who knew me and took over my name and identity when I left the city. But the creepy thing," Meg went on, "is that she claims she met me again recently. I mean, after I was Lisa. She says she talked with me and told me all about herself, claiming to be Megan Howell. Apparently, I was really drawn to her."

"No wonder," Jim said dryly. "You'd certainly be drawn to the woman if she was using your old name and identity."

"But I have no idea who she is. I don't remember talking to her at all."

"But if that really happened," he said at last, "then whoever this woman is, she's not only a criminal, she's an incredibly bold one. I can even see why the doctor was convinced."

"I know. And then there's my..." Meg trailed off.

"What?" he asked.

"Nothing." She squared her shoulders and looked up at him. "It's so wonderful that you remember seeing me with my daddy. It means I'm real. I really exist."

"If I tried hard, I could probably even remember your daddy's name."

"Hank," she whispered. "His name is Hank Howell."

Jim frowned and rubbed his chin thoughtfully. "Hank Howell. You know, I think that rings a bell. Where's your daddy now?"

Her eyes darkened with worry. "I don't know. I think maybe something happened to him, but I can't remember...."

She gazed at the distant sky while Jim watched her covertly, unable to take his eyes off her.

"I'm so glad you told me this," she said at last. "It's like everybody's been trying to take my life away from me, and now you've given it back."

"I didn't do anything. I just remembered seeing you in Arizona."

"But that's..." She paused, looking troubled. "If I was living the kind of life I remember, why would Lisa have appeared so suddenly like that? I have no memory of her at all."

"There must be some point in your life where your memory just stops. Some kind of trauma, or problems you needed to escape from?"

Meg nodded, frowning in concentration. "I have lots of clear memories from my childhood," she said slowly. "And some after Mama died, and Daddy and I started traveling around so much. But then it all gets kind of hazy." She looked at him. "Especially for the past few months, it's really confused. I don't remember much of anything. I think we were at a dude ranch for a while, helping with the horses, and I have some memories of working in the kitchen at the casino, but nothing's very clear."

"The books I read on the subject say that most multiple personalities have those hazy memory patterns because they're usually not aware of times when the other personality takes over until they've been in therapy for a long time."

"So you think for the past few years both personalities have been taking turns?"

"Well, that seems to be the standard pattern, doesn't it?"

"But when I came up here to Salt Lake, and married Victor and moved to this house... it must have been just Lisa for all those years. I have no memories of being in this place before."

"So at some point, your life was interrupted. Your consciousness of being Meg just stops?"

"Not really. It's more like..." She twisted her hands together, looking down at them in silence, then turned to him again. "It's really just a blur. Like somebody dropped a...curtain onto the middle of my life, and everything on both sides went hazy."

Jim looked down at the pale curve of her cheek. "When you were living next door," he said, "you used to go to Las Vegas a lot, all by yourself. Do you think that Lisa went away during those times and Meg came out? Maybe you were Meg while you were in Vegas, and that's why you have all these confused memories."

She nodded slowly, gazing at the two horses as they cropped grass near the trail and swished their tails lazily.

"But then..."

"What?" Jim asked.

"My cousin... I have a cousin who comes to visit me. His name's Clay Malone."

"So?"

"He's *Lisa's* cousin," Meg said. "He has all kinds of memories of our childhood together in Provo, and our mothers and everything. But if what we're saying is true, Lisa never had a childhood, right?"

"Not if I saw you with my own eyes when you were sixteen, shoeing horses in Arizona."

"But I don't understand. Why would Clay invent a whole elaborate story?"

"I don't know," Jim said. "What do you actually know about this guy?"

"Just..." She raised her hands helplessly, then let them fall into her lap again. "Clay says our mothers were sisters. He used to be a policeman in Miami, but now he's a private investigator. He doesn't want Victor to know that he visits me." she added, giving Jim a quick glance.

"Why doesn't he want Victor to know?"

"He says Victor's jealous of him because we've always been so close."

"But you have no memory of him?"

"None at all."

Jim nodded and took his cap off to run a hand through his hair, wondering what to tell her. "This guy...he's been coming to visit you for quite a while," he said at last.

"Ever since I got out of the hospital."

Jim took a deep breath. "No," he said. "I mean, he used to come before, too. When you were Lisa."

"I know."

"Trudy's never believed he was your cousin," Jim said quietly.

Her shoulders tensed, and she turned to stare at him. "What do you mean?"

Jim shrugged, feeling uncomfortable. "Trudy's always thought maybe you and this guy were..."

Her cheeks flamed. "I don't want to talk about that," she said, getting up and moving toward the horses.

Jim followed her. "Okay. But just bear in mind that he might have some motive you don't know about. Especially if he's lying to you about the past."

"Sometimes," she said bitterly, "I feel like everybody's lying."

Jim put an arm around her to give her a brief, comforting hug, but she stiffened and moved away.

"I'm going to go to Las Vegas," she said.

He paused with the reins in his hand. "Why?"

"I have to find out if any of this is true. I want to look at the farm where I grew up to see if I recognize it. I need to find some people who knew my parents, and see if they remember me."

"Maybe that's not such a good idea," Jim said. "What about this woman who's taken over your old identity? She wouldn't be all that anxious for you to pop up and announce yourself, would she?"

"She's not there anymore. When the doctor called back to talk to her, she was gone. I guess she got scared, knowing somebody's found out what she's doing." Meg gripped the stirrup and swung herself onto the horse. "I have to find out what's going on. I can't keep living this nightmare."

Jim mounted and sat erect in the saddle, looking over at her. "When will you go?" he asked.

"Right away. Tomorrow, if I feel strong enough to drive."

"What will Victor say about that?"

Her face hardened. For a moment, she looked almost like her old self, the Lisa he remembered. "I don't care what Victor says."

"How about the doctor?"

"I don't have another appointment until late next week. I can be back by then."

She looked at him directly and the hardness vanished. Magically, she was Meg again, gentle and sweet, tugging powerfully at his sympathies. "Please don't tell anyone about this, Jim," she said. "Please let me go and see if I can get my memories back. I have to find a way to make my life bearable."

He nodded, moved his horse over beside hers and started down the path toward the buildings. "I won't tell anybody what you're doing, but I want you to promise me something."

"What's that?"

"Don't do anything dangerous. Don't be alone with anybody, and remember that you've still got a lot of gaps in your memory. You can't believe everything people tell you. Okay?"

"Okay."

"And one more thing," he said.

"What's that?"

"Don't tell your cousin where you're going."

She cast him a quick, measuring look. "Why shouldn't I?"

"I just think it's better if you don't. For now, at least."

"All right. I won't tell Clay."

Jim looked down at Cochise's twitching ears, wondering why he felt so worried. Meg was quiet and gentle, but she was a grown-up, intelligent woman. And if she got to Las Vegas and Lisa's personality came to the fore again, that was no problem, either. Lisa Cantalini could certainly take care of herself....

"Look, I'm leaving home the day after tomorrow," Jim told her. "I go away every fall for about three weeks to do the rodeo circuit through Nevada and Arizona, getting to as many rodeos as I can. It's my big holiday of the year."

"That must be fun," she said wistfully.

"I'll be passing through Vegas next weekend and I'd like to call you. I want to make sure you're all right. Will you be staying at your condo?"

She shook her head. "I don't even know where it is. I have a few memories of Las Vegas, but nothing about that condo."

"So where will you stay?"

"I don't know. Maybe I'll get a room at the Willows." She gave him a wry smile. "I only remember washing dishes down in the kitchen. It should be a real novelty to stay upstairs in one of the fancy guest rooms."

"Just be careful, all right? Promise me you'll be careful."

She spurred her horse into a canter, then a full gallop, and flashed ahead of him down the trail.

14

Meg woke before dawn and quietly hurried around her room, packing toiletries and clothes into a couple of the soft leather cases she found at the back of her closet.

When she touched the silky blouses and trim, pleated slacks, the delicate sandals and low-cut sundresses, all chosen to fit her body and flatter her coloring, her anxiety deepened.

She could almost feel Lisa in the room with her, waiting and watching....

Meg fastened the larger suitcase, opened the door and peered down the hallway. Far below, she heard Victor's gruff voice and Dommie's laughter, then the sound of a door closing.

She went back into her room and watched from behind the drapes while Victor's Lincoln pulled out of the garage, turned in front of the house and rolled up the tree-lined drive toward the highway. She forced herself to wait a few minutes longer in case he changed his mind and came back for something he'd forgotten. At last she grabbed a sweater from the closet, took a shoulder bag and the two suitcases and dragged them down the stairs as fast as she could.

There was no sign of Filomena or her little boy. Meg took her luggage through the hall and into the garage, stowing both cases in the trunk of the Thunderbird. She paused at the driver's side with a brief shudder of reluctance, then opened the door and got in.

Immediately, she was conscious of the car's lush interior, and the glitter of chrome in the door handles, window cranks and old-fashioned dashboard fittings. The vehicle had a standard transmission, she noted absently, toying with the gearshift. She knew she was able to drive it, but she couldn't remember where she'd learned.

Meg gripped the wheel and looked through the windshield at the garage wall, breathing deeply. Both front seats had been newly upholstered, making the car smell pleasantly of fresh leather. She searched through the bunch of keys Victor had given her, looking for an ignition key.

The first two she tried didn't fit. Meg began to panic, fearing that Victor had played some kind of trick on her. Maybe none of the keys worked, and she was trapped here until...

At last, one of them caught and turned, and Meg heaved a sigh of relief. She dropped the keys into her handbag, got out of the car and went quietly back into the house, making her way through the wide hallways to the kitchen.

Dommie was apparently finished his breakfast. He sat in a corner of the kitchen playing with a truck while Filomena cleared the table and stacked plates in the dishwasher.

The housekeeper looked up in surprise when Meg came in. "I'll bring your breakfast to the dining room," she said curtly. "I thought you were still in bed."

"That's all right." Meg crossed the room, took a red cup from one of the hooks and filled it with coffee. "I'll just make myself some toast and eat it here at the table. Hi, Dommie. Let's see your truck, sweetie."

The little boy scrambled to his feet, brought his toy over and handed it gravely to Meg. She squatted on the white tiles and made a few circles with the truck, growling engine noises, then filled the back with a handful of cereal and ran it gently over Dommie's little shoe while he squealed with delight.

Meg stood and smiled back as she leaned against the counter and sipped her coffee. "I don't think the truck driver's supposed to eat his cargo," she said, bending to ruffle the little boy's dark hair.

She took a loaf of bread from the fridge and put a couple of slices into the toaster while Filomena looked on with disapproval.

"Where's the peanut butter?" Meg asked.

Filomena gestured at a cabinet, then went back to rinsing an iron skillet in the sink.

"Filomena," Meg said, opening a cupboard door.

"Yes?"

"I'm driving to Las Vegas today. I likely won't be back for a week or so."

"Mr. Cantalini didn't say anything about that." Filomena turned to stare at her.

"I didn't tell him," Meg said, trying to sound casual. "He'd just make a big fuss and say I wasn't well enough to go away."

"Will you be staying at the condo?"

Meg looked down at the toaster. "I'm not sure. Maybe I'll stay with some friends. Tell Victor not to worry about me, that I'll call when I get there. Oh, and Filomena..."

"Yes?"

"If my cousin should ask where I am, don't tell him, all right? I don't want him to be concerned and come looking for me. Just say that I went away for a couple of days and I'll see him when I get back."

Filomena nodded and averted her head, but not before Meg saw the look of distaste on the housekeeper's face.

She recalled Jim's comment and suddenly realized that Filomena, too, believed that Clay Malone was Meg's lover, not her cousin. The housekeeper probably thought she was planning to meet Clay in Las Vegas, and lying about it to cover her tracks.

Meg sighed and put her toast on a plate, carrying it over to the table. Dommie left his truckload of cereal by the counter and came to lean against her chair.

"Dommie ride a horsey?" he whispered.

Meg scooped him onto her knee and held him while she buttered her toast, resting her chin on his sleek dark head.

"Not today, sweetheart," she murmured. "I have to go away. But as soon as I get back, we'll ride the horse again, all right?"

Filomena stalked across the room and lifted the little boy in her arms. She carried him out while Dommie twisted in his mother's arms to give Meg a wistful smile before they disappeared.

On the freeway between Salt Lake City and Las Vegas, several hours later, her mood began to lift. The sporty car was responsive and powerful, and the autumn sun was dazzling. After a month spent in a hospital bed, then convalescing at home, Meg had a heady sense of freedom as she flew toward the south.

She considered lowering the convertible top, but decided against it. Despite the warmth of the morning sun, there was a chill in the air at these higher altitudes.

Toward noon, she neared Cedar City and began to feel nervous. Somewhere around her, she knew, was the spot where her car had plunged over the cliff a month ago, but nothing looked particularly familiar to her. It was almost as if she'd never driven this stretch of highway in her life.

Her stomach gnawed with hunger, but she was reluctant to stop at Cedar City for lunch. She decided to press farther south, maybe get all the way to Mesquite before stopping. Her heart pounded with sudden excitement, and she pressed her foot down harder on the gas pedal.

She remembered Mesquite. A year-round rodeo operated in the little Nevada border town. She and Hank used to go there with their horscshoeing gear when work was thin in other areas.

Meg skimmed along the freeway, thinking about Jim Leggatt's validation of her own theory.

It was gratifying in one sense, but in another way, the truth was far more chilling than Dr. Wassermann's theories.

What secret hidden deep in her past had caused her personality to fragment so drastically? And what part of her mind could possibly have created an alter ego like Lisa Cantalini?

Meg could tell how Lisa had behaved by watching the faces of the people around her. She recalled the hatred in Filomena's eyes, Victor's attempt to hide his dislike and even the way little Dommie had looked at her so fearfully the day Victor first brought her home from the hospital. Nobody had much liked Lisa Cantalini, it seemed.

Nobody except her cousin, Clay Malone.

Meg frowned, trying not to think about Clay and the disturbing relationship that both Jim Leggatt's words and Filomena's attitude kept hinting at.

Instead, she pondered the nature of the personality that had somehow usurped her own. She recalled the closetful of expensive clothes, and that luxurious bedroom with the pictures of herself displayed on every available surface.

The blatant narcissism of those images was embarrassing and upsetting.

Meg's own memories were of a shy, self-conscious child who'd hated her looks because they made her different from her parents, a little girl who had fiercely rejected admiration and yearned to be exactly like her mother and father.

Where, then, had Lisa come from? Had that personality evolved as a protection against Meg's own insecurities and self-doubts? If so, there was nothing to prevent Lisa from appearing again if Meg began to find her life too upsetting.

But now that she'd somehow managed to take back her existence, Meg wasn't at all willing to fade away again. She wanted to remain, to hold Lisa at bay. And in order to do that, she needed to find out the secrets of her past and come to terms with whatever horror was blocking her mind.

And then there was the matter of Clay Malone. Reluctantly, Meg considered the possibility that he really had been her lover while Lisa was the dominant personality. Perhaps his whole charade was a calculated assault on Meg, an attempt to draw Lisa's personality back into ascendancy.

If so, the man certainly was accomplished in the art of deceit.

And if *that* was true, Meg realized suddenly, then maybe he'd also lied about Jim Leggatt. She realized for the first time just how upset she'd been by Clay's accusations against the genial cowboy next door.

She didn't want to believe that Jim Leggatt was a violent and unstable man. Meg liked everything about him, from his crinkled smile to the easy, confident way he sat a horse. She liked his quiet speech, his intelligence and warmth.

The two men, Clay Malone and Jim Leggatt, were very different, yet powerfully attractive in such dissimilar ways. But only one of them was telling the truth.

Which one?

Her head started to ache with the effort of concentration. She looked around, trying to think about the drive. The town of St. George fell away behind her car, along with the high ruggedness of southern Utah. The freeway bisected the northwestern corner of Arizona for a few miles, snaking through a canyon splashed with afternoon sunlight. The rock walls glistened with vivid hues of gold, crimson and chocolate.

Abruptly, the canyon ended and she emerged onto the dry plains at the approach to Mesquite. Meg left the freeway and headed into town. She stopped on the busy main thoroughfare and went into a little restaurant.

She could remember coming to this restaurant with her father years ago. She would have been a teenager at the time. Nothing had changed. The booths were still upholstered in the same faded red vinyl, and the plastic napkin holders sported yellowing insets of garish rodeo scenes. Each table was equipped with a miniature jukebox, where patrons could page through the metal tabs to select their favorite country songs.

Meg knew this wasn't a borrowed memory. In fact, it felt so real, she almost expected to look up and see Hank come strolling in, along with a crowd of slow-talking, tobacco-chewing cowboys...

Hank! Her mind shied away automatically, but she forced herself to picture his weathered face and easygoing smile, his gentle callused hands.

Where was her father? Somebody, perhaps the doctor, had told Meg that Hank was dead, but she couldn't believe it. She had a vague fear that she would discover something terrifying if she allowed herself to pursue her memory of Hank.

Where had the fear come from? Was Hank in some kind of danger, and was his fate somehow tied to the baffling confusion of her own life? Was he...

"What'll ya have?" a waitress asked, holding her order pad.

Meg glanced up at the woman who looked about fifty, with a mound of brassy golden hair and a tight uniform. She was wearing a fan-shaped lace hanky in the pocket over her left breast, and a pair of beaded earrings that almost brushed her shoulders.

"What's the special?" Meg asked.

"Bacon and tomato sandwich, home fries, soup and beverage, four dollars."

"That's fine. Iced tea, please." Meg watched as the waitress wrote down her order. "Have you worked here long?" she asked.

"Twenty-two years this coming January."

Meg looked at the woman's wise, tired eyes.

Do you know me? she wanted to ask. Do you remember when I was a girl, and came here with my father?

Have you seen my father?

"Anything else?"

"No thanks," Meg said, riffling aimlessly through the jukebox selections. "I guess that'll be all."

"Okay. Coming right up."

"Excuse me," Meg said as the waitress turned away.

"Yeah?"

"Is there a rodeo performance this afternoon?"

"Just evening rodeos this week," the waitress said, examining her wristwatch. "First one starts at five o'clock. You got lots of time to eat your meal before then."

"Thank you," Meg said, smiling.

She ate her sandwich, then left the restaurant and drove over to the rodeo grounds, entering through the contestant's gate and parking the Thunderbird on a patch of dusty grass near the bucking chutes.

The grounds were littered with trucks and campers—an impromptu village that bustled with activity in the afternoon sun. Clotheslines were strung between the horse trailers, and young rodeo wives rinsed out tubs of dirty jeans on tailgates while their children scampered amongst the horses and riding gear, playing noisy games.

In the corrals nearby, bucking horses milled and galloped, sending up dense clouds of dust into the blue desert air. Brahma bulls paced along the fences, pausing occasionally to lower their massive horns and bellow menacingly.

It was all so familiar that Meg had a joyous sense of homecoming. She felt her strength come flooding back, along with more surges of memory. She hurried over to the bucking chutes, looking eagerly at the groups of men in boots and Stetsons lounging behind the corrals. The cowboys were preparing for their upcoming performances, chatting casually while they practiced their roping and worked over horses and equipment.

Several of them glanced at Meg with speculation and warm admiration as she approached, but there was no recognition in their eyes. She shrank back, suddenly terrified by their blank faces and lustful, appraising glances. She hesitated awkwardly, then turned and ran back toward her car.

She spent about an hour driving around Mesquite, warmed by the memories that kept coming back to her with increasing clarity. For the first time since her accident, Meg began to feel like a real person again. But she recalled the empty looks of those cowboys at the rodeo grounds, and knew that the answers to her questions didn't lie in this bustling rodeo town. Finally, reluctantly, she pulled back onto the freeway and headed for Las Vegas.

The sun was dropping low in the western sky as she crossed the desert and approached the sprawl of the gambling mecca. The beam of light atop the black Luxor pyramid already stabbed the air, so massive and brilliant that on a clear night it could be seen as far away as Los Angeles.

Suddenly, Meg experienced a chill of panic, but she also felt an increased sense of familiarity. She drove through the outskirts of the city with ease, heading for the Strip, and merged into the streams of early-evening traffic flowing down the wide streets.

The casinos drifted past, glittering brightly in the deepening twilight. She saw the Mirage with its massive waterfall, and Treasure Island's fantastic open-air sea battle. She looked with pleasure at the huge pink neon birds outside the Flamingo, the golden opulence of Caesar's Palace and the towering blue-eyed lion at MGM

Grand, with hundreds of tourists passing between its outspread paws.

At the Willows casino, Meg drove into the outdoor parking lot and gazed up at the immense tree above her head, where thousands of neon leaves glittered against the desert sky.

Her heart pounded suddenly and her hands clenched on the wheel. She had a surge of pure terror, an almost unbearable urge to drive out of this place, head north and flee back to the safety and silence of that pink granite mansion in Salt Lake City.

At last, she took a deep breath and forced herself to climb out of the car. She locked the doors, grabbed her suitcases and headed for the hotel lobby.

15

The Willows was the newest casino-hotel complex in Las Vegas. It was an impressive creation even in a city where gorgeous, overdone opulence was standard fare.

The building of rough quarried limestone sprawled over a vast expanse near the southern end of the Strip, illuminated at night by a soaring neon tree almost a hundred feet tall. This famous tree, one of the world's most photographed modern wonders, was made up of thousands of electric leaves that shimmered and glistened a dozen brilliant shades of green against the black Nevada sky.

Inside the lobby, though, was the really awe-inspiring feature of the Willows, the one that was talked about as much as the massive moving walkway at Caesar's Palace, or the white tigers in their huge glass cage at the Mirage, or the vast indoor trapeze dome at Circus Circus.

At the Willows, an actual river flowed through the whole complex, bordered by tall trees full of living, nesting birds. The river wound its way from the enormous central lobby down to the meeting rooms, past the glittering casinos and showrooms and luxurious dining areas.

Meg waited her turn in the middle of the check-in line, looking around at the lobby with its murmurous sound of cool running water, its huge murals of desert scenes, the deep soft carpets in every imaginable shade of green and brown, the discreet rich gleam of gold in fixtures and appointments.

Somewhere in the depths of this vast building, people labored in the kitchens, scrubbing grease off stoves and clearing mountains of dishes. Meg knew that she belonged among them, not up here with the hotel guests. But the unfamiliar luxury and comfort was so beguiling that she almost hated to think about the lower kitchens where she remembered working.

A short while later, she reached the desk and booked a room in the tower, enjoying her own audacity.

"How long will you be staying, ma'am?" the desk clerk asked.

"I'm not sure," Meg told him. "At least a week, I think."

He made a notation on the computer. "And how will you be paying?"

Meg gripped her handbag tensely. She had more than five hundred dollars in the bag, money she'd found in one of the bedroom drawers in Salt Lake. But she wanted to hold the cash in reserve for possible emergencies. And she was fairly certain that she also had a savings account at a downtown bank in Las Vegas, in the name of Megan Howell, with almost three thousand dollars, but no cheques or charge cards on the account...

"Ma'am?" the clerk asked, fingers poised over his keyboard. He glanced up at her with narrowed eyes. "Your method of payment?"

"I'll be using my credit card," Meg said reluctantly.

"Could I take an imprint of that number, please?"

She nodded and rummaged through her handbag, extracting Lisa Cantalini's gold card. When she handed it to the clerk, Meg felt an irrational chill of fear, as if an armed policeman was about to materialize and arrest her for fraud.

She'd spent some time up in her bedroom at Salt Lake, practicing how to forge the signature on the card. It hadn't been too difficult. Lisa's handwriting was very similar to her own, a dashing, slanted style with blunt downstrokes and small gaps between the letters.

"Do you want me to sign for it now?" she asked, flexing her hand under the counter.

The clerk shook his head. "I just need to take an imprint. You can sign off on the total bill when you check out."

Meg smiled with relief. "Thank you," she murmured, taking the room key and dragging her suitcases toward the bank of elevators.

Inside her room, she looked around with a growing sense of unreality. It was so hard to believe that this was the same building she remembered. Meg knew the Willows casino, but her recollections were of gritty service entrances, stained concrete corridors and windswept parking lots where rows of metal containers overflowed with kitchen waste.

This room, though, was the height of tasteful luxury. Meg moved around hesitantly, touching the gleaming wooden surfaces, fingering the rich linen of drapes and bedspread, testing the brass fittings in the bathroom. She stood at the window looking out over the glittering expanse of the city and thought of herself slaving away in the kitchens below, dreaming about having enough money one day to stay up here.

And all the time she'd been . . .

Meg shook herself abruptly and crossed the room to pick up the phone. She dialed the number in Salt Lake City and waited, listening to the hollow ring.

"Cantalini residence," Filomena said. "May I help you?"

"Hello, Filomena," Meg said, then paused awkwardly. She still hadn't settled the matter of what name to use with the housekeeper. She hated being called Mrs. Cantalini, but Filomena had obviously never called her anything else.

"Mrs. Cantalini?" Filomena asked.

"Yes," Meg said. "I just wondered...could I speak with Victor, please?"

"He's not home yet."

Meg nodded, not at all surprised.

Victor was seldom home before ten or eleven at night. She had no idea whether her husband worked or played during the evenings, but whatever he did to occupy himself, it had nothing to do with his home life.

"Would you tell him that I've arrived safely in Las Vegas?"

"Is there a number in case he needs to contact you?"

Meg hesitated, looking at a pair of oil paintings above the bed. She felt a growing reluctance to let anybody know where she was. She was picking her way cautiously through a deepening mine field of lies and confusion, and there was no way to know who could be trusted.

"I'm staying at my friend's house," she said at last, improvising rapidly. "Her name...her name's Dana," she added, recalling the haughty supervisor in the Willows kitchen. "I don't think Victor's ever met her."

"And the number?"

Meg's mind raced. She obviously couldn't give the number for the casino kitchen, and she couldn't remember any other local numbers. Finally, she made one up, reasoning that if Victor tried to get in touch with her, he'd simply assume that she'd made a mistake about the phone number and wait to hear from her again.

Filomena wrote down the false number and read it back. It was time for Meg to terminate the conversation, but she found herself reluctant to say goodbye. The pink granite mansion in Salt Lake City, once so alien and forbidding, now seemed almost homey in contrast to this impersonal hotel room, high up in the starry darkness.

"How's Dommie?" she asked wistfully. "Is he in bed yet?"

"Not yet."

Meg smiled, thinking about the little boy's eager dark eyes and beautiful face.

"Give him my love, Filomena," she said. "Give him a big hug for me and tell him he can ride the horse again when I get home."

"Yes, ma'am." The housekeeper sounded startled and wary. "I'll tell him."

"Good night, Filomena."

"Good night, Mrs. Cantalini."

Meg hung up and wandered into the other room to run a bath. She soaked in a froth of steaming bubbles, thinking about Jim Leggatt who'd told her he planned to be in Las Vegas the following weekend.

She remembered his blue eyes, his broad shoulders and lithe, springing walk, and the way his hands looked when he fastened a saddle cinch or held a currycomb.

I wish he were here right now, Meg thought, forgetting all of her cousin's dark warnings as she sank into the bubbles and closed her eyes. I wish he were coming by in an hour to take me out to dinner.

She woke early the following morning and stirred anxiously in her bed, thinking about the day ahead. The logical first step, of course, would be to go down to the kitchens and look up some of the people she remembered.

But Meg was reluctant to approach the kitchens until she learned more about the mysteries that surrounded her past. She frowned, gazing at the drapes that shadowed the broad window, trying to concentrate.

Finally, she got up and went out for breakfast in one of the hotel dining rooms, then hurried to the parking lot to retrieve her car. She put the top down to enjoy the brilliant morning sunlight, and headed across the city.

Somewhere in the downtown area, just off the busy thoroughfare known as Glitter Gulch, she could remember a small apartment. The recollections were misty and confusing, but Meg was almost certain she'd lived there quite recently. She drove around the streets until she recognized a building, then parked and sat looking up at its stained brick facade.

The apartment was old and shabby, with sagging, unpainted window frames in which some of the panes were broken, and a few tattered clotheslines attached to the metal fire escapes at the rear. She got out of her car, went up to the building, pushed open a peeling front door and walked into a shadowed vestibule.

At once she was assailed by an odor that was a strange mix of old grease, floor wax and cleaning fluid. The smell was so powerfully evocative that Meg's mind flooded instantly with memories.

She *knew* she'd lived here. She'd ridden downtown on the bus after her shift and come into this vestibule with dragging steps, worn-out from kitchen work. Time after time, she'd climbed those shabby stairs to her own little apartment. She could remember what the apartment looked like, even its number.

"It was 4C," she murmured aloud. "I lived in apartment 4C."

But when she approached a board where the tenants' names were listed, there was no indication that either Megan Howell or Lisa Cantalini had ever lived in 4C. The occupant's name was an untidy scrawl, impossible to read.

Meg was standing uncertainly in the lobby, when a woman descended the stairs carrying a mop and a bucket full of cleaning supplies. The woman paused at the foot of the stairs to set her equipment down and rub the small of her back, then gave Meg an inquiring glance.

"You need help, or something?"

"I was just..."

The woman was wearing a yellow bandanna around her head and a pair of stained blue jeans. She lit a cigarette and inhaled greedily, leaning against the scarred newel post. "Yeah?" she asked, blowing out a gust of smoke.

"I wondered who lives in apartment 4C. I can't make out the name."

"Kozinski," the woman said, taking another drag on her cigarette. "Young guy, long blond hair, deals blackjack over at the Four Queens."

"Has he lived here long? Do you happen to know who had the apartment before?"

"I've only been janitor here since the first of the month. Kozinski was here when I came."

"I see." Meg turned and started for the door. "The people who lived in the apartment before him...what would have happened to all their things?"

"I reckon they took 'em," the woman said dryly. "Don't you?"

"I mean, if somebody just disappears and doesn't come back to clean out his apartment, what happens to his belongings?"

"We junk 'em," the woman said. "We got no fancy storage lockers around here, if that's what you're asking. The stuff's held in the janitor's room for two weeks, and then somebody comes to haul it away to the dump."

"All of it?"

"Every bit of it," she said with gloomy satisfaction, exhaling another long plume of smoke. "Every single bit. I load them boxes on the truck myself."

Meg nodded, feeling defeated. "Thanks," she said.

"No problem." The woman tossed her cigarette butt into the pail, shouldered her burden once more and headed for a hallway at the back of the lobby.

"Megan Howell," she said to the young man in the teller's wicket about an hour later. "The account's in the name of Megan Howell. It's one of those accounts that pays daily interest if you have a balance over a thousand dollars. I think it's getting close to three thousand by now."

"What's the account number?"

"I can't remember it," Meg said.

"It's really hard without the number," the teller said. "Don't you have your passbook, some checks or something with the number on it?"

"I was in a car accident recently," Meg told him. "All that stuff was destroyed. I was hoping you could look up the account for me."

"Howell, you said?" He squinted at his computer screen.

"Yes. Megan Howell."

"There was an account," the teller said at last. "It was terminated after all the money was withdrawn."

Meg stared at him. "*Terminated?* When?"

"There's no record of the date. All I have is the customer name and the code that indicates your account was terminated."

"But... that's ridiculous!" Meg said. "Who would have closed my account?"

"If you think there's been some kind of irregularity," the teller said, "you have to file a complaint. I can give you the form."

"No, that's... When was the account closed?" Meg asked. "Do you have a date?"

"It's not recorded."

Meg drew a deep breath. "Is there any way to find out?"

"That information is stored on computer at the head office. I'd have to send in a memo to have a search done."

"How long would it take?"

He shrugged, looking bored. "I don't know. It can be as long as a week, depends on how busy the terminals are. Look, if you want to file a complaint..."

"Never mind. I'll check it out and come back later."

Meg stood on the sidewalk outside the bank, feeling chilled, though the desert sun was warm on her face.

Somebody had recently closed her bank account and withdrawn all her money. The few bits of furniture and personal things once stored in her apartment had been hauled to the landfill. All traces of her past life had been systematically removed, as if she had never existed.

Slowly, inexorably, Meg sensed a trap tightening around her in ever-narrowing circles. She had no idea who was doing all this, or why, and the very invisibility of the danger made it seem all the more sinister.

On the southern outskirts of the city, the glitter ended and the Strip turned into a broad desert highway, streaking its way through rocky wastes of sand and cactus. Lavish new housing developments stood next to messy little truck farms and dilapidated trailer houses. A few movie sets dotted the landscape, complete with false storefronts, ornate saloons and tumbleweeds artfully arranged along the fences.

Meg peered around her, looking for landmarks, but nothing seemed familiar. Finally, she passed a deserted baseball diamond with a sagging backstop made of chicken wire, and her pulse began to quicken. Yes, she was sure of it. She turned down a side road and into a dusty farmyard where a few goats nosed through some wisps of hay near a water trough. When she saw the trailer house her mind flooded with memories.

Meg parked her car in front of the trailer and went up to knock on the door.

She heard a furious storm of barking, quickly hushed, then the sound of footsteps. A young woman answered the door, carrying a baby on her hip. Both of them had curly red hair and cheerful smiles.

"Hello," Meg said, returning their smiles. "Do you... is this your place?"

The woman nodded. "My husband works over there at the marshmallow factory. I'm Tessa, and this is Ashley."

"Hi, Tessa. And hello to Ashley." Meg smiled at the fat baby, who bounced in her mother's arms and made some unintelligible sounds.

"Can I help you?" Tessa asked, shifting the baby to her other hip.

"I... used to live here." Meg took a deep breath. "I just wanted to look around a bit, if you don't mind," she added shyly.

"Hey, no problem," the woman said, sounding pleased. "The place is kind of a mess, but feel free." She stepped aside and gestured at the porch.

"Oh, I won't come inside," Meg said. "I just wanted to see the barn, and some of the—"

"Come in," Tessa repeated firmly. "I'm stuck alone here all day with this kid. I'd love some company. Come in and have a cup of coffee."

Meg stared at her in surprise, then at the little girl. "Aren't you afraid of strangers?"

Tessa opened the kitchen door to reveal a fierce white pit bull who stood with his legs aggressively bowed and his pink muzzle quivering as he stared at the newcomer.

"Stay, Marshmallow," Tessa murmured. "Nice doggie."

Meg smiled cautiously at the brutal-looking animal. Marshmallow sat down and shifted on his haunches to watch as she stepped into the porch, a narrow space crowded with fishing gear and various pieces of baby equipment.

"Ron... that's my husband... he's a real fishing nut. We used to live in Oregon and he was out every weekend, but this place doesn't exactly have great fishing. How long ago did you live here?"

"About...we left about ten years ago, after my mother died." Meg followed her hostess into the kitchen, trying to remember. Nothing seemed familiar, although this must have been the same kitchen where she cuddled in Glory's arms and listened to bedtime stories.

"I can't remember anything," she said when the other woman gave her an inquiring glance.

"Hey, don't feel bad," Tessa said. "It probably isn't even the same trailer."

"Really?"

"We've only been here two years." Tessa lowered her baby into a high chair. The little girl grasped a spoon and began pounding on the plastic tray. "This trailer was here when we moved in, but it might still be a different one than when you lived here."

Meg nodded, struggling to make some sense out of her jumbled memories. Marshmallow waddled into the room and fell heavily at her feet, still watching her with one ear cocked.

"Can I pet him?" Meg asked.

"I wouldn't," Tessa said laconically. She brought two mugs of coffee and sat down, chatting about her baby and her life, clearly glad of the company. They drank their coffee and ate chocolate brownies filled with marshmallows.

"Ron gets them free over at the factory," Tessa said. "Sacks of them."

Meg smiled at the baby, whose plump face was soon smeared with chocolate from eyebrows to chin.

"What a mess." Tessa glared at her laughing daughter. "You need a bath, missy."

"I'd better go," Meg said reluctantly. "Thanks for the coffee."

"Hey, no problem. Drop by anytime."

Meg hesitated in the doorway. "Could I just...walk around a little?" she asked. "I'd like to go out in the pasture, see if I can remember anything."

"Sure." Tessa hauled her baby out of the high chair and carried her toward the back of the trailer. "Take all the time you like."

Meg smiled again and left, escorted all the way to the door by Marshmallow, who showed no visible signs of warming.

She closed the porch door in his face and picked her way among the goats and chickens, heading for the pasture at the rear of the trailer. Then she opened a wire gate and edged through, closing it with haste to block the goats who followed closely at her heels. In the field she paused to study the dusty horizon, deep in thought.

This was the place, but none of her memories were definite enough to prove that she'd actually lived here. She might simply have seen the farm in the past, maybe even visited here with somebody else during those confused years she couldn't remember.

If only there was something she could recall with absolute certainty that would confirm her theory. Something from Megan Howell's childhood that nobody else would know...

Suddenly, Meg remembered the Indian rock.

She started to run, stumbling in the desert sand as she headed for a gravel-filled ravine at the foot of the pasture.

The ravine was little more than an irregularity in the desert landscape, a shallow depression where water sometimes flowed after a heavy rainfall. But Meg remembered it as a magic place where she'd gone when she was a child to daydream and make up fantasies about pirates and cowboys.

In the floor of the ravine, near a dusty stand of stunted mesquite, there was a boulder about three feet in diameter, covered with rusty stains that she'd once fancied were Indian paintings. She bent and touched the rock, tracing the stains, remembering how she'd made up stories about each of them.

With a sharp intake of breath, she saw a rock pushed against the foot of the boulder. The smaller rock was gray and flat, wedged in the sand, half-buried under dusty gravel.

Meg knelt and clawed at the dirt, panting with exertion, then tugged on the smaller rock. It came away in her hands, revealing a dark cavity at the foot of the boulder. Inside, she could see a glint of brightness. She reached into the cavity and pulled out a mayonnaise jar with a rusty lid.

Meg held the jar, tears stinging her eyes. She grasped the lid and tried to twist it, but it wouldn't budge. Finally, she took a smaller rock and smashed the jar, stowing the jagged pieces of glass carefully back in the cavity.

Then she lifted the small notebook that had fallen out of the jar, opened it and read the message inside.

"My name is Megan Elizabeth Howell and I'm eleven years old," the childlike writing said. "I'm leaving this as a message to future generations that this rock is a special Indian rock, and the paintings on it should be protected. Do not ever move this rock away from this place, or the Indian spirits will come back and haunt you!"

The message was signed, "Megan Howell," and dated March 3, 1982.

16

Jim Leggatt led his horse behind the chutes and across the rodeo grounds to his trailer. He removed the saddle, then knelt to examine the horse's rear fetlock.

"Looks pretty good," he murmured, standing erect and patting Cochise. "That Mrs. Cantalini's done a real nice job on you, hasn't she, old boy?"

He whistled through his teeth as he brushed the horse's glossy hide, thinking about his neighbor. For some reason, he couldn't seem to get the woman out of his mind.

This was supposed to be Jim's holiday, a time to get away from everything and enjoy himself. But his head was filled with thoughts of home, and a host of nagging worries that persisted in spite of the easy companionship on the rodeo circuit and the beautiful scenery around him.

He thought about Victor Cantalini's wife, and realized with a touch of uneasiness that he'd begun to think of her as Meg, not Lisa.

Jim recalled their final conversation, and the happiness in her eyes when he'd confirmed that those childhood memories really belonged to her, not to some stranger in Las Vegas. There was a touching quality of sweetness and vulnerability about the woman, completely at odds with all his memories of Lisa Cantalini.

He squinted at the horizon. It was late afternoon and the sun was drifting low in the sky, shimmering like molten gold through a pall of dust and haze that lay across the busy fairgrounds.

He was at a small rodeo west of Phoenix, at the southernmost end of his trip. Tomorrow, he'd start heading back, working his way north toward Las Vegas, then on to Mesquite for a few days and back home to Utah.

He tossed his currycomb into the storage compartment of the trailer and took out a set of heavy leather pads, fitting them over the gelding's hind legs and strapping them in place. When he stood up, he found a couple of cowboys leaning against the neighboring trailer, watching him with cheerful speculation.

"You made a pretty good run, Jimbo," one of them said, chewing reflectively on a wad of tobacco. He was young and blond, with a round boyish face and an expression of innocence. "Won the day money, right?"

Jim grinned, knowing this young man well enough to understand that the cherubic expression concealed a wild and reckless nature.

"I guess I did, Brad. What bull did you draw for tomorrow?"

The boy scowled and spat into the dust. "I'm ridin' ol' Grasshopper. He don't spin too good these days. Gettin' tired."

"That bull can still hurt you, kid," the other cowboy said. He was tall and thin, with a dark, sad face and eyes that had seen too many rodeo grounds in the past few years. "Cain't he, Jim?"

"I reckon." Jim lifted a bale of hay from one fender and broke part of it open on the ground for Cochise. "Hey, Mel," he added.

"Yeah?" the dark-haired cowboy said as he lit a cigarette.

"Do you remember a fellow called Hank Howell? He used to travel the circuit in Nevada and down this way, shoeing horses."

"When?"

"About ten years ago."

Mel flicked his cigarette ash into the dirt. "Tall, kinda shaggy yellow hair?"

"That's the man."

"Yeah, I remember now. What about him?"

"Do you recall the girl that traveled with him for a few years? Did you ever talk to her, or anything?"

Mel looked at his friend in surprise. "Hell, Jimbo, she was just a little kid. I think she was his daughter, for God's sake."

"I know she was. I just wondered if you could tell me what she looked like."

"I never looked at her much. Skinny little thing, as I recall. All eyes and hair, that kid was."

"But she helped him a lot with the horses, didn't she?"

"Yeah. I guess she got pretty good at it. Old Hank, he started drinkin' pretty heavy after his wife died. Last time they were around, seemed like the kid was doin' most of the work. Real good hand with a horse, that girl."

"How long ago?"

Mel shrugged, his face furrowed with concentration. "Last time I seen 'em, musta been six or eight years ago, maybe more. They didn't travel the circuit after that."

"Did you ever hear what happened to them?"

"I guess they got some work at ranches and quit traveling."

"Where did they go?"

"Look, it ain't easy to recall all this," Mel complained.

"Just give it a try."

The cowboy gazed at a Ferris wheel circling ponderously against the dusty sky. "Last I heard, they was at some dude ranch up in the Amaragosa, I think. Seems to me somebody told me ol' Hank was gettin' real far out of control, makin' himself a whole heap of trouble."

"How?"

Mel shrugged again. "I don't recall the details."

"Do you know what happened to the girl?"

"Hell, Jim, how should I know? And how come you're so interested in this girl?"

"Jimmy likes girls," the young cowboy said. "Don't he?"

Mel's tired face lighted up with humor. "Oh, yeah," he said, nodding. "Jimmy likes the girls, all right."

"Well, good," Brad said with sudden purpose. "Come with us over to the beer garden, Jimbo. We got a nice trio lined up, an' we need a spare hand."

"What kind of trio?" Jim stored his saddle away in the trailer and began to coil his ropes.

"A nice little herd of high-steppin' fillies," Mel said with satisfaction. "They work over at the city hall here in town, wanted to see a rodeo on their day off. They just *love* cowboys," he added soulfully, tipping his Stetson low over his eyes.

Jim shook his head. "I don't think so. I've gone out with enough of those cute little secretaries in my time. Anyhow, I'm not really in the mood to party, boys."

"Aw, hell," Brad said with a winsome smile. "You don't need to be in the mood, Jimbo. You just need to come along and flash those ol' blue eyes of yours. Come on. The girls are waitin' for us."

Jim started to protest further, then gave up and followed the other two into the beer garden, which was nothing more than a dusty compound filled with trestle tables and a planked area at the front for dancing. A few couples two-stepped in time to canned music blaring from a set of amplifiers nearby, but most of the people sat at tables, drinking beer and talking in loud voices.

Brad waved with enthusiasm and hurried across the matted grass to a table where three young women sat watching the gate with expectant faces.

Jim's heart sank when he saw them. They all had long masses of crimped and frizzled hair, a lot of bright makeup and the tight blue jeans and checked shirts that were their attempt to "dress western." They couldn't hide their excitement at having won the attention of three genuine cowboys.

He sat down next to the pert blonde who had apparently been allocated to him by Brad and Mel.

She said she'd watched him rope a steer during the afternoon performance. "It was *wonderful,*" she murmured, touching his arm. "You were so *fast.* And your horse is just . . . he's absolutely beautiful."

Jim smiled automatically, pleased that she'd thought to mention the horse. But when he looked into her eager blue eyes, his gloom increased. He sipped his beer, trying to make conversation.

There was nothing really wrong with this pretty young woman. He'd just seen her too many times over the years, at rodeos all the way from Calgary to Corpus Christi. He'd listened to her chatter, whirled her around the dance floor, charmed her and dazzled her and taken her to bed.

He didn't want to do it anymore.

"Come on, sweetheart," Brad said to his companion, a dark-haired girl in a clinging black tank top, with a lush bosom that drew the attention of every man nearby. "I feel like dancin', don't you?"

He dragged the girl to her feet and headed for the dance floor. She followed him, clutching his hand and laughing breathlessly.

Jim watched them as they merged with the crowd and two-stepped their way around the floor. The young cowboy's knees were stiff as he danced, his body thin and muscular in jeans and a brightly colored shirt. The girl melted against him, gazing up at him with an adoring smile. Jim looked at her big breasts as the soft black cotton pressed and flattened against Brad's chest. He felt a surge of wayward sexual desire, but his lust had nothing to do with these giggling women in the beer garden.

In the misty twilight, through the smoke and the dust, he saw a gentle face, a pair of wide blue eyes and a tousled head of dark hair. He saw a woman on a horse, swaying gracefully in the saddle, and heard her quiet voice...

"Pardon?" he asked, realizing that the woman at his elbow was looking at him earnestly.

"I was just asking about your life. It must be so exciting."

"Not that exciting," Jim said bluntly. "I'm a building contractor in Salt Lake City. My company puts together warehouses and buildings for industrial clients."

"But you're..." She drew away and examined him cautiously. "You're a cowboy. Aren't you?"

"Sure I am." Jim took a long gulp of beer. "But you can't spend all your time being a cowboy. Not once you grow up and learn a bit about life."

She smiled uncertainly.

These cowboys, he could see her thinking. You just never know if they're telling you the truth.

Again he felt that depressing flood of weariness.

He was lonely. He needed a woman badly, wanted one in his bed tonight. But not this woman. The one he really wanted was in Las Vegas, searching for the truth about her past.

Jim realized with horror that he was beginning to have a lot of these adulterous thoughts about his neighbor's wife. Furthermore, he was increasingly afraid that he would act on his thoughts. He'd be driving into Las Vegas in a few days, and as soon as he arrived, he intended to get in touch with Victor Cantalini's wife, all alone up there at the Willows casino.

And God help me, he thought grimly, but if she gives me any kind of encouragement, I won't be able to help myself. I'm going to do something that both of us will regret.

He hated himself for his thoughts, knowing how vulnerable the woman was. In all decency, a man should stay away from her if he couldn't control himself. But the desire to see her was too strong.

He nursed his beer and listened politely to the woman's chatter, wondering how soon he could decently extricate himself and head across town to his lonely motel room.

Meg huddled in the stillness of her room, gazing out the window at the street below.

Dusk had fallen and Las Vegas Boulevard was coming to life, filled with quickening streams of traffic, masses of people walking between the casinos and neon lights flashing in the darkness. But up here in the lofty tower room, all Meg could hear was the gentle hum of the air conditioner and the clamor of her own thoughts.

She drew her legs up in the chair, hugging them and resting her chin on her knees. The best thing to do, she decided, was to organize all the facts she knew for certain, and forget about speculation for the moment.

First of all, Meg knew now that she and Jim Leggatt had been right. Megan Howell wasn't just a borrowed life, or some long-term fabrication of Lisa's mind. Meg was undoubtedly the primary personality, and Lisa was the latecomer. Meg had actually lived the life she remembered. She'd grown up on that dusty little farm south of the city, and Glory and Hank had been her parents.

Glory had died when Meg was fourteen, just as she'd told her therapist, and she and Hank had traveled on their own for a few years. Meg finished high school by correspondence and never went on to college. She'd always wanted to take a course in veterinary science, but Hank couldn't get along without her in those later years when he started drinking heavily.

There was always so much work to do. Her own work and Hank's, too, a lot of the time.

Her memories, clear enough during childhood, grew confused and hazy as they approached the present. She could remember a lot of details about her childhood and their life on the rodeo circuit. But she recalled very little about the ranches they'd worked on in recent years, or the miserable trauma of Hank's drinking. And at the end...

Meg frowned and rocked on the chair, distressed by the confusing gaps in her memory.

Those early gaps must surely have marked the time when Lisa first appeared. But where had she come from, and why? And what had happened during the past spring and summer down here in Las Vegas, where she had a few clear memories of living in that shabby apartment and working in the casino kitchen?

Apparently, Meg had continued to have some kind of sporadic existence after Lisa's first appearance. Meg still had no clear memory of Victor or the house in Salt Lake City, but something must have driven her Lisa personality to come back to Las Vegas regularly. During the time that she spent here, Meg must have come out and managed to reestablish herself. She'd even landed a casual part-time job, rented an apartment, opened a bank account.

To this point, the situation was bizarre but not impossible. After her research into multiple personality disorder, Meg was able to understand some of these things that had happened in her life. But she was completely baffled and terrified by the woman still claiming to be Megan Howell, the woman Dr. Wassermann had spoken with on the telephone.

Meg's only knowledge of that mysterious woman was through Dr. Wassermann, which frightened her even more. Why did Dr. Wassermann cling so stubbornly to her own theory, which now, in the light of truth, looked farfetched and contrived? Could she perhaps have some motive beyond a merely professional ambition to research and document a rare psychiatric condition?

And now, after her visit to the farm, Meg was also haunted by a growing concern about her father. Was Hank really dead, as Clara seemed to assume? And if not, where was he? Meg was beginning to feel that the whole mystery turned on that question.

If she could find out where her father was, she would know the answer to everything. But she couldn't even remember the last place they'd worked. She had a dim recollection of a few dude ranches in Nevada and eastern

California, a winter in Death Valley, some time at Virginia City.

But she couldn't remember anything beyond that.

"Daddy?" she whispered, rubbing her temples. "Daddy, where are you? I'm getting so scared...."

Ashamed of her weakness, Meg got to her feet and hurried into the bathroom to wash her face. She changed her T-shirt, put on a pair of running shoes and went down to the lobby, peering through the screen of willow trees along the artificial riverbank.

She had no idea how to get to the kitchen from here, though there was probably a connecting corridor somewhere. After a brief hesitation, she went outside and walked all the way around the huge compound to the rear of the casino, adjacent to the parking lot, where a metal gate stood open and a few service vehicles passed by with loads of fresh linen and kitchen supplies.

This, at least, was familiar territory. She moved forward with more confidence, heading for a ramp and a white metal door controlled by an entry buzzer. After a moment's concentration, Meg buzzed in her employee number and waited for the door to open, then stepped inside.

The door clanged shut behind her and she moved down a concrete corridor, past a time clock banked by rows of yellow punch cards and into a scene of frantic activity.

People in uniforms and hair nets worked over banks of long tables, preparing salads and dessert plates. Chefs toiled at the stoves, filling the room with clouds of steam and leaping flames. Kitchen helpers scurried around with loads of supplies, while dishwashers bent over their sinks, arms buried in suds.

Meg's senses were assaulted by the noise, heat and familiar smells. She stood hesitantly, looking around.

Habit was so strong that she had to stop herself from crossing the room, taking an apron and hair net from the rack and assuming her usual position among the dishwashers.

A few people glanced up at her and smiled timidly in recognition, then returned to their work.

"Well, what the hell," a voice said at her elbow. "Look who's here."

Meg turned around, startled, and found herself staring into a pair of hostile brown eyes. A woman stood watching her, hands on hips. She was tall and heavy, with dark eyebrows that met over her nose and a threatening scowl on her face.

"Dana," Meg said, recognizing her old supervisor. "I'm . . . I just came by to—"

"If you're looking for another paycheck, there won't be one," Dana said. "You already got everything that's coming to you. And if you want me to sign some damn letter of recommendation," she added, "you can forget it, honey. Just forget it."

Meg shifted nervously on the tile floor, taken aback by the woman's venom. Her memories of Dana were cloudy and erratic, but she had the impression they'd gotten on well enough while Meg worked in the kitchen.

"I've been...sick, Dana," she said awkwardly. "I had a car accident and couldn't come back to work. I'm sorry if I—"

"A car accident," Dana mimicked. "Well, ain't that just too bad." She studied Meg in silence. "You really had me fooled, you know," she said at last. "I thought you were a nice kid and a real good worker. But you showed your true colors at the end, didn't you? When I took you off waitressing and made you wash dishes, you didn't like it a bit, did you, Meggie?"

"What do you mean? I can't remember a lot of things, Dana. I honestly don't know what you're talking about."

"Oh, I see," the supervisor said with heavy sarcasm. "You've had a little accident, right? You don't remember the things you said to me. You can't recall how you swore at me in front of everybody and walked out of here in the middle of a Saturday shift, the busiest night of the week?"

"I..." Meg licked her lips and stared at the big woman in growing alarm. "Dana," she said urgently, "when did I do that? When did it happen?"

The supervisor made a brief angry gesture and turned away. Meg grasped her arm.

"Please, Dana," she said. "I need to know. I honestly can't remember any of this. Please tell me when I walked off the job."

Dana hesitated, looking back at her with a flicker of uncertainty. "Three weeks ago," she said at last. "You left right around the first of September."

Meg's hand fell away. She stared at the tall woman in horror.

The car accident had been well over a month earlier, in mid-August. Three weeks ago, she'd been lying at home in her bed in Salt Lake City, almost too weak to get up and go to the bathroom.

Hadn't she?

17

Meg got up before sunrise the next day, weary and hollow-eyed after a sleepless night. She packed her shoulder bag with a toothbrush, her nightgown and a change of clothes and underwear. Then, leaving everything else in the hotel room, she got into her car and headed north to Reno.

By the time she passed through Indian Springs, the sun was rising above the mountain range to the east. Stands of cottonwood trees along the creek beds gave way to a forest of tall cactus that spread across the arid valley. To the west, the Amaragosa range was already dusted with an early snowfall, its peaks glistening like pale marble in the sunlight.

Meg approached the Amaragosa Valley with rising dread, a feeling so powerful that it was almost nauseating. Her father, too, seemed very close to her now.

Something had happened to Meg and Hank in this place, but she couldn't remember what. There was nothing in her mind but an urgent need to escape. She stepped down harder on the gas pedal and her little car flew northward past the barren Amaragosa, heading toward Scotty's Junction, then Tonopah.

The day was cool and windy. Jagged mountains on both sides of the highway were blue-gray in the distance, rearing up from the valley floor in vertical rifts of stone. Every mile of the trip had an eerie sense of familiarity.

"It's over four hundred miles from Las Vegas to Reno," she heard Glory's voice saying, "and Hank and I must have flew, because I don't recall that old truck touching the ground even once..."

Tears burned in Meg's eyes. She brushed them away and continued to drive.

Hunger forced her to pull over at Hawthorne. She ate an egg salad sandwich in a truck stop, then took the road across the Indian reservation to Fallon and headed west through Sparks, pulling into Reno late in the afternoon.

She looked around at the glitter of the mountain city, searching for something familiar. But nothing here triggered any strong memories, not the way Las Vegas did. The stores and casinos, the streams of traffic and brilliant lights looked bright and impersonal.

Meg checked into the Desert Inn, offering the credit card with Lisa Cantalini's signature. She stored her sparse belongings in her room, checked her watch and headed out again, reaching the law office a few minutes before closing time.

"Hello," she said to the receptionist. "I'd like to speak with Mr. Clifton, please."

The young woman's eyes widened in astonishment. "I beg your pardon?"

"I'd like to see Mr. Clifton. This is Clifton, Rhodes and Burkitt, right?"

"Well, yes, it is. But Mr. Clifton hasn't been with the firm for a number of years."

"Could you tell me where I might find him? I need some information about a case that Mr. Clifton handled a long time ago."

"Mr. Clifton died last year at his home in Los Angeles," the receptionist said flatly.

"Please... I really need to speak with somebody. Is there another lawyer in the firm who could help me?"

"I'm sorry. You'll need to make an appointment." The receptionist turned off her computer and rummaged under the desk for her handbag.

Meg gripped the edge of the desk, leaning forward urgently. "Please," she said again. "I've driven all the way from Las Vegas today. Can't you find somebody who'll give me just a few minutes? It's really important."

The young woman looked at her, then got up and started toward the hallway. "I'll see if one of the lawyers is working late," she said over her shoulder. "Could I have your name, please?"

"It's Megan Howell. Thank you." Meg sank into one of the leather chairs in the reception area and looked around, clenching her hands nervously.

"All fancy oil paintings and dark wood," Glory used to say.

Apparently, the decor hadn't changed much in a quarter of a century. Meg studied a hunting scene under a gold spotlight, wondering if these were actually the same paintings.

"Miss Howell?"

Meg got up and followed the receptionist down the hall to a paneled oak door and into an office.

"Mrs. Abrams will help you," the receptionist said to Meg, then faded outside and closed the door softly.

Meg seated herself opposite the lawyer. "Thank you so much for seeing me without an appointment. It's really important to me."

"So I gather," the lawyer said dryly.

Meg looked at the woman's eyes behind the dark-rimmed glasses, took a deep breath and began to speak, "My name is Megan Howell. I was...I'm adopted, Mrs. Abrams," she said. "I was born here in Reno on September 15, 1971. My parents arranged the adoption through this office, and Mr. Clifton handled all the details. My mother always told me that if I wanted to know more about my birth family, I should come here."

"I see." Mrs. Abrams put down her pen and looked at Meg in silence for a moment. "What is it you want to find out?"

"Just...anything you can tell me." Meg took another deep breath, her heart pounding. "A lot of strange things have been happening in my life lately," she went on. "I seem to be having some kind of identity crisis. I thought it might help if I could go back to the beginning, and start by trying to find out who I really am."

"I understand," the lawyer said, her voice softening. She got to her feet and came around the desk, placing a hand gently on Meg's shoulder for a moment. "I'll have to go and search the old files. It could take a while, because they haven't all been transcribed to our computers. Do you want to wait, or would you prefer to come back tomorrow?"

Meg turned in her chair and looked up at the woman, touched by the unexpected kindness. "I'd rather wait," she said. "If it's not too much trouble."

"It's not much trouble to search an old file," the lawyer said with a cheerful grimace. "It's just tedious. Help yourself," she added, waving at a stained coffeepot and a motley collection of mugs on a wooden console nearby. "I'll be back as soon as I can."

Meg poured herself a cup of coffee and sipped it, trying to control her impatience. She looked out the window at the autumn colors in a park along the banks of the rambling Truckee River.

The lawyer reappeared about ten minutes later, carrying a file. She seated herself behind the desk and gave Meg a glance full of sympathy. "I'm afraid I can't help you much," she said.

"There's no record of my adoption?"

"Oh, there's a record, all right," the lawyer said. "But it's pretty scant."

"Don't you have to register all the names and personal details in an adoption case? I thought that was the law."

"The law wasn't as strictly enforced back in the early seventies," Mrs. Abrams said. "In fact, there was a thriving black market in babies. They sold through private adoption mills for anywhere from ten to twenty-five thousand dollars, which was a fairly hefty sum in those days."

"I thought that sort of thing was...a little more recent."

"I guess there's nothing new under the sun," Mrs. Abrams said. "It was illegal, of course, and a pretty awful situation. There was no attempt to screen adoptive families and no follow-up on the baby's welfare, or recourse for the adoptive parents if something went wrong, for that matter."

"And you're saying that I was one of those babies?"

The lawyer shook her head. "Not quite. There was also something called a 'gray market' in babies, which wasn't illegal...still isn't, actually. Doctors, lawyers and other professionals can arrange a private adoption for a finder's fee, and there's no official supervision of the transaction. Over the years, this office has apparently handled a few of those situations for our clients who..."

She paused, looking uncomfortable.

"Yes?" Meg leaned forward tensely. "What clients?"

The lawyer looked down at her desk. "People who were embarrassed by an unexpected pregnancy and needed to..."

"To dispose of the baby discreetly," Meg said.

"Yes. Something like that."

"So Mr. Clifton arranged to dispose of me after I was born?"

"Among others, I gather. It must have been known that he did this on occasion. According to the file, your parents had contacted him several years earlier and requested to be put on his waiting list."

"My parents?"

"Henry and Gloria Howell, from Las Vegas."

"Yes," Meg whispered, closing her eyes. "They were my parents. They were really good parents."

"But not the ones you're looking for, I gather."

"I just want to know a little bit about my birth family," Meg said. "I want to know who my mother was."

"Well, I'd help you if I could, but I'm afraid I can't."

"Why? It's not illegal to disclose that information, is it? I thought you were able to give it out on request."

"There's no information to give you, Meg," the lawyer said quietly.

"But...you've got the file right there."

Mrs. Abrams frowned at the papers, then closed the file. "This must have been a really favored client. Mr. Clifton seems to have handled the case very carefully. Every single trace of your birth family has been removed from the records. It would be impossible to find them now."

"How can that be?" Meg looked at the closed file. "I don't understand."

Silently, Mrs. Abrams handled the file across the desk. Meg took it and read the date of her birth, the details of the Howells' application to adopt and the lawyer's signed confirmation of the arrangement. Wherever the birth mother's name appeared, the record had been cleared and all signatures except for Hank's and Glory's had been obliterated with heavy black lines.

She studied the faded papers, then looked up at the lawyer again. "What can I do?" she whispered.

Mrs. Abrams removed her heavy glasses and rubbed her forehead. "Did you have a happy childhood, Meg?" she asked gently. "Did you love your parents?"

"Yes," Meg said, thinking about the dusty little farm, the baseball games and fresh bread and Glory's arms around her. "Yes, I did."

"Then why don't you remember that, and let the rest go? Don't torture yourself by searching for something that's gone forever. Henry and Gloria Howell were your parents. This—" the lawyer leaned over to tap the papers in Meg's hand "—doesn't mean anything. The people who've loved you all your life, they're the ones who really matter."

Meg looked down at the file. Finally, her shoulders sagged in defeat.

"I guess you're right," she murmured, reaching for her handbag. "Thanks for your trouble, Mrs. Abrams. How much do I owe you?"

The lawyer waved her hand in dismissal. Meg left the office, conscious of the woman's sympathetic gaze as she closed the door behind her. She walked slowly through the deserted reception area and out onto the darkening street.

* * *

A few hours later, Meg stood looking around at a hospital lobby decorated in soothing desert colors.

She tried to remember when she'd ever been in a hospital, except for the recent two weeks after her car accident when she'd mostly been too sick and feverish to be aware of the surroundings.

Her growing-up years had been healthy and uneventful. Neither of her parents had ever been confined to the hospital, and they had no close relatives in the Southwest. Meg wasn't accustomed to sickness, and she was unfamiliar with the reality of hospitals.

She'd expected a colorless, sterile kind of place, but the newly renovated hospital in Reno was bright and bustling, crowded with visitors, children's toys, flowers and laughter. Meg walked through the lobby and approached a reception desk where a pretty young woman sat behind a curved panel of glass block, surrounded by file cabinets and computer equipment.

"May I help you?" she asked when Meg paused at the desk.

"I wondered if you... Please, look after them first," Meg said, standing aside to make way for a woman holding a fretful baby and a suitcase.

She waited while the receptionist offered the mother myriad pink and yellow forms, then filled out an admitting slip. The woman disappeared down the corridor with her baby, and Meg approached the desk again.

"I'm looking for some information," she said.

"Well, I'll be happy to help if I can," the receptionist told her.

Meg smiled. "I'd like to find out about somebody who might have been a patient here a long time ago."

"How long?"

"Twenty-four years," Meg said.

The woman's eyes widened. "And this person *might* have been a patient here? You're not even sure?"

Meg shook her head. "I think she might have come here to. . . to have a baby."

The receptionist looked up at her thoughtfully. "I see," she said at last. "But you're not sure it was this hospital?"

Meg shook her head. "This one looks the oldest. I thought it might be a good place to start."

"I don't know if I can help very much. Let's see, what's the date of birth?"

"September fifteenth, 1971."

"There was a fire here in 1986," the receptionist said, giving Meg a sympathetic glance. "Most of the original lobby and storerooms were destroyed, along with all of the old files that were never transferred to the computer system."

"That's all right. I didn't really expect to find anything in the files," Meg said with touch of weariness. "I think the names would probably have been removed or altered, anyway. I was hoping to find somebody who worked here at the time, maybe a doctor or a nurse who might remember something. You see, I was born in Reno on that day and I was given away. I'd like to know something about my birth parents."

Again the young woman looked at her in silence. "My husband's adopted," she murmured after a while.

"Is he?"

She nodded, looking down at her keyboard. "He's gone through so many years of wanting to know who he is, and not being able to find out. I tell him he should let it go, but he can't."

"It's hard," Meg said quietly. "It's really hard, not knowing."

"I guess it is." The receptionist glanced up at Meg. "Look, I'm not even sure who's worked here for that long. I know we had a party last year and a few of the nurses got long-service awards, but most of them were for fifteen or twenty years. There's Dr. Evans, of course, but I doubt if he..."

"Dr. Evans?" Meg prompted when she fell silent.

"He retired about ten years ago. He's such a sweet old thing, almost eighty now, I guess."

"So he would have been working here in September 1971?"

"Oh, absolutely. Dr. Evans spent his whole career at this hospital, more than fifty years. Of course, he might have been on vacation at that time, or busy with other patients. It's still a pretty long shot."

"Well," Meg said gratefully, "it's a place to start. If he doesn't know anything, he might be able to tell me about somebody who would."

"That's true," the woman said, looking hesitant.

"Could I have his address?"

"I'm afraid I can't give that information out."

"Do you think it might be listed in the phone book?"

The receptionist smiled. "Well, I can't stop you from looking, can I? But," she added, "I should warn you, if you manage to find him, Dr. Evans has good days and bad days. He's got a condition something like Alzheimer's, I guess. His wife looks after him at home."

"Thank you," Meg said, and headed for the lobby in search of a phone book and some answers.

Next morning, Meg stood on the wide, pillared veranda of a stately home along the river. "Are you Mrs.

Evans?" she asked. "My name's Meg Howell. I called you yesterday evening from the hospital."

"Oh, yes. Come in, Miss Howell." The doctor's wife was a trim little woman in her seventies, wearing a checked apron over a pair of bright blue cotton slacks. She stood aside to let Meg enter.

"This is very kind of you," Meg said, pausing in the foyer and looking at a brass-bound wooden chest holding a bowl of yellow chrysanthemums.

"John likes to have visitors. He's in the sun-room, watching his game show."

Meg followed the woman into a sunny room furnished with a couch and chairs upholstered in a bright floral pattern. An old man was sitting in one of the armchairs, wearing corduroy slacks and a tan cardigan. He looked well-groomed and cheerful, and his eyes were bright with interest.

"Miss Howell," he said, extending a withered hand. "Gladys told me you might be dropping in. Pardon me if I don't get up, but my left knee's been giving me a lot of trouble these days."

"That's fine, Dr. Evans. Thank you for taking the time to speak with me."

The doctor took her hand and gripped it with surprising strength, looking up at her keenly. His eyes widened in recognition.

"I've seen you before," he said. "Gladys," he called to his wife, who was vanishing through the doorway, "I've seen this girl before."

"I don't think so, John," she said gently, then smiled at Meg. "I'll just make a pot of tea," she said.

Meg nodded. She was suddenly aware of the game show blaring from a television set in the corner.

"You can turn that off if you like," the old doctor said, gesturing at a remote control on a coffee table nearby. "I'd rather talk to a pretty girl any day than listen to all that foolishness."

"Your wife said it's your favorite show." Meg switched off the television.

"It's all right. But attractive company's even better," he said with a shy, courtly smile. "I wish I could recall where I've seen you before. Were you a patient of mine?"

"No, I wasn't. But," she added hesitantly, "it's possible that... that my mother was."

The old man regarded her with bright speculation.

"I was born on September fifteenth, 1971, here in Reno," Meg told him. "I was given up for adoption immediately afterward. I'm looking for anybody who might know something about my birth, and about my...my real family."

"When did you say you were born?"

She told him the date again. He leaned back in his chair and closed his eyes, remaining silent for so long that Meg wondered if he'd drifted off to sleep. At last his eyes flickered open, looking at her vaguely.

"What were we talking about?"

Meg's heart sank. "About my birth," she told him patiently. "I was born twenty-four years ago, on September fifteenth. I thought it might have been at your hospital, and you'd remember something about it."

The doctor's eyes focused on her with a faraway look. "You were pregnant," he said. "So young, and pregnant. Poor little girl, they weren't very kind to you, were they?"

Meg's throat tightened, and her mouth felt dry. "Was that my mother, Dr. Evans?" she asked, leaning forward tensely. "Did you look after my mother?"

He shook his head, looking fretful. "Nobody did. They wouldn't even take her to the doctor. Fools!" he added, fixing Meg with an angry glance. "A lovely young girl like you, and treating her that way. Damn fools."

The doctor's wife came in with a tray and set it quietly on the coffee table. "Does he remember something?" she asked.

"I believe he does. He seems to think I'm...somebody else," Meg whispered.

"I see. Sometimes he can't remember what we had for breakfast," the woman said. "Other times, he produces these amazingly vivid recollections that are decades old, and so detailed that I can hardly believe my ears. But he does need a little prompting." She touched her husband's arm. "John," she said gently. "John, listen to me, dear."

The doctor turned and looked blankly at his wife.

"John," she said, bending toward him, "I've brought you some of those fruit biscuits you like."

"With butter?" he asked, looking interested.

She nodded. "Real butter."

He leaned forward with childlike eagerness. "I want my biscuit."

"In a minute, dear," Mrs. Evans said. "First, I want you to answer Meg's questions. All right?"

The doctor's gaze swiveled back to Meg. He looked clear-eyed and alert once more, his face full of humor and calm intelligence. "That girl...she was your mother, I suppose?"

Meg nodded, a little unnerved by the rapid shifts in his mental state, though his wife seemed to be accustomed to them. "I think it might have been. Can you tell me something about her?"

He looked hungrily at the biscuits on the tray, then rested back in his chair and began talking with the ease and lucidity of a natural storyteller.

"It was a rainy night in September," he began. "I was alone in the emergency room, the only doctor on duty. The admitting nurse called me from the front desk."

The old doctor paused, remembering . . .

18

Rain had begun to fall in the Sierra Nevada during that September night so many years ago. A cold autumn rain that rustled the dying cottonwood leaves and swelled the Truckee River as it flowed down the mountains into Reno. At three in the morning, the city was almost silent in the chilly downpour. Casino lights glistened forlornly on the damp pavement and traffic slowed to a trickle, crawling up Virginia Street and out through Sparks toward the desert.

Across town at the hospital, the emergency room was also unusually quiet. The doctor on duty, weary after three days of eighteen-hour shifts, lay on a couch in the staff lounge and tried to catch a few minutes of sleep. He stirred and muttered when the house phone jangled on a table nearby, then heaved himself upright and fumbled for the receiver.

"Dr. Evans?" The admitting nurse's voice was sharp. "Can you come down here, please?"

"Some kind of problem?" he asked.

"They won't give me a *name,*" the nurse said.

The doctor sighed, rolled off the couch and headed down the hall to the admissions room. Three people waited at the desk, a middle-aged man and woman and a young girl huddled on a chair. Dr. Evans took the situation in at a glance. The girl was probably no more than sixteen or seventeen, and heavily pregnant.

"Is she in labor?" he asked the older couple.

The woman nodded uncertainly, casting a timid glance at the man beside her. "Her... her water broke an hour ago. We thought she was only about seven months along, but she's been getting so..."

The man made an angry gesture and the woman fell silent.

"Just get it over with," he said to the doctor.

"They claim she's their daughter, but they won't give me a name," the nurse repeated from behind her desk.

Dr. Evans gave the girl's father an inquiring glance. The man was tall and heavy, wearing a good topcoat and a costly gold watch.

"I'll pay cash," the man said, taking out a wallet and displaying a wad of bills. "And we'll take her home as soon as it's over. There's no need for you to know our name."

"What about the baby?"

"That's all been looked after," the man said curtly. "Somebody will be coming to get it."

Beside him the woman tensed and gripped her handbag, but said nothing. Dr. Evans moved closer to the girl on the chair who was doubled up in pain, her long dark hair falling over her face. He put a hand on her shoulder, waiting for the contraction to pass, then leaned closer to her.

"How far apart are the pains?" he asked.

She looked at him with a blank, terrified expression, and he caught his breath sharply.

The girl was lovely, even in pain. Her face was pale and delicately oval, her eyes large, dark blue and slightly tilted above high cheekbones, giving her an exotic look. She bit her lip and stared at him in confusion.

"The pains," he said. "Can you tell how far apart?"

She shook her head and turned away.

Dr. Evans stood erect. "Call her Jane Doe," he said to the nurse. "Mr. Doe, here, can stay and give you all the information you need," he added with a mirthless smile. "I'd like you to come with us to the labor room, ma'am," he told the woman, rolling a wheelchair over from behind the desk and helping the girl into it.

The father's beefy face tensed with concern. His wife cast him a beseeching glance and he subsided, frowning a warning at her.

"He's not usually like this," the woman murmured to Dr. Evans as he pushed the wheelchair down the corridor. "He's just...he's terribly upset. This has all been so hard for him."

In the chair, the girl doubled up in the grip of another contraction, whimpering softly.

Dr. Evans gave her a comforting pat and wheeled her into an elevator. At the obstetrics floor, he handed the girl over to a duty nurse, issued some terse instructions and escorted the mother to an alcove fitted with couch and chair.

She seated herself on the edge of the couch, casting quick nervous glances down the hall at the room where her daughter had been taken. Dr. Evans sat in the chair and looked at her curiously. She was a thin woman with well-cut clothes and a subdued manner, clutching her leather handbag in her lap.

"What's your daughter's name, ma'am?" he asked gently.

She looked at him in terror. "Oh, please," she whispered. "My husband doesn't want me to..."

"All right. How old is she?"

"She just turned seventeen."

"And you're not sure of her due date?"

The woman shook her head. "We thought it must be...about December. She won't tell us anything."

"But surely you have some idea when she conceived."

"It must have happened in the early spring. She and her boyfriend were..." The woman bit her lip and fell silent, then forced herself to continue. "We didn't know anything about it. She's always been tall and slender. In June when school was out, she went away to spend the summer with a girlfriend at their place up in Tahoe. The other girl's parents must have known, but they never even told us she was..."

The woman shivered with emotion. Dr. Evans thought about the father's overbearing anger and the girl's silence, her delicate loveliness.

"So when she came home...?" he prompted.

"She didn't come home. When summer was over, she...ran away. Both girls did. They went to Las Vegas and tried to rent an apartment. We...my husband got the police to find them."

"I see," the doctor said quietly. "So the police brought her home?"

"No, we went down and got her."

"And that was the first time you realized she was pregnant?"

She gave another tight, jerky nod. "My husband...we're churchgoing people, Doctor," she whispered. "Nothing like this has ever happened in our family. He's so terribly upset."

"Has your husband been keeping the whole thing a secret? Her condition, I mean?"

The woman looked down at her handbag. "We never told anybody she was back, or anything about her. We said she was spending the final term at a prep school in California."

"So you've been hiding her at home?"

"Yes. For almost a month now."

"Have you taken her for a prenatal examination?" he asked with sudden suspicion.

The woman shook her head, still toying nervously with the leather straps of her bag.

"So, she's had no medical attention at all," Dr. Evans said flatly.

She licked her lips and gave him a look of miserable appeal. "My husband is . . ."

"Never mind. It's too late now to be concerned about it, I guess. What arrangements have been made about the baby?"

"There's a . . . We know a lawyer in town. He offers a placement service. He has a list of people who—"

"I'm familiar with the lawyers and their placement services. But there are still some regulations that we need to observe, you know. Your daughter will have to sign release papers a few days after the birth."

"The lawyer told us all about it. He'll bring the papers to the house. He says the hospital doesn't have to be involved after the . . . after the baby is gone."

"So you're planning to take your daughter home as soon as the baby is delivered?"

The woman gave him another look of naked pleading. "We've hired a private nurse to come to the house. She'll make sure there are no problems."

"I see. All the important things have been taken care of, haven't they?"

Tears filled her eyes and began to trickle down her cheeks. "I'm sorry," she whispered. "I'm just so sorry..."

Dr. Evans immediately regretted his sharpness. The poor woman probably had little control over her household, after all. And it was evident that she was suffering enough from her daughter's pain, let alone the imminent loss of her grandchild.

He patted her shoulder awkwardly.

"Dr. Evans?" the nurse said from the hallway. "She's fully dilated, and the baby is crowning. We've taken her into delivery."

The woman's face turned ashen. She whimpered and began to sob. The doctor got to his feet, looking down at her with sympathy.

"I have to go and scrub. It won't be long now," he murmured. "I'll let you know when she can leave."

The girl's father strode down the hallway and acknowledged the doctor with a curt nod, heading for the alcove where his wife huddled, her face in her hands.

In the delivery room, the girl lay on a stirrup table, still silent in the grip of her pain. Her beautiful eyes were fixed on the ceiling. She seemed remote and detached from the bustle of activity all around her.

Within a mercifully brief time, the doctor delivered her of a baby girl, very small but perfectly formed, with a dusting of silky dark hair.

"It's a girl," he said. "Do you want to see her?"

She shook her head and continued to stare at the ceiling with that remote expression, but he could see the pain that darkened her eyes. Suddenly, her face contorted with agony.

"She's having another contraction," one of the nurses muttered while the other tended the baby. "A really strong one."

The doctor turned hastily back to his job.

"Jesus," he whispered in amazement as another dark head appeared, followed almost immediately by a second tiny, well-formed body.

The nurse looked over at him curiously, then at the girl on the table, who shuddered in relief and turned her head away.

"They're small, but they look almost full-term, don't they?" Dr. Evans muttered, lifting the slick little body and watching the baby take its first breath. "Identical twins, practically an effortless delivery, and she never even saw a doctor."

The nurse took the second baby from him and cleaned its eyes and mouth, then wrapped the flailing body in a blanket and tucked it into a nursery cot next to the other child.

On the table, the girl's eyes were closed, her beautiful face pale and cold. She seemed oblivious, wrapped in a loneliness and sorrow so profound that the doctor felt a painful surge of sympathy. He watched as she was wheeled from the labor room, then looked down at the two babies cuddled together in their nest of blankets.

"Pretty little things, aren't they?" he said to the obstetrics nurse. "I wonder what's going to happen to them..."

The old man's voice trailed away into silence and he closed his eyes again, resting his head against the back of his chair.

Meg stared at him, appalled, her mind reeling.

"Twins?" she whispered. "I have an identical twin? Dr. Evans, nobody told me anything about that. My mother never said a word. I'm sure that if she..."

The doctor opened his eyes again and looked at Meg in confusion. His face cleared when he caught sight of his wife on the opposite couch.

"Gladys," he asked, "who's this girl? Where did she come from?"

"She's visiting us for a little while, John," the older woman said. "You delivered her at the hospital, years and years ago. Come, now. Have your biscuit."

He sat up in the chair. "With butter?"

"Yes, dear. With butter."

Meg watched, still dazed with shock, as Mrs. Evans spread butter on a biscuit and handed it to her husband. He looked at it happily, then stuffed it into his mouth and began to chew. Crumbs spilled down his chin, and his wife got up to clean them away with a napkin.

"Mrs. Evans," Meg said, "do you think he'd be able to remember anything else?"

"Probably not," Gladys said. "He does have some fairly long spells of complete lucidity, like the one you just saw. But most of the time..." The little woman shrugged, looking weary.

"I'm so sorry," Meg said. "I hate to bother you like this. But I..."

"It's quite understandable, my dear," Gladys said gently. "John," she said, leaning toward her husband. "John, try to remember. Do you know what happened to those little girls?"

"What little girls?" He looked over her shoulder at the tray on the coffee table.

"The twin babies you delivered all those years ago. Remember, John? It was raining, and they hadn't taken her to a doctor at all?"

His eyes flickered briefly with indignation. "Criminal," he muttered. "Damn fools, treating the poor child that way just because she was pregnant. Where are my slippers, Gladys? My feet are cold."

"They're right here by your chair. You took them off a while ago."

The old man bent and fitted a leather slipper onto his foot. When he looked up at Meg, his face was clear and full of interest, almost humorous. "Funny thing about those twins of yours," he said.

"What about them, Dr. Evans?"

"A fellow came by to see me just a while ago, asking a whole lot of questions about those same twin girls. Wanted to know all about them."

"What?" Meg's heart started to pound, and she stared at the old doctor in horror. "Someone was asking about the same twins? Who was it?" she asked, getting to her feet and moving closer to him, leaning urgently over his chair.

The doctor didn't answer. He bent to struggle with something, and Meg saw in despair that he was trying, slowly and methodically, to fit a second slipper on his right foot over the first one.

"Now, John," his wife said calmly, "you know that's not right." She bent, took the slipper from him and put it on his other foot.

Meg watched, feeling numb and sick.

"I'm afraid he's getting tired now," Gladys said apologetically. "He'll likely drift off to sleep for a little while."

Meg nodded, got to her feet and moved toward the door.

"I'm sorry he couldn't help you a little more."

Meg paused in the foyer, taking a deep breath to calm herself. "Mrs. Evans...do you know anything about this man he mentioned? The man who was asking about... about my birth?"

"I know he had a visitor one day last spring, but it was on a Wednesday, so I couldn't tell you anything about the man."

"Why not?

"On Wednesdays," Gladys explained, "he goes over to the hospital for a day of respite care so I can look after chores and shopping. Apparently, this man visited John while he was there."

"Would anybody at the hospital remember what the man looked like?"

Gladys shook her head. "I asked later. I was curious, you know, after John mentioned he'd had a visitor who was asking about an old case. Somebody remembered a man coming to see him, but nobody could give me a description. John spent the afternoon in the common room at the auxiliary unit, and people were in and out all day."

"I see." Meg gripped the door frame with shaking fingers.

"I'm very sorry," Gladys repeated. "I hope you find your sister."

Meg murmured something in reply and fled down the walk to her car.

I hope you find your sister...

Meg was on the highway, heading back to Las Vegas, before she could even begin to grapple with the story she'd just heard. It was distressing enough to learn the truth about the sad family trauma that had surrounded her birth.

But the fact that she had an identical twin, a sister she'd never seen or even heard about...

Meg struggled to comprehend and analyze the full import of this knowledge.

First of all, she wasn't insane or psychologically unbalanced. She didn't suffer from multiple personality disorder. She was herself, Megan Howell, and she always had been.

And Lisa Cantalini wasn't a manifestation of a fragmented personality. Lisa was a completely different person, a girl who'd lived a separate life, entered beauty pageants, married a rich older man and squandered his money.

Lisa was her sister.

In that case, Meg realized, Clay Malone wasn't a liar, after all. He'd been telling the truth about his relationship with Lisa. All the things he remembered from their shared childhood were events that had actually happened.

But somebody was certainly lying, because there was a man who knew the truth about Meg and Lisa. Somebody had found Dr. Evans, probably the same way Meg had. He'd heard the same story about the identical twin girls born on that rainy September night.

How had he used that knowledge?

An icy chill crept down Meg's spine and curled into her stomach.

She was just beginning to realize that the car accident which plunged her into the center of Lisa's life couldn't have been as random as it seemed. After all, it could hardly be a coincidence that Meg Howell had driven over a cliff in a car belonging to a sister she'd never met, on a stretch of freeway that she had no memory of traveling.

Her mind worked slowly, wrestling with the incredible sequence of events, increasingly frustrated by the gaps in her memory.

How had she got into her sister's car? Had somebody put her into it? If so, why couldn't she remember? Maybe she'd been drugged, then taken up the freeway to Utah, put into Lisa's car and sent over the cliff.

Meg's fear began to mount, and she gripped the wheel so tightly that her fingers ached.

If the car crash had been deliberate, where was Lisa Cantalini? Had she been kidnapped, as well? Was she dead by now, or being held prisoner somewhere while this bizarre plot, whatever it was, unfolded?

Meg frowned and shook her head, trying to concentrate.

Why had Dr. Wassermann been so quick to believe the theory about multiple personality?

Part of the reason, Meg realized, was that she had so little memory of the past year or so. It was probably easier for the doctor to believe Meg's personality had become fragmented because she had no strong sense of belonging or identity.

Something had happened in Meg's life to obliterate most of her recent memory. She remembered describing the feeling to Jim Leggatt as being like "a curtain dropped into the middle of my life, shading out everything on both sides."

Meg gazed at the highway, struggling with an inexplicable fear. Her mind didn't want to explore this, or deal with the past at all. There was something she couldn't bear to remember...

Desperately, she forced herself to marshal all her thoughts. She could remember Glory's death clearly, and the years she and Hank had wandered from place to place, picking up work as they went. And she recalled a lot of detail about the dude ranches they'd settled at...except the last one. This was where her memory went fuzzy and she felt a growing anxiety when she tried to remember the details. Meg knew that Hank had been drinking more heavily, and it was a daily struggle to protect him and cover for him.

She'd obviously left the ranch at some time and moved to Las Vegas, but she couldn't recall the circumstances or whether Hank was with her. And the memories of Las Vegas, of her job at the casino and her life in the city, were similarly blurred.

Had something happened in those final weeks at the dude ranch—an event so awful that her mind refused to deal with it? And had the shock left her vulnerable to this nightmare that had happened afterward? Maybe the trauma of her car accident, coupled with a general sense of loss and disorientation, had allowed her to be convinced that she really was a fragmented personality.

Meg gripped the wheel in despair. If only she could *remember....*

The sun was setting over the mountains to the west, lighting the sky with a soft violet glow by the time she reached the Amaragosa Valley. Again she felt that sickening chill of nausea she'd experienced on the drive north to Reno two days earlier, but this time, finally, she understood the emotion.

Memories began to wash over Meg, so sudden and so lucid that she had to pull over. It was here in the Amaragosa, only a few miles from this stretch of highway, that she and Hank had settled for the last time.

She parked on the edge of the highway and huddled over the wheel, shaking and crying as she relived that final day at the dude ranch . . .

19

The coming of spring had been almost imperceptible in the Amaragosa Valley. Late-March snowfalls still blanketed Reno to the north, while a few miles to the northwest across the Sierra Nevada, Death Valley shimmered in ninety-degree heat. But the Amaragosa was cool and sunny, with only a dusting of pale green leaves on the cottonwoods to show that spring had arrived.

Meg was working in the ranch corral, training one of the two-year-old colts on a halter and line. The colt was a high-stepping sorrel, gleaming in the sunlight like a new copper penny. He whinnied nervously and rolled his eyes as Meg tugged gently on the line, slowing him to a walk, then a standstill.

Meg gripped the rope in gloved hands and wrapped it snugly around a post in the center of the round corral, picked up a gunnysack from the foot of the post and edged her way down the line toward the colt, murmuring gently as she walked.

"Easy, boy," she said. "Easy, now. Nothing to worry about. See this in my hand? This is just an old sack. Nothing to be afraid of."

The colt trembled and strained at the end of the taut rope, but didn't move as Meg came up beside him, grasped the halter and stroked his head and neck.

"See?" she murmured in a soothing monotone. "Nothing in the world to be afraid of. Not a thing...."

Slowly, she lifted the sack and drew it over the colt's quivering back, down his flanks, across his rump and hind legs, talking to him all the while. His trembling lessened and he stood quietly, enduring her touch.

At last, Meg dropped the sack at her feet, patted the colt and praised him softly, then unclipped the line from his halter and turned him loose. She watched with a smile as he tossed his head and trotted around the circular corral, kicking up his heels in relief.

"I never seen anybody break horses the way you do," a voice said from the fence as Meg unwrapped her line at the snubbing post.

She turned and glanced at the man, then coiled the rope and bent to retrieve the sack. "I don't break horses," she said curtly. "I gentle them. There's a big difference."

Carl Trapper grinned, and hoisted himself onto the top rail where he sat eyeing Meg with lazy interest. "Is that so? And what's the difference?"

"You wouldn't understand, Trapper," Meg said, walking past him toward the gate. "You're the kind of man who likes to break things."

He flushed with annoyance and glared down at her.

Carl Trapper had narrow, foxlike features that were strangely at odds with his bulky shoulders and torso. He had arrived at the ranch only a couple of months earlier to take over as foreman. Meg had been unimpressed with him right from the start.

Trapper just looked like the kind of man who was likely to throw his weight around. And she'd soon discovered that the new foreman was vicious with animals, especially when he thought himself unobserved. Her coolness had turned to an active dislike that made her job uncomfortable.

The foreman slipped down from the corral rail and fell into step beside her, unlatching the gate and holding it open for her with exaggerated courtesy.

"You sure don't show much respect," he complained, "for a girl who needs a job."

"There are lots of jobs for a good hand with horses, Trapper."

"So how come you hang around this dump?"

"I like the place, especially in the summertime when the dudes come. I get a big kick out of all the little kids."

"How long you been here? I looked up your records, but I forget."

Meg walked into the barn and headed for the tack room, annoyed by this reminder that Trapper had access to her employment records. It was just one of the heavy-handed ways that he exercised his power over her.

"Howell? How long you been here?"

"Three years," Meg said curtly.

"And how old are you now?"

"I'm twenty-three," Meg said calmly. "As you know very well."

The foreman leered at her. "Yeah, I remember now. Too old for a pretty girl like you to be all alone without a man. It's just a damned waste of raw material, that's what it is."

"It's my own business, and none of yours." Meg hung her rope on a peg, put the sack away and moved to the chop bin where she measured out a pail of oats.

"You and your daddy came here three years ago, did you?"

"Yes, we did. Four years, actually, this coming summer."

"What were you all doing before that?"

Meg closed and latched the door to the chop bin and bent to lift the pail. "We traveled the rodeo circuit doing horseshoeing at county fairs and such, worked at a few other dude ranches, trained colts at the racetrack...odd jobs like that."

"Your daddy never stays in one place very long, does he?"

Meg thought of Hank, with his slow drawl and his dazed expression, and the increasing struggles he had with the bottle. "Daddy likes to keep moving on," she said briefly.

"So why's he staying here?"

Meg controlled her impatience with an effort. "We're both getting tired of traveling. We came to shoe horses here one summer and liked the place, so after that first season we just stayed on."

"Poor old Hank," the foremen said with a gusty sigh. "Not much good for anything, is he?"

"Shut up, Trapper!" Meg said, goaded into anger. She looked at the grinning foreman, her eyes flashing in the shadowy interior of the barn. "Drunk or sober, he's a better horseman than you'll ever be, with a lot kinder heart than the likes of you."

She lifted her pail and moved toward the door, conscious of Trapper following close behind.

In Meg's opinion, her father's poor loyal heart had broken the day Glory died. Hank shambled through life, ate and drank and visited with other cowboys. But his soul was gone, and his big body was only a shadow of what it had once been.

"Pretty Meg," Trapper breathed, pressing closer to her as she paused in the dusty sunlight by the door. "You're sure a pretty thing, Meggie Howell."

He reached for her with disconcerting swiftness, pulled her arms behind her back and pinned her wrists with one callused hand. While she shouted in surprise and outrage, Trapper shoved her back against the wall. Breathing hard, flushed with emotion, he unsnapped the buttons on her old denim shirt, pulled the cotton fabric roughly aside and ripped her bra open to reveal her breasts.

"God," he whispered, staring down at her hungrily as she cursed and struggled. "What a pretty sight them things are."

Meg swore at him and wrenched herself away. Crimson with fury, she grabbed hastily at the front of her shirt while Trapper stood back and watched her, laughing at her distress.

"A real little hellcat," he whispered. "Just a spittin' hellcat. You're gonna be a lot of fun in bed, Meggie Howell. I can hardly wait."

Meg glared at him fiercely while hot tears pricked behind her eyelids. "If you ever touch me again, Trapper," she said, her voice trembling, "I swear I'll kill you."

His eyes glittered. "Yeah? We'll see about that, sweetheart. We'll just see."

He turned and strolled off through the gate and into the ranch yard while Meg watched him, still clutching her shirt. When he finally disappeared, she felt a rising tide of nausea. Her body began to shake so violently that she had to lean against the barn for a while until the sickness passed. She looked up and saw her father standing at the corner of the barn, watching in silence, his weathered face pale beneath the tan.

"Daddy," Meg whispered, fumbling with her buttons. "Daddy, don't look like that. I'm all right. He didn't hurt me."

"I should kill the son of a bitch," Hank said heavily. He moved closer and touched her hair with a clumsy hand. "I should kill him, Meggie."

"Daddy, don't go near him! Promise me you won't do anything. I'm fine. Really I am. He's not going to hurt me."

"Not even man enough anymore to protect my own little girl," Hank muttered, turning away to squint at the horizon with his faded blue eyes. "Not even man enough to look after her."

"Daddy," she said, agonized by his pain. "Please, please, don't talk like that. Come help me with the colts. I can use a hand at the snubbing post."

He followed her without saying anything more. For a few hours, they worked companionably in the corral, gentling and brushing the colts....

It was a nice memory, sunlit and peaceful. And it was the last time she ever saw her father alive.

In the white Thunderbird by the side of the road, Meg buried her face against her arms on the steering wheel and sobbed as if all the pain was happening now, raw and fresh.

Reluctantly, her mind went back to that awful day and the terrible thing that had happened later, long after dark.

She'd finished mending a pair of Hank's jeans, then read for a while in bed, alone and cozy inside the small house trailer that the ranch had supplied them so Meg wouldn't be required to bunk with the men. She was intensely grateful for this consideration, and loved the little trailer, which was the first real home she'd known since Glory's death.

All those years she'd traveled with Hank and lived out of tents and truck campers, doing her high school correspondence lessons in bars, horse corrals and service stations. Now she had an actual kitchen, tiny but serviceable, equipped with table, chairs and recipe books. There was a small bedroom at each end, a bathroom with a shower and a homey central area with a television, couches and piles of books. Trees rustled overhead, a creek flowed by just beyond the window and even a few flowers and vegetables had been coaxed into existence in the dusty garden plot.

Meg thought her home was the best place on earth.

She switched off the reading lamp by her bed and lay in the dark, thinking about Trapper's attack earlier in the day and his harsh threats. The episode reminded her of a long-forgotten image, a summer baseball game and the boy who'd grabbed her, kissed her, said she was pretty...

Meg grimaced and turned over, burying her face in the pillow.

Men never changed. When they saw something that struck their fancy, they wanted to grab it and squeeze the juice from it. Somehow, they believed they had the right to, just because they were male. And a man like Trapper, so strong and brutal...he was going to do more than grab.

Meg rolled over again to stare at the ceiling.

Suddenly, her eyes widened and the fine hair prickled along her arms.

She could hear somebody coming to the door, approaching rapidly along the path.

Meg sat up in bed and looked around for a weapon, but there was nothing at hand.

If she screamed . . .

But there was no use screaming. The trailer was located well away from the other ranch buildings, in a grove of poplars near the creek. A scream coming from this distance would sound like a hunting bird's cry, or maybe just the natural roar of the stream.

She got up, pulled an old sweater over her T-shirt and jogging pants and went to the door. Cautiously, she looked out through the screen.

The ranch manager stood there in silence, with the moonlight casting an eerie glow on his face.

"Mr. McPhail," she said in alarm. "What is it? What's the matter?"

"There's been an accident, Meg. It's your father."

"Tell me," she said tensely. "Tell me what happened."

"He was in town with a bunch of the men. Carl Trapper was there, too."

"Trapper?" she whispered. "Oh, God . . ."

"Trapper had too much to drink, so Hank offered to drive him home."

"Daddy?" she asked in confusion. "How could Daddy drive anybody?"

"Apparently, your father was stone-cold sober, Meg. He never had a drink all night."

Her mouth went dry with terror. "What . . . what happened, Mr. McPhail?"

"Hank got into Trapper's truck with him, pulled out of town and started for home. But they never got here. Hank drove in front of a freight train on a level crossing about two miles out of town. They were both killed instantly."

Meg licked her lips, staring at him. "It could have been an accident," she whispered. "They could have . . ."

"It was the opposite direction from the ranch, Meg. Three other people saw Hank turn off the road and head up onto that crossing while the train was roaring down the track."

Sorrow mounted in her, an empty, anguished despair that was far too deep for tears.

"Oh, God..." Meg's teeth started to chatter and she pressed a hand against her mouth.

"Meg, I think you should get in your truck and leave right now," the manager said urgently. "There's going to be a whole lot of ugliness over this. Trapper's wife and family will raise some hell tomorrow, you can count on it. But if you're out of sight, maybe we can cover things up somehow."

"But the police...won't they..."

"They know you had nothing to do with it. I'll tell them it was my idea for you to leave. It's better this way," he added. "For you and for your daddy's memory. Just go away and leave it behind."

"I don't want to run away. I want to stay and do my job."

"I'm sorry, Meg. You don't have a job anymore," he said gently. "We can't afford a scandal like this, right at the start of the season. I want you gone from the ranch before morning. Here's a couple months' pay to help you out."

She looked at the envelope he offered, then at the cozy little trailer behind her. "Keep it," she said, struggling to hold back the tears. "Please see that he gets a decent funeral. Mama would have wanted..." Her voice broke.

After a moment's hesitation he nodded and pocketed the envelope. Meg hurried inside to grab a few clothes, books and personal belongings. She jammed everything into a duffel bag and ran out to the old truck while the man stood watching, his face grave and sad.

Meg put the truck in gear and careened out of the ranch yard and down the lane by the hay meadow, past the main ranch buildings and onto the highway. She headed south, into the darkness, while the first glow of dawn began to touch the mountaintops.

Near the level crossing, truck remains still littered the railroad tracks and a couple of uniformed men worked in the fading moonlight among the bits of twisted metal. Meg averted her eyes. Somewhere in that wreckage was her father's body, but Meg knew that Hank Howell's gentle, battered spirit was far away from this sad place.

"I love you, Daddy," she whispered through her tears. "I've always loved you..."

She squinted past the dusty windshield at the sprawling glitter of Las Vegas to the south, where the mighty beam of light atop the Luxor penetrated the darkness like a sign from heaven.

Maybe somewhere in all that dirty, noisy, corrupt city, there was a safe hiding place for a runaway horse wrangler whose father had just committed murder.

20

For a long time, Meg sat in the Thunderbird, shaken by her flood of memories. Hank's kind blue eyes smiling into hers. The way he'd let her ride on his shoulders when she'd been a child. His strong brown hands shoeing a horse. And then his death, his sacrifice. Too horrible to think about. Which was why she'd managed to block it out for all this time. She'd repressed the memory whenever it crept into her mind and, after a while, her recollection of that night had vanished completely, leaving nothing but a dull ache and a vague sense of unease.

At last, Meg put the car into gear and headed south toward Las Vegas, feeling hollow and shaky.

But the recollection of that last terrible night at the ranch seemed to have released a floodgate in her mind. A lot of other things were coming back to her. She could recall everything about their final months at the dude ranch.

She remembered her strange, predawn journey to Las Vegas, even the way she'd stopped at a stock tank in the fading moonlight to wash her face and hands, and how lonely she'd felt, arriving in the city in the gritty light of dawn.

Functioning automatically, numb with despair, she'd moved her bank account the next day, rented a shabby apartment and found her job at the Willows, waiting tables and working in the kitchen.

She couldn't bring herself to drive back up the highway north of Las Vegas, and she'd never been able to make friends or feel at home in the city. Her days had followed one another in a fog of weariness, and she'd been utterly alone.

Then, one August morning, she'd opened her eyes and found herself lying in a hospital bed in Salt Lake City, battered and dazed with fever, being called by a different name. Ever since, her life had been one long, confusing nightmare.

And the nightmare wasn't over.

She reached the sprawling outskirts of Las Vegas, drove down the Strip to the Willows and parked outside, being careful to leave her car under the bright glow of an overhead light and in full view of the service attendant. She wasn't going to take any chances. The person who had sent her over that cliff could be waiting for another opportunity to sabotage her car.

Up in her room, Meg closed the door and looked around cautiously.

It was clear to her that whoever had snatched her from a Las Vegas street and put her into that car certainly hadn't been operating at random. Somebody wanted her injured or dead, and had almost succeeded. It wasn't unreasonable to expect that he would probably try again.

But what could anybody possibly hope to gain by her death? Or was it *her* death they wanted? After all, someone had gone to great lengths to make it look as if Meg's twin sister had been the one who died.

Briefly, she considered going to the police with her story, but discarded the idea almost at once. It was all too fantastic. They'd no doubt react with skepticism, maybe even amusement. Victor Cantalini, her "husband," was a powerful, respected businessman. And if they consulted Lisa's therapist, Clara Wassermann would tell them her patient was delusional, suffering from emotional trauma and multiple personality disorder. As for the bizarre story about identical twins, what proof was there, really, except for the memories of a senile doctor?

If only the old doctor had been able to remember something more about that man who'd visited him in the spring...

Meg hesitated by the door. Then, holding her breath, she made a careful examination of the room, checking the closet, the bathroom, even kneeling to look under the bed.

The room was exactly as she'd left it, and none of her belongings had been disturbed. Finally, she moved over to the little fridge and took out a sack of fruit and a sturdy paring knife she'd bought earlier in the week, just after she'd arrived in the city.

She sat in an armchair by the window and gazed out at the Strip in brooding silence as she ate an apple, carving it into neat wedges with the little knife.

The weekend was approaching, and laughing throngs passed by on the street below. All of them were casually dressed and ready for fun. Meg looked down, feeling as if she were a whole world away from that happy crowd below. Here alone in the luxurious tower room, she was caught in some nightmarish plot that she couldn't comprehend, and that she couldn't escape.

She switched off most of the lights, went into the bathroom and had a long, hot shower, then pulled on a nightshirt and padded back into the room, pausing by the door once again. The night was dark and moonless, and fingers of neon light from outside flickered against the walls and ceiling with a ghostly radiance.

Meg checked the lock on the doorknob and set the dead bolt that barred all entry from outside, even with a key.

She stood looking at the lock for a moment, then crossed the room abruptly, took the paring knife and wedged it firmly into the gap between the frame and the door.

At last, she climbed into bed and huddled under the blankets. Her head whirled with thoughts and speculation, and myriad questions that were impossible to answer.

And through it all she saw the face of Lisa, the sister she'd never known.

Who are you? Meg thought. What are you like? And where are you right now?

She thought of the beautiful house in Salt Lake City, decorated in all the colors that she loved. And the wardrobe of clothes that flattered Meg, fit her body perfectly...

She and Lisa were alike in so many ways. Apparently, Lisa's own husband and cousin, even her therapist, weren't able to tell them apart. They had identical faces and figures, wore their hair the same way, even liked many of the same things.

Egg salad sandwiches, Meg thought, staring moodily at the ceiling. She and Lisa both liked egg salad sandwiches.

She felt a wave of longing for her unknown sister, and a growing concern for Lisa's welfare. She got out of bed wrapped the light blanket around her, then switched on one of the bedside lamps and sat in the armchair again hugging her knees and gazing at the wall.

Victor would help, she decided. The man might be cool and blunt at times, but he wasn't entirely without compassion. One just had to see him with the housekeeper's little boy. If Meg told him the whole incredible story, he would take it seriously and make an attempt to find Lisa.

After all, Lisa was his wife and he clearly loved her. He'd visited regularly while she was in the hospital even though he hated the place. And he'd tried to please her by getting her car repaired promptly.

And he'd come to her bed that night...

Meg shifted in the chair, thinking about her sister's husband and his powerful, naked body pressing against hers. She'd been so shocked and terrified.

She'd even called him Trapper...

Meg buried her face on her knees, then looked up in sudden alarm.

The doorknob was turning. She could see it clearly in the dim glow of the lamp. Meg watched, horrified, as the knob shifted to the left, then back again.

She sat frozen in the chair, gripping her knees, eyes glued to the door. The doorknob stilled. She could hear a key being inserted into the lock, and the tumblers rotating softly.

It was somebody who'd gotten lost, she told herself frantically. Just another hotel guest, probably drunk and confused, trying to get into the wrong room.

But even as she watched, the lock clicked.

Whoever was out there had somehow obtained a key to her room. But the dead bolt was still in place. She was safe. Nobody could defeat that bolt. It was two inches long, embedded in a heavy steel casing...

Meg held her breath, straining to listen, as the intruder began to work on the dead bolt. She heard the key being removed from the lock, a slight rustling outside in the corridor and a new movement toward the door.

Then, with infinite slowness, the dead bolt began to turn. She saw the lock rotate on its metal axis and realized with a flood of pure terror that the person out there in the hallway had a key to the dead bolt, as well. How could that be?

Suddenly galvanized into action, Meg grabbed the telephone and punched a button on the dial.

"Front Desk. How may I help you?"

"Somebody's trying to get into my room," Meg whispered.

"Ma'am, nobody can get into your room if you have the dead bolt in place."

"He's got a key to the dead bolt!"

"I don't really think that's possible, ma'am."

"I'm siting here and watching it move!" Meg whispered. "Please, can't you send somebody up here?"

"Room number?"

"It's..." Meg gasped in panic, watching the sinister movement of the dead bolt. "It's...1411," she said at last. "Please hurry!"

"Somebody will be right up."

Meg hung up the phone and watched, paralyzed with horror, as the dead bolt clicked softly into the off position. The doorknob moved again, turning slowly, then stopped.

Somebody pushed heavily on the door. The paring knife quivered against the frame, but held. Meg heard a soft scuffling noise outside as the intruder braced himself and pushed again. The knob turned sharply, jerking a little with the effort of the shove.

Again the knife held.

Meg licked her lips and stared at the wooden knife handle, then at the gold-rimmed peephole in the middle of the door, realizing that if she got up and crossed the room, she could look through the little glass eye and see who was out there.

But she knew that nothing in the world could make her approach that door.

"Hurry," she whispered in agony, glancing wildly at the telephone. "Oh, God, please hurry. . . ."

The doorknob moved a third time, and the knife strained and quivered.

Then there was silence. Meg huddled in the chair, hardly daring to breathe.

After what seemed like hours, a knock sounded on the door.

"Ma'am?" a male voice called. "Hotel security. Are you all right?"

Meg got up and stumbled toward the door. She looked at the little fish-eye with a reluctant grimace, then leaned closer and peered through it to see a worried face, a blue hotel uniform and a holstered revolver.

Sobbing with relief, she worked the knife out of the frame and opened the door.

The security guard was a heavy graying man with burly shoulders and a scarred face. He looked at her uneasily as she appeared in the doorway, trembling in her thin nightshirt and clutching a knife in her hands.

"Ma'am," he asked, peering over her shoulder into the hotel room, "what's going on in there?"

"There was . . . Somebody was trying to get into my room. They unlocked the door, then the dead bolt . . ."

"What's the knife for, ma'am?"

Meg looked down at the paring knife. "I . . . was afraid," she murmured. "I stuck it into the door frame before I went to bed. If I hadn't," she added, taking a deep, shuddering breath, "he would have been in my room. He had a key to the dead bolt."

The guard smiled down at her with gentle skepticism. "Now, ma'am, I don't think that's possible," he said. "The dead bolt is fully secure. Nobody can get through it."

"But the hotel must have a key, right? I mean, what if somebody got sick inside the room, had a heart attack, or something? You'd need a key to get in."

"Of course there's a key," he said patiently. "But it's kept in a vault down in the office, and it has to be signed out through security."

"Maybe somebody could copy it, or take an impression from the lock," Meg argued, feeling increasingly foolish under his thoughtful gaze.

"It's a very secure system," he repeated. "Now, what probably happened was that somebody just mistook your room number for theirs, and tried to use their key in the lock."

Meg leaned against the door, trembling and biting her lip.

"Ma'am," the guard asked, "are you afraid of somebody? Have you had threats lately, or something that's alarmed you?"

Meg looked at him in silence for a moment, then shook her head. "No," she murmured. "I had a car accident a while ago, and I've been...kind of nervous, ever since." She tried to smile. "I'm really sorry I bothered you."

"That's fine." He smiled back and turned to leave. "Don't be afraid to call the desk if you're concerned about anything," he said over his shoulder. "I'm on duty all night."

"Thank you," Meg whispered.

She stood in the silent hallway, watching until the man was out of sight. Then she went back into her room, jammed the knife firmly into the door frame again, set all the locks and went to bed.

She lay in grim silence with the telephone at her side, not even trying to sleep, and watched the door until the first light of dawn washed through the linen drapes.

In the morning, Meg ate the last of her fruit, packed her bags with nervous haste and hurried down to the lobby to pay her bill. Then she went outside to the parking lot, glancing around fearfully.

But the streets of Las Vegas, normally so crowded and busy, were silent. Scattered bits of paper drifted on a cold morning breeze. The sky was steel-gray and chilly, with an autumn storm gathering over the mountains to the east.

Meg went to her car and looked at it hesitantly, wondering if it was safe. She visualized explosives wired to the steering column, severed brake lines...

But that was nonsense, she told herself firmly. Complete paranoia. Things like that only happened in the movies, not in real life. Besides, the car looked untouched, and the parking attendant had been on duty all night just a few steps away.

Finally, taking a deep breath, she unlocked the trunk and stashed her luggage, then opened the door and got in. She bit her lip and turned the key in the ignition. The engine roared to life and settled to a warm, reassuring hum, and Meg began to feel better.

She was relieved to be inside the car, heading for Victor and that pink granite mansion in Salt Lake City. Victor would know what to do. Even though she knew she was probably still a target, she had to cling to something that represented even a little hope of ending this nightmare.

In truth, it was surprising how quickly the house in Salt Lake City had begun to feel like a refuge rather than a prison. She thought about Filomena and Dommie, and the beautiful yard that surrounded the pink granite mansion, of plump little Trudy next door with her goats and cinnamon buns, and Jim Leggatt and his horses . . .

Meg entered the freeway just past the Sahara and headed north on the I-15. The downtown casinos were still visible to her right, rearing up against the pale skyline. She could see the huge lighted signs on Lady Luck, Fitzgerald's and Union Plaza.

She whipped past the housing complexes, motels and industrial areas that bordered the freeway. Within fifteen minutes, she was in open country, heading northwest toward Arizona and Utah. Salt Lake City was a little over four hundred miles away. If she didn't stop along the way, she'd be home by midafternoon, just as Dommie was getting up from his nap.

When she thought of home, something nagged at her mind, some wayward bit of information that she couldn't put her finger on. It wasn't until she neared Mesquite and saw the rodeo grounds that the memory leaped into her mind, stark and terrifying.

Jim Leggatt was traveling the rodeo circuit this week. He'd told Meg that he planned to pass through Las Vegas and Mesquite. And Jim Leggatt was the only person in the world who knew that Meg had been staying last night at the Willows casino.

She remembered telling him her plans, and his promise to call her when he reached Las Vegas on the weekend. But what if he'd been lying about his schedule? Had it been Jim Leggatt out in that hallway last night, trying to get into her room?

Maybe she'd been fooled by his easygoing cowboy manner and his sympathetic warmth. Because, after all, he was the one who'd confirmed the theory that had taken her to Las Vegas, far from the safety of the big house in Salt Lake...

Meg gripped the wheel, staring out at the highway as she drifted across the Arizona border and the canyon walls closed in around her.

If Jim Leggatt was the man who'd been threatening her all this time, what could his motive be? Had he developed some kind of fixation on his beautiful neighbor, Lisa Cantalini, and somehow learned the details of her birth? Everyone spoke of her dislike for the man. Maybe he'd made an approach toward Lisa and been angered by her rejection, and this elaborate plot was some kind of revenge.

But why...

Meg shook her head in despair. She was tired of running on the same weary treadmill of speculation and doubt, of endless questions that brought her up against solid walls. Nothing made sense. Everybody around her seemed to tell conflicting stories, and she had no idea who could be trusted.

Now the pink granite house in the canyon began to feel like less of a sanctuary. Meg also found herself becoming reluctant to confide in Victor. The best thing, she decided, would be to wait awhile, bide her time and try to discover what was going on.

It would be easier, now that she knew who she was and had no doubts about her sanity. Meg had power over the person who was stalking her because he didn't know that she knew the truth about Lisa and herself.

But somewhere in Lisa's room, among those messy cartons of bills, photographs and newspaper clippings, there must be some clues to this bizarre situation.

Meg realized that she had to keep up the charade, pretend to be a woman tormented by her mental problems, weak and dependent on others. But while she was doing that, she also had to find out what had happened to Lisa.

Once she'd learned where her sister was, perhaps she'd know the answers to everything. Maybe together, she and Lisa could put an end to the sinister threats that dogged their lives. Lisa could come back home, and Meg could return to Las Vegas and go on with her life.

Her life . . .

She thought about Dana in the casino kitchen, and the supervisor's bitter anger at Meg who'd quit her job just weeks ago.

It seemed highly likely that whoever abducted the twins had forced Lisa to assume Meg's role for a brief time, just as Meg had been dropped into the middle of Lisa's life.

No wonder Dana had been so upset. Meg smiled without humor, thinking about a woman accustomed to the kind of luxury that Lisa Cantalini was, being forced to work in that greasy kitchen. Lisa probably hadn't been much of an employee.

I'll bet she was as scared and confused as I was, Meg thought with sympathy.

She drew her breath sharply, struck by another thought. Could Jim Leggatt have arranged everything simply to put Lisa in a position he knew she'd hate? Meg's mind was reeling with the implications. And what about Lisa? She had to know about Meg's existence by now. She couldn't possibly have gone to work in that kitchen without understanding the truth, that Megan Howell was her exact physical double.

But how had they forced her to cooperate? More important, *why* was it happening?

It all kept coming back to that same question. Somebody had learned about the existence of those identical twins and decided to exploit the knowledge for some reason. He or she had gone to bewildering lengths to arrange and carry out the kidnapping of both women.

But Meg Howell's footloose, simple childhood was hardly the kind of thing to arouse the interest of sophisticated criminals. She was certain that the answer to the whole mystery would be found somewhere else.

Somewhere is Lisa's life, not hers. . . .

21

Early the following morning, Jim Leggatt drove up the freeway toward Las Vegas in a heavy autumn rain. His wipers slashed at the downpour, and the horse trailer wallowed behind the truck, its double axles sending up huge plumes of muddy water.

He squinted through the smeared windows, barely able to see the vehicles ahead of him. Finally, he drew close enough to distinguish the Luxor beam and the irregular, spangled outline of the city as it glimmered through the rain.

He'd been driving all night, and he felt tired and empty. He badly needed sleep, a shave and a hot breakfast, but the hollowness wasn't just from lack of food.

Jim Leggatt was getting lonelier with each passing day.

Increasingly, he was surprised at himself and the wistful images that kept haunting him. Jim had always traveled light and fast, enjoyed people when they were nearby and then moved on. But the woman who lived next door was a different matter. He could never recall being so utterly wrapped up in any woman, so fascinated and protective and full of deep, deep tenderness.

Maybe back when he was a teenager, with his first real crush on Bonny Harper who worked behind the counter at the Dairy Maid...

He smiled absently, then gripped the wheel as a semi-trailer roared past him into the streams of traffic heading toward the city.

But those boyhood crushes had only been fantasies, a confused jumble of immature yearnings. The feeling he was developing for his neighbor's wife was something different altogether. The emotions were sweet and romantic, all right, but there was also a thrusting power behind them that had nothing to do with childhood, and he couldn't pretend otherwise.

Jim wanted this woman. He wanted to hold her and kiss her, to undress her slowly and gaze at her body. He wanted to touch her breasts, caress her hips and thighs…

He moaned aloud and gripped the wheel, picturing the way she'd looked on that spring morning by the pool in her topless bikini. The memory seemed to grow sharper and more unsettling with every day that passed, even though his stolen glimpse hadn't bothered him much back when it happened. But now that he'd spoken with her at length, learned more about her feelings and problems, he couldn't seem to get her out of his mind.

Jim pulled off an exit ramp and drove down a service road to a little farm south of the city where he'd made arrangements to stable his horses. He got out and turned up the collar on his long yellow slicker, then plunged through the streaming yard to inspect the buildings. The barn was dry, clean and airy, well worth the rental fee he'd negotiated by telephone.

He waded up to a house trailer near the corrals to pay an advance on the rent and was greeted by the owner, a fat red-haired woman in a rubberized olive green wading suit and floppy yellow hat.

"Hell of a storm, ain't it?" she commented genially. "Happens about once every ten years around here. Gonna have some high water, this keeps up."

"Will my horses be safe in the barn?" Jim asked, taking off his dripping hat.

"That barn's never had a drop of water in it. Safest place in the county."

"That's good. You sure keep it nice." As Jim paid the woman his deposit, a small girl about ten years old slipped out from one of the rooms in the trailer and stood watching. Jim smiled at her.

The child had carroty hair, obviously a strong family trait, and bright eyes that were almost lost in a drift of freckles. She, too, was wearing a baggy rain suit and a pair of black rubber boots.

"Are you an outdoor girl?" Jim asked.

She flushed and squirmed, ducking her head shyly.

"She surely is," the girl's mother confirmed. "Won't nothing keep that child away from the horses. Caroline takes care of every animal that boards here. She feeds them horses, exercises 'em, even doctors them when they need it."

Jim thought of Meg, who'd been traveling the rodeo circuit with her father when she wasn't much older than this freckled child.

"Hey, Caroline, I'll pay you ten bucks," he offered, "if you'll come out in the rain to help me unload my horses and get them settled."

The child's eyes widened in disbelief and excitement. She cast a glance at her mother, who nodded. Then she grabbed a rain hat from a peg near the door, jammed it on her head and followed Jim outside.

It wasn't long before the two horses were safely stabled. Jim paid the little girl, said goodbye and drove back onto the highway heading for the Strip.

He took a room at Bally's where he usually stayed, just up the street from the Willows. Gratefully, he shed his wet jeans and jacket and put out some clean clothes on the bed. He shaved in the elegant bathroom, studying his reflection, wondering what Meg saw when she looked at him.

Did she see a footloose, restless cowboy like her father? Or just another dull businessman like her husband?

Jim frowned, thinking about her husband, and shook cream from his razor into the marble sink.

He'd never before been involved with another man's woman. It had always been part of his personal code of honor, the concept that if a woman was with somebody, you left her alone. He had nothing but contempt for the kind of men who crept around to back doors and made secret phone calls.

But this was different, he told himself. Technically, Meg wasn't Victor's wife at all. She hadn't consented to the marriage. The marriage had happened while Lisa's personality was in control of the body. Lisa had deliberately chosen a rich man who could give her all the luxuries she craved.

Meg would never...

Jim groaned aloud and sat on the edge of the tub, burying his face briefly in his hands. The nightmarish thing about this experience, he realized, was that he was beginning to accept it so readily. The idea that two women lived in the house next door, sharing a single body, had begun to seem much less bizarre. And from there, it was a small step to the realization that while he despised one of those women, he badly wanted to go to bed with the other.

"God help me," he whispered, looking bleakly at his torso in the big mirror. "I don't even know if she exists."

He got up and finished shaving. After he was dressed, he looked up the number for the Willows. As he dialed, his heart was pounding like a teenager's.

But the desk clerk's response wasn't encouraging. "Megan Howell? I don't think so, but let me just check..."

After a brief, tense silence, the clerk came back on the line.

"We have no record of a Megan Howell registered here, sir."

Jim frowned, feeling a twinge of uneasiness. "She could be using her other...her friend's room," he corrected himself hastily. "Could you check for a Lisa Cantalini, please?"

"Certainly."

Again there was a silence while Jim watched the rain splattering on the window.

"Sir? We had a Lisa Cantalini registered. As a matter of fact, she checked out yesterday morning."

"I see. Thanks," Jim said, feeling hollow with disappointment. Only now, knowing that she was gone, did he realize how desperately he longed to see her.

He hung up and sat gazing blankly at the window once more, trying to think.

Why had she used Lisa's name when she registered at the hotel? Maybe the stimulation of Las Vegas had caused Lisa to emerge once more as the dominant personality. If so, was Meg now lost to him forever?

"This is so crazy," he whispered, shaking his head. "God, what am I supposed to do?"

After a moment, he picked up the phone again and dialed Trudy, listening to her cheerful accounts of Crystal's behavior and of the dandelion wine, which would be ready to taste as soon as Jim came home.

"How's the new boyfriend?" Jim asked.

"I think it's about time you quit calling him that. He has a *name,* you know," Trudy said with dignity.

"So what's his name?"

"Oswald."

Jim grinned. "Can I call him Ozzie?"

"Certainly not. And I'm inviting him for Sunday dinner as soon as you're home, so you'd better be nice to him, you hear?"

"I'm always nice," Jim said. "Right?"

"Right," she agreed fondly. "You're a pretty nice man. How was your trip?"

"You know, it's getting kind of long," Jim confessed. "I'll be glad to be home." He hesitated. "How's the weather up there? Has it been raining?"

"Just started a few hours ago, but it looks like it's going to settle in and pour for a while."

"That's good. The pasture can use some rain."

Again there was a silence on the line.

"Look," Trudy said at last, "I don't think you called all the way from Vegas to talk about the weather. Is something wrong?"

"Oh, nothing much. I was just wondering," Jim said awkwardly, "if anything's been happening next door."

"Like what?"

"You know. Just anything... interesting."

"My goodness," Trudy said with a chuckle. "You're getting to be quite the gossip."

"I guess you've corrupted me," Jim said. "So, what's happening?"

"Well, let me think," Trudy began. He could hear her settling more cozily into her padded chair. "Filomena took Dommie to the doctor the other day. He was really sick with a cold and earache."

Jim sighed and forced himself to sound interested. "The poor little guy. What did the doctor say?"

"He said Dommie probably has to have his tonsils out. Filomena's practically beside herself. You'd think it was brain surgery, or something."

"Well, it can't be much fun," Jim said reasonably, "having to take a little kid in for surgery, no matter how minor it is."

"I guess you're right. Anyhow, when Victor called the other night, he promised to pay all the expenses and give Filomena a whole week off whenever they can schedule the surgery."

"That was nice of him. Where was Victor calling from? Is he away somewhere?"

"Seems like everybody's away. I forget where Victor is. At some auto convention somewhere, I guess. He left right after Lisa did, according to Filomena."

"Really?" Jim asked, trying to be casual. "Where did Lisa go?"

"Actually, she's been gone a few days. Filomena said she took off for Las Vegas, just like she used to in the old days. Victor never even knew she was going."

"I guess she must be feeling better, then," Jim ventured.

"Oh, yes. I'd guess she's a lot better," Trudy said darkly.

"Why?" Jim asked, alerted by the housekeeper's tone. "What do you mean, Trudy?"

"Well, there was no sign of the cousin after Lisa went away. Maybe he went down there with her. Or at least, met her down there."

Jim's throat tightened. "What makes you think that?"

"Just a feeling, I guess. Anyhow, their little holiday is all over now. The lady's back."

"Are you sure?"

"I saw her pull into the garage yesterday, late in the afternoon when I was milking my goats."

"Have you seen her or talked to her since?"

"No. I told you, it's raining," Trudy said patiently. "Nobody's left that house since I got up. But," she added with relish, "somebody just arrived."

"Who?"

"The cousin," Trudy said. "Big as life and twice as handsome. He parked out front a few minutes ago in that snazzy little red car of his."

"I thought he always drove a motorcycle."

"I *told* you," Trudy said again, "that it's..."

"Raining," Jim concluded wearily. "I know. So he's inside the house now?"

"Kind of early for a family visit, isn't it?" Trudy said meaningfully. "But I guess it's okay if you're real *close* relatives."

Jim was silent, staring at the deserted streets below where a few neon lights reflected dismally in the puddles.

"Will you be home by next weekend?" Trudy asked, interrupting his gloomy thoughts.

"Probably," he said. "Maybe even earlier. I'm entered in a couple of rodeos here in southern Nevada on Monday and Tuesday. I'll be at Mesquite later in the week, and then I'm heading home. Unless I decide to..."

"What?" Trudy prompted when he trailed off.

"I don't know. I might come home a little earlier."

"Jim?" Trudy asked. "Is everything all right?"

"Sure," he said. "Everything's fine. I've been driving all night and I'm pretty tired, that's all."

"Well, get some sleep," she said firmly. "And have yourself a good hot meal, you hear?"

He thanked her and hung up, then lay back on the bed, staring at the ceiling. Weariness washed over him, pressing against his eyes and making his body ache.

Jim pictured the pink granite mansion up in Salt Lake, silent and withdrawn in the pouring rain. He thought of Meg, tucked away inside the house with her handsome visitor.

Trudy and Filomena continued to gossip and speculate about those two, but Meg claimed to have no memory of the man who called himself her cousin...

On impulse he sat up again, then levered himself from the bed and crossed the room to drag one of his suitcases from the closet. He rummaged through it, extracted a small leather-bound address book and thumbed the pages until he found the Cantalinis' address and telephone number in Salt Lake.

He placed the call and waited, listening to the ring of the phone and the hiss of rain against the window.

"Cantalini residence," a voice said.

"Filomena? It's Jim Leggatt, your next-door neighbor. I'm calling from Las Vegas."

"Yes, Mr. Leggatt?"

"Is Mrs. Cantalini there?"

"Just a moment," Filomena said tonelessly. "I'll tell her you're calling."

After a long pause, a different voice came on the line, quiet and tentative. "Hello?"

Even the sound of her voice affected Jim so powerfully that chills licked up and down his spine, and his hand tensed on the receiver.

"Meg?" he asked. "Meg, is that you?"

He held his breath, waiting.

"Yes," she said at last. "This is Meg."

"It's Jim Leggatt."

"I know. Filomena told me."

He hesitated, wondering what to say. Was the man sitting next to her as she spoke?

"Where are you?" he asked abruptly.

"I beg your pardon?" she asked, sounding startled and wary.

"In the house. Which room are you in?"

"I'm in my bedroom," she said in surprise. "Looking at some old pictures and things. Why?"

"Are you alone?"

"No," she said in a guarded tone. "My cousin is here with me."

"Your cousin Clay?"

"Yes. Clay is here."

He paused again, aching with frustration. Jim Leggatt was a man used to being in charge of situations. He hated the uncertainty and helplessness that seemed to surround all his dealings with this woman.

"I'm in Las Vegas. I was hoping to see you down here," he said at last. "Maybe go out for a meal, or something. Why did you leave so soon?"

"I just got tired of the place," Meg said in a strained voice. "It wasn't all that pleasant, actually."

"Why not?"

"When did you get in?" she asked abruptly, ignoring his question.

"To Vegas?"

"Yes. How long have you been there?"

"I just arrived a few hours ago. Drove all night to get here from Arizona, and left my horses at a little farm outside town. It's pouring right now. I've never seen rain like this in Vegas."

"I guess," she said in that same remote tone, "that I got away just in time, then."

"Meg?" he asked, feeling an inexplicable tug of fear. "Is everything all right?"

"Everything's fine," she said. "I'm home and safe now."

"Safe?" he asked with growing anxiety. "What do you mean?"

"Goodbye," Jim," she said distantly. "Thank you for calling."

Before he could respond, she hung up and he sat listening to the hum on the line. He swore under his breath and replaced the receiver, then lay back and stared at the rain-smeared windows.

22

Meg looked up from the telephone at Clay, who sat by her little desk amid a pile of newspaper clippings and old photographs. She'd asked Clay to help her go through Lisa's papers. She wanted to learn anything Clay could tell her about her sister.

"So, your cowboy friend's started calling to check on you?" he asked with a smile.

"He's never called me before," Meg said.

Her voice was calm, but she still felt unsettled by Jim's voice, and by her memory of his eyes and hands and the warmth of his smile.

Most troubling of all, though, was her fear that Jim Leggatt might have been the midnight intruder out in that hallway at the Willows hotel. She pictured him turning the key in the dead bolt in stealthy silence, then trying to shoulder his way into the room...

"So, where is he?"

"In Las Vegas." Meg shifted uneasily. She was sitting in the middle of the wide bed, also surrounded by news clippings and other papers. "He's down south on a little holiday, going to a few rodeos in Arizona and Nevada. When I happened to mention that I'd be down there at the same time, he suggested we might be able to...get together for a meal, or something."

"Oh, I'll just bet he did," Clay said with another smile. He turned to look fully at her, placing one arm along the back of the chair.

Lisa's cousin looked especially handsome this morning. His crisp dark hair was still dusted lightly with raindrops, and his chiseled features had a healthy, outdoor look. So mild and engaging was his smile that Meg began to regret her earlier doubts about him.

She, who'd always trusted people too much, felt suspicious of everybody these days.

She had a sudden longing to confide in Clay, to tell him the whole baffling story and enlist his help in finding Lisa. But something held her back. Eager as she was to learn more about her sister, she wanted to feel a little more confidence in her understanding of past events, before she revealed the truth.

"Doesn't the guy even care that you're a married woman?" Clay asked, twirling a pen idly between his fingers.

"Who?" Meg picked up a folder containing copies of airline boarding passes from a year-old plane trip, and a handful of receipts carrying the logo of a luxury hotel in Barbados.

"The cowboy. Jim Leggatt, your neighbor. What the hell's he doing, making arrangements to meet his neighbor's wife in Las Vegas?"

"He was just being friendly."

"Really friendly," Clay agreed. "You know what I think, kid?"

"What?"

"I think he's just taking advantage of a poor girl who's pretty mixed-up right now. I always thought that bastard was bad news," he added, his face darkening.

"Clay..."

"Look, stay away from him, kid. Just do it for me, all right?"

"All right," Meg agreed.

She bit her lip and looked down at the hotel receipts, briefly overwhelmed by the thought of her twin.

She and Lisa had to be absolutely identical. Even Clay, who'd been close to Lisa since childhood, apparently had no suspicion that Meg wasn't actually his cousin.

Of course, she thought with a frown, there'd been the car accident and subsequent bruising to her face, and then that long spell of feverish disorientation caused by the infection she'd picked up in the hospital. Obviously the transition had been gradual enough that Clay and Victor hadn't been able to detect any differences between the two women.

Two women. Once again Meg was surprised at how readily she'd adapted to the fact of her sister's existence.

She remembered hearing once that identical twins separated at birth often carried a sense of duality throughout their lives, a distant awareness of the absent sibling. But she remembered nothing like that, no consciousness of a missing part of herself.

Still, Meg was astonished by the strength of her desire to see and talk with her twin. Ever since she'd sat in the old doctor's house and heard the story of her birth, she'd felt an urgent need to find Lisa, to touch her sister and look into her eyes . . .

"What's that?" Clay was asking.

Meg pulled herself together and examined the bundle of papers in her hand. "Some receipts from a hotel in Barbados. They're dated last January."

"That's right. I remember when you and Victor went down there. You had a great time, and came home with a terrific tan for once. We went out for a drink the first weekend you were back, and the guys couldn't stop looking at you. You wore this silky white dress, low-cut..."

He fell silent, smiling at the memory.

"Clay..."

"Hmm?" He picked up a white envelope and held it, glancing up at her.

"All these times when you and I went out together... Victor never knew anything about it?"

"I told you, Victor doesn't know I've ever been in Utah."

"I can't believe he'd be that upset if he were to meet you. Why don't you just..."

Clay shook his head and peered inside the envelope. "No way, kid. If you were a little more conscious of reality, you'd understand why it's impossible."

"But I don't—"

Clay looked at her directly, his gaze level and sincere. "I'm afraid of what Victor might do," he said simply. "The man's not exactly what he seems. If you could remember everything from the past, you'd be scared, too."

Meg hesitated, struggling through her tangle of thoughts and memories, vague impressions and nagging suspicions.

Clay took something from the envelope and glanced down at it, whistling softly. He gave her a quick, teasing grin.

"Hey, look at this, kid," he murmured. "What a knockout."

Meg looked at the photographs in his hand, showing Lisa sunbathing topless on a white sand beach. Her cheeks flamed and she rushed to snatch the pictures from his hand.

Underneath the topless photos were those others, the darkly erotic nude poses that Victor must have taken in the hotel bedroom. Meg felt as embarrassed as if her own body were being displayed.

Clay watched her with that teasing, brotherly grin while she tossed the pictures into a drawer and began to page through the newspaper clippings.

"I wish there were just a few things about the beauty pageants," she murmured distractedly. "If I could only see them, I might be able to..."

Clay toyed with a handful of drapery samples stapled to a piece of cardboard. "I guess none of this is helping," he said. "Is it?"

"What do you mean?"

"You still don't feel like you're Lisa? You're not starting to recover a few of those memories and get your personality back?"

Meg hesitated, feeling uncomfortable about all the lies she kept telling. "Sometimes," she began cautiously, "I feel as if Lisa's...very close to me. I really feel as if we're one person. If I could only..."

Clay picked up another pile of clippings and glanced at it with idle interest. "Here's a picture of Pauline," he said, handing it to Meg. "You were asking about her a while ago, remember?"

Meg tensed when she saw the plump, gentle face of Victor's first wife. Clay held the paper while Meg stared in fascination at the yellowed clipping.

"Poor lady," Clay said casually, putting the clipping down again. "Now, there's somebody who probably should have been a little more afraid of Victor."

Meg's skin prickled with sudden alarm. "Why?" she asked. "What do you mean?"

Clay shrugged and turned away, getting up to prowl around the room as he frequently did.

"Nothing, really," he said. "Just that Victor broke her heart, I guess. He fell in love with a gorgeous younger woman and dumped his wife. Middle-aged ladies should watch out for guys like that, shouldn't they?"

Meg was silent, watching him. He paused by the window and stared down at the rain as it washed over the lawn.

"Why did you go to Las Vegas, kid?" he asked without turning around.

"I just... I wanted to see if..."

"What?" Clay prompted gently, coming back and sitting next to her on the bed. He put an arm around her and gave her a comforting hug. "What did you want to see?"

"If going there could help me remember anything about all these things that have been happening to me."

"And did it?"

"Not really."

"Nothing seemed familiar at all?"

"It was the same as everything else," Meg said. "Just a jumble of impressions and memories that seem to be all tangled up and confused. Some are real and some are fantasies, I guess."

"You've been really quiet since you got back," Clay said, looking at her with sympathy. "Like you're unhappy about something. Did anything bad happen in Las Vegas? Somebody scare you or upset you?"

Meg thought again of that key turning slowly in her lock in the midnight stillness. She shivered and gripped her hands tightly in her lap.

"No, it was fine. I just felt lonely, I guess. It was really nice to get back home."

"At least this place is starting to feel like home to you," Clay said, obviously trying to be encouraging. "That's some progress, right?"

"I guess so," Meg said. "Maybe," she added, glancing at him cautiously, "if I could have talked to the real Megan Howell, the one whose life I've borrowed..."

"But you didn't?"

"She quit her job a while ago and dropped out of sight. The woman at the kitchen where she worked seemed pretty upset with her."

Clay shrugged and got up again, moving over to sit at the desk. "From what you told me, she was really a drab, ordinary kind of person. I could never understand why you were so fascinated with her."

Meg looked up at him sharply.

"Kid?" he asked. "What's wrong?"

"I don't know," Meg said, weary of the dark twists and turns her life was taking. She was so tired of all the questions that had no answers, and so terribly worried about her sister.

Again she told herself that she had to confide in somebody if she wanted to find Lisa.

And Clay was a policeman, a trained private investigator. He was used to dealing with missing people and criminal investigations.

"Clay," she said with sudden decision.

"Hmm?" He glanced up at her, smiling.

Meg took a deep breath. "Listen, Clay, there's something I want to—"

"Mrs. Cantalini?" a voice said, interrupting her.

Meg looked up, startled, to see Filomena standing tensely in the doorway. "Yes?" she asked. "What is it, Filomena?"

"The doctor just called," the housekeeper said in the expressionless voice she always used when she found it necessary to speak with one of her employers. "About Dommie's surgery."

Meg nodded encouragement. "I see. What did he say?"

"They've scheduled the operation for Wednesday morning at eight o'clock. I'd like to leave on Tuesday night and have the rest of the week off so I can be with him."

Meg nodded. "Of course. Mr. Cantalini already told you that would be fine, didn't he?"

"Yes, he did," Filomena said, gazing fixedly at the window.

"Will you be staying in town?"

Filomena nodded. "They said I could sleep on a cot in the hospital and help to look after him. I'll be away for three nights."

"All right." Meg said. "And I'll come to visit him every day. You'll have to be sure and call me if you need anything."

Filomena gave her a startled glance, then nodded abruptly and turned away.

"Filomena," Clay said.

The housekeeper's back stiffened as she paused in the doorway. "Yes?" she asked without turning around.

"What's the matter with Dommie?"

"He needs to have his tonsils out," Filomena muttered, her voice almost inaudible.

Clay nodded, looking thoughtful and concerned. "Poor little guy," he said, winking at Meg. "I'll come along with Mrs. Cantalini when she visits and bring a present for him, Filomena. We all care a lot about Dommie, you know."

Meg was puzzled by the contrast between his words and Filomena's reaction. The housekeeper turned slightly and looked briefly at Clay, her face pale and twisted with an expression Meg couldn't quite decipher. Part anger, part fear. The woman seemed on the verge of saying something.

But she turned away without speaking and vanished into the hallway.

Clay got to his feet and paused to drop a casual kiss on Meg's cheek. "Time to go," he said with regret. "Sorry we couldn't come up with anything to jog your memory, kid."

She submitted to his embrace and watched quietly as he took his leather jacket from a chair near the door, shrugged into it and left the bedroom, following the housekeeper down the stairs to the foyer.

Dark clouds rolled up from the south and brooded over the valley. Rain continued to fall all during the weekend, settling in with such a desolate rhythm that it seemed the sun would never shine again.

On Sunday night, Meg was sitting in the dining room, picking listlessly at a plate of roast beef and Yorkshire pudding. From time to time, she glanced up at Victor, who'd arrived home earlier in the day from another of his business trips.

Lisa's husband was wearing a casual pair of pleated slacks and a yellow cashmere pullover. His rugged face was softened by the candlelight, but he looked tired and dispirited, and his voice was curt when he spoke to her.

Meg watched his hands as he put down his knife and fork and reached for a tall crystal water glass.

He was so strong, she thought. He had the bulky arms and shoulders of a wrestler, and his hands were like iron, dusted with springing dark hair on the backs of his blunt fingers.

She looked away when their eyes met, wondering why Lisa had married him. Was it just for the money and prestige he offered, or had there been a genuine attraction between them? After all, those nude photographs certainly hinted at some kind of sexual excitement.

"How was Vegas?" he asked, setting down the goblet and wiping his mouth on a linen napkin.

"Fine," Meg murmured. "The weather wasn't great, though. It was cold and windy, looking really stormy when I left. They're getting all this rain down there, too, I guess."

"So did you stay at the condo?"

Meg glanced at him quickly, but he was looking down at his plate, digging amongst the vegetables with his fork.

"No," she said distantly. "I stayed at the Willows hotel."

"Why?"

She shrugged. "No reason. I just wanted to be near the Strip, that's all."

"Is it nice? I've never been inside the place."

Haven't you? Meg asked silently. Or were you there the other night, Victor, out in the hallway with a key to your wife's room?

She thought about Clay's obscure warnings, and especially his suggestion that Pauline Cantalini would have done well to be more afraid of her husband.

Did Victor know where Lisa was right now? Had he been the one to put Meg into that car and send it over the cliff?

If he'd engineered this whole bizarre plot, it was difficult to understand what he hoped to gain. And his bewildered impatience with Meg's "medical condition" seemed too genuine for such a bluff, hard-edged man to be faking the reaction . . .

"Victor, where did you go last week?" Meg asked abruptly.

He stared up at her in surprise, arching his heavy eyebrows.

"These last few days," she said. "You were still at home when I left for Las Vegas. Where did you go?"

"To a leasing seminar in Seattle. Why?" he asked with a humorless smile. "Since when have you been interested in what I do, Lisa?"

"My name is Meg," she said quietly. "I'm not Lisa."

"Oh, hell," he muttered.

Meg watched silently while he lifted the gravy boat from its little tray, looking annoyed.

"Filomena!" he shouted.

The housekeeper appeared in the doorway.

"The gravy's all gone," Victor said. "Get some more, okay? And make sure it's hot."

Filomena took the gravy boat and vanished without a word.

"I'll be leaving again in the morning," Victor said, helping himself to more broccoli.

"I see," Meg said in a neutral voice. "Where are you going this time?"

"I'm taking a swing up through the Northwest, going to a few dealer auctions and looking for used cars to restock some of the lots. Our inventory's dropped off since summer."

Filomena returned with the gravy boat and set it carefully on the tray.

Victor nodded his thanks, tipping the jug over his mashed potatoes. "When does Dommie have the surgery?" he asked the housekeeper.

"Wednesday morning at eight o'clock."

"I'll try to be back by Wednesday," Victor said. "Tell him I'll bring him a nice present if he's a good boy in the hospital."

Once again, Meg was surprised by his change in tone, and the tender look on his face when he spoke of the little boy.

She waited until Filomena left the room and she heard the kitchen door close.

"Victor," she said.

"What?"

"Who was..." Meg leaned toward him and lowered her voice. "Who was Dommie's father?"

23

"What did you say?" Victor looked at her in astonishment, the gravy boat suspended in midair.

"I asked you who Dommie's father was."

"You know who it was."

"No, I don't. I still have no memory of this place, remember? I only know that Filomena is all on her own with this little boy, and everybody seems to..."

"Seems to what?" he asked, his eyes glinting with amusement.

"I don't know. I just...wondered, that's all."

"Well, I'll tell you, then. It was Sam." Victor dug into the steaming mashed potatoes.

"Who's that?"

"Jim Leggatt's gardener. He was always out there mowing lawns and trimming hedges."

"That little wiry man?" Meg asked, bewildered. "The one who wears denim overalls and a black T-shirt?"

Victor chuckled. "No, that's Manny. Sam worked for Jim a few years ago. He was a handsome devil, old Sammy, with a real eye for the ladies."

"And Filomena..."

"The poor girl didn't know anybody around here when Pauline hired her. When Sam started flirting across the back fence, she fell for him like a ton of bricks. She got pregnant almost right away, and then she was scared to tell us for fear she'd be fired."

"But didn't he..." Meg paused in confusion. "Didn't he know about the baby? I mean, if he lived right next door..."

"Hell, no. Apparently, the son of a bitch denied everything right from the beginning, and dropped poor Filomena like a hot potato as soon as she told him. She couldn't tell anybody else, and she was practically beside herself with worry."

"So what happened?"

"She tried to kill herself when she was five months pregnant," Victor said, his smile fading. "Pauline found her down in the basement with a razor, getting ready to slash her wrists."

"Oh, *no,*" Meg whispered. "The poor woman."

"Pauline got the whole story out of her," Victor went on. "Then she told Filomena not to worry, that it didn't matter whether or not Sam did his duty by her, because she and the baby would always have a home with us."

"So what happened to Sam?"

"Pauline went and told Jim the whole story. When Jim confronted Sam, the man refused to take any responsibility. The two had a blowup and the next day Sam was gone. Nobody's heard from him since."

"Poor Filomena," Meg said again. "It must have been awful for her."

"It was pretty bad at first, I guess. But Pauline started taking her to the doctor every week, made sure she had everything she needed and looked after her like a daughter until Dommie was born."

"That was very kind of her."

"Pauline was so excited about that baby," Victor said with a faraway look. "She always felt bad that we didn't have any kids."

"She must have been . . . a very nice person," Meg ventured.

"Don't you remember her at all?"

Meg shook her head, frightened by the impatience on his face.

"Well, it's true." He got to his feet and started for the door. "Pauline was a nice person, all right. She was a good wife, too." He paused in the doorway and gave Meg an enigmatic, intent look that made her feel sharply uncomfortable. "Sometimes I miss her a lot."

The damp weather continued throughout the weekend. On Monday morning, rain was still falling steadily, washing through the canyons and flowing across the highway in muddy streams.

Meg parked downtown in the business section and got out, pulling up the hood of her jacket. Through a gap in the tall buildings, she could see the golden angel atop the lofty spire in Temple Square, glistening faintly in the mist.

She stuck her hands into her pockets and hurried toward a three-story building nearby. Pausing in the lobby, Meg looked nervously at the directory. This was the first time she'd ever come downtown to Clara Wassermann's office. She had an uneasy sensation of being on unfamiliar—possibly dangerous—ground.

Meg stared blindly at the numbered list of offices, trying to think.

Why had the therapist been so quick to believe the bizarre diagnosis of multiple personality disorder? The suspicion that dogged all her thoughts these days kept reminding Meg that Clara Wassermann had been Victor's choice.

Victor had been the one who'd sent Lisa to see this particular doctor in the spring. And immediately after his "wife" was hurt in the car accident, he'd called Clara to come and talk with her.

Victor thought you seemed confused, Clara had told her that first morning in the hospital. *He thought I might be able to help...*

But the therapist hadn't helped, she'd hindered.

If it hadn't been for Clara Wassermann, the truth would have come out at the beginning. It was the doctor's analysis, combined with Meg's memory loss and confusion, that had allowed this fantastic situation to develop. The doctor had even made a point of telling Meg and Victor that Lisa had shown symptoms of multiple personality disorder back in the spring.

But how could that be true?

"Ma'am?" the doorman asked, approaching Meg courteously. "May I help you?"

She pulled herself together and turned to him. "I'm looking for Dr. Wassermann's office."

"Third floor, down the hall to your left."

"Thank you." Meg went into the elevator and rode up to the doctor's office, feeling a little awkward in her jeans and sweatshirt when she saw how luxurious Clara's waiting room was.

"Well, hello," Clara said, appearing in the doorway and beckoning Meg into the consulting room. "How are you today?"

"I'm fine," Meg said. "Where should I sit?" She looked uncertainly at the chairs and the soft leather couch.

Clara smiled. "You're still Meg, I take it?"

Meg nodded, avoiding the doctor's keen glance. "Yes," she murmured. "I'm still Meg."

"Because I remember having this same conversation with Lisa a number of times. I'm afraid Lisa considered it quite old-fashioned of me to use the couch. But I still prefer it for therapy sessions, if you don't mind."

Clara settled into a handsome tapestry-covered wing chair, while Meg lowered herself gingerly onto the couch, gratified to realize that she wouldn't have to face the doctor.

"So," Clara asked after a brief silence, "are you comfortable there, Meg?"

"I'm fine," Meg repeated. She crossed her legs and stared at the tips of her handmade brown loafers. Lisa's feet were exactly the same size as hers, with a narrow arch and high instep.

"And how have you been? You're looking much stronger today."

"I feel better. I've been able to stay up all day for quite a while now."

"That's excellent."

There was another silence while Meg fidgeted uneasily on the couch, wondering what to say. This session felt so different from the earlier times when Clara had come to the hospital, then to Meg's room at the house.

She was afraid that the doctor would hear a telltale inflection in her voice or see something in her face that revealed the truth. Meg wasn't ready yet to have the whole story exposed, not until she knew who could be trusted.

"I beg your pardon?" she asked. "I didn't hear what you said."

"Las Vegas," the doctor repeated. "I understand you took a little trip last week."

Meg tensed. "How did you know that?"

"Victor told me."

"When did he talk to you? I thought he was away all last week."

"He called yesterday and left a message. I got back to him later in the day."

Meg was silent, frowning.

"Meg?" the doctor asked gently. "Is something bothering you? Did something happen in Las Vegas?"

"No," Meg said. "It was fine. I was just trying to understand why..."

"Yes?" Clara prompted.

"Nothing," Meg said. "It's all right." She shifted nervously on the soft leather.

"So why did you make the trip?"

"Just to...see if I could remember anything. I thought it might be good for me to look around down there."

"I really wish," Clara said gently, "that you had told me before you left."

"Why?"

"I might have been able to help you, Meg. I could have directed your search a little. And," Clara added, "Victor was very concerned. He's not sure that you ought to be traveling alone."

"Why not? I'm a grown-up, aren't I? There's no reason for everyone to keep treating me like a baby, or some kind of invalid."

"You're sounding more like Lisa all the time," Clara observed. "Have you had any further awareness of her, Meg?"

"Some," Meg said cautiously. "I feel as if I...know a little about who she is, now."

The doctor said nothing, but Meg could feel the other woman's silence like a physical force that pressed and tugged at her, forcing her to go on speaking.

"I... talked with my neighbor last week," she said at last, her cheeks turning warm. "The one who owns the horses."

"Yes, I recall the horses. What is his name?" Clara asked.

"Jim Leggatt."

Meg waited, listening to the faint sound of the doctor's pen as she made notes.

"He thought maybe we had it backward, the multiple-personality thing. He suggested perhaps I'd always been the dominant personality and actually lived the childhood I remembered, and Lisa was the one who'd been suppressed and only appeared recently."

She could sense Clara being jolted from her cool analytical mode. "What made him suggest a theory like that?"

"The way I can ride and handle horses. He thought I must have had a lot of training and childhood experience with horses, and Lisa never seemed to exhibit anything like that."

"I've told you, Meg, how alter personalities can frequently exhibit skills and knowledge completely unrelated to those of the host. You understand that, don't you?"

"Yes. I do. I guess it can seem really strange to people who don't know about it, though."

There was another long silence while Meg lay and watched streams of rain flow down the window behind the venetian blinds.

"Also," she went on, "there's the fact that I could never find any traces of Lisa's childhood among our belongings. Pictures or anything."

"We discussed that," Clara said. "We talked about Lisa's hostility toward her mother, and her strong sense of alienation."

"I know. But it still seemed..." Meg paused, wondering how much to say.

"I can understand how you felt," Clara observed calmly. "It would be extremely encouraging to receive that sort of validation, especially when there still seems to be considerable competition for dominance between you and Lisa. So," she added, "that's why you went to Las Vegas?"

"Partly. I wondered if maybe..." Meg paused again and took a deep breath. "I wondered if Lisa had come out and taken over as the dominant personality a few years ago, but maybe I kept on appearing from time to time and that's how I had all those memories of Las Vegas and the casino."

"And what did you learn?"

"Well, of course it was impossible," Meg said wit forced casualness. "The whole theory was just silly. If I' had any sense, I would have realized it right from th start and not wasted the trip."

"Why?"

"For one thing," Meg said, "there really is a Mega Howell. Apparently, she's left the city now, but I talke to the supervisor at the casino where she worked."

"I see," Clara said, her voice relaxing. "I spoke wit her, as well, you know."

"Yes, I remember. But I think I needed to hear it fo myself. And besides," Meg went on, "there's Clay."

"Your cousin?"

"Yes. He's a person who actually remembers ou childhood. I mean, Lisa's childhood. That's more ev dence than an album full of photographs, right?"

"I would think so. Have you talked with Victor about your neighbor's theory?"

"I hardly ever see Victor. He left about the same time I went to Las Vegas, and he was only home for a little while on the weekend."

"Is he gone again?" Clara asked in surprise. "I don't believe he mentioned another trip."

"Yes, he's gone. I'm not sure when he'll be coming back. Dr. Wassermann..." Meg hesitated.

"Yes?"

"I'd really like to learn more about Lisa. I'm not...not so afraid of her anymore."

"That's very good news," the doctor said approvingly. "Perhaps in our next session, we can begin discussing some integration therapy."

"All right. But I think it would help," Meg said as nonchalantly as she could, "if I could only find out a few things from her past."

The doctor didn't respond, making notes. Meg shifted in the chair to glance around at her, then looked away quickly.

"You said you have tapes of your sessions with Lisa," she ventured. "I wondered if I might be able to hear some of them."

"Meg, I couldn't allow you to listen to those tapes. That might compromise the entire progress of your therapy."

"I'd just like to understand more about her childhood," Meg pleaded. "About what she's like, and why she entered all those beauty pageants. Maybe if I could see some pictures from the pageants..."

"I'm sure there would be old newspaper articles and pictures on file at the library," Clara said casually. "I gather that you were quite a local celebrity in your earlier years."

"Of course," Meg breathed, her eyes widening. "Of course there would be things in the papers. Why didn't I think about that?" Impulsively, she climbed from the couch and rushed toward the door.

"Meg," Clara said in surprise. "Our time isn't up. We still have almost half the session left."

Meg paused in the doorway. "I'm sorry," she said. "I just remembered that I have to . . . I have to pick up Filomena and take her and Dommie to see the doctor," sh said, improvising hastily. "Dommie's had a bad case o tonsillitis," she added. "He needs to have surgery late in the week. On Wednesday morning, in fact. Filomena's going to be staying with him at the hospital."

"Will you be alone at the house, then? I believe yo mentioned that Victor was away, as well."

Meg fell a brief, prickly chill of alarm, and suppresse it quickly.

"Oh, Victor will probably be home by then," she sai with deliberate casualness, "and Dommie and Filomen will only be gone for a couple of days."

"Well, I'm sorry to hear of Dommie's illness," Cla said. "I hope he'll be all right."

"So do I. Everybody loves Dommie. He's such a litt darling," Meg agreed. "I'll come back for my regul appointment next week," she said. "And we can sta talking about personality integration. Dr. Wasserman I think I'm finally ready to meet Lisa. In fact, I'm loo ing forward to it."

"That's wonderful news," Clara said, watching h intently.

Meg ducked her head, still frightened of that penetrating dark gaze, and hurried out to the waiting room to get her jacket. She rode downstairs in the elevator, ran through the lobby into the rain and over to her parked car.

24

In spite of her sporadic formal education, Meg was no stranger to books and studying. During all the years she and Hank had traveled the dusty plains of Nevada and Arizona, she'd spent many hours in small-town libraries, doing research on assignments. Often she would finish her correspondence lessons in a library somewhere in the desert, and mail them at a post office five hundred miles away from the one where she'd picked them up.

Better than most students at the high school level, Meg knew how to read a card file or a microfiche, how to cross-reference a topic, how to exhume ancient yellowed articles from the newspaper-clipping morgue and follow their trail of information.

Still, she wasn't accustomed to a huge and efficient operation like the downtown library in Salt Lake City, with its tiers of reading areas and conference rooms, its potted plants and discreet lighting and endless shelves of books.

She consulted a chart on the wall and discovered the reference and clipping rooms on the lower floor, then located an elevator and went downstairs. Meg edged her way nervously into a silent, windowless chamber where a couple of staff members worked behind a long desk, surrounded by people reading bound newspapers or studying plastic-covered bindings of old clippings.

She found a chair and settled there, tore a request form off the pad on the table and jotted down some topics. She forced herself to concentrate on her task, trying to think of any topic headings that might generate news articles on Lisa's past.

She listed beauty pageants, Utah child stars, Lisa Bauer, Victor Cantalini, automotive dealerships, and important local weddings, September, 1992. After a brief hesitation, she added local television advertising campaigns, and took the whole list up to the desk, handing it to young librarian.

"Could you please run a search for me on these," Meg asked, "and let me know how much you can pull on any of them?"

The girl examined the list. "We don't usually get much on specific names, although both of these look kind of familiar. And the files on car dealerships and local television advertising are going to be very extensive. Would you like me to break them down?"

"Actually, you could cross-reference. I'm particularly interested in the television advertising done by automotive dealerships."

The girl laughed. "Now, that's still going to be pretty extensive," she said, looking at Meg's name at the top of the request form. "Please have a seat, Miss Howell. I'll call you when I've put something together."

"Thanks." Meg watched as the librarian disappeared into a back room filled with stacks of old newspapers and bound clippings, then settled down to wait, leafing through a magazine.

"Megan Howell?" the librarian called at last. "I have a file for you."

Meg hurried up to the desk, brought the heavy file back to her table and opened it, tense with anticipation.

She was surprised to find that the information on beauty contests was the most extensive, including news items on state and local pageants going back at least fifteen years. She paged through the clippings and found a picture of Lisa.

Local Girl Crowned Miss Provo, the headline said. The article went on to describe how Lisa Bauer, aged seventeen, had defeated an impressive field of contestants, enchanting both the judges and the audience with her grace and beauty. The winner told the news reporter that she planned to enter Miss Utah the following year, then Miss America.

Meg studied the picture of a radiant, smiling Lisa, then read the article describing the pageant. The Miss Provo competition apparently placed great emphasis on the talent component, as well as the contestant's interview skills.

I wonder what you did for talent, Meg asked her sister silently, gazing down at the face that was so uncannily identical to her own. Because we sure can't sing or dance. At least I can't, and I doubt if you're any different . . .

Evidently that was the case, because Lisa's skill in the Miss Provo competition had been poetry. The winning contestant had recited a poem of her own creation, called "Flowers in the Stream," and many audience members had reportedly been moved to tears.

Meg, who'd secretly been writing poetry all her life, was stunned by this information. She gazed hungrily at the photograph of her twin sister.

"What's happened to you, Lisa?" she whispered. *"Where are you?"*

She forced herself to continue reading, trying to reconstruct the details of Lisa's life. She found a few more articles about beauty pageants, and a couple of pictures from earlier years. Except for her long cloud of dark hair and dainty feminine clothes, Lisa had looked exactly like Meg.

In addition to the stories about Lisa's childhood, there were a few articles in the file about Victor, most of them dealing with the aggressive success of his business. A few pictures showed him with his first wife, Pauline, and the articles recounted various charitable organizations with which the Cantalinis had been involved. There were also copies of the same clippings that Lisa had kept up in her bedroom, the ones recounting Pauline's death.

At the bottom of the file, Meg found a brief description of Victor's wedding to her sister, along with the photograph that was on the dressing table in Lisa's bedroom. She read the accompanying text describing Victor as a prominent local businessman and Lisa as a former beauty queen.

Meg pushed aside the untidy mound of clippings and stared at the opposite wall. She frowned, wrestling with a nagging sense that something important was missing from the mass of details in front of her. After a moment, she realized what it was. She gathered the files and clippings and carried them back to the front desk.

"How would I find out the details of an inquest?" she asked the librarian. "For a death that happened locally, I mean."

"How long ago?"

"Two or three years."

"We should have clippings on file if it was that recent."

Meg shook her head. "I already saw some clippings about the death in this material you gave me. They indicate that the inquest proceedings were closed to the public, and none of the details were being released to the media."

"That's interesting. Somebody must have had a lot of influence," the girl said in surprise. "But they certainly couldn't hide it altogether. I'm sure it would still be possible to look up the transcript."

"Where would I do that?"

"At the courthouse just down the street. You ask for the coroner's office and tell them which inquest you want to look at. They'll let you read the transcript, either in print or on computer disk. I think you probably have to pay a search fee, though."

"That's all right. Thanks so much, you've been very helpful."

The girl took the folder and opened it to sort the clippings for replacement in their various files. She caught sight of the picture of Lisa in her sash and gown as Miss Provo and gave it a startled glance, then looked up at Meg.

"This is you, right?" she asked. "But you've had your hair cut since then."

Meg shook her head. "That's not me." Her throat tightened with emotion. "It's my sister," she murmured, saying the words aloud for the first time.

Meg had been mildly surprised to learn how easy it was to obtain a transcript of the inquest into the death of Pauline Cantalini. She'd simply made her request, paid the fee and soon afterward found herself installed in a comfortable small room with a window overlooking the parklike grounds of the old courthouse. She sat for a moment in front of a blank computer screen, turning to watch the rain fall through the trees.

A couple of gray squirrels frisked among the wet, dying leaves, apparently heedless of the raindrops that glistened like diamonds in their soft fur.

Meg took a deep breath, punched a few keys that brought the court transcript onto the screen, then began scrolling slowly downward.

It was tedious but fascinating, like reading the account of an actual trial. The court recorder had included everything said by witnesses, even their pauses, repetitions and grammatical errors. Oddly enough, the dry, ponderous tone of the text brought the whole scene to life, even years later.

Meg could almost see Victor, looking powerful and uncomfortable in an expensive suit and tie. And Filomena, terrified by the proceedings as she stood alone in the witness box, longing to be at home with her new baby...

She settled in to read the portion of the transcript in which Filomena was being questioned by Mr. Michael Kraft, the court attorney.

Q: Now, Miss Morales, Mrs. Cantalini was very good to you. That's what you told us, isn't it?

A: She was wonderful. She looked after...and gave me and the... my baby, you know... and she gave us everything.

Q: And how did you feel about your employer, Miss Morales?

A: I loved her.

Filomena went on to describe how she and Pauline were alone in the house that day. The housekeeper recalled being worried because she suspected that Pauline had begun drinking again. She was in the kitchen when she heard a cry, then a "big noise" and ran into the foyer to find Pauline lying at the foot of the stairs in a pool of blood.

Q: What did you do then, Miss Morales?.

A: I called 911. I was so scared, and crying...I was...and I didn't know what to do.

Q: That's certainly understandable. And you say there was nobody else in the house at the time?

A: Only Dommie.

Q: That's your child?

A: Yes.

Q: And how old was he at this time?

A: Ten weeks. He was ten weeks old.

Mr. Kraft: Thank you, Miss Morales. You may step down. Calling Mr. Victor Cantalini, Your Honor.

Victor took the stand, his speech so rambling and incoherent in the transcripts that the court record was almost impossible to follow until the lawyer took him in hand and led him gently though the details of his whereabouts at the time of his wife's death.

Q: Where were you on the ninth of June of this year, Mr. Cantalini?

A: I was on a fishing trip. We were...we'd gone into...packed in by horseback to fish along the Green River, back in the Uintas. God, if only I'd stayed home...

Q: You say 'we,' Mr. Cantalini. Does that mean there was someone else with you up in the mountains at the time of your wife's accident?

A: Yes, I had a buddy with me. We were planning to stay up there in...in the mountains for the whole week, but they...until they came in and found us so they could let me know about...oh, my God...

Q: We'll give you a moment to compose yourself, Mr. Cantalini. Now, could you tell the court the name of the person accompanying you on this fishing trip?

A: It was Clay. An old friend and business associate of mine, Mr. Clayton Malone. Clay was . . . he was with me the whole time.

Meg stared at the computer screen in horror, too shocked to breathe or think clearly. She pressed her hands to her forehead.

When she'd talked with Jim Leggatt up on that peaceful autumn hillside with the horses grazing nearby, Meg had told him that she suspected everybody of lying. Now the proof of that deceit was in front of her eyes.

She sat back in her chair and looked blindly out the window, trying to clear her mind so she could concentrate.

If Victor and Clay had been partners all this time, then why had both of them taken such pains to keep the knowledge from her?

Suddenly, her skin began to crawl with fear.

She rubbed her arms and leaned forward to examine the text on the computer screen. If they'd worked together so skillfully to deceive her, it was entirely possible that they'd done the same thing during this inquest. Meg scrolled rapidly back and forth through the pages of text.

But she knew she wasn't going to find the truth anywhere in this dry transcript. The truth was elsewhere, locked inside the minds of the people who knew what had really happened to Pauline Cantalini.

And one of those people, Meg was certain, was Filomena Morales.

During most of the following day, Meg searched for a chance to draw Filomena into conversation. But the housekeeper was absorbed in her work, flying around the big house as she made preparations for her upcoming absence.

"I made some casseroles that just need to be heated up," she told Meg, hurrying down the hall with an armful of laundry. "They're in covered dishes in the fridge, and, by the way, Mr. Cantalini called earlier from Boise. He says he won't be home till tomorrow."

"That's fine. Please don't go to any trouble on my account, I can eat peanut butter sandwiches if I'm hungry. Look, Filomena, I need to ask you something."

"Mama, can Teddy go to the hospital?"

Both women looked at Dommie who stood in the hallway near the kitchen door, looking frightened. The little boy was still pale and fragile after his sickness, and his eyes were shadowed with worry.

"Of course he can," Filomena said, moving forward to lift her son tenderly in her arms. "Teddy would be lonely if you left him at home while you went away. Now, please be a good boy and go play in the kitchen, Dommie. We have to leave in just a few hours and Mama has so many things to do."

"Come on, Dommie," Meg said. "I'll play with you, okay? We'll make a whole big city out of boxes, and drive trucks around on the streets."

Dommie's face brightened and Filomena gave Meg a shy, grateful smile before she hurried away to take her laundry upstairs.

In the kitchen, Meg watched while Dommie stacked cereal cartons and other boxes into rows of elaborate skyscrapers. After a while, he paused, squatting back on his heels. One of his overall straps fell off his shoulder and Meg bent to straighten it, kissing his soft cheek.

"Will it hurt?" he asked timidly.

"What, darling?"

"The doctor. Will he hurt me?"

"Of course not," Meg said, hugging him. "You'll be sound asleep. And Mama will be there when you wake up, and the nurses will give you ice cream and make a big fuss over you, and you'll be back home in just a few days."

"Will you be there?"

Meg shook her head. "Not all the time, like Mama. But I'll come to visit every day."

"Where will you be?" the child asked.

"I'll be right here just like always, sleeping in my room and eating my breakfast in the kitchen."

Dommie's eyes widened. "All alone?"

Meg looked down into his face and felt a chill of uneasiness. Once again, she realized that after she dropped the housekeeper and her little boy at the hospital, she'd be coming back to a completely empty house. She stared at the window, trying not to let Dommie see her face.

If only it would stop raining...

But the sky was gray and sullen and rain fell without ceasing, swelling the banks of the creek and lying in sodden pools across the yard.

Meg was relieved when the long afternoon finally ended and it was time to drive Filomena into town. She pulled the four-wheel drive out of the garage, glad to escape from the big granite house standing silent and withdrawn behind a dark curtain of rain. As they drove off, Meg thought briefly about taking a room in town for the night, telling herself that it might be better to be close to the hospital in case Filomena needed her.

Immediately she rejected the idea. After all, the house was equipped with all kinds of sophisticated alarms and protective devices. She couldn't be any safer if she were inside a fortress. Besides, her terrifying experience in Las

Vegas had shown her that a motel room didn't offer much protection if somebody really wanted to get in.

She cast a glance at Filomena who was sitting in the passenger seat, gazing fixedly out the window at the sweeping movement of the windshield wipers. Dommie was behind them, strapped into a car seat, hugging his teddy bear as he hummed tunelessly under his breath.

"Filomena," Meg said.

"Yes?"

Meg hesitated, then said, "That day when Pauline died..."

Filomena glanced over at her, then looked away. "What about it?"

"I went to the courthouse yesterday and looked up the transcript of the inquest. I saw the testimony you gave."

She could see how the woman's thin body stiffened and her hands curled into fists, the fingernails digging into her palms.

"What's the matter, Filomena? What are you afraid of?"

"It was so awful," the other woman whispered. "It was an awful thing."

Meg took a deep breath. "In the transcript, you said there was nobody else in the house when she died."

"Yes. That's what I said."

"Is it true?"

Filomena turned away to stare out the window.

"Is it true?" Meg repeated gently.

Filomena looked down at her hands, twisted painfully in her lap. "Please," she muttered. "Please don't ask me."

"Somebody forced you to say those things, didn't they?" Meg asked quietly. "They made you tell a lie."

Filomena's sharp intake of breath was all the confirmation Meg needed.

"Somebody else was there that day. You and Pauline weren't alone in the house."

Filomena made a strangled noise and buried her face in her hands. Meg stared at the rainwashed highway, listening to the rhythmic sweep of the wipers and the hiss of the tires as they splashed through small lakes of water on the road.

"Filomena?" she said.

The housekeeper nodded, keeping her face hidden as she mumbled through her fingers, "He said..."

Meg reached over and patted the woman's thin shoulder. "Don't be afraid," she murmured. "I'm not going to cause any trouble for you, I just want to know the truth. I need to find out, Filomena. I need to know what happened. Were both of them at the house? Clay and Victor?"

Filomena looked up, her eyes huge and dark in her pale face. "He said he'd kill Dommie," she whispered. "He said if I didn't tell those lies to the police, and at the inquest, Dommie would be..." She shuddered, her whole body wrenched with a long, trembling spasm. "He said a baby would be easy to drown, just like a kitten."

"My God," Meg whispered, staring through the smeared windshield. "Who said that, Filomena?" she asked urgently. "Which of them was it?"

"He was there when I came out of my room after giving Dommie his noon-hour feeding," the housekeeper went on tonelessly. "I was in the hallway and he asked where she was."

"Pauline, you mean?"

Filomena nodded, jerking her head awkwardly. "I said she was up in her room, lying down. She'd been sick all morning and didn't want to be disturbed. He pushed me away and went upstairs, and I could hear them arguing. Pauline was screaming," she said, her eyes staring into the past. "Then there was a horrible noise and I ran into the foyer and . . . and found her there. He was still at the top of the stairs. He came down and told me . . ." She shivered again, wringing her hands. "He told me what I had to say when the police came."

Meg gripped the wheel, swallowing hard. "Who? Was it Victor?" she whispered.

Filomena went on as if Meg hadn't spoken. "He left right after that. I tried to help her, but she was . . . there was blood coming out of her ears and nose, and I could see—" Her voice broke. She began to cry softly, hiding her face again.

"Please," Meg said, aching with sympathy. "Please don't cry. It's all right."

"But I should never have told those lies. It was wrong to lie. I was just so...so afraid of him, and what he might do to Dommie. I still am."

"Why didn't you run away?"

"Where could I go? I didn't know anybody. I didn't even know Trudy in those days. And Sam wouldn't . . ." Filomena took a deep breath. "He wouldn't have anything to do with me."

"But couldn't you have found a job somewhere else? How could you stay in that house, knowing what happened to Pauline?"

"He said I had to stay or he'd kill Dommie," the housekeeper told her simply. "He said if I tried to run away, he'd follow us and find us no matter where we went."

Meg's stomach churned with nausea and terror. "Who was it?" she asked again. "Who said those things to you?"

Filomena shook her head and looked away. "You're different now," she murmured. "You don't remember anything about him. If I tell you, maybe he'll hurt you, too. I don't want to say any more."

"But I have to know," Meg said. "I have to know what's going on, Filomena. Can't you see that it's—"

Just then, they reached the hospital and Meg drove around the circular driveway to the front entrance, swerving to avoid an ambulance that came careening past them with flashing lights and siren blaring.

She parked and looked over at Filomena, who gathered up her handbag and packages and climbed hastily out of the van. Meg followed, taking a small suitcase from the back and standing in the rain while Filomena reached inside to undo the fastenings on Dommie's car seat.

The housekeeper carried her son toward the front entrance, her coat flapping around her thin legs. Meg followed with the suitcase, pausing inside the big glass doors while Filomena set the little boy down.

The smaller woman looked up at Meg, her face pale and urgent. "Don't go back there tonight," she urged. "Don't trust him. He's a monster."

"I'll be careful," Meg told her. "Nobody else is around, and Victor's not home. I'll set the alarms and keep my eyes open, but I need to know who..."

"No, I'm sorry. It's too dangerous. Just stay away from that house."

But Meg needed to be there in case Lisa somehow escaped her captors and found her way home, and of course she couldn't say that. Instead, she summoned an encouraging smile for Filomena, then knelt to give Dommie a hug and some whispered encouragement.

When Meg turned to leave, Filomena walked beside her toward the door. "Please . . . be careful," the housekeeper whispered, as she gripped Meg's sleeve and stared up at her.

Then she was gone, lifting the little boy into her arms and hurrying across the lobby toward the admitting desk.

25

On Tuesday, while Meg was preoccupied with Filomena and her little boy, Jim Leggatt was passing another idle, restless day in Las Vegas. He'd been scheduled to compete in a rodeo at a small town west of the city, but the relentless downpour had canceled events for a second day. Jim found himself at loose ends, and he didn't enjoy the feeling.

Around midafternoon after spending a couple of hours at the Willows casino playing blackjack, Jim went into the coffee shop and ordered a club sandwich and some apple pie. Halfway through the pie, he stopped eating and put his fork down, struck by a sudden thought.

The waiter came by to refill his coffee cup and glanced at the unfinished pie.

"Anything wrong with your dessert, sir?"

Jim looked up at him. "No, it's delicious. I was just thinking..."

"Yes, sir?"

"How many kitchens are there in the casino?"

"Three. One on the eighth floor that services the dining rooms, one here at lobby level for the coffee shops and another on the lower floor that handles room-service orders, plus most of the bar and casino deliveries."

"How would I get down to the lower kitchen?"

The waiter gave him directions and moved away with his coffeepot. Jim finished his pie abstractedly and counted out enough money to pay the bill. He added a ten-dollar tip from his morning's blackjack winnings and left the coffee shop, heading for the bank of elevators in the lobby.

At basement level, he made his way through a maze of corridors that were a stark contrast to the luxurious upper floors of the casino complex. He paused at the entrance to the kitchen, and looked in at the noisy, steam-filled room and the bustling crowds of workers in aprons and hair nets.

A couple of young women at the sinks caught sight of him. They stared in frank admiration, nudging each other and giggling. A woman passed by and spoke sharply to them, then glanced at Jim and came over to him. She was tall and broad-shouldered, with a grim expression and dark eyebrows that met above her nose.

"Can I help you?" she asked brusquely.

"I'd like to speak with the supervisor," Jim said, giving her one of his engaging cowboy grins. "If it's not too much trouble, that is."

She softened visibly. "I'm the supervisor. My name's Dana Kirsch. Come with me," she said, leading the way down a corridor to a cluttered office that was taken up with a desk, a huge file cabinet and a couple of bulletin boards containing charts and schedules.

The supervisor seated herself behind the desk, while Jim leaned casually in the doorway. "I was hoping you could tell me something about a former employee," he said.

"I'll do the best I can, but I have to get back to the kitchen pretty soon. Those kids don't work at all if I'm out of sight."

"The employee I'm wondering about is somebody who worked here a while ago. Her name is Megan Howell."

The woman's dark eyes narrowed and her face turned hard. "What about her?"

"I was hoping you could tell me a little about her," Jim said mildly. "What kind of an employee she was, that sort of thing."

"Is she in some kind of trouble? She was down here a few days ago, you know, and I wondered if she'd gotten herself into something. She looked kind of sick. Pale as a ghost."

Jim stared at the woman, suddenly alert. "She was here? Meg Howell?"

"Big as life. And after everything she did, too. The girl's got some nerve, you have to give her credit for that."

Despite her words, Dana Kirsch didn't look as if she was inclined to give Meg Howell credit for anything. "Wasn't she a good worker?" Jim asked.

"Why do you want to know? Are you a cop?" The woman eyed Jim's blue jeans, his riding boots and tooled leather belt.

"No, I'm just an old friend who's concerned about her. I was passing through the city, going to a few rodeos down here, and I thought I'd see if I could find out how she's doing."

There was a brief uncomfortable silence while the supervisor stared grimly at the shift schedules on the opposite wall.

Finally, Jim repeated his earlier question. "Was her work all right?"

"Oh, sure," Dana said with a heavy sigh. "She was a good worker. At least back in the spring when she first started, she seemed keen enough. But that changed later on."

"She started in the spring? This past spring?"

"March, I guess it was. Turned up one day looking for a job. She had no references or anything, but I was shorthanded so I took a chance and hired her part-time. I had no regrets, either. As I said, she was a real good kid at first."

"At first?" Jim prompted.

"She didn't have any kitchen experience, but she was a hard worker, kept to herself and didn't talk much, took any job I gave her. A good worker, Meg was. I put her on waiting tables a few shifts besides the kitchen work, and she got real nice tips."

"Did she ever seem...moody?" Jim asked cautiously. "I mean, sort of...different? Did she miss a lot of her shifts, or anything like that?"

"Not that I recall. She was just real quiet. Then one day in August..." Dana paused, frowning.

"She didn't show up," Jim suggested, trying to keep her talking. He was puzzled by the woman's story.

Jim couldn't recall how often his neighbor's wife had been away during the spring and summer. But it didn't seem possible that Lisa Cantalini had been able to hold a job in Las Vegas, even part-time, without somebody getting suspicious.

Hadn't Meg told him that someone was using her name? Maybe he and Dana were talking about two different people.

The supervisor looked at him in surprise. "Didn't show up? What makes you think that?"

"I just wondered if she might have missed a few shifts. She's been...having some problems."

Dana gave a harsh laugh. "So she told you that story, too, did she? Well, I don't know why she's been telling all those lies, but it's not true. She never had any car accident, that's for sure. She was here at her job all through August, big as life, but she wasn't the same girl. Not at all."

Jim felt an icy chill lick along his spine. "What do you mean?"

"I *mean,*" the supervisor said with heavy emphasis, "one day Meg Howell just changed like a shot. Overnight she was a different person. She was rude and chippy at work, and she acted like she was above it all. She caused trouble with the other kids, too, because she wasn't doing her work. I tried to talk to her, but she just ignored everything, so I took her off waiting tables and put her at the sink full-time. Around the beginning of September, she got upset about something and walked out on a Saturday night, the busiest shift of the week. No warning at all."

"What did you do?"

"I fired her," Dana said with satisfaction.

"And you never saw her again?"

"Not till she came back a few days ago, telling me she'd had an accident and asking a lot of questions. She tried to look all sweet and innocent, like butter wouldn't melt in her mouth."

Jim's head began to spin. He leaned forward urgently, resting his hand on the desk.

"Look," he said, "this is really important. The woman who worked here during late August, are you sure it was the same person? I mean, the woman you hired in the spring and the one who came to see you a few days ago...she was the same person who worked here in late August?"

"Well, of course I'm sure. If it wasn't Meg Howell," Dana said with a mirthless smile, "then it must have been her twin. That's all I can say."

Jim stared at the woman, and the hair began to prickle along the back of his neck.

"Jesus," he whispered.

"Hey, what's going on?" Dana asked, her eyes narrowing again. "What the hell is this?"

But Jim didn't hear her question. With a last frantic glance at the woman behind the desk, he turned and ran down the echoing corridor, heading for the lobby and the rainy street.

Back in his room at Bally's, he looked up the Cantalini number and dialed the house in Salt Lake City, then swore fiercely under his breath when he heard the empty ringing on the other end of the line.

Finally, he grabbed his keys and hurried out through the lobby again, wondering how long it would take him to drive up the freeway to Salt Lake if he didn't stop at all. He tried not to think about what might be happening in the pink granite house next to his own, but the dark fears gathered and pressed at his mind with tormenting urgency.

Jim knew he'd taken far too long to recognize the truth, even though it had been staring him in the face for such a long time.

And there was a very real possibility Meg was in danger.

After Meg left the hospital, she drove around aimlessly for a while, reluctant to go back to the empty house. The sky darkened and the wind began to howl down from the mountains to the east, driving the rain so hard that it fell almost horizontally across the road.

She passed a little Italian restaurant on the way out to the canyon, and remembered that she hadn't eaten. Meg turned around and drove back, parked in the lot and splashed across the pavement to the front door, entering gratefully into the fragrant warmth and brightness of the restaurant.

She lingered over her spaghetti and garlic bread, taking a long time to finish the meal. At last, reluctantly, she paid her bill and left, ducking her head as she hurried through the rain to her van in the parking lot.

By now, it was dark and the storm raged fiercely. The rain was pouring down with such force, it was impossible to keep the windshield clear. As she drove, Meg leaned forward to peer at the road ahead where trees groaned and swayed in the wet glow of the headlights, and long stretches of highway were under water.

At last she pulled into the yard and entered the triple garage, grateful for the interior lights that came on automatically. She parked the van and checked the lock on the garage door, made sure the security devices were still activated, then went into the house, turning lights on as she went.

The first thing that struck Meg was the emptiness. She realized that she'd never been completely alone in this house. Even though her life since the accident had often seemed like a solitary, miserable existence, there had always been somebody else under the roof with her. Even Dommie would have been welcome company at the moment, she thought wistfully as she went through the foyer and paused by the curved staircase.

As she'd done every day since she heard about the accident, she looked up toward the landing, shuddering when she imagined Pauline Cantalini plunging down these stairs to her death.

And a man standing at the top, watching her as she fell...

Meg hugged her arms, gazing bleakly at the shadowed upstairs landing where rain pounded against an octagonal window of leaded glass.

Had Victor Cantalini slipped back from that fishing trip to dispose of his wife, leaving his "old friend" behind at their camp in the mountains to furnish him with an alibi?

His old friend Clay Malone, Meg thought bitterly. The man who'd told her several times that Victor was unaware Clay had ever been in Utah.

But why had Clay been so insistent that she not tell Victor about his visits? Was he really Lisa's cousin, or was all that a lie, too? And if so, why didn't he...

The thoughts whirled through her mind in a weary circle of questions that had no answers. Meg moaned and pressed her hands to her temples. Finally, she turned away to hang her jacket in the hall closet, then began to climb the stairs.

A sound caught her attention, a soft distant thump that echoed in the stillness. Meg paused on the stairs and gripped the railing, her heart pounding. She strained to listen, trying to pinpoint the source of the noise. But the wind howled around the eaves of the big house, driving the rain so hard against the windows that the world was filled with sounds.

She shook her head and hurried upstairs to her bedroom, comforted by the familiar warmth and luxury. Meg felt very close to Lisa now that she was alone in her sister's house. She wandered around the room, touching the smiling face in the photographs, opening the closet door to look at the expensive clothes hanging in rows.

Then she moved back out into the room and studied the huge oil painting above the bed.

Meg was no longer surprised at how easily the psychiatrist had been able to convince her that she was suffering from a divided personality. In a way, it was the truth. She and Lisa really were one person, somehow divided into two separate parts. In Lisa, Meg saw many aspects of herself that she'd recognized but never understood.

Her longing for her sister almost overwhelmed her. She couldn't bear to think that Lisa might be in danger somewhere.

Lisa could already be dead, a voice whispered inside her mind. Maybe she's dead, like Pauline, and you never even got to meet her...

"No!" Meg said aloud. "No!"

Suddenly, she froze, lifting her head, her eyes wide and fearful. She could hear footsteps on the lower floor, moving quietly across the foyer. Meg stared wildly around the room, then edged out into the hallway and peered over the stair railing.

"Who's there?" she called. "Victor, is that you?"

But the house was silent again, the only sound was the wind shrieking outside. She'd left all the lights on when she came upstairs, and the brightness seemed to mock her. Outside the little window on the landing, a dripping tree branch swayed and tapped rhythmically on the leaded glass. Meg sagged against the railing.

It hadn't been footsteps at all. The noise from downstairs had been nothing more sinister than this gentle tapping. The house was empty, and the security system was functioning. Nobody could break in without triggering the alarm.

Except Victor, she thought. Victor knew the security code...

But that was ridiculous. Victor was away on a business trip. If he'd come home while she was gone, his car would have been in the garage.

Meg forced herself to go back to her room. She ran a bath and soaked for a long time. Then she went down to the kitchen in her nightgown and housecoat to make herself some hot chocolate.

Afterward she rinsed her mug, climbed the stairs to her room again and selected a book from a pile of paperbacks on the desk. She lay on her bed reading until her eyes were gritty and her head began to throb with weariness. Finally, she switched off the light and lay in the blackness listening to the howl of the wind and the breathing silence of the big house.

She was wakened from a fitful sleep by another noise. Again she heard footsteps moving toward the stairs. Her breath caught in her throat, and her heart began to thud noisily as she waited for the sound to get closer. But the steps seemed to recede a little, then stopped altogether.

Meg sat up in bed and switched on the light, looking at the telephone. She needed to call somebody—anybody—just to hear a comforting voice on the other end of the line.

The hospital, she decided. She'd call the hospital and ask how Dommie was doing, and if Filomena needed anything. Nobody would mind if she called, because people were on duty all night. Filomena was probably spending a sleepless night, too. It would be so good if she could talk to the housekeeper for a little while and hear a familiar voice.

She rummaged through the list of emergency numbers on a card in the top drawer of the night table, found a listing for the hospital and lifted the receiver. But there was no dial tone.

The lines must have blown down in the storm, Meg told herself.

Her words did nothing to stop the wave of terror that gripped her. A wave so intense that her stomach churned with nausea. She replaced the phone and huddled in her bed, hugging her knees as she stared at the drapes pulled across the window.

Her lips began to tremble and she choked back a soft whimper of panic.

Suddenly, she had an overwhelming urge to be away from this house. Her mind darted around feverishly, wondering where she could go.

Jim Leggatt's house! She would go next door.

Trudy was over there, just a few hundred yards away, plump and comfortable and sensible. Trudy would give her a bed for the night and a glass of homemade wine to chase away her fears. And in the morning, when it was light again, these midnight terrors would look as silly and childish as the bad dreams that sometimes wakened Dommie at night.

Meg dressed hastily, took her keys from the dresser and ran downstairs. She pulled on her raincoat and went down the hall to the garage, planning to slip through the side door and go across the yard to the neighboring house.

Inside the garage, she looked around, wondering again if Victor could somehow have returned home while she was away. But only two vehicles were parked in the garage, the muddy van Meg had driven home earlier in the evening, and her little white Thunderbird.

Lisa's Thunderbird, she corrected herself, pausing by the car.

The car someone had somehow put Meg into. Had that person or persons drugged her before they'd sent her and the car over the cliff?

No matter how confusing later events had become, Meg was becoming utterly convinced of one thing. The person who engineered that accident had wanted her to die.

She hurried toward the door at the side of the garage, remembering to punch in the security code before she switched off the lights and reached for the doorknob.

"Meg?" a voice called softly, from somewhere inside the house.

Meg turned and stared into the garage, where the door to the house was still open. She stared through it at the lighted hallway, wondering if she could have imagined that ghostly call.

"Who is it?" she asked, her words sounding loud and frightened in the stillness. "Is somebody in there?"

"Meg, come and help me! Please, help me..."

The voice was her own.

26

Meg's hand fell away from the doorknob. She took a ew steps back into the garage.

"Lisa?" she whispered, peering through the darkness it the open door and the carpeted hallway beyond. 'Lisa, where are you?"

"In here," the voice called, "I'm in the house. Please urry, Meg."

Meg started toward the open door, passing the Thunlerbird and edging around the mud-smeared side of the ig van. Suddenly, she dropped to one knee and crouched t the front of the van, holding her breath.

Footsteps sounded behind her, cautious and muffled n the concrete floor. They slowed when she did, then topped altogether.

Meg huddled against the van's heavy front bumper, igging her fingernails into her palms as she strained to sten. Even through the noisy pounding of rain on the led roof, she could hear someone breathing, a conolled, regular sound that was unspeakably menacing.

Wildly, she tried to gauge the distance to the open door here a bright wedge of light from the hallway spilled to the garage. The person behind her in the darkness ust still be a few feet away, hiding somewhere near the ck of the Thunderbird. If she got up and ran, she could reach that open door before he did and slam it closed, locking him in the garage.

She squinted at the door, wondering if she dared to whisper a warning to Lisa before she made a run for it. Desperately, she searched the floor for something, anything to use as a weapon.

An old tire iron would do, or even one of Victor's golf clubs.

But there was nothing within reach except a pile of concrete blocks stacked untidily near the door. Meg remembered the crew who'd been at the house earlier in the day to fix a retaining wall weakened by the steady downpour. They must have stored some extra blocks in the garage...

Her scattered thoughts were interrupted by a furtive noise behind her, coming around the side of the van. She had a sense of some large predatory animal creeping forward in the darkness, muscles rippling as it gathered itself to spring.

Meg took the bundle of keys from her pocket and gripped them in her hand, pushing the long, heavy ignition key out between her fingers to use as a gouge. Then with a final galvanizing surge of terror, she burst from her hiding place and flung herself toward the open door.

Arms gripped her from behind. She was pulled into fierce embrace, held so tightly that her struggles were as feebly ineffectual as the wriggling of a child. A black gloved hand closed over hers and wrested the keys away from her, then twisted one of her arms brutally behind her back.

Meg screamed in pain and her body went limp.

"That's better," a voice whispered against her ear, the breath hot on her neck. "That's better, Meg. Just take easy and this won't hurt at all."

There was a silence, then a soft, mocking laugh.

"Well, maybe I shouldn't say that," the voice went on. "It might hurt a little bit, kid, but it'll be over real soon."

"Clay," Meg said, struggling to twist her head and get a look at her assailant. "It's Clay, isn't it?"

He gave her arm another vicious yank. "Shut up!"

Meg's hands were seized and tied firmly behind her back with some kind of tape that felt like an elastic tensor bandage.

She bit her lip and stared at the light flowing through the hallway door, trying to calm herself. "Where's Lisa?' she asked.

"Lisa's inside you, kid," the voice whispered against her neck.

This time it was unmistakable. The intruder who held her was the same handsome young man who'd been so warm and affectionate during all those afternoon visits, the man who called himself Lisa's cousin.

"You're a multiple personality, remember?" he added with sneering emphasis. "Even your shrink believes that."

"But it's not true. Lisa's my twin sister, and you know it, don't you?"

"Twins?" he said in mock surprise, still holding her from behind with a grip of steel while he checked the tapes on her wrists. "Well, isn't that an interesting theory? Whatever gave you that idea, sweetheart?"

"I went to Reno just like you did, and talked to the old doctor who delivered us."

"What a smart girl. It's a pity you don't have anybody to confide in, isn't it? Because nobody else is ever going to know about those little twin babies."

Meg panted and struggled against his grasp, twisting again to get a look at him.

"Where's Lisa?" she asked. "What have you done with her?"

She had a confused impression of darkness, a black sweater and knitted cap and black smears of greasepaint on a hard tanned face. He squeezed her neck with his thumb and forefinger, making her scream aloud.

The man released the pressure slightly, still holding her with his other arm. "What's taking you so long?" he called toward the door. "We can't stay here all night."

"I'm coming," a woman's voice said from the hallway. "Where is she? I don't want her to see me."

"She sees you every day in the mirror," Clay said, yanking Meg's arms again. "Come on, when did you get so squeamish?"

But he pulled Meg around and turned her away, facing her into the gloom of the garage while someone else came through the hallway door.

"What took so long?" he asked tensely.

"I was trying to find something big enough," the woman said, coming nearer. "Dommie only has a bunch of little stuff."

"Lisa?" Meg whispered, straining in Clay's grip as she tried to look over his shoulder toward the light. "Lisa, is that you? Help me!"

"Make her shut up, can't you?" the woman's voice said nervously. "It gives me the creeps listening to her."

The man drew Meg into another forced embrace, then reached around and stuffed her mouth full of bunched fabric, wedging it so hard between her teeth that her jaws ached.

"Now she won't talk," he said with cold satisfaction. "Put it over there, right by the door. No, a little more to the side. Remember, she's already been in and out a cou ple of times and the kid isn't home. It has to be off to one side where she wouldn't have noticed it unless she—"

"I know, I know," the woman said impatiently. "We've been over this a million times." Meg trembled, gagging against the mass of fabric bunched inside her mouth. She felt herself being pulled forward, hauled toward the doorway that led to the house, while footsteps followed close behind, the man's and the woman's.

One of Dommie's trucks stood near the doorway, its chunky red wheels looking bright and incongruous in the wash of light. Meg could even make out the little driver with his tiny plastic hard hat, and the green pull cord lying on the concrete floor.

"See that truck?" Clay whispered behind her. "Little kids shouldn't leave their toys lying around, should they, Meggie? A person could trip over that thing and take a nasty fall. It's really dangerous."

With those words, he pushed her forward harshly. Her feet blundered against the truck and sent it skittering across the floor. Meg felt herself plunging forward. The side of her head banged with sickening force against the pile of concrete blocks and she fell to her knees.

"Poor Meg," the man's voice said behind her. He knelt above her, pushing her down onto the floor. "She tripped over the nasty old truck and banged her head, and now she can't get up. And you know what? She left her van running. Now what's going to happen to her?"

Meg lay on her stomach with her cheek pressed against the gritty concrete. She rolled her eyes wildly to look up at him. He was bending close to her, holding her down with a knee pressed hard between her shoulder blades. They were closer to the lighted doorway now, but Meg could barely make out his face through the waves of pain.

"Does she have the keys?" the woman's voice asked. Meg strained to see her, but Clay's looming torso blocked out everything else.

"They were right in her hand," he said with amusement, pressing harder against Meg's back. "She was all set to use them as a weapon. She's a feisty little thing, this sister of yours."

"Shut up, Clay," the woman whispered urgently. "God, it almost seems like you're enjoying this."

"Aren't you enjoying yourself, kid?" he asked, looking over his shoulder into the darkness. He grinned, his teeth flashing white against his skin. "After all the planning, don't you think it's fun to be doing it?"

"Just shut up and give me the keys."

He dug into his pocket and handed the keys behind him, still kneeling on Meg's back.

Meg choked into the gagging mass of cloth, listening in confusion as the van engine roared to life beside her. Hands worked busily at her ankles, binding her legs together with more of the heavy medical tape.

"Do you see what's going to happen, Meg?" Clay asked, leaning down close to her. "It's one of those rea sad things. Just a tragic accident. Lisa Cantalini was home all alone tonight, see? She's been pretty mixed-up lately, and she must have got scared and had a sudden urge to go for a drive, even though it was storming. She came down and started her van, then remembered some thing she'd forgotten and decided to run back into the house to get it. But she tripped over the kid's truck, fel down and knocked herself out."

Meg listened to his voice in growing horror. Beside her she could see the toy truck near the wall and a pair c slender feet and ankles next to the man's body.

"Of course, the coroner might be a little suspicious if he saw this gag and the bindings on your wrists and ankles, wouldn't he? But they won't be there anymore, kid. They'll just stay on long enough for you to fall asleep. Then we'll take them off and get out of here, and you'll be one more statistic. Poor Mrs. Cantalini, just a tragic accident."

Meg grunted and flailed, trying to work the bindings loose from her wrists.

"And poor Victor," Clay said in a gentle musing voice. "His first wife falls down the stairs and the second one is asphyxiated. It might look a bit odd, but there's going to be no problem. It's another accident, that's all. Just a real sad accident." He slapped the side of Meg's head and she lay still.

"For God's sake, stop it, Clay," the woman's voice said nervously. "Quit talking to her."

"Hey, relax. There's nothing to be worried about," he said, getting up.

Meg felt a brief moment of relief to have his weight lifted from her back. She moaned and turned her head on the cold concrete.

She saw the slim ankles again, clad in black tights. A dark form hovered nearby and Meg looked up to see a woman's face, so much like her own that she felt another flood of sickness. She stared wildly up into those dark blue eyes, choking on the gag in her mouth. For a long moment, Lisa crouched beside her, gazing into her face with an unfathomable expression. At last she reached out and touched Meg with a thoughtful gloved hand, lifting the tumbled hair away from her sister's forehead.

Lisa whispered something, but Meg couldn't make out the words. Then she got to her feet and hurried out of the garage without a backward glance, followed by Clay.

The door closed behind them, cutting off the light. Meg lay in the blackness next to the roaring vehicle, trying to breathe shallowly as the killing fumes seeped through the air and swirled across the floor of the garage.

She heard a noisy, insistent ringing and wondered if the phones had been connected again. Then she realized that the ringing was inside her own head. Her eyelids drooped and her body felt heavy and inert. After a long, long time, she sensed movement. Dimly she felt the gag being removed from her mouth and the bindings unwrapped from her wrists and ankles.

Finally, she was alone in the dark again, with the purring of the van's engine sounding gentle and soothing in her ears. She understood vaguely that she was untied and she could get up if she wanted, but she was far too sleepy.

"Too sleepy," she murmured aloud, nestling cozily on the floor. "I'll just sleep a while longer, and then I'll get up. Just sleep a little while..."

She smiled, drowsy and contented, and let herself drift away into nothingness.

Jim's truck pounded through the rain on the freeway, heading north. After nightfall, he passed Cedar City and kept going, trying to comfort himself with the knowledge that the trip was half over. He peered down the edge of the freeway where the grade steepened, and thought about the way Lisa's car had been sent over the cliff with Meg inside.

He shook his head in despair, wondering how he could have been so blind, so easily deceived. He should have understood right from the beginning that there were two separate women, not a divided personality.

It was because of the psychiatrist, he decided, frowning through the streams of water on the windshield. People were so ready to believe the opinions of a professional.

He should have listened instead to the reactions of his own body. Though he'd never liked Lisa Cantalini, Jim had been powerfully drawn to Meg the first time he saw her. At some level, he must have sensed the difference, but he hadn't paid enough attention to his instincts.

He groaned and pressed down harder on the gas pedal, hoping desperately that he'd be able to get there in time. He tried not to torture himself by thinking about what might be happening in Salt Lake. All he knew was that Meg was in danger. The car going over the cliff had certainly not been an accident. And whoever had tried to kill her, would no doubt try again. He had to get to her first. Of course, if Meg wasn't at home to answer the phone, she could be anywhere. How would he ever find her in this storm?

But there was no point in brooding over the possibilities. All he could do was get there and start looking for her. Grimly, he drove through the streaming night, his hands tense on the wheel, his face hard with purpose.

Rain was still pouring down and the wind howling fiercely in the trees when he reached the farm around midnight. He splashed through the water to his house, letting himself in and startling Trudy. The housekeeper was watching television, sitting next to a small balding man in corduroy slacks and a cardigan.

"Jim," she said in surprise. "I didn't expect you home for days."

"Something came up," he said tersely. "Trudy, do you know if—"

"This is Oswald," Trudy said, indicating the man beside her. "Oswald, this is my boss, Jim Leggatt."

Jim gave the man a distracted nod. He saw the glow on Trudy's face and realized with detached sadness that his housekeeper was in love. No doubt, she would be leaving soon, along with her milking goats and jugs of homemade wine, her gossip and laughter and lively opinions, and he was going to miss her terribly.

But right now, he had no time to think about the future.

"Trudy, is anybody home next door?" he asked from the doorway.

"Dommie's in the hospital," Trudy said. "And Filomena's staying in town tonight. Why?"

"Is Victor home?"

"I don't think so. His wife is over there, though."

Jim tensed. "She is? How do you know?"

"All the lights are on," Trudy said. "And I saw her come home a few hours ago in the van. Right after supper, I think it was. She must have taken Filomena into town, then come right back."

"You haven't heard anything from over there?" he asked urgently. "No other vehicles coming and going, nothing like that?"

"Not that I recall." Trudy got to her feet and moved toward him. "Why, Jim? What's the matter?"

"I'm not sure. Are the phones working?"

Trudy picked up the receiver from a table nearby and listened, then nodded. "Ours sounds fine."

"Dial the Cantalinis," Jim said, heading for the locked cabinet in the office where he kept his guns.

Trudy glanced at him in alarm, then obeyed. After a few moments, she came down the hall and watched as he selected one of his rifles, a workmanlike Winchester carbine with a dull wooden stock.

"Their phone just rings and rings," she said. "There's no answer."

Jim checked the sights, then unlocked a drawer and took out a handful of shells. He loaded the gun and pocketed some more ammunition.

"But you never saw her leave?" he asked.

Trudy shook her head. "Oswald came around eight o'clock and we've been watching television ever since. She could have driven away without my noticing."

"If the phone lines were cut," Jim said, "and you dialed in, the phone would still ring, wouldn't it?"

"Probably. Jim, what's going on?" Trudy's eyes wid-ened as he shouldered past her and headed for the door vith the gun in his hands.

"Wait a few minutes," he said. "If you don't hear nything from me, call the police."

"Jim!" she wailed while the other man stood next to er in the hallway, looking bewildered. "Jim, for God's ake..."

He closed the door and plunged out into the rain, hur-ying across the muddy yard toward the neighboring ouse. At the edge of the property, he crouched in the hadows of a tall cedar tree.

Most of the lights were on in the stone mansion, glim-ering through the storm. He could see the illuminated itchen, the downstairs lamps, even a light from the sec-nd-floor bedroom window where Meg had sat and watched him so often during the summer, silent and sad in her blue housecoat.

Meg had been a virtual prisoner up there, trapped and isolated, somehow made to believe that she'd lost both her mind and her identity.

Rage stabbed through him, and a wave of emotion so urgent and powerful it made him shudder. Then he took himself in hand and made a rapid assessment of the situation.

The garage was at the rear of the house, so he couldn't tell if it, too, was lit. Of course, if Meg had been frightened and left, she wouldn't have needed to leave the garage lit because those lights probably came on automatically when the door was activated.

Maybe she wasn't home at all, Jim thought hopefully Maybe she'd driven back into town to spend the night at the hospital with Filomena, and all his worries were fo nothing.

If so, he'd never let her out of his sight again. Not un til he knew who was threatening her, and why.

He gripped his rifle in both hands and sprinted to ward the front door, checking all the windows as he went They were secure and the house was silent.

Jim hesitated, wondering whether to ring the door bell. He decided against it, reasoning that if Meg was in side and in some kind of danger, a ringing doorbell woul alarm her captors and threaten her even more.

He slipped around the side of the house and starte edging toward the rear of the house between the pool an the terrace, hoping to get a look inside the garage and se which vehicles were there.

Suddenly, he heard something. He caught his brea and flattened himself against the wall of the hous straining to listen. Voices came to him from the terra-

next to the garage, muffled and distorted by the heavy downpour.

Jim shrank back under the dripping eaves in the shadow of a leafy trellis. He held his rifle and peered cautiously through the vines at the terrace.

27

A brass-framed coach lamp shone through the wet shrubbery at the far side of the terrace, casting a faint glow on the flagstones and the two people who huddled under the overhanging roof.

They seemed to be arguing. Jim moved around the trellis and edged closer to them along the wall of the house. He crouched in the shadows and strained to hear what they were saying.

The taller of the two made an angry gesture and moved aside, turning briefly to face the dark alcove where Jim was hiding.

Although he'd only seen the man a couple of times, Jim recognized him as Clay Malone, Lisa's "cousin," whose visits caused Trudy such displeasure. Clay was wearing dark clothes and a close-fitting knitted cap. His face was smeared with some kind of black greasepaint, making him look like a jungle fighter.

Jim gripped his rifle and peeked through the tangle of vines. A woman came into view, also wearing black. Jim sagged with relief when he saw that it was Meg.

But when she spoke, he tensed again and gripped the rifle more tightly. There was something odd about the way she held her head, the look on her face...

Suddenly, his skin prickled with horror and he edged deeper into the shadows. Instinctively, Jim knew that the woman wasn't Meg at all. It was Lisa Cantalini.

"I can't do it," she was saying. "I just can't do it, Clay."

"Can't do what? Come on!" He yanked harshly at her arm.

"I don't want to leave her like that. It's not... not right."

"Not right!" he jeered. "Since when did you give a damn about right and wrong, kid? We sure as hell can't turn back now. We've been planning this for months."

"I know we have. But when I saw her like that, it felt... different."

"What do you intend to do?" he asked furiously. "Let her go, so she can run around telling the whole story? Is that what you want?"

Jim relaxed a little, still gripping his rifle. At least Meg was still alive. Whatever they were planning to do, they hadn't carried it out yet.

"I don't want to do this," Lisa repeated stubbornly.

"Well, I don't care what you want," Clay told her. "Look, this isn't kid stuff, you know."

He moved closer to her, turning so Jim could see both of them clearly, and went on speaking.

"That woman in there is my beloved cousin, name of Lisa Cantalini. She's got a life-insurance policy for a million dollars naming me as her beneficiary. And there's a double-indemnity clause in case of accidental death," Clay added, his face twisting unpleasantly. "So she's worth two million dollars. For that kind of money, you'd damn well better forget your squeamishness."

"But what if the insurance company refuses to pay? We can't be sure they'll give you the money without an argument."

"They paid for Pauline, didn't they? Come on," he added, grabbing at her arm again.

Lisa jerked away from him. "What does Pauline have to do with this?"

"Nothing. Come *on,* kid. We don't have any time to waste."

"Tell me!" she shouted. "What did you mean about Pauline?"

He smiled coldly. "Well, think about it. Pauline died, right? And Victor collected a tidy pile of money and you got the rich husband you always wanted. Accidents can be real profitable, kid."

"But..." She rubbed her arm slowly. "But Pauline fell down the stairs. Filomena saw her."

"Sure she did," he said with a cold smile.

"Why would Filomena say that if it wasn't true?"

"Filomena's a smart girl. She knows what's good for her, and for that little kid of hers, too. Look," Clay added, leaning toward her, "nobody ever said a thing about that accident. And they aren't going to connect me with this one, either, as long as we both stay cool. That's the important thing."

Lisa's face turned even paler. "Was it *you,* Clay?" she whispered. "Did you push her down the stairs?"

"Come on," he said. "Stop talking and let's get out of here."

She resisted, standing tensely at the edge of the terrace while the rain flowed off the roof in silvery torrents.

"Why?" she asked. "What did you ever have against Pauline?"

"Nothing," he said curtly. "I was just doing Victor a little favor, that's all."

"But..." She stared at him in confusion. "But you didn't even know Victor when Pauline died. You never met him until we..."

Clay laughed harshly. "God, you're stupid, Lisa. You've always been so wrapped up in yourself that you couldn't even see what was happening in front of your own eyes."

"I don't know what you mean."

"Victor and I go way, way back, kid. He and I, we've had a lot of business dealings over the years."

Lisa turned away, frowning.

Clay gave her a mocking grin. "Remember that night you first met me at the bar? You thought you were pretty bold, didn't you, hitting on a handsome dude and taking him home behind your husband's back."

She listened in appalled silence.

"Victor set the whole thing up, kid. He sent me down to that bar to meet you."

"*Victor* sent you? Why?"

"He figured you were probably getting ready to have a little fling. Victor wanted somebody around to keep an eye on you, maybe even give you a taste of what Pauline got if you strayed too far."

She looked up at him in horror. "Victor wanted you to *kill* me?"

"It was an option," Clay said casually. "You and I weren't the only ones with a big life-insurance policy on you, kid. Victor had one, too. And he'd already found out that it wasn't so great to have a beautiful young wife. He wasn't about to be made a fool of, not after what he'd sacrificed. Don't forget, he'd killed for you."

"But why did he..." She twisted her hands together nervously. "Did Victor know about everything else, too? Did you tell him you were going to Reno to find my birth parents?"

"Of course. He was paying for it, remember? You thought you were so smart, pretending I was your cousin and making Victor pay for my investigation into your past. And all the time, he and I knew exactly what was going on."

"Even Meg?" she asked tensely. "Did Victor know about Meg?"

Clay shook his head. "When I found out about your twin, I thought maybe you and I should keep that little secret to ourselves. What Victor didn't know wasn't going to hurt him. Lisa could die, her husband and cousin could both collect the insurance money and nobody would ever be the wiser."

"What about me, Clay?" she asked bitterly. "Were you keeping secrets from me, too? Were you going to dispose of her, then kill me and keep all the money for yourself?"

"Come on, kid," he said with another mocking smile. "You know how much I love you."

She watched him coldly. "Did Victor ever find out about Meg?"

"No. He thought she was you. And you know what?" he asked with a broad grin. "Poor old Victor started to like his wife again. I guess your sister's a whole lot nicer than you are, sweetheart." His smile faded. "Victor called me a few days after the accident, told me his wife wasn't feeling well and I should stay away from her. The bastard," he added with a vicious scowl. "After all we've been through, he tried to throw me away like I was nothing more than a hired thug."

She hesitated for a moment longer, then turned abruptly and started running through the rain, heading for the other side of the house.

Clay shouted in outrage, plunged after her and caught her easily. He hauled her back to the terrace, gripping her arm while she kicked and fought. He turned her around and began hitting her with such force that her head flopped from side to side like a doll's.

Jim had seen enough. Within seconds, he was behind Clay, jabbing the rifle sharply against the man's ribs.

"Okay," he said quietly. "That's it. Let her go and put your hands up. Start moving toward the house."

Clay released the woman. She dropped to the flagstones, moaning. Jim glanced down at her briefly, and Clay made a grab for the rifle.

Jim held on to it and swung fiercely, hitting the other man's head with a glancing blow. Clay staggered backward, then lunged toward him again. Jim crouched and braced himself, reversing the rifle in his hands. He swung the wooden stock, connecting with Clay's head and shoulders. The man fell to his knees and Jim struck him again.

Clay crumpled onto the floor and lay still. A pool of blood began to seep from under his body, running across the stones and into the damp grass.

Jim looked down at him, feeling sick, then crossed the terrace to kneel beside the woman. He lifted her to a sitting position and she grimaced in pain.

"Lisa," Jim said urgently. "Where is she? Where's Meg?"

Lisa looked up at him blearily. Her face was dark with bruises, and blood trickled from her swollen mouth.

"Lisa," Jim said, resisting the urge to shake her. "Tell me! Where's Meg?"

"Garage," she whispered at last. "Please...please hurry!"

Jim ran across the wet grass and fumbled for the garage door. It was locked. He swore in frustration, then pressed against the window where he could hear a dull roaring sound that throbbed above the noise of the storm.

Confused, he cupped his hands and peered through the glass. The garage was dark and silent, but one of the vehicles seemed to be running.

Suddenly, Jim shouted aloud in horror and smashed wildly at the glass with the stock of his rifle. He climbed through the jagged opening, heedless of the sharp edges that tore at his skin and clothing, and tumbled onto the concrete floor. Then he picked himself up and moved between the parked vehicles in a running crouch, pausing beside the van to switch off the ignition.

"Meg," he whispered, peering into the hot darkness, his mouth dry with terror. "Meg..."

When he moved toward the door to find the light switch, he tripped over her body.

He turned on the lights and knelt to look at her, then ran back to press the switch and open the garage door. Fresh air poured in, along with a cold gust of wind.

Jim hurried back inside the garage and lifted her in his arms. He carried her to the open door and knelt beside her.

She was limp and still. Her face was very pale under the harsh fluorescent light, her lips cherry red. Blood trickled through her hair from a wound in her scalp, smearing her neck and ear.

"Oh, God," he moaned, holding her and rocking on his heels. "Oh, Meg..."

Tenderly, he set her down on the floor and bent to press his mouth against hers, trying to breathe life back into her body. Somewhere in his desperate thoughts, he was aware of the bitter irony, the fact that he'd never even had the chance to kiss her.

She was immobile. He kept working, breathing and releasing, pressing his hands rhythmically on her body while tears ran down his cheeks.

Rain pounded and slashed against him, soaking his clothes and plastering his hair against his face. Time passed, but he was unaware of it. He didn't even pause or look up when he heard, above the roar of the storm, the faint wail of sirens speeding toward him through the night.

Epilogue

Winter blanketed the canyon with white, then gave way to the tender green of spring. The seasons rolled on, painting colors on the hillside and transforming the creek bed as they passed.

A second year went by, and another summer. Cold weather flowed down the mountains again, dusting the valley with snow that covered the frozen surface of the creek and weighed heavily on the branches of the evergreens. The big house in the canyon was decked out for Christmas, glowing with holly boughs and colored lights, fragrant with the scent of pine and fresh baking.

Meg woke in the pearly, frost-sparkled stillness of early morning and stretched drowsily in her bed, as contented as a kitten. But when she remembered what the day held, her face sobered.

She rolled over to switch on the bedside lamp, then sat up against a mound of pillows, thinking. A small dark head appeared at the doorway and Dommie peeped in at her, smiling shyly, still dressed in his yellow pajamas.

Meg smiled back at him and patted the mattress beside her, watching as he hurried across the room to climb onto the bed.

Dommie was approaching his fifth birthday this Christmas, losing his round baby look and beginning to display the leggy tallness of childhood. He carried a large notepad and a handful of felt pens, which he showed her when he was settled in the bed.

"I'm writing a letter to Santa," he said.

"Are you, sweetie?" Meg pulled the covers cozily up around the small boy and drew him close to her. "What are you asking for?"

"A new sled and a Super Builder set. How do you write 'Santa'?"

Meg considered. "I think maybe you should just draw a picture," she said. "Santa will know. Do a picture of him, then draw the things you want and write your name at the bottom."

He looked dubious. "Will Santa know what the pictures are?"

"Santa always knows what pictures are."

Dommie nodded, apparently satisfied. He bent over his notepad, gripping the pen firmly in his hand.

Filomena appeared in the doorway, her dark face softening with affection as she looked at the two.

"Trudy just called," she reported. "She and Oswald are coming over for Christmas dinner."

"Oh, wonderful!" Meg said. "I thought they were going to Barbados this year."

"They're leaving a few days after Christmas. Trudy likes sunshine. She's always hated the clouds and snow in January."

"Well, it's going to be nice and sunny today," Meg said. "Perfect for driving."

The housekeeper came into the bedroom and peered out the window. "I'm not happy about this," she said. "I still don't think you should go. Not in your condition."

"I know you don't," Meg said cheerfully. "But I'm going just the same. Don't worry about me so much. I'll be home before you know it."

Filomena drew back the curtains, then stood looking down at Meg. "He's going to be upset when he finds out where you've gone," she said.

Meg thought about her husband, and her body warmed with tenderness.

"Maybe," she agreed, slipping out of bed and moving toward the bathroom. "But he'll get over it. Tell him I love him, and I'll try to be home before dark."

Two hours later, Meg was driving steadily north, heading across the state line into Idaho and up toward the remote country beyond Pocatello. She munched on egg salad sandwiches Filomena had packed and, soon after noon, she began to check the road signs with increasing nervousness.

Finally, she pulled off the freeway and headed down an obscure side road for several miles, driving toward a barbed-wire fence beyond which a sprawl of concrete buildings formed a large compound.

She was checked through a security gate and subjected to a cursory search in an entry port, then ushered into a visiting room with long banks of cubicles, each containing a wooden shelf and single chair.

Meg sat down in one of the chairs, her heart pounding, grateful for a pair of tall fabric-covered screens that separated her from the adjacent cubicles. She rested her arms on the scarred wooden shelf and looked at the window in front of her. Sturdy wire mesh was contained within the glass, pierced by a neat pattern of small holes about twelve inches above the shelf that allowed voices to carry to the other side, where another chair sat empty.

Meg looked up as the door opened and a group of women in faded blue dresses were ushered into the room. One of the women separated herself from the group and crossed the floor to face Meg through the glass-covered wire mesh.

Even without makeup and in shapeless prison garb, Lisa Cantalini was beautiful, her stride was fluid and graceful. She seated herself, and gazed through the glass at her visitor.

"Well, well," she murmured as she leaned back in the chair. "Look who's here."

Meg shifted uneasily. She hadn't seen her sister face-to-face since that autumn night more than two years ago, when Lisa and Clay had left her alone in the garage. She was astounded all over again by the uncanny similarity between them, as if her personality had somehow divided and taken on separate but identical forms.

Lisa watched her, smiling slightly, and made no move to say anything further.

"You look...you look really good," Meg said at last, clearing her throat awkwardly.

Lisa laughed with genuine amusement. "Well, I have a private hairdresser and makeup artist in this luxury spa," she said. "And I have nothing to do but look after myself."

Meg was silent, wondering what else to say.

"Actually, I'm getting used to having my hair like this," Lisa went on casually, ruffling her short-cropped dark hair. "I always kept it long before."

"I know. I saw the pictures. But," Meg said, "you had it short when I...when you were..."

"I had to," Lisa said, glancing at her in surprise.

"Why?"

"So I'd look like you," Lisa said, as if puzzled by her sister's obtuseness.

Meg shifted in the chair once more, battling another wave of sickness. She'd been steeling herself for over a year to make this visit, but she still wasn't prepared for the reality of sitting across from her sister, close enough to touch her if the glass and steel were removed.

"I never understood everything that happened," she said at last. "That's why I decided to come. I wanted to ask you about... about what you did."

Lisa shrugged. "Too bad we plea bargained and never went to trial. You'd have learned the whole story."

"I couldn't bear the thought of a trial," Meg said with a shudder. "I was so glad when they told me I wouldn't have to testify. Besides," she added, looking down at a set of initials scratched into the wooden surface of the self, "I was... By the time the case was ready to go to trial, I was pregnant, and not feeling very well. We hadn't planned on it, but it just happened."

"So, what did you have?" Lisa asked, sounding bored.

"I miscarried at four months." Meg bit her lip and looked up at her sister. "It was twins," she said. "Twin girls."

"No kidding?" Lisa asked. "Probably just as well, then," she added with a faint smile.

Meg nodded, briefly overcome by her memories of that terrible time, of her husband's sorrow and her own pain.

"I'm pregnant again," she said after a moment. "I'm due in May."

"Twins again?"

Meg shook her head. "Not this time."

"Did you have any bad effects?" Lisa asked. "From the gas, I mean?"

"Nothing permanent. The garage was so big that the concentration near the floor wasn't too bad, and I hadn't breathed enough of it by the time they found me to do any real damage. I guess it wouldn't have taken much longer, though."

Meg fell silent, almost unable to believe that they were actually having this conversation.

"So," Lisa said at last, "I heard you married the cowboy."

"Yes," Meg said smiling. "I married Jim Leggatt."

"And you're living in his house?"

"Of course."

"Doesn't it feel weird to look at the other place, right next door?"

"It used to," Meg said. "But Victor's house was cleared out and sold a long time ago. A dentist owns it now, and they have five kids. It's pretty lively over there."

Lisa grimaced. "Five kids. I can imagine what the inside must be like. I loved that house, you know," she said with a faraway look.

"So did I," Meg said. "I guess we have the same taste in a lot of things."

"Except for men."

Meg thought about Clay Malone's strange green eyes and cruel, handsome face. He was so utterly different from Jim, with his boyish warmth and kindness and his wholesome blond looks.

"Funny how the cowboy would be so attracted to you," Lisa said. "He never liked me very much. But then, you and I are different people, aren't we?"

"Yes," Meg said quietly. "I think we are."

"I'm certain Clay was planning to double-cross me, you know," Lisa said. "He probably would have disappeared as soon as he collected the insurance money."

"I want to know why you did it," Meg said at last. "I want to know if it was just for the money."

Lisa looked down, tracing a design on the shelf top with her finger. "Yes," she said. "That's why we did it."

"The only reason?"

"When we found out about you, the whole thing seemed perfect. You could die in my place and I could collect my own insurance money. What a great idea, right?"

"But how did you find out about me? Did you know all along, or what?"

"Clay found you."

"Why did you say he was your cousin?"

"I had to make something up to explain why he was around so much, and why he was the beneficiary on my insurance policy. I thought I was fooling Victor," Lisa said bitterly. "And all the time, it was Victor who'd arranged for me to meet Clay. He actually had Clay following me, keeping an eye on what I was doing. The sneaky bastards," she added darkly.

"But you never knew about Pauline, did you?"

"That they killed her?" Lisa shook her head. "I didn't have a clue. Not ever. I actually believed the poor old thing just fell downstairs when she was drunk. Victor was so stupid," she went on scornfully. "He never needed to kill her. We would have got married no matter what she did. I think he just felt guilty. He wanted me so much but every time he looked at Pauline he felt rotten about what he was doing. He killed her just so he wouldn't have to look at her anymore. And then he blamed me for making him do it."

"Victor didn't kill her," Meg said quietly.

Lisa shrugged, "Same thing. He got Clay to kill her." Her face hardened. "They fell all over themselves to implicate each other after they were arrested, didn't they? And now," she concluded with satisfaction, "both of them will be in jail for a long, long time."

"You're happy about that?"

"Of course I am. They deserve to go to the electric chair."

"I thought you loved Clay."

"I didn't know he was lying to me right from the beginning. I believed the whole story about how he'd never met Victor, all that crap."

"So did I. Clay kept telling me not to say anything to Victor about his visits."

"It was risky for him to keep seeing you after Victor told him not to," Lisa said. "But we had to know what you were doing, and what was happening inside the house. We couldn't afford to have our plan falling apart at that point."

"And it almost worked," Meg said in wonder. "If it hadn't been for Jim..."

"Jim Leggatt was a problem right from the start. Clay did the best he could, telling all those lies about the guy to scare you away from him, but your cowboy was just too persistent."

"How did you find me in the first place?" Meg asked again. "You must have known about me for a long time if it took so much planning."

"After I met Clay and fell in love with him, I told Victor he was my cousin, which was a lie, and that he was a private investigator, which happened to be the truth. I told Victor I wanted my cousin to find my birth parents. That was the truth, too, but it was also a good excuse to keep Clay around and give him some money. Victor was so tight with money," she said resentfully. "If I'd divorced him like I wanted to, I wouldn't have got a cent. That's why we had to think of something else. We were hoping maybe my birth family would have money, and we could do some kind of extortion thing."

"So Clay went to Reno."

Lisa nodded. "My mother had kept the address of that lawyer's office where I was adopted. Clay found the lawyer, then the hospital. He talked to the crazy old doctor and found out there'd been twin babies born that night. When he came back and told me, I was so—" Lisa fell abruptly silent.

"What?" Meg leaned forward tensely. "How did you feel when you found out?"

Lisa shook her head, looking down at the shelf. "It drove me crazy," she muttered. "I couldn't stand it. You were like all my worst nightmares coming true."

"Why?"

"Because I knew about you. I'd always known."

"Your mother told you we were twins?"

Lisa laughed harshly. "Terry? Hell, no. Terry never told me a thing. She didn't even have the guts to tell me I was adopted."

"Then how did you..."

"I think I remembered you," Lisa said. "You were always there. I'll bet I was born first, and I had about ten minutes of attention before you came along and spoiled everything."

"But..." Meg looked at her, bewildered. "We were never together. We must have been separated right away, and adopted within a week or so."

"It didn't make any difference. At some level, I always knew you existed, that you looked exactly like me but you were better than I was. God," Lisa said with a bleak smile, "I hated you so much when I was a little kid."

"I've been reading books about twins," Meg said, a little shaken by Lisa's intensity. "Apparently, it's fairly common for a separated twin to be aware of the other sibling. It's called 'shadowing.' I never felt it at all," she added.

"Why should you? You were growing up in a loving home, playing baseball and being treated like a normal kid."

"Maybe that's it." Meg was silent a moment. "So it wasn't just a calculated thing," she said at last. "You didn't just want to kill me for the money. It was partly because of the anger you'd always felt."

Lisa stared at the wall above Meg's head. "Maybe," she said. "I only know that when Clay told me I actually had a twin, I almost went out of my mind. Especially after he got a look at you and started raving about how identical we were."

"How did he find me?"

"It wasn't hard. Clay's a private investigator, remember? He was good at his job. He traced you and your father to that dude ranch and found out how you ran away after your father killed some guy."

Meg thought about poor Hank, with his faded blue eyes and clumsy goodness.

"I was so confused," she said at last. "That whole period after I ran away from the ranch became a kind of blur. I couldn't remember much when Dr. Wassermann questioned me. And I didn't know anybody in Vegas."

"Clay found all that stuff out, too. Our plan wouldn't have worked if you'd been in control of your life and had a lot of friends and family around. We didn't even start to consider it seriously until Clay saw how isolated you were in Vegas, all lost and pitiful like a hurt little puppy."

"So," Meg said, "the plan was to kidnap me and put me in your car, then send it over the freeway and kill me, right?"

"Right. But you didn't die. Uncooperative all the way," Lisa added with a grin.

Meg didn't return the smile. "That's one of the things I've always wondered about. Why take the chance? Why not kill me before you put me into the car?"

"We talked about it," Lisa said seriously. "It was all we talked about for months," she added with a faraway look. "We kept working out the whole plan, going over and over it from different angles. We planned how we'd snatch you and I'd go to Vegas right afterward and take your place in that kitchen so nobody would report you missing. After a while, none of it even seemed real any more. I mean, it wasn't like killing a real, breathing person. The whole thing was just an interesting challenge like figuring out a detective story. You know?"

Meg nodded silently.

"We couldn't risk killing you before you went in the car," Lisa went on, "because Victor's first wife had already died under suspicious circumstances so the police would be looking at it very carefully, especially with a the insurance on your. . . my life. We absolutely couldn't afford having them investigate and find out you were dead before the accident. We had to hope that you'd die in the crash, but we couldn't be sure that would happen."

"And that's where Dr. Wassermann came in," Meg said dryly.

Lisa gave a contemptuous wave of her hand. "Clare was so easy. We knew that if you didn't die, you we going to wake up and start telling people your name, so I had to plant a few seeds of doubt. When Victor suggested in the spring that I should get some counseling, I met Clara and I could see right away that she was a cold, ambitious bitch. I guess," she added cheerfully, "it takes one to know one, right?"

Meg didn't answer.

"What happened to Clara, anyhow?" Lisa asked.

"She left the city right after the three of you went to prison," Meg said.

"Didn't she lose her license or anything?"

"Nobody ever learned much about her part in the whole business. I was hardly inclined to sue her for malpractice. Anyway, she could always have argued that she nade an honest mistake. After all, you were prettyconincing."

Lisa looked amused. "So where did she go?"

"I think she moved to Los Angeles."

"Not such a bad idea, right? Maybe out in California ne can still find that fantastic case she's been looking or."

Meg looked away, reluctant to discuss the psychiatrist hose professional ambition had caused her such misy.

"Anyhow," Lisa went on, "I studied a lot about mulple personality and learned how rare it was. I knew lara would love to have a genuine, interesting case that e could write up and publish, so I laid the groundwork ring my therapy sessions, just in case you survived and arted talking about how you weren't Lisa Cantalini. I gured that after a few sessions, Clara would have you confused you wouldn't know who you were anymore. ot that Clay planned to let you go on talking for very ng," she added.

"It was all very, very clever," Meg said slowly. "I'm just beginning to understand how clever it was."

Lisa shrugged. "Like I told you, Clay and I spent months planning the whole thing. It was like a game."

"Who was the woman in Las Vegas? The other Megan Howell?"

"It was me," Lisa said. "Who else would it be?"

"But..." Meg looked at her in confusion. "You tolc Clara that Meg Howell talked to you in the spring, lon before any of this happened."

Lisa laughed with genuine amusement. "I was *lying*, you dummy. I had to say that, so there'd be some expla nation why Lisa Cantalini was suddenly claiming to b this completely other person."

"So there was never a time when you and I actuall met each other in Las Vegas? I kept wondering if mayb I'd seen you somewhere and then forgotten it along wit everything else."

"No," Lisa said, "we never met. Pretending that I' talked with Megan Howell in the past was just anothe part of the plan, that's all."

"It's all so incredible. Sometimes," Meg confessed, " lie awake at night and try to figure everything out, an the details still slip away from me."

"I told you, for months, Clay and I did nothing b plan. We'd spend hours making love and talking abo how we'd get that insurance money, and what we'd d with it after you died. But when I..."

Lisa paused, toying with a ragged bit of fabric at t edge of one of her pockets.

"What?" Meg asked. "What were you going to say?

"That night when I saw you in the garage..." Li looked up and met her glance, then turned away quick "It was different then," she murmured. "When I act ally saw you and looked into your eyes, it wasn't a game anymore. I didn't . . . like the feeling."

"But you'd seen me before, hadn't you? You must have been there the night Clay pushed your Thunderbird over the cliff."

"You were unconscious the whole time, and it was so dark. It wasn't the same."

"I don't remember anything about that night except or leaving the casino after work, but he must have given ne a really powerful dose of something. It's a long way ıp the freeway to Cedar City."

"Clay knew how to handle people, and to make them ınconscious if he wanted to."

Meg remembered those fingers on her neck, the delicate, exquisite pain of his grip. She shuddered and ıugged her arms. "It was him outside my room that night n Las Vegas, wasn't it? How did he get the keys?"

"It was easy. I pretended to be you and got an extra oom key from the front desk. Then Clay bribed a girl in ne office to make him an imprint of the dead bolt key. ut you'd found some way to bar the door," Lisa went n with a reminiscent smile. "Clay was so furious."

"Jim told me . . ." Meg paused awkwardly, then went n. "He told me how you fought with Clay that last ight, trying to help me."

They were both silent, avoiding each other's eyes in ıdden awkwardness. Faintly, scraps of other conversaons came to them from elsewhere in the visiting room, ıd they heard the hands of a big clock on the wall click ward the hour.

Finally, Meg cleared her throat and looked up. What's it like in here?" she asked. "Is it awful?"

"At first it was. But I'm getting used to it, and it's not bad anymore. Actually," Lisa said reluctantly, "it's kind of interesting. We have discussions and support groups, and I've made some friends. I never had friends before," she added with surprising candor. "Not even when I was a little girl."

"Why not?"

Lisa shrugged. "Terry kept me dressed up all the time and told me I was better than the other kids. And when I started winning a lot of pageants, the girls at school didn't want anything to do with me. I grew up seeing other women as competitors, not friends. But now it's different."

Meg nodded thoughtfully.

"And I'm taking college classes," Lisa went on sounding almost shy. "I hope to get my degree nex year."

"Really? I didn't know that."

Lisa smiled. "I got so interested in all that multiple personality stuff, I think I'd like to study more. If some body like Wassermann can be licensed to treat people maybe I can, too."

A female guard appeared in the doorway behind Lis and called something that was inaudible through th glass-covered wire mesh. Lisa got to her feet and Me stood up as well, bending toward the holes in the glass.

"Lisa," she said.

Lisa was already moving away. She paused, then toc a few steps back.

"I brought some things for you," Meg said. "Th warden needs to look at them before you can have them but they thought it would be all right."

"What kind of things?"

"Some makeup and chocolate, and a few books a magazines, and some...some Christmas presents," M said, flushing when she saw how her sister's eyebrows went up.

Lisa smiled at her through the glass. "You're really something, aren't you, Meg?" she murmured. "Really something."

"Lisa, I'd like to come back again sometime."

"Why?"

"Just to see you. To talk some more. Not about what happened," Meg added. "Just about . . . life."

Her sister's eyes shadowed and she turned away quickly before Meg could see her face.

"If you want to," Lisa said over her shoulder as she walked away, her voice so muffled that Meg could hardly make out the words. "I guess you can come back if you want to."

Then she was gone, disappearing through the door ahead of the guard without looking back.

Meg watched the closed door for a moment before she turned and left, wandering outside into the late-afternoon stillness. She left the prison compound, drove back onto the freeway and headed toward Utah.

The winter sun dropped low in the west, casting long blue shadows across the fields. Inside her, the baby stirred and fluttered. The movement was as gentle as the brushing of butterfly wings, so sweet and full of promise that tears gathered in her eyes. She gripped the wheel, watching a red-tailed hawk as it skimmed the fields near the road.

The sun slipped over the horizon and its last fading rays tipped the hawk's wings with bright gold.

Meg smiled through her tears and followed the golden wings south, toward home.

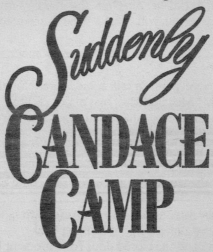

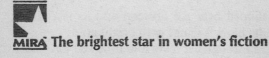

Award-winning author!

DEBBIE MACOMBER

They say opposites attract. Find out this March in

The Playboy

Cliff Howard drove an expensive sports car and was on a first-name basis with every maître d' in town. A confirmed bachelor, he wasn't prepared to trade in the fast lane for car pools.

The Widow

Diana Collins drove a ten-year-old station wagon and was on a first-name basis with teachers and ice-cream vendors. A widow, she wasn't prepared to trade in her nice safe life for high heels and small talk.

They had both become adept at playing their roles. Until the playboy met the widow.

The brightest star in women's fiction MDM3

In the public eye, nothing is kept sacred.

BARBARA BRETTON

STARFIRE

Sara Chance, the wealthy widow of celebrity Maxwell Chance, is in the spotlight. And she wants out.

Sam Berenger, an unforgotten love from Sara's past, enters the scene. And he wants Sara.

Sara is desperate to change her life, especially when she discovers that someone close to her is trying to destroy her reputation and her wealth. But can Sam be trusted? Because the enemy is often the one you least suspect....

Available this March at your favorite retail outlet.

MIRA The brightest star in women's fiction

MBB

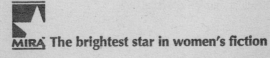